Praise for

"*The Eaton* is an astonishing debut. A tense and suspenseful thriller set in Mid-Michigan, filled with historical information, I could not put this down! Fresh, original, and truly terrifying." - *Kirk Montgomery, ABC-TV*

"It's not often I find myself so absorbed in a book that grabs my attention from the onset up until the last page. It's fast-paced, macabre and full of gritty atmospheric settings, along with a relentlessly chilling plot from an author who's mastered the genre!" - *Catherine Rose Putsche, Author of The Surgeon's Son*

"*Journey to Cassiopeia* is not only a remarkable tale, but also shines a light on our own mortality and that nothing can be taken for granted in this world, especially the safety of the ones we love." - *Rosie Malezer, Readers' Favorite*

"Reminiscent of an old-school Stephen King novel, *The Eaton* will hold you captive from its first paragraph to its shocking conclusion. This spell-binding thriller kept me guessing all the way through, and left me anxiously hoping for a sequel." - *Jenn Carpenter, Violent Ends Podcast, Author of Haunted Lansing*

"*The Bells of Beaumont Tower* covers all bases of film from horror to drama to tell one hell of a story. I really can't begin to express how cool I felt that this film was." - *Tracy Crockett, Unspeakable Magazine*

"Addis pens plenty of suspense, gore, disturbing imagery, and edge-of-your-seat tension throughout the entire text. The book, as a whole, is inviting, intriguing, and worth investing in. Plus, Addis manages to create independent, smart female characters, not something you see every day in a horror novel." - *Julia Gaskill, Portland Book Review*

"Amazing debut by a really talented author. This is one of those books that will stick with you after you read it—Addis does a great job of putting you in the action." - *Alec Drachman, Goodreads*

"What Addis does best is convey to the reader the slow rising terror as the characters realize their situation. I don't want to give anything thing away because finding out what is in the hotel, where it came from and how it works is part of the creepy fun. It is hard to creep me out and this one did it."
- *Sharon Stogner, I Smell Sheep Reviews*

"*The Eaton* is a great book. I would recommend *The Eaton* to anyone who loves a good horror story with rich, well-developed characters who all have their secrets they would like to keep hidden, but are faced with a horror they've never met." - *Melanie Marsh, FangFreakinTasticReviews.com*

"Out-and-out thrilling horror and an absolute page-turner—it had me wanting 'just another chapter.' But it is, I think, also a little more than that. Addis explores a number of very contemporary and relatable concerns here regarding the relationship between the characters and their pasts. This is a great read and I guarantee horror fans are about to be as hooked in as I was." - *Lit Amri, Readers' Favorite*

# The Paper

19 of 50

*[signature]*

John K. Addis

FIRST EDITION
Version 1.0

Also available in hardcover and ebook.

Copyright © 2024 by John K. Addis.

All rights reserved.

Cover artwork by Ryan Holmes.
Book layout by John K. Addis.

*Learn about additional titles at*
johnkaddis.com

ISBN-13: 978-0-9983656-4-0 (AE Press)

To my mother, the journalist,
for teaching me empathy.

## Prologue

I'll keep this short, because it's not fashionable to have prologues these days, so I'm told.

My name is Jimmy Logan. And the following story is true.

Well, at least to the best of my ability it's true. You see, this book takes place when I was 12 and 13 years old at the end of the 1980s. Decades have passed since then.

Most of the memories I'll be sharing with you here are absolutely as they happened, in perfect detail. These parts are seared into my brain and created who I am today. Other parts of this story are at least a decent approximation of the truth. In such moments where I don't have a flawless recollection, I'm relying on a combination of memory, conjecture, and even connecting with old friends to help me fill in the gaps. These story elements are probably close enough to the truth to qualify as memoir, but not close enough to hold up in court.

I've changed all names to protect the proverbial innocent, so if you think you recognize yourself in this book and disagree with my depiction of your personality or of any events you witnessed, well, you're being ridiculous because it's just a story. Any similarities to any persons living or dead, blah blah blah, totally coincidental.

This is a work of fiction.

And here's how it happened.

# I

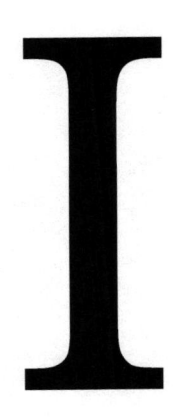

## One

"Dale Dunkle?"

I perked up in my seat and looked around. I had known a Dale Dunkle from my neighborhood, but he was a year younger than me. He would be in sixth grade now, not seventh.

"Present," replied a weak voice from the far right of the classroom. A few students giggled. The first five or so kids called for attendance had said "here," not "present." No one said "present." But it was exactly the kind of thing Dale Dunkle would say. I strained to get a better look, but being in the back row I had a bad angle unless he turned around.

Mr. Gilbert said nothing for a few moments. He just sat there, slouched in his old brown chair behind a grey metal desk, half-moon granny spectacles balanced on the tip of his nose. I thought perhaps he was trying to figure out how to pronounce the next name on the roll sheet. Instead, a grin crept across his face and the attendance pad fell into his lap.

"Dale Dunkle. Would you stand up for us, please?"

Dale stood up.

It *was* him. My God, he still had the same bowl cut from when he was five. Poor bastard. Only now he also had glasses. With *green frames*. All he needed was a "kick me" sign on his back. He looked like a geekier version of Ben Seaver from the first season of *Growing Pains*, though I suppose I'm dating myself with that reference.

"Class," said Mr. Gilbert, "I'd like to introduce you to Dale Dunkle. He's a transfer student from Roeper City and Country School in Bloomfield Hills. Has anyone ever heard of this school?"

The class hadn't.

"Roeper City and Country School is a *private school*. A private school for *gifted children*." Mr. Gilbert looked right at Dale. "I guarantee that this kid is the smartest student in this class. How old are you, son?"

Dale looked down at his no-name brand shoes. "11, sir."

There were a few murmurs at this. The rest of us were 12 at least. Hell, Marco was nearly 14.

"11," Mr. Gilbert repeated. "Are you turning 12 soon?"

"No, sir, I turned 11 last month."

More giggles now. Was this kid in the wrong class?

Mr. Gilbert leaned forward and pivoted his attention to the rest of us. He seemed pleased with himself, like a lawyer who had extracted a confession in open court.

"Dale is 11," Mr. Gilbert explained, "because he had to skip a grade when he left Roeper to come back to New Haven so he wouldn't be too bored in his classes. We're dealing with a real *Einstein* here, you understand. Which is why I want to make sure that none of you treat him any differently. Just because Dale is smarter than you, and younger than you, doesn't mean it's okay to pick on him. Maybe he can even teach some of you a thing or two. But there will be no bullying of Dale *in my classroom*, got it?"

A few kids nodded their heads. We got it, alright.

"Dale, you let me know if this class is too easy for you," Mr. Gilbert said in a syrupy tone. "You may sit back down now."

Dale did.

Mr. Gilbert slumped back into his chair and continued homeroom roll. When he got to my name, Jimmy Logan, I was horrified to catch Dale smiling at me from across the room. I was probably the only one in the whole school that he knew. *Great*.

Dale and I had grown up on the same street, Chennault, in an affordable New Haven subdivision called "The Heights." This was New Haven, Michigan, you understand, not Connecticut—I always feel the need to make that clear, even when talking to other people in our state. No one has heard of New Haven outside of Macomb County, and on the rare occasion people claim to know where I'm talking about, they inevitably begin describing *Grand* Haven instead. I'm sad to correct the error, since Grand Haven's a gorgeous lighthouse-filled vacation spot on Lake Michigan, with a state park that boasts the most beautiful freshwater beach in the Midwest. Not the worst place to be from, in other words. *New* Haven was an anonymous mile-square village centered around Gratiot and 27 Mile Road, about halfway between Detroit and Port Huron, with no claim to fame at all. New housing developments have tripled the size of the town in recent years, but back in 1988, when I started seventh grade, the village had barely 1,800 residents. Unless you lived there, or your nearby small-town school competed against us in track or football, you'd never have known we existed. We didn't even merit our own exit ramp off the interstate.

Anyway, The Heights was a neighborhood consisting of about fifty bi-level homes mostly built in the late 1960s. There were two long parallel streets, Chennault and Stevens, and two small connecting streets, Shirley Ann and Clawson. An uninspiring wooded area with a creek separated the subdivision from Gratiot Avenue, the only busy road in town. Mom and I had moved into our Chennault house when I was a toddler to be closer to my grandma, who would eventually move in with us. Dale and his parents had moved into the neighborhood a few months afterward, eight houses down and across the street. As a single mother anxious to arrange a playdate, Mom made a point of walking up and down Chennault with me until she could run into this new family and make a proper introduction.

"Nicole Logan," she had said by way of greeting. "I live with my son on the other end of the block. Your boy seems to be about the same age!"

"Alice Dunkle," Dale's mom had replied. "Dale, come and meet your new friend!"

And that was that. At least that's how it was explained to me.

From the time I was three years old until I was seven, Dale and I played together several times a week, and often every day. My mom and his parents would take turns babysitting, so I got to know his house as well as mine. Although Dale was a year younger, his language skills had developed early, and I remember getting jealous at the way he could communicate with my own mother better than I could. Once, in what may be my first negative memory of my mom, she said "I hope Dale's brains rub off on you." I stormed off and barricaded myself in my room, which she didn't know I had figured out how to do, and I refused to come out until she apologized, though she never did. I went to kindergarten a year before him, of course, and he was super jealous, but I told him we'd be in the same school soon enough. And we were the next year, but first graders don't see kindergarteners during the day. We still played together almost every day after school and on weekends, though, so when Dale and his family moved away the summer before *his* first-grade year, I was devastated.

I hadn't thought about the kid in years, and wasn't ready to be his friend again at the expense of my own shot at popularity.

"Jimmy!"

Damn. I had tried to slink out of the classroom before he could see me, but he caught me in the hallway.

"Oh, hey," I said, noncommittal.

"Do you remember me?"

"Yeah, sure," I shrugged. "You used to live on my street when we were babies."

Dale smiled. "I do again, my friend. Same house."

My eyes went wide. "Really?"

"Yep! My dad never sold the place. He just rented it out when we moved to Pontiac for his teaching job. But now we're back, so our families are neighbors again. Isn't that neat?"

"Radical," I deadpanned. I still wasn't sure what to make of this enthusiastic former friend, and I became quite aware that other students were staring at us. At least that's how it felt.

I had been a somewhat popular kid in school the last few years, all things considered, but this was my first day at the high school. No, seventh grade wasn't "high school" in the technical sense, but since New Haven High School held grades 7-12, it sure *felt* like high school. I mean, I had seen two teenagers making out by their lockers before the first bell, and no one even asked them to stop. This was a level of grown-up culture I had never experienced before. One wrong move and I could be stuck at the nerd table for the next six years.

"Your hair's changed," Dale observed.

"Uh, yeah," I said, reaching up to feel my new undercut. I had straight brown hair like my mom, which could get boring, so I'd insisted on a modern style for the schoolyear. "Yours...hasn't," I noted.

"This is so different than my last school," Dale babbled cheerily, ignoring my slight. "At Roeper, we didn't have bells. Or desks. It was an excellent learning environment. But my dad said this is what everyone else does, so I have to get used to it. It'll be a challenge. A different kind of challenge, anyway. But I'm so glad I know someone! This is going to be great."

"Yeah, well, speaking of bells..."

"Oh, that's right! We only have four minutes to get to class. So sorry to keep you waiting. What are you going to next?"

I was flustered. I couldn't remember. I just hoped it was a different class than Dale. I fished the crumpled half-sheet of paper out of my front pocket and replied "uh, English."

"Ah, okay," said Dale, disappointed. "I have Science. See you around!"

And with that, he practically skipped down the hallway.

*He's going to get his ass kicked,* I thought.

—

At lunch I sat at a crowded table with my three closest friends: Marco, Zach, and Benny. I don't think Dale saw where I was sitting, and if he did, he would have noticed there wasn't room for him. My friends and I talked about the last days of vacation, made fun of our new teachers, and gossiped about a girl named Sarah, who we decided had "blossomed" over the summer, because we were adolescent idiots.

Marco asked about Dale. "He's the kid who used to live next to Mrs. Regan, right? Like, three down from the Black House?"

"Yeah," I agreed.

"I remember him," Marco said. "Didn't he move away forever ago?"

I shrugged. "He's back. And apparently in our grade."

"Man, I can't imagine being a year younger than everyone else."

"He's two years younger than you," I reminded him. "At least."

Marco stuck out his tongue. "You know that whole held-back thing was total bullshit. I could read fine in first grade. That old racist hag just didn't want to let me through."

"If she hated you so much, why would she want you back in her class another year?"

"Hell, I don't know. I just know it was a race thing. My momma said so."

I had been in Marco's first grade glass (my first time, his second) and thought Mrs. Ladrido was quite nice. Besides, a third of the kids in the New Haven school system were Black, and Marco was the only one I knew to have been held back a grade. Lucky for him, Marco was small for his age, so he fit in okay.

I resisted the urge to tease him further.

Zach, on the other hand, couldn't let it go. "It can't be a race thing. T-Too never got held back and he's darker than you."

"Shh," I said, looking around the room. "He's probably in here and you don't want to get punched in the back of the head."

"I ain't afraid of T-Too," said Zach, unconvincingly. "Just sayin' he didn't get held back. Besides, if Ladrido hated Black kids so much, she should have at least sent Benny to summer school."

"Go to Hell!" laughed Benny, who then did his own nervous sweep around the room to make sure no adult overheard him.

Benny's dad was Black, but his mom was an Irish redhead so fair-skinned she was almost a ghost. New Haven in the 1970s and 1980s was racially diverse, with a high number of interracial families, so Benny wasn't unique among our friends in that regard.

Zach smiled. "She probably thought you were Mexican, Benny."

"Maybe you're right," Benny said. "Sorry, Marco! Mrs. Ladrido loved me!"

Marco still looked grumpy over being teased and mumbled something about setting the school on fire. Zach made a peace offering of his remaining tater tots.

When I went to clear my tray, I noticed Dale sitting with a few kids I didn't know. Perhaps he had met them in his last class, or he'd just sat down alone and was joined by strangers. Either way, I was relieved. My fear that he would cling to me as his only "friend" had been premature.

Another class we ended up having together, not counting homeroom, was Social Studies with Mr. Wright. Dale had tried to sit next to me, but Mr. Wright assigned seats, which landed Dale a seat in the front row and myself in the back. Of course, this is where each of us would prefer to sit anyway.

"Sucks to be in the back, doesn't it?" whispered a girl a desk over. She had dark brown hair and wide eyes. I wasn't sure she was talking to me, but when I cocked my head she smiled.

"Uh, yeah, I guess," I said.

"I'm Emilia Jankowski. I'm new here."

"I'm Jimmy Logan. I'm not."

She giggled. It was an adorable sound. I glanced up to see if Mr. Wright had noticed. He hadn't. He was droning on about the Soviet Union.

"Nice to meet you, Jimmy," she said. Then she must have heard something important from Mr. Wright, turned back to her desk, and started taking notes.

I had to force myself to look away.

—

As new experiences go, seventh grade seemed fine. It was fun to see certain friends again, like Zach who didn't live in my neighborhood, and the lockers were bigger. None of my classes were interesting yet, but both band and gym started the next day, and I suspected those would be my two favorite periods. True, I had never been in band before, but I liked loud music, and as a drummer I would get to hit things.

On the bus I sat with Marco who lived two doors down from me. Dale was late coming onto the bus and we caught each other's eye, but seeing everyone partnered up, he sat by himself behind the driver. The bus made two stops on our street, one near Dale's end of the block and one near mine and Marco's. Dale got off first, turned around, saw me looking at him from my window seat, and waved. I didn't wave back.

I heard Mom doing dishes as I walked in the house. It smelled like she had been cleaning. I called "hi, Grandma" up the stairs, heard "hi, Jimmy" back, then joined Mom in the kitchen.

"Mike coming over tonight?" I asked. Mike Healy was a pretty cool guy she had been dating the better part of a year. He had red hair, like Benny's mom, only he was big and burly, whereas Benny's mom was a waif like Benny himself. Mike worked at the New Haven Foundry, though I didn't know what a foundry was exactly, and the one time I asked him he had claimed he was in charge of "foundring."

"Hello to you too," Mom said, smiling. "And yes he is, so tidy up your room for me, please."

"Aw come on mom," I moaned. "He's not going to come up to my room."

"You never know," she said. "Besides, your room is

next to the bathroom and your door might be open."
"Can't he use the downstairs bathroom?"
My mom shuddered. "No one is allowed to use the downstairs bathroom."
"I use the downstairs bathroom."
"No *company* is allowed to use the downstairs bathroom."
I laughed. "Guys don't care if places are gross."
"I care," she said. "Now clean your room."
"Don't you want to know how school was?"
"I do, but you're stalling."
I went up and cleaned my room.

We ate dinner late on nights Mike came to visit, because his shift ended at 5:30 and he always had to shower and change before feeling presentable. At 6:30 sharp, just like dozens of times that summer, he was at our door.

"Ah, Nicole," he said to my mom. "So good to see you after a long, hard day."

"You as well," she cooed. "And looking so handsome."

"Gross," I called from the other room.

"You don't think I look handsome, sport?"

"I have no opinion on that, Mike!"

He laughed a big, full laugh that reminded me of Santa Claus.

Over meatloaf and mashed potatoes, I finally got to describe my first day of seventh grade. I told them all about my classes, teachers, lockers, and friends. I didn't bring up the cute Polish girl, obviously, but I did mention Dale.

"You mean the Dunkle boy you used to play with years ago?" Mom seemed genuinely interested.

"Yeah, I guess they moved back to town. Same house, even."

Mom turned to Mike. "Dale was the only white kid besides Jimmy on the block," she explained. "Probably Jimmy's only white friend since we've lived here."

"*Zach's* white," I said, annoyed that she seemed to be color-grading my friends.

"Well yeah, but he's just a school friend. He's not

in the neighborhood."

Zach wasn't just a "school friend." We were bonded for life since I had saved him from being run over by a giant riding lawn mower back in grade school.

Mom frowned. "Wait, wouldn't Dale be a grade below you?"

I sighed, annoyed. "Yeah. I guess he skipped a year."

Mom thought about this for a moment as she scooped mashed potatoes onto a plate for Grandma. "You know," she said, "I bet you could skip a grade too if you tried harder."

Mike shot her a look. "Now Nicki, I'm sure Jimmy's doing just fine. And you wouldn't want him to skip a grade anyway. Can you imagine being the youngest kid in your class by a whole year? That Dale kid might not be able to drive to his own Junior Prom."

I couldn't imagine Dale Dunkle dressed up and on a date. Then again, I couldn't imagine me on a date either. I wondered what Emilia would look like in a few years.

"All I'm saying," Mom protested, "is that anything Dale can do, Jimmy can do." She turned to me. "Don't you forget that. Especially if you start playing with him again. I wouldn't want you thinking you're not as good as he is."

"Don't worry," I said. "I won't."

## Two

New Haven in the late '80s was unlike anywhere I've lived since. In many ways, it was similar to a number of its neighboring small towns like Capac, Dryden, or Romeo. But unlike those towns, which were considered safe and crime-free, New Haven was perceived as having a problem with drugs and the violent crime that came with it. The police chief once explained to us at a school assembly that this was due to the "Detroit-Port Huron drug pipeline" which New Haven was smack in the middle of. Apparently, it was difficult to get hard drugs into Canada through the heavily guarded Detroit-Windsor border, but was easy through the lax security of the Port Huron crossing into Sarnia. So, drugs would travel from Detroit to Port Huron via I-94 on their way to our northern neighbor, and sometimes dealers would pick up customers in the towns along the way, including ours.

When I'd talk to outsider kids at county fairs or regional camps, it became clear that the stereotype of New Haven as "unsafe" had more to do with our demographics than our crime rate.

"Oh, you're from *New Haven?* Bet you have locks on your doors."

"Well, sure."

"My dad says New Haven is a *dirty* city."

"You mean because of the foundry?"

"No."

I guess if you grew up in one of the nearby all-white small towns and went to an all-white school and had all-white friends and family, and the only two things you knew about New Haven is that it had crime and that it had Black people, well, maybe it was just too easy to assume New Haven had crime *because* of its diversity. The only truly big city in the state was nearby Detroit, where the crime explosion of the '70s and '80s had coincided with the collapse of its white population. Bigotry often lurked beneath the surface of even the friendliest Midwesterner; to say I had personally observed racism against my Black friends by residents of neighboring towns would be an understatement.

I used to believe New Haven itself had avoided such tensions. There were cliques at school, sure—popular kids, athletes, geeks, bullies, and so on—but all were mixed. The whole village marched in the Martin Luther King Jr. parade each year, and prominent business owners and elected government officials reflected the town's racial makeup.

I was hanging out with an old friend from New Haven a few years back, and he thought my perception of growing up there was a bit rose-colored.

"Well, of course you'd think that everything was great. You're white."

"So?"

"I'm Black. It was different for me."

"It couldn't have been *that* different."

"How many times have you been in jail, Jimmy?"

"Well, once I spent a few hours locked up for driving with a suspended license."

"So, never."

He then proceeded to list off every Black kid we grew up with and every white kid we grew up with, comparing their life stories. Some of the details he knew, and others we had to look up on free background check websites. I was shocked to see that most Black kids from my neighborhood had spent time in jail or prison at some point in their teenage or adult lives, mostly for stuff like marijuana possession or simple assault which I knew damned well my white friends were equally guilty of. A couple names we entered were still locked up today. We couldn't find any record of a white kid with a significant criminal history, except for Pax.

# THE PAPER

Now, I know I've already overloaded you with tons of exposition and a dozen names to keep track of, but this is important. Pax was a tall, blond-haired, blue-eyed dude who lived a block away from me. And he was, for many of us in the neighborhood, The Bully.

I know now that the scariest bullies are those consumed by a voice convincing them they are special, and that rules only apply to others. You can't explain to this type of bully why they shouldn't be a bully. It's who they are. It's who Paxton Jenner was. And Pax was, and apparently still is, an evil fucking bastard.

This means Pax also could not be scared off by someone "standing up" to him. That only works on bullies with low self-esteem. Pax thought he was a God. And Derek and T-Too, his loyal goons, were happy to worship him.

The good news was that these guys weren't the type of bullies to roam the neighborhood looking for trouble. It's not like you'd run into them when you least expected it. The bad news was that their hangout, the Black House, was at the edge of our street, making it almost impossible to go anywhere without, at a minimum, being glared at by Pax and his crew.

"Yo, Jimmy," he called to me. I was on my bike, as always, on my way to Huck's Party Store.

"Yeah, Pax?"

"Stop for a sec."

If I biked past him, he'd make my life miserable later. If I stopped, he'd make my life miserable now—but maybe without the added anger of having been previously shunned.

I stopped.

"You going to Huck's?" he asked.

"Yep."

"Can you bring me some Redpop?"

"Uh, sure, Pax," I responded. Behind Pax, I saw Derek and T-Too sitting on an old tree stump. They were taking out cigarettes from a pack and barely seemed to notice me. I gestured their way. "I suppose they want some too?"

"Yeah, buy three. Thanks, man."

"Alright. Faygo's a quarter a bottle. Ya got seventy-five cents?"

Derek and T-Too looked up from their cigs. They noticed me now.

Pax just smiled. "Aw, man, you know I'm good for it. I'll catch ya next time."

This would be the third time I had bought something for him this month and he had never paid me back. But I couldn't say this. I thought maybe I could claim I didn't have enough to cover it, but then when he saw me biking back a few minutes later with my own items, he'd know I had been lying.

"Is there a problem?" asked T-Too. T-Too had been trouble as long as anyone could remember. I couldn't even count how many toys of mine he had stolen over the years, and he wasn't afraid of getting physical.

"No. No, man, I got you. It's, uh, cool." I tried to look nonchalant about it all, like seventy-five cents was nothing to me.

"Good," Pax said, a touch of malice in his voice, which always sounded like he was speaking through clenched teeth. "Now get off your ass. I'm thirsty."

I began to pedal, turning east on Clark (our local name for 27 Mile Road), leaving the Black House and its punks behind me. I had half a mind to just buy my own stuff and take the long way back, up Gratiot and around into the far entrance to The Heights, but that was a mile out of the way. Besides, it's not like he'd believe me that I forgot his request. I was stuck.

"I wish they'd tear down the Black House," I told my mom once after an earlier bullying episode.

"The Black House?"

"You know, the house at the end of the street."

"Oh. That's the *White* House."

"But it's black."

"Yes, but the guy who built it and lived there was Jerome *White*. He plowed the fields behind the house and sold his food to local supermarkets. Everyone my age and older knows it as the White House."

"Oh."

## THE PAPER

"Back then, he was the only Black farmer in Macomb County. That's not why you call it the Black House, is it?"

I laughed. "No. It's the Black House because it's painted black!"

Mom explained the house hadn't been sold when Farmer White died, and he had no heirs, so no one in town seemed to know who owned the place. It was creepy and abandoned, with boarded-up windows and a collapsed front porch, and a few spots in the roof where the shingles had rotted away. It was the only house on that side of Clark for a mile, too, with nothing but untilled farmland behind and around it. If you stood at the corner of Chennault and Clark and looked north, you'd feel like the Black House was in the middle of nowhere, and if you turned around and looked south, you'd see the rows of nearly identical houses that comprised our neighborhood. Mom said they just kept that creepy house around to make the rest of our homes look better by comparison.

I was thinking of this conversation as I made it to Huck's, which was as typical a specimen of a Michigan party store as you could imagine. If you're not from the state, a "party store" is a convenience store that sells pop, beer, magazines, chips, candy, and a few overpriced toiletries and stuff. For kids old enough to bike around town but too young to drive, a party store is where you'd get everything you ate and drank outside of mealtime. On this day, I was going there for a Kit Kat candy bar. And apparently three Faygo Redpops.

I was in line with my items when I heard a Dunkly voice behind me.

"Hey, Jimmy!"

"Oh, hey Dale."

"Whatcha getting?" He looked at my Faygos. "You must be thirsty."

I didn't want to tell him the truth, so I ignored the comment, and peeked to see what he was buying.

"Garbage Pail Kids?" I asked, shocked. Never in a million years would I have thought Dale Dunkle would collect the same hysterical, vulgar trading cards that I did. I assumed he just read the encyclopedia all day.

"Yeah! It's Series 13. The only ones I still need are Ampu-Ted and Undead Ned."

I nodded. "I have those but can't find Corkscrewed Drew."

"Is that the twin of Champ-pain Dwayne?"

"Yep."

"I might have an extra. Do you have any extras of the ones I need?"

"Hmm. I'm not sure. I can look."

Dale grinned. "That'd be awesome! Maybe we can complete each other."

"Uh, okay."

I bought my stuff with a couple singles from my jeans pocket. Dale motioned for me to wait while he paid for his cards, which I did. He opened the pack as we walked out. None of the cards were anything either of us needed.

I got on my bike and was amused to observe what Dale was riding. Even by the standards of our neighborhood, all cheap Huffy bicycles and hand-me-downs, it was the ugliest bike I had ever seen. It was a hideous shade of orange and completely unbranded, as if no self-respecting manufacturer would dare be associated with it. It wasn't a girl's bike, for it had the center crossbar, but it was undeniably feminine.

"What kind of bike is that?" I asked.

Dale shrugged. "Donno. My mom got it for me."

"Does your mom decide everything for you?"

Dale nodded, sadly. He knew what I was referring to. It had been the first day of band, although we didn't get a chance to play anything. It was mostly talking about music and what interested us all about our chosen instrument. When Ms. Campbell asked me what I was excited about, I made the class laugh by saying "hitting stuff." When she asked Dale about why he chose to be in band, the kid got choked up. "I didn't choose band. My *mother* chose band." Then he stopped talking so he wouldn't cry. There were some murmurs, and the teacher must have been a bit irritated at this response, but she moved on. I didn't know what had made Dale so upset, but now I thought I understood.

"It's alright." I wasn't sure what to say. "What's your instrument, anyway?"

"French horn," he said.

I had no idea what that was. But it sure sounded nerdy.

"Uh, cool."

"We'll see. You ready?"

I couldn't think of any way out of riding back to our street together, so that's what we did.

I'm sad so many kids these days won't know what it was like to ride a bike around town before the world got paranoid. Even with someone riding beside you, and even with a clear destination, nothing beat that sensation of freedom. I mean, I'm a grown-up now, with even more freedom than I had then. I can bike wherever I want, right? But I don't. I wouldn't leave work early to explore an old trail, or check out the loading dock of some industrial building, or ride through a cemetery looking for the tallest monuments, or any of that. True freedom is wasted on those who have lost the desire to be free.

As we crossed the bridge over the small creek and approached the Black House, I began to hope that maybe Pax and his group had taken off. But they were still there, thirsty as ever.

"Hey Jimmy," Pax called out. "Who's your girlfriend?"

"It's Dale Dunkle, from the red house over there." I gestured in the general direction of our street, but as I needed both hands to brake the bike, I doubt they knew which house I meant.

"Nice to meet you," Dale said, cheerfully.

Pax looked Dale up and down. "What the fuck are you riding, there?"

Dale seemed confused. "My bike."

"Why is it orange?"

"I donno. It came that way."

"Bikes are black, dude," offered Derek. "Or blue. That's not a bike."

Dale wasn't sure what to say. "Well, it gets me

places," he argued. "It has wheels. And pedals. It's obviously a bike."

"Holy shit, dude," said Derek, wide-eyed. "Is that a *single-speed* bike? Like a first grader would have?"

"It's a t-two-wheeled tricycle," stuttered T-Too. "You hang out with little kids, Jimmy?"

"We're not hanging out," I snapped.

Pax looked uncharacteristically thoughtful. Then, it hit him. "Hey, wait a minute! You're the kid who cried when he had to get a tardy slip! I saw you in the office!"

Dale stammered. "I...forgot where I was supposed to go."

"The crybaby! I knew you looked familiar."

"Crybaby on an orange juice bike!" laughed Derek.

"*Orange* juice!" added T-Too, helpfully.

Dale turned to me, his eyes pleading for me to be on his side, to defend him against these taunts. Instead, I said: "don't look at me, Tropicana!"

The bullies roared with laughter.

But Dale was crushed. I think he knew we weren't going to hang out and trade Garbage Pail Kids now. Without another word, he peddled his hideous bike toward home.

"I gotta run, too," I said, turning my bike toward the street. Before I knew what was happening, Pax had sprinted toward me and grabbed the front of my shirt.

"Hey asshole," he hissed. "Aren't you forgetting something?"

"Oh, shit! Sorry guys." I gave them the plastic bag with the three Faygos. "Sorry, really."

Pax passed the drinks to Derek and T-Too. Then, his face brightened. "Ah, no worries, man. *Tropicana!* That shit's funny."

"Uh, thanks."

I realized too late that the bag I had handed over also contained my candy bar. But the boys had resumed whatever discussion they were having before Dale and I had pulled up, and now that they had their drinks, I was invisible. The chocolate was gone.

As I started to bike home I noticed a little dark-haired girl, maybe five years old, standing in the front yard of the small yellow house on the southwest corner of Chennault and Clark. She was dirty and sweaty, wearing a white play dress and holding a beat-up old doll. I thought I had maybe seen her before but couldn't be sure. I didn't know anyone on this end of the block, but I smiled in a neighborly way just the same. Instead of smiling back, she gave me a disappointed, judgmental stare. I got it in my head that she must have seen the way I had teased Dale. The desire to spit "what the hell's your problem" at the girl was almost overwhelming.

Shame is a strange feeling for a 12-year-old. The part of you becoming a man wants to be defensive, angrily so, at anyone's attempts at judging your behavior. But this new testosterone can't quite override the programmed need to avoid getting into trouble, to be a "good kid," and to make grown-ups proud. What if I had barked at the little girl and she told her dad, who then called my house to complain about my behavior? I'd be grounded for sure.

Nothing was worse than when parents tattled to other parents. It had happened a few months earlier with Marco's mom Lorraine, a stern but quirky Black woman with a penchant for romantic comedies. Marco and I had been trying to light ants with matches after we were unsuccessful with a magnifying glass, and Marco had burned his finger pretty bad. He told his mom the matches had been my idea, which wasn't true at all, but she called my mom and, well, no video games for a week. And I hadn't even done anything wrong. Imagine if I'd yelled at a preschooler.

In the end, I didn't say a word, and neither did the dirty girl. But something about her disapproving look unsettled me, maybe because it reminded me of my mom's similar expression whenever I let her down. I thought about it all the way home, and was considering talking to Mom about it, to admit the guilt I felt over teasing Dale.

By the sounds of the shouting I could hear from two houses away, I knew that wasn't going to happen.

# Three

The front door of our split-level house opened onto a small landing connecting two short staircases: one leading up to the bedrooms, the other down to the living room and kitchen. The nice thing about this layout was that if I did hear Mom and Mike fighting on one level, I didn't have to pass them on the way to the other. Since it sounded like they were going at it in the kitchen, I snuck upstairs.

I hated when they were like this because I felt like a traitor for not taking my mom's side by default. After all, Mike was just some guy she was dating, right? A good son would say "you're perfect, Mom—you need to dump that loser!" But back when I used to listen to their fights, it rarely seemed like Mike was in the wrong. Mom had a tendency to harp on things, to bring up disagreements that happened months ago just to start something. Mike was the strong and silent type at first, taking as much as he could without raising his voice, but eventually he would snap and start screaming back at her, sometimes even punching walls and throwing plates and all that. Rather than escalating the tension, Mike's fury seemed to be what my mom was after. No matter how calmly Mike would try to talk her down at first, the fight could never be over without the explosion that was happening now.

"I said I was fucking *sorry*," I heard Mike yell.

"That apology was like everything you do," Mom spat back. "*Half-assed.*"

Something got punched. The counter, maybe. I don't think Mike ever hit my mom, but I couldn't rule it out. I did see her slap *him* once, though she apologized afterward.

## THE PAPER

I had almost made it to my room when I heard Grandma calling me.

"Jimmy? Is that you?"

I thought maybe I'd pretend to not hear her and shut my door, but that seemed wrong. She might need water or something.

"Yeah, Grandma?"

"Can you come here a minute?"

"Sure, Grandma."

My mom's mom was my only living grandparent, and she'd lived in our third bedroom since I was in fourth grade. A frail, hunched-over woman, she wasn't in good enough health to live by herself, but didn't need a nursing home either, so here she was. I don't think I ever knew what was wrong with her—if it was disclosed to me, I don't remember now—but I knew her moving in with us was a one-way trip. She wasn't that old or anything, 60 or so, but Mom would say things like "wow, your grandma's still hanging in there" which made me guess that she had outlived at least one doctor's prediction.

I walked into her room. She was sitting on the bed, a glass of water on a TV tray beside her. The room smelled vaguely antiseptic, as always.

"Sit down, there." She gestured to the chair opposite the bed. I sat.

The only times I tended to see Grandma were in the mornings, when I said hi before running to school, and after dinner, when it was my job to bring her a plate of whatever we were having. I thought it was kind of sad that she couldn't make it down for dinner and eat with us, but going up or down stairs was difficult for her. She couldn't even get up and reach the floor lamp by herself, so she had The Clapper, a sound-activated outlet controller Mom bought off a TV commercial. Whenever we ate, I imagined Grandma would be smelling the food, and hearing the conversation, and just sitting alone waiting for me. So, I tried to spend at least a few minutes with her each night when I brought the meal, and maybe share a laugh as well. Grandma could be pretty funny. She seemed serious today, though.

"Yeah, Grandma?"

We could hear the shouting from downstairs again. I knew what this was going to be about.

"Jimmy, your mom is a very stubborn person. I was stubborn at her age, too. I used to yell and scream at her daddy. He never could do anything right."

"I can't imagine you yelling at anyone, Grandma!"

She smiled. "Well, I can't imagine yelling at my only grandson, that's for sure. But I did have a temper back in the day."

Her voice was soft in volume, but it wasn't weak. And I had indeed heard her snap at my mom a few times, so I believed her.

"She doesn't yell at me much," I said, looking down.

"No," Grandma agreed. "She doesn't need to yell at you. She has Mike to yell at."

I nodded. "She's going to scare him away."

"She might."

Grandma was looking at me curiously. I realized she was reaching out and giving me an opportunity if I needed to talk. But it's hard to talk seriously to family, you know? I mean, sometimes I would talk to Benny about my mom's temper if we were bitching about our folks. There was this old giant wooden spool in the woods behind his backyard, probably left over from the construction crew who wired the neighborhood. Two slats on the inside part of the spool had been removed, so you could crawl inside and sit in this cool wooden cylinder. When we were little, four of us could squeeze in, but now it was quite confining to be in there with even one other person. I knew this was the last year we could hang out there, getting so big and all. But Benny still called it "The Clubhouse" and he and I would use it to talk about stuff you wouldn't admit to anyone else.

Grandma was still looking at me.

"It's how she is," I finally said. "She can't get over things."

"Some people live in the present," Grandma explained. "Like you. You're always in the moment. It's why it's hard for you to plan for something in the future, like having a test the next day, or recalling the past, like where you left your backpack. People like you are happy for the most part. Your grandpa was like that, and it drove me crazy. I would fight with him and bring up things he had done wrong years earlier, and he would have no memory of what I was talking about. He held no grudge against anyone, even if they deserved it. It meant he kept making the same mistakes. And he was late for everything, because he never gave himself the right amount of time to get ready."

"Sounds like I would have liked him."

She smiled. "He did get to meet you, you know."

"Really?"

"I wish we had taken a picture. But we didn't know that first time would be the last time. We knew he was sick, of course. Just didn't quite plan ahead, I guess."

I thought about this. "Can you be a future-based person?"

"Oh yes. Like your Aunt Sharon."

Sharon was my mom's only sibling, and the most successful person in our family. She was a college professor out in Pittsburgh and super smart.

"See, with Sharon," Grandma said, "she always knew everything that was coming. Planned for every possibility. Turned her homework in a day early when she could. The kind of kid who planned a week's worth of outfits for herself in grade school."

I laughed.

"But that's not without its own problems," she went on. "It's hard to give yourself over to the present when your mind is racing about the future. How do you truly relax and enjoy a sunset if you're counting down the minutes before you have to be asleep so that you get eight hours because you have to wake up exactly at 6:35 am to have time to beat traffic? It all sounds a little exhausting to me."

"You're not a future person."

"I'm afraid I'm like your mom, stuck in the past. Probably held me back, to be honest. I was born in New Haven and I'll die in New Haven. It's hard for people like us to move on sometimes. We like things to be familiar, so we replay everything in our minds. Every fight, every slight, everything we ever did wrong, and every wrong ever done to us. We stew over things most people would forget about. That makes it very hard to trust people, which makes it very, very hard to have friends."

"Why?"

"Think about it. Hasn't Marcus ever hurt your feelings? Teased you or made you angry?"

"Marco."

"Yeah, Marco."

"Well, sure. He broke my Optimus Prime Transformer and wouldn't apologize. And, like, a year ago he got to take one friend to Cedar Point and he chose Benny over me. Oh, and he got all the other guys to tease me about that bad haircut last summer. I thought I'd never talk to him again."

"But you forgave him."

"Yeah."

"And you probably forgot about those times until I asked you to think about them, right?"

"Yeah, that's true."

Grandma nodded. "People like your mom and I would love to have that ability to forget and forgive. But we can't. Anytime we're thinking about something in the past, it's like it just happened, just now. It's still raw."

The muffled shouting from below was increasing in intensity.

"But you're calm these days, right?"

"Eventually," Grandma said, "you make your peace with living in the past and try and empathize with other points of view. Do you know what empathy is?"

"Like, sympathy?"

"Kind of. Sympathy is feeling sorry for someone. But empathy is the ability to understand another person's point of view because you can share their feelings. Which means you should have empathy for your mom, because this is how God made her, and it isn't her fault."

"Yeah. Well, it's not Mike's fault, either."

Just then, we heard Mike scream "fuck you!" loud and clear. Instantly, the room became dark.

"The Clapper!" exclaimed Grandma. It was set to turn off the lights with two loud claps. Mike's two words must have been perfectly spaced.

We both burst out laughing.

—

Mike didn't stay for dinner that night, and I knew enough not to ask about it. Mom looked like she had been crying, and I thought it would be a good time to try out some of that "empathy" by not complaining about a thing.

After the late meal, I told Mom I had homework and went to my room. I didn't have any homework, but figured it was the best way to get some alone time without being bothered. Sometimes, when Mom and Mike fought, she got all clingy with me afterward and insisted we watch TV together or something. I was still a bit mad at her, so I wasn't in the mood to be her friend.

I liked my room, for the most part. It was painted blue, though not the kind of blue I wanted. I had asked for a deep, midnight blue, with little white dots painted on the ceiling, so it looked like a night sky at all times. I'd seen a show on Nickelodeon where a kid had his bedroom painted that way, almost like a planetarium, which was the coolest thing. Mom had bought baby blue paint instead, which sucked, but at least she let me get glow-in-the-dark star stickers. I put them everywhere, not just on the ceiling, but on the walls and the bed and my desk and even a few on the floor. After they charged up a while, I'd close the curtains and turn off the lights and lay on my bed and imagine myself falling through space.

I was about to do this tonight, too, and had already

brushed my teeth and put on a baggy t-shirt to sleep in, when I heard the front door open. It was Mike, I knew. I stayed in my bedroom, listening to the muffled voices below. I didn't hear any fighting, which was good.

Before I could get into bed, he knocked on my door.

"Hey, sport."

"Hi Mike."

"You turnin' in?"

"Yeah, I guess. Why, do you wanna play a game?"

"I'd love to."

I heard my mom calling from her bedroom. "One game, guys. It's a school night."

"One game," Mike confirmed.

We went downstairs to the game shelves. I had a Nintendo, like most kids my age, but Mike wasn't a video game guy. He liked board games. Lately we'd been playing Battleship or Sorry, so I expected him to grab one of those. Instead, he moved some boxes around and found the chess board.

"Checkers?" I asked, hopefully.

"Oh, you're in seventh grade now. I think you're old enough for chess. Do you know how to play?"

"Kind of. The horsey moves in an L-shape, right?"

"You're a regular grandmaster."

Mike set up the board for us, explaining that the queen started on her own color, and detailing the power behind each piece. I had forgotten we even had a chess set. I think Benny and I had tried to figure it out a couple times, but I doubt we ever finished a game. Mike was patient, and waited until I knew how to use all the pieces before we began.

He beat me almost immediately.

"It's okay," he said, sensing my disappointment. "That was a practice round. You have to try and think ahead. Think of the game from my point of view. Put yourself in my shoes."

"You mean using empathy?"

"What?"

"I was talking to Grandma and she was telling me to have empathy for Mom."

Mike was silent for a moment. I wondered if I had embarrassed him.

"You know, I care for your mother very much."

"I know." Then, dumbly, I added: "Me too."

Mike laughed. "Well, I should hope so."

"I think she's mean to you sometimes."

"Well, just between us, I think she's mean to me sometimes too." He began resetting the pieces.

"Mom said one game."

"I said that was a practice round."

We played again. This time, I tried to anticipate what he would do on his turn. I even took two of his pieces, though I suspected he knew I was going to take them. I don't think he was letting me have small victories, but rather he saw sacrificing certain pieces as part of his plan. He still beat me the second time, but at least it took longer.

"My dad and I used to play chess," Mike said as he began putting the pieces back in their box.

"The game's that old?"

"Yeah, it's that old."

"Did you ever beat him?"

A sly smile crept across Mike's face. "You know, my dad and I played a lot of games when I was your age. And he always beat me. And after each game, he'd say: 'The day you beat me at chess is the day you become a man.'"

"So, did you ever beat him?"

"Of course."

"Will I ever beat you?"

Mike finished putting the last piece away and shimmied the lid onto the box. He gave me a serious look.

"Jimmy, listen to me carefully. *The day you beat me at chess is the day you become a man.*"

I snorted. "I guess I'll be a kid forever."

"That," he said with a wistful smile, "doesn't sound so bad."

Grown-ups were always saying things like that.

# Four

I understand why classrooms need to have windows. But man can they be a distraction during a boring class. I remember this one time, in sixth grade math, when I was staring out the window and became fixated on a squirrel that was getting ready to jump from the branch of one tree to the branch of another tree. You could tell he was trying to psych himself out, tentatively walking back and forth on the limb, then approaching the launch point, concentrating and shaking his back legs a bit, like revving up an engine, before taking the leap. I gasped as he went airborne, certain he would plunge to the ground, and to my surprise a dozen or so other students gasped as well. All of us thought we were the only one watching the squirrel, and so all exploded into laughter upon realizing we were fixated on the same scene.

Our math teacher turned from the chalkboard, perplexed. He didn't know what he had done to deserve a synchronized gasp and laughter. We didn't tell him.

The squirrel made it, by the way.

"Mr. Logan, what do you think?"

Oops. Caught looking out a window remembering another time I was looking out a window.

Mr. Wright was staring at me from behind his desk.

"Uh, sir?"

Emilia giggled. She knew I hadn't been paying attention.

"Your thoughts, Mr. Logan." After a pause, he took pity on me. "On the worker's strikes. Will they lead to Poland abandoning communism?"

"Uh, no sir."

I knew next to nothing about this, but had at least done the reading last night, which was an opinion column from *The Detroit News*. The writer of the article believed the strikes wouldn't lead to much of anything in the end.

Mr. Wright nodded. "And why not?"

"Well, I guess I don't think the Ruskies will give up that easily."

He looked at me for a while, and I wasn't sure if that meant my answer was really smart or really stupid. Then he looked over at Emilia.

"What about you, Miss Jankowski? You're Polish, right?"

"Yeah."

"Think your people will get the whole democracy thing figured out?"

"Yes, sir."

"Why?"

"Well, we invented paczki. We're clever!"

Mr. Wright chuckled. "Okay, then."

One of the weird things about Mr. Wright was that he barely taught us anything in class. He assigned homework, sure, but spent most of the class period just asking us all what we thought about things. It seemed to be his way of making sure we were doing the assignments, but he wouldn't really tell us if we were "right" or "wrong" in our answers. It was kind of maddening.

Mr. Wright turned to his next victim. "How about you, Moriah? Any thoughts on this?"

I had heard of Mr. Wright as early as grade school. He was a somewhat legendary track coach who led the high school team to regular regional championships and two state titles. But he sure couldn't have demonstrated any techniques himself, for he could barely walk, even with his cane. Rumor had it that he used ancient paper flipbooks to show his team proper stance and form. The only time Mr. Wright stood up during our class was to pull down the retractable world map behind him, which took considerable effort on his part and involved the use of a large wooden dowel rod with a cup hook screwed into one end.

I bring this up because his perpetually-seated position made it hard for him to notice kids passing notes.

"Psst."

I looked up and around. Emilia was smiling at me. The cutest dimples, seriously. She was holding a folded piece of paper. When Mr. Wright glanced down at his book, she passed the note to me and I opened it.

It read "iyay amyay oredbay" in blue bubbly letters.

I don't know if this was the first time someone had passed me a note in class, but it's the first time I remember. I stared at the words, uncomprehending.

"Polish?" I mouthed to her.

"Pig Latin," she whispered back.

—

The ditches on either side of Clark were filled with a variety of rocks and stones. None of them was larger than an egg, so they fit perfectly in our 12-year-old palms. Benny didn't have a great home life, though at least his parents were still together. When he used to complain about his dad, or his asshole older brothers, he loved to stand on the bridge up the road from our neighborhood and chuck those rocks as far as he could into the creek below. I liked to join him, and throw rocks of my own, though I listened more than talked. Sure, I had my own problems, but never liked gabbing about them much.

"Maybe I'll run away," Benny said.

"Nah," I said, after a pause. "Where would you go?"

"I donno. These woods here, I guess." He threw a rock.

"Not very big woods. I think they'd find you."

"Yeah. I'm just talking."

"I know."

"You don't have a dad. And your momma doesn't whup you when you mess up. You got it easy."

I stiffened a bit. "I have a dad. Well, I mean, I assume he's alive somewhere." My mom had me pretty young. She was only 19 or 20, and it was a college fling. She was going to school to be a teacher but dropped out when she got pregnant. She'd been a waitress as long as I could remember, but at a diner in nearby Mt. Clemens that only serves breakfast and lunch, so she was usually home by the time I was done with school. My dad was out of her life before I was born.

"You never hear from him at all?"

"Nah."

"Not even a birthday card?"

"Nope."

Benny considered this. "My dad loves me. He's just strict."

"I know."

Benny threw his last rock. It was a flat stone and got a decent skip off the surface of the water before it disappeared. I was impressed. Normally from this angle they just sank.

Let me describe Benny for you. Like I said, he was half-Black and half-white, which gave him light brown skin and tight, curly black hair up top. He was skinny and a bit short for his age, and his eyes were a little too close together. He appeared to have a big nose, too, but maybe it only looked that way 'cause his head was small. All-in-all he was a slightly awkward, squirrely kid who was fun to hang out with, but wouldn't be the leader in any group of friends, if that makes sense.

He turned to me.

"What would you rather have?"

"What do you mean?"

"Well, *my* dad, or *no* dad?"

I laughed. "Shit, I don't know. Would I have to get your brothers too?"

We heard a bike approaching. It was Dale. I hadn't seen him in a few days, and it took me a second to realize what was different.

"Hey Dale," I said, trying not to sound too welcoming. "Looks like you got a new bike."

Dale beamed. "Yep! Well, not really. My dad painted it black when I told him I was being teased."

"How about that."

Dale pushed his green glasses up his nose and turned to my friend. "You're Benny, right? Benny Roberts?"

"That's me," Benny said. "And you're the boy genius."

"I'm Dale Dunkle," he beamed. Jesus, it's like he didn't even realize what a dorky name that was. Though who knows what you'd pair with "Dunkle" to make it sound cool. Maybe something like Malachai or Burt? Anything but *Dale*. It'd be like if my mom had named me Louie Logan.

"*I'm Dale Dunkle!*" came an effeminate, mocking echo. Pax, for sure.

We turned around. Pax and T-Too were walking toward us from the direction of Chennault.

I turned back to Dale. He had gone a bit white.

"What are you losers doing," Pax continued, casually. "Throwing rocks?"

"We're all done," Benny said.

T-Too pointed at Dale's bike. "Hey! L-look, it's not orange!"

Pax frowned, studying the situation. "Yeah. It's not orange, but it's the same ugly bike." He glared at Dale. "What, you think you can throw some spray paint on that shit and we wouldn't remember what's under there, *Dale Dunkle?*"

"Dale Dunkle!" echoed T-Too, mockingly.

Even *Tyrone* Dunkle wouldn't be such a bad name, I thought. T-Too's real name was Tyrone Thomas, which isn't so bad as names go. But everyone called him T-Too, which I should clarify was pronounced "tee-two," a reference to his initials, not his stutter. It's how he wrote his name on his homework assignments, and even how the teachers spelled his name on the chalkboard when he got in trouble. I knew this because he was in a couple of my classes. Pax and Derek were in eighth grade so we didn't share anything, but T-Too was in seventh with us, though he was a bit taller than most. It occurs to me just now that Tyrone Thomas should have been T-2 or T-Two, not T-Too, but it was probably his own idea for how to spell the nickname and he wasn't that bright. Honestly, I was impressed he'd noticed the bike change.

"My dad painted it," Dale offered, looking miserable.

"Oh, I bet," Pax said. "You're a bit too young to use spray paint. Would get all over your dick." He turned to Benny. "Got any more rocks?"

"Uh, no," Benny responded. "We threw them all in."

Pax turned to T-Too. "Hey, get me some." T-Too nodded and ran down to the ditch.

This wasn't good.

"Want to throw rocks with us?" asked Benny, hopefully.

"No," Pax sneered. "I want to throw them at Dale's bike and see if I can chip the paint off and bring the O.J. back."

Dale looked horrified. "Don't do that!"

"Yeah, that's not cool, man," said Benny.

I was shocked. Benny never stood up to anyone. Not to his old man or his brothers, or even to his friends. Why the hell would he stand up to a bully, and in the defense of *Dale Dunkle*?

"You shut the fuck up, kid," Pax spat. "Or I'll throw rocks at you too and see if I can't knock the black off, Oreo."

T-Too was walking back toward us. He had cupped his t-shirt in front like a basket so it could hold a dozen stones.

"Oreo?" asked Dale.

Pax scoffed. "Black on the outside, white on the inside, dipshit. Like your bike. Pretending to be something it ain't."

T-Too dropped the rocks at Pax's feet. Then both hooligans leaned down and grabbed one. Before we could turn to run, Pax had thrown a rock at Benny, hitting him in the leg. T-Too had thrown a rock at Dale's bike but missed.

"Run!" Benny yelled.

You're not supposed to run. Like I said, you're supposed to stand up to bullies. Teach them a lesson so they'll leave you alone. Pax was only a year older, after all. And we had them outnumbered, three to two. Somehow, though, fighting back just didn't work in the real world. At least not in our world.

It occurred to me, as I was about to turn and flee, that Pax hadn't made any threat to me personally. Only to Dale and Benny. And as Pax stood there glowering, the Black House and the entrance to our street visible behind him, a strange thought popped into my head. What if I took a single step over to Pax's corner, picked up a rock, and pelted Dale's bike myself?

Pax gave me a look like he was reading my mind, and I remember seeing small bugs flickering around his body. In a flash, I had a graphic vision of pelting a rock straight at Dale's head, slicing through his cheap glasses and sending sharp shards into his left eye. I could imagine it so clearly, his eyeball popping out of its socket, dangling from its half-severed connecting tissue, crimson blood pooling on his cheek.

Now, don't go thinking I'm a bad guy just yet, because I didn't do that—but I wasn't sure where the dark, fleeting thought came from, either.

Before we could attempt an escape, and risk being pelted in the backs of our heads, we were saved by an approaching pick-up truck. A simple drive-by would have bought us a little time by itself, but miraculously, this driver slowed and lowered his window.

"You kids ain't throwing stones at each other, are ya?"

I didn't recognize the driver, but Pax seemed to. The guy was a big, stern-looking dude, with bulging biceps and serious stubble. Must have been one of Pax's neighbors on Stevens.

"Nah, we just playin', sir," Pax answered.

"You know you boys could hurt someone that way."

"Just messin' around, I promise."

The man's eyes narrowed. "Why don't you and your

friend hop in the back, and I'll drive you home. Your daddy'll be happy to see you in time for dinner, for once."

Pax and T-Too exchanged a look. It didn't seem to be a suggestion.

"Alright, thanks," Pax said. Then, to us: "See you babies later."

The bed of the pick-up was missing its tailgate, so it was easy for them to hop in. As the stranger drove away with the bullies in tow, Dale, Benny and I exchanged relieved glances. To say we had lucked out was an understatement. I didn't know if Dale had ever taken a rock to the head, but Benny and I sure had. My nose was crooked from taking one to the face two years earlier. I prefer people sit on my left side, my "good" side, to this day.

"That was close," said Benny.

"No shit," I agreed.

"Thanks for defending me," Dale added, to Benny. I couldn't tell for sure, but I thought he said this a little pointedly, to shame me for not doing the same a week before.

"Ah, well," Benny said, shyly. "Getting sick of those dudes."

Dale smiled. "And you know what else? You're not an Oreo."

"I'm not?"

"No," said Dale. "You're mixed, right? So you're more like S'mores. Tan on the outside, both black *and* white on the inside."

Benny blinked. He looked at me, then back at Dale. Then he burst out laughing.

"Alright man," Benny said to me. "I guess your friend's okay."

I still had made absolutely no determination on whether or not I wanted to be Dale's friend. But under the circumstances, it'd be a dick move to correct him.

Dale brightened. "Hey, you two wanna come over and play video games?"

Benny shook his head. "Nah, pick-up-truck guy is right. It's getting close to dinner. And I'm not gonna get out of having my ass kicked by Pax just to get my ass kicked by my dad."

"How about you, Jimmy? We eat dinner late, so there's time."

"Us too," I admitted. "I can swing by."

"Super-duper!"

Seriously, dude.

Neither Benny nor I had our bikes, so Dale walked his bike beside us as we traveled west on Clark back toward our block. After a few minutes, Benny started to get more nervous about the time, and so said an early goodbye and jogged ahead of us toward his home.

"His dad must be pretty strict," Dale observed.

"You could say that."

"What about your dad?"

I shrugged. "My dad's not around."

Dale looked concerned. "I'm sorry. I should have remembered that."

"It's cool, man. It's been a long time."

We were silent for a bit. Then I thought of something to ask him.

"Hey, you're real smart, right?"

"Boy genius," Dale responded, dryly.

"Ya ever hear of Pig Latin?"

"Sure."

I fished Emilia's note from my pocket. "What's this say?"

He looked at it. "It says 'I am bored.' Hey, if you know it's Pig Latin, then you must know Pig Latin, so how come you couldn't read it?"

"She told me it was Pig Latin. Never heard of it."

"She, eh?" Dale flashed me a little grin. "I suppose I could have guessed from the pretty penmanship. Not a teacher, I assume."

"Nah, some chick in Social Studies. Where'd you learn Latin?"

Dale laughed. "Pig Latin isn't *Latin*. It's fake. You take the first letter of whatever word you want to say and put it to the end, and then add 'ay'. So, Dale would be Aleday. And Jimmy would be...?"

"Immyjay," I answered.

"That's right. And if it's a word starting with a vowel you don't move the first letter, but add 'yay' at the end. That's why you get 'iyay' and 'amyay' for the first two words."

"Huh."

"We talked in Pig Latin a lot at Roeper."

"The nerd school?"

Dale looked embarrassed. "Yeah."

We had turned the corner onto Chennault. I could smell someone cooking chicken on a charcoal grill. I did wish sometimes that we ate dinner earlier. I was usually riding my bike around town this time of day when the weather's nice, and there was always someone making barbeque or burgers every few houses, which killed me. Ding Dongs and Ho Hos from Huck's were tasty and all, but you were hungry a few minutes later.

"Why do you eat dinner late, Dale?"

"My Dad works in Detroit so he doesn't get home until after six. You?"

"My mom's boyfriend wants to shower after work before coming over, so we've gotten in the habit of eating at six thirty whether he's joining us or not."

"That's nice of you."

We approached his house. I know I must have been there a thousand times when I was a little kid, but it barely seemed familiar to me. At the front door, I hesitated a bit, somehow realizing that crossing the threshold meant I was agreeing to...well, not agreeing to becoming *friends* necessarily, but at least *friendly*. I wondered what I'd say if Dale waved me down in the lunchroom tomorrow. Would I ignore him like I did the first week? Or just accept the fact that one of my friends was a nerd?

"Say," I said, stalling. "What computer games are we playing? You got a Nintendo?"

A huge grin swept across Dale's face. "No. Something *better*."

# Five

Dale's house looked a lot like ours from the outside, and like ours, when you entered the front door, you immediately had to make a choice to go up or down a half-flight of stairs. Both houses had the living room downstairs, but ours had the kitchen downstairs, too, whereas his had the kitchen and dining room upstairs. This seemed to give his house a lot more downstairs room, and his family had divided the space into a living room side and a home office side. He motioned for me to sit on the floor.

"That's a nice TV," I said, sitting.

He beamed. "27 inches!"

Bastard. Ours was 25.

The television sat on a short walnut entertainment center with a cable box, a VCR, and the "something better" nestled in an open shelf.

"Is that a computer?"

"Yep. It's a Commodore 128. It's like the Commodore 64 but, well, twice as good. Get it?"

"Uh huh." I squirmed. I had used a school computer (an Apple IIe) a couple times for a math testing program, but I couldn't believe Dale would have brought me over to play *educational* games. How much of a nerd would this kid have to be to think a *computer* was better than a Nintendo?

I must have looked disappointed, for Dale laughed. "Trust me, you'll love it. I always keep it in Commodore 64 mode. I have over 200 games, including *Aliens, Ghostbusters, Summer Games, Bruce Lee, Skate or Die, Karateka...*"

"Really?"

"Yeah, check this out."

He handed me a huge plastic container filled with 5.25" floppy disks. Most of them had hand-written labels.

"I don't get it."

"It's easy to make bootleg copies of Commodore games. My mom works for General Motors and they swap games all the time on the assembly floor. She's always bringing me new things to try, and if I hear of any game that's supposed to be good, I ask her and she can usually get it for me."

This was admittedly cool. I had a decent Nintendo game collection, but cartridges were expensive, and there was no way to copy them.

"What do you want to try?" he asked.

"I donno. What's good?"

Dale thought about this. "Well, there's a cool two-player motorcycle racing game. I always play against the computer, but since you're here..." He rummaged through the large box until he found it. "Here we are. *Kikstart II*."

He put the large floppy disk into a disk drive and typed "Load '*',8,1" on the keyboard. At least, I assumed he was typing that, since that's what appeared on the screen, but his fingers moved so fast it seemed like he was mashing keys at random.

I don't want to get into too many specifics here or you'll be bored to death, but let's say the game was kind of like *Excitebike* on NES, but with a two-player split screen for racing a friend. It also had the ability to build your own courses using all the ramps and springs and obstacles you wanted. The graphics were about as good as my Nintendo, but the music was better. Although Dale kicked my ass the first few games, I won the last game by a couple seconds.

"What else ya got?"

For the next hour Dale let me go through the massive number of disks and pick out a few titles that sounded fun to try. My favorite was *One on One*, a two-player basketball game pitting Dr. J against Larry Bird. Though I had never played this title before, Dale didn't stand a chance. I realized that for a lot of these two-player games, even if Dale had played them against the computer, he hadn't played them against an actual live person before me.

"Didn't you have friends at your old school?"

"Of course! But we lived far away from everyone, so I didn't have people over much."

"Does your dad ever play with you?"

"Nah, not really. He liked a Star Trek game I had on the old computer, but it wasn't two-player."

"This isn't your first computer?"

Dale laughed like this was the funniest thing he had ever heard. "Of course not! My first was the Timex Sinclair 1000. We used to get a newsletter mailed to us that had code you could type in in order to build a game. But you had to type every character exactly right for the code to work, and some of the games were over a hundred lines long."

"That sounds awful."

"Well, it made me a faster typist, so that's good. But the next computer we had was a TI-99/4A. That one I loved. I bet you've used one of those—they have one at the library in town."

I nodded, but as far as I knew, I had never been to our library.

"That was my first computer with a speech synthesizer," he went on. "Some of the games talked to you which was awesome. I still have that one in a box under my bed and plug it in once in a while to play old games like *Parsec* and *BurgerTime*."

"We've never had a computer," I said. "We went from Atari to ColecoVision to Nintendo. Have you ever had any of those?"

"No. But with a computer like this, I don't need one!"

We heard someone coming down the stairs. It was Dale's mom.

"Food's almost ready, boys!"

I stood up. "I guess I better get home myself."

"You're welcome to stay for dinner," Mrs. Dunkle offered.

"Can you?" asked Dale, a hint of pleading in his

voice.

"Uh, I donno."

Mrs. Dunkle smiled. "We have plenty of food. It's beef stroganoff, and we have apple pie for dessert."

"Can you call my mom and ask?" I was thinking Mom might appreciate a one-on-one dinner with her boyfriend. She didn't get many of those. And besides, the stroganoff smelled amazing.

"Sure thing!" She nodded to Dale. I think she was proud that her son had made a new friend. Or, rather, rediscovered an old one.

My mom said yes.

Dinner was good, and I was so glad it wasn't awkward. Dale's little sister Debbie had been a newborn when they moved away, but now was a talkative kindergartener. "I'm going to be a scientist," she declared at one point, which struck me as a highly unusual career prediction for a five-year-old. (At that age, I just wanted to be an ice cream truck driver—and still hadn't ruled it out.) Dale's dad was a geeky but funny guy who had a couple good puns about food that made me laugh.

Mr. and Mrs. Dunkle weren't overly nosy or prying like some parents. Mostly, they listened to Dale and I talk about school and didn't mind when we made fun of our teachers. When they did join the conversation, they asked good questions and listened to our responses. It was a nice change from my normal routine, to be honest. Don't get me wrong, I loved my mom—I just sometimes felt she was always picking at me, nagging me like I was a little kid no matter how old I got. The Dunkles treated Dale and even Debbie more like peers, and treated me that way, too.

Over pie, Mr. Dunkle asked what we had been doing downstairs.

"Just computer games," Dale answered.

Mr. Dunkle shook his head. "Kids and computer games. You should play real games. Maybe Scrabble, or chess."

"I play chess," I said, a bit too excitedly. I felt a weird need to impress these people.

Dale's dad raised an eyebrow. "Oh?"

"I'm not very good yet," I admitted. "But I play games with Mike—that's my mom's boyfriend—and I'm getting close to beating him." This was an exaggeration. We'd only played a dozen times at that point. But, I wasn't losing as badly as I had the first few games.

"Then I have something you'll like," said Dale, shoving the last bite of pie in his mouth. "It's called *Archon*. Let's go back downstairs!"

Now, on the off-chance that you're not familiar with 1980s 8-bit consumer video games, *Archon* was a sort of battle chess. Instead of pawns, you had knights and goblins. Instead of a King or Queen, you had a Sorcerer or a Wizard. Different pieces, like unicorns or manticores or phoenixes, had different weapons and powers, and when you landed on another player's piece you had to fight them in combat to determine which piece survived.

I did like *Archon*. A lot. Though it drove Dale nuts that I beat him four out of five attempts.

"Maybe we should play something else," he pouted.

I found two disks that had professionally printed labels, rather than the handwritten scribbles adorning most of the pirated collection.

"What's this?" I asked.

"Ah, that's *The Newsroom*."

"*The Newsroom*? Is it a game?"

A wistful smile overtook him. "Oh, no. Not a game. Let me show you."

With that, he stood and ran up the stairs. I didn't think I was supposed to follow him, so I just sat there. Eventually he returned with a cardboard box.

"I was editor of the school paper at Roeper," Dale bragged. "Check these out."

The kid proceeded to show me issue after issue of *The Roeper Free Press*. It was a student-run newspaper from his old grade school, and contained articles, comics, word searches, and everything else you'd expect a newspaper to have. The issues were printed on standard letter-size paper, stapled in the top left corner and folded in half to create the proper newspaper "look." To my 12-year-old eye, they seemed pretty legit.

"Kids made all these? How?"

"With *The Newsroom* software. See, we had this big computer lab, and each student was tasked with writing certain articles, or making cartoons, or typing up Letters to the Editor, that sort of thing."

"And the teacher laid everything out?"

Dale shook his head. "No, we did that too. I mean, Terry taught us how to use the software, of course, but we did it all ourselves, and she answered questions if we got stuck."

"Terry?"

"The journalism teacher."

"You called your teachers by their first names?"

Dale shrugged. "Roeper was all about teaching students that we were equals to everyone, even grownups. We didn't call anyone by their last names. It's a bit hard to get used to that at New Haven."

"I can't imagine calling my teachers by their first names. I don't think I know most of their first names."

"I don't think I knew all of my teachers' last names," Dale said.

I ruffled through more of the papers. It was cool to think of a group of kids being given the training and tools to create something uniquely theirs. New Haven High School had a school newspaper, too, but it didn't look as good as this one from Roeper, written and designed by 8 to 11-year-olds.

"*The Roeper Free Press*," I said, thoughtfully.

"I wanted to call it *The Roeper Report*, but was outvoted," Dale complained.

"You should join our school paper," I said. "You could improve it."

"My parents asked about that," Dale admitted. "But at New Haven you have to be in the tenth grade or higher to participate."

"That sucks. These are awesome."

Dale was bursting with pride at my being impressed. "Let me show you how we did it!"

He inserted the first floppy disk I had found and booted up *The Newsroom*. The start screen was a cute depiction of, well, an actual newsroom, with a darkroom, a printing press, an artist at a drafting table, a guy with a typewriter, and a woman assembling panels on a broadsheet. These drawings were entitled Photo Lab, Press, Banner, Copy Desk, and Layout, respectively, and Dale explained that each of these five parts of the software mimicked each of the five crucial components of developing a complete paper. He clicked "Copy Desk," which opened a blank white square with some icons beside it.

"What do you want to write about?" he asked.

"Huh?"

"Your first article! What do you want it to be about?"

I thought for a moment. "How about how bullies suck?"

Dale beamed. "Oh yes," he agreed. Then he typed "How Bullies Are Ruining the New Haven Heights" as the title. "Now what?"

"Earlier today, two bullies bothered three innocent kids who were minding their own business," I dictated. Dale typed almost as fast as I could speak. It was super-cool seeing my own words appear in black type on the screen before us, like some sort of science fiction movie with a voice-to-text computer. His fingers moved so fast on the soft plastic keys it sounded like gentle rain falling on cement.

"Go on," he urged.

"The bullies were Pax and T-Too, two losers from Stevens street. They hang out with Derek as well, but, uh, he was probably grounded or something."

Dale laughed, but typed it all, except for the "uh".

"The good citizens of New Haven are committed to seeing bad guys brought to justice," I concluded, finding my stride. "If you have any information about these bullies, please contact the New Haven Police Department at once."

I smiled, pleased with myself.

"That's it?"

"That's it."

"It's a little short," said Dale, gesturing to the half-filled white square. "But we can add some clip art."

He clicked the save icon, then opened the Photo Lab from the main screen. Using the arrow keys on the keyboard, he browsed through pages of cheesy black and white line drawings until he found an image of a stereotypical tough guy burglar with a black mask over his eyes. He copied this image into my bully article to fill the extra space.

"There you are, Jimmy. Your first complete article. You're officially a reporter!"

"Ha. If you ever published that, I'd get my ass kicked."

Dale sighed. "Well, it's not like anyone will ever see it but us."

"It really is too bad you're too young for the school paper," I said. "Our town doesn't have a paper, right?"

"That's right. It used to, though. It was called *The New Haven Herald*. I found the archives at the library. Its last issue was printed twenty years ago."

"I wonder why it shut down."

"I think it was because *The Macomb County Chronicle* covers all of Macomb County, including New Haven, so it wasn't needed anymore."

"Makes our town feel small, though," I mused. "Pretty lame that we're not important enough for our own paper."

"We're important enough. It's just a lot of work to publish a newspaper."

"That didn't seem like that much work," I said, pointing to the screen. "Especially with how fast you type. And your school paper was printed on normal-sized paper, right?"

"Right."

"Last year we had a field trip to *The Detroit News*," I recounted. "The best part was the big printing press. It took huge pieces of paper and cut and folded them so fast you could barely see what was happening. But with this program you wouldn't need a press or anything. Just a printer and a Xerox machine. Well, and a bunch of articles."

Dale and I glanced back at my short little article on the screen, then stared at each other for several seconds. We were both thinking the same thing.

"I do hate that I can't be on the school paper for three more years," he said. "I love writing. I'm constantly thinking of cool things to write about. And I miss doing the layout."

"You already have the software," I said. "And I could write articles too, as long as you could type them up for me."

"And we publish it ourselves?"

"Why not?" I actually could think of several good reasons "why not" but kept them to myself.

"But would anyone read it?"

I shrugged. "My mom says people will read anything."

Dale studied the screen for a while, then looked back at the box from his time at Roeper. You could tell he was tempted. Then he made up his mind and grinned.

# Six

By October of '88, Dale and I were hanging out after school a couple times a week. Sometimes we just played video games, and I could bore you to death if I described all our favorites. Especially don't get me started on *Paradroid*—one of the greatest video games of all time and the reason I have a Commodore 64 emulator on the laptop I'm typing this novel on right now.

But we worked on the paper a lot, too. It was sort of a secret project that even my closest friends didn't know about. Although it was still a concept at this point, we had written a dozen articles about various things happening in the neighborhood, along with movie reviews, a fake advice column, and so on. Admittedly, Dale did most of the work, including all the typing and layout, but I still felt like I was contributing quite a bit. He knew nothing about sports, for example, and I talked him into letting me write articles about the Detroit Pistons and Detroit Tigers. I even tried my hand at creating a Word Search.

"We need a name," Dale said one day.

"A name?"

"For the paper. If we're going to actually publish it, it can't just be *The Paper*."

"Might be kinda cool that way," I considered. "Everyone reads *The Paper*."

We laughed.

"How about *The New Haven News*?" I offered.

"Nah, there's already a *Detroit News*."

"*New Haven Chronicle*?"

"Already a *Macomb County Chronicle*."

"*New Haven Free Press*?"

"Well, now you're being silly."

I shrugged. "Well, what was the name of that old New Haven paper?"

"*The New Haven Herald*," Dale replied, perking up.

"Can't we just call it that?'

"I donno. It's not the same paper. People might get confused."

This seemed unlikely.

"Didn't you say that paper went out of business in the sixties? Man, everyone who even remembers that paper is probably dead." My math sucked there, but he didn't call me on it.

"Maybe *The New Haven Herald Two*?"

"Like, a sequel?"

"Sure."

I nodded. I dug this idea. And besides, everyone knew that sequels were better than the originals.

Dale loaded up *The Newsroom*. He created a masthead with a big bold font declaring *The New Haven Herald Two*. We both looked at it for a while. Something didn't feel right.

"I don't think I like the 'Two'," Dale said.

"Yeah," I agreed.

He tried the number "2" instead of the word. Nope, that was worse. Then he tried the roman numeral. This was better, but seemed stuck-up.

Dale had a thought. "What if we did something that acknowledged that we're kids?"

"You mean making the 'R's backward, like the Toys R Us sign?"

"No," Dale laughed. "I mean like this." He deleted the "Two" and replaced it with "Jr."

"*The New Haven Herald Jr.*?"

"NHHJ for short."

"Huh. So not a sequel, but, like, a spinoff."

Dale beamed. "Exactly! An homage."

"A what?"

"We're saying we've been inspired by this earlier thing, *The New Haven Herald*, but we're taking it a different direction. And, we're kids!"

"Is it *for* kids?"

"No, I don't think so. But, we should acknowledge

that it's *by* kids so that we don't get looked down on when we have typos and mistakes or whatever."

"I can live with that."

"Great! Let's make business cards!"

Dale proceeded to use the same program, *The Newsroom*, to design business cards for the two of us. He was Dale Dunkle: Owner & Editor and I was Jimmy Logan: Reporter. Each card had our respective home telephone number. The cards were printed on regular paper, and so were kinda floppy, but Dale cut them very carefully with his mom's paper cutter, which made them look official enough.

"Why do we need business cards, anyway?" I asked while admiring my stack.

"Same reason as grown-ups," Dale replied. "So people take us seriously when we're talking to them."

—

Zach, Marco, Benny and I sat together most lunches, and Dale joined us sometimes too. He held back, though, seeming to understand that our in-school friendship wasn't as strong as our after-school friendship. Dale would often sit alone at lunch, head buried in a notebook, or occasionally he'd eat with another geeky kid I didn't know. I'm finding this a bit hard to explain without making me sound like a popularity-obsessed douchebag, but I sometimes had to let him know his place with me in public. I suppose I felt my Junior High reputation could survive being a sometimes-friend to Dale, but not an always-friend to Dale.

Besides, the rest of the gang didn't get Dale the way I did. They tolerated him, but were a bit distant.

I remember one day it was all five of us, devouring grilled cheese sandwiches, fries, and chocolate milks.

Zach held up his slightly burnt sandwich.

"This chick is *toast!*" he said, and we all laughed at the reference.

"Don't cross the streams!" added Benny. "Especially when taking a piss!" More laughter.

The nice thing about *Ghostbusters* is that everyone

loved it for different reasons. If you enjoyed a good comedy, there was plenty there for you. If you liked action and adventure, well, plenty of that as well. If you were like Dale and had typed up your own *Tobin's Spirit Guide* on a Smith Corona Electric Typewriter, including original research on spirits you had conducted at the Lenox Township Library...well, you get the idea.

"Last night, I had a fart that qualified as a class 5 full-roaming vapor!" said Dale. This got a communal chuckle, but damn his jokes were nerdy.

T-Too approached our table. It was always weird to see him without Pax and Derek, but eighth grade ate lunch the next period, so we rarely saw them all together in school.

"W-what are you girls laughing about?"

"*Ghostbusters*," said Dale. "Ever see it?"

"The cartoon?" he asked.

"No, the movie!" explained Dale. "But the cartoon is awesome too. Did you see the one where they went back in time and accidentally trapped the ghosts of Christmas past, present, and future?"

I nudged him to say *why are you talking to him* but I don't think he got it.

"I don't watch cartoons anymore," T-Too said, disgusted. "You really are a baby."

Dale looked confused. He thought everyone watched Saturday Morning cartoons. And, truthfully, we all did. T-Too probably did, too; he was just trying to pick on Dale for being the youngest one in the cafeteria.

There was a moment of silence before Dale said "well, you're missing out," and began to take a sip of his chocolate milk. T-Too knocked the carton out of Dale's hand and into his lap. Dale immediately tried to rise but T-Too stopped him.

"Don't move," he snapped.

Dale froze. There was something in T-Too's voice that scared the hell out of him. They eyed each other for a moment, then Dale looked down at his pants. The milk had pooled in the plastic chair and the liquid was making a large wet spot in his jeans.

"Come on, man," said Marco. "Lay off the kid."

T-Too jerked his head to Marco. It allowed Dale a moment to stand up and start wiping his crotch with napkins.

"What's it t-to you?"

Marco had no response. T-Too looked back at Dale, then at Dale's crotch, and grinned.

"Looks like someone p-peed their pants," he observed. Then he turned and left.

I passed Dale my extra napkins. He used them to sop up the remaining milk on his jeans and the chair. But it really did look like he had pissed himself, and we weren't the only ones to notice. A few in the cafeteria had begun whispering and pointing at Dale, who was standing, waiting for his chair to dry. I didn't know if T-Too had started the rumor, or other people had noticed on their own, but people at the nearest table began making a "pssssssss" sound and laughing.

"It's chocolate milk," Dale said, weakly.

It didn't matter.

By next period, half the people at school were making "pssss" noises when Dale walked by. I saw his face in the hallway between classes and he seemed lost and pathetic.

Even Emilia asked about it at the start of Mr. Wright's class.

"Hey, is it true your friend peed his pants at lunch today?"

I wasn't sure how to respond. I should have said "nah, a mean kid dumped milk in his lap." That would have been the truth. But I couldn't tell if that's what would have impressed her. Another part of me wanted to say "oh, he's not really my friend," like I would have a month ago, but that ship had sailed. I had let too many people see us together at this point. I was tempted to say "yeah, what a loser!" since she was so interested, and maybe thought it was funny and wanted to laugh with me about it. Since I couldn't read her, that too might be risky. I wouldn't want her to see me as someone without empathy.

Finally, I said: "well, he *is* pretty young."

This was not a lie, I told myself. In fact, it didn't answer the question at all. Sure, maybe it *implied* that he had peed his pants, but it had that thing Mr. Wright just taught us about: plausible deniability.

Emilia shrugged. "That's too bad," she said.

As class began, I began to feel a bit guilty about my response. Maybe not as guilty as when that dirty girl on the corner had given me a disapproving stare, but guilty just the same. I thought about passing Emilia a note explaining the situation, that it wasn't pee at all, but that would admit that my first response had been evasive. I guess it wouldn't have made a difference one way or another, but I didn't like this feeling. I suppose Grandma would call it my "conscience" bugging me. Though, she was a past-oriented person, as she explained. I wasn't. I was present-oriented. I needed to stop thinking about it.

—

Dale was the last kid to get on the bus. He looked miserable. I was sitting with Marco, as usual, but there were plenty of empty seats. Then people started making the "pssss" sound, and some put their backpacks next to them to block Dale from sitting. No one wanted to ride next to someone who, allegedly, would smell like piss. Dale was ready to cry. Then his eyes caught mine.

"Jimmy, tell them! You were there! Tell them it was chocolate milk!"

Quite a few heads turned my way.

I opened my mouth to speak, but froze. Running through my head were all the pros and cons of publicly siding with the geeky kid with a stain on his jeans. I felt bad for Dale, I did—and I knew he needed my help. Maybe I could say something that didn't take a clear side, like "come on everyone, stop picking on him," which Dale would hopefully see as coming to his defense, but that wouldn't spoil the fun of people laughing at the clown. Before I could say anything, Marco spoke up beside me.

"It was just spilled milk, guys." Marco turned to me. "We both were there."

I was a bit stunned to be outed but nodded in affirmation.

There were a few "awws" of disappointment in the crowd. Dale looked relieved, but gave me a sort of quizzical look. Someone finally let him sit down beside them.

When we arrived at Dale's stop, I got off with him rather than waiting for my own stop. He walked to his house, not turning around to acknowledge me.

"Dale, wait," I said, catching up.

He had reached his driveway before he spun around.

"What?" he asked, coldly.

"Well, uh," I stammered. He had never been angry with me before. I wasn't sure how to take it. "I thought we could work on the paper!"

Dale stared at me for a long time. Finally, his face softened, more in defeat than forgiveness.

"Ya know, I was really popular at Roeper."

I must have looked surprised.

"No, it's true. Everyone knew who I was. Everyone liked me. The teachers even let me run cool projects when I had a creative idea. Like writing and directing my own movie, during the school day, with other students and other teachers as the actors. It was amazing. I had no idea…" his voice broke.

"…how different public school would be?" I offered.

Dale nodded. "How lucky I was."

I guess I had assumed Dale had been a geeky loser everywhere. Only now did I realize that at a school for gifted students he might have been King of the Nerds in a *good* way.

We stood there in his driveway in silence for a bit, and I got why he was disappointed. I should have been the one to defend him, not Marco. I was the one who was supposed to be his friend, even at a distance. But I didn't apologize and he didn't ask me to.

"Come on in," he said at last. "I do want to show you your new sports page."

Mom had corned beef bubbling in the crock pot all day, so the whole house smelled like heaven when I got home. Mike was there already setting the table, humming along to Elton John playing in the other room. He flashed me a smile.

"Hey sport," he said.

"Hey."

"Hanging at Dale's again?"

I nodded, taking my normal seat. I had decided to finally tell them, and this was as good an opening as any.

"Dale and I are starting a newspaper."

Mom and Mike exchanged a glance. "For school?" Mom asked.

"No," I admitted, hoping it didn't sound too lame. "For the neighborhood. New Haven hasn't had a newspaper in over twenty years. We thought we'd, uh, make one."

"How are you going to make a newspaper?" Mom asked while serving the food.

"Well, Dale's got this computer program they used to make the newspaper at his old school, and we've been writing articles and seeing what we can do by ourselves."

"How many pages have you written?"

"Oh, I donno. Maybe three or four so far. We're hoping for eight pages altogether."

Mom smiled. "So, just for fun then?"

"Not really. We've been talking about printing it and selling it for a quarter at local stores like Huck's. We figure if it's cheap, like *The Macomb County Chronicle*, people might give it a shot."

"You think Huck's will sell a kid's newspaper? What's in it for them? Do they get some of the money?"

"I hadn't thought of that."

Mom shook her head. "It'll cost more than a quarter to print each copy. You'll lose money on every sale."

"Well hang on," Mike protested. "Don't crush his

dreams yet with practical stuff."

"One of us has to be practical. Lord knows it's not going to be you."

Mike stiffened. "I think it's a cool idea."

"I'm not saying it isn't," Mom said. "I just don't see how they're going to make any money, so what's the point?"

I hadn't really thought the money was important. It would just be exciting if people were reading what we wrote. But if it cost our entire allowance to put an issue out, maybe it wasn't a good plan.

I must have looked dejected, for Mom softened a bit.

"Well, you could sell ads, I suppose."

"Ads?"

"Yeah. I mean, most newspapers are only 25 cents, and they have thirty or forty pages every day. I'm sure it costs more to print them than they're selling for. Which means they must make their money from the advertisements inside. All those car dealerships and restaurants and grocery store coupons. Businesses pay tons of money to advertise in papers. It's worth it to them to reach that many people."

"Hmm. Do you think anyone would want to advertise in our paper?"

"What's the circulation?"

"Huh?"

"How many copies will you be printing?"

"I have no idea."

Mom gave me a patronizing look I didn't appreciate. "Well, it sounds like you have a lot to think about before you're serious."

Mike came to my defense again. "Hey, I think it's cool if he wants to be an entrepreneur. We should encourage this. Besides, it might look good for colleges for Jimmy to have a successful hobby under his belt."

Mom chuckled. "You think Jimmy's going to college?"

"Why wouldn't he?"

"I'm sorry, you're right." She turned to me. "*Of course* you can go to college if that's what you want to do. It would be good for you to think of the future for once. Just don't expect me to pay for it."

I was going to tell Grandma about the paper, too, but was feeling a bit embarrassed about it by the time I brought up her food. Instead, we talked for a few minutes about school and some soap opera she watched that day. She could tell I didn't seem very talkative and just gave me a nod and a smile when I left.

Mike caught me in the hallway.

"Chess?" he asked.

We played the first game in silence, as I was still a bit moody, but by the second game I came out of my shell when I realized I was winning.

"Hey, you're getting better at this," he said.

"I've been playing *Archon*," I explained. "It's a computer game Dale has which is like chess, but when you land on a piece, you have to battle them with lasers and magic powers and stuff."

"That does sound fun," Mike agreed. "Though it might be making you over-confident. Checkmate."

"Wait, what?" I couldn't believe it. "You said I was getting better!"

"You are! You're taking more chances. Just remember that in the real game, if someone lands on you, you don't have the opportunity to out-shoot them."

"Yeah. I'm not as good without my lasers."

Mike smiled. "The day you beat me at chess..."

"I know, I know."

"...is the day you become a man."

I sighed. "One more?"

"Sure thing. This time, try not to be so focused on the present. Think more about the future."

He must have been talking to Grandma.

We set up the pieces again. Somehow, I had to balance being aggressive, going after his important pieces even if it meant sacrificing some of mine, with keeping an eye on my own vulnerabilities, anticipating Mike's possible moves more than one turn in advance. I almost wished I could step around to his side of the board between turns to better imagine what I would do in his position. But I realized I'd have to do that in my head instead.

"I wanted you to know," Mike said, "that I think the newspaper idea is cool."

"Yeah?"

He nodded, then took my last bishop.

"I bet I can get the foundry to place an ad," he said. "We're always hiring for something. What would a quarter-page ad run?"

"I donno," I said. "Two bucks?"

"Make it four," Mike countered. "I'll tell Patty that we can place a quarter-page help wanted ad in the new local paper for only four bucks, and if we don't get any calls, she can take the four bucks out of my paycheck."

I laughed. "You don't have to do that, Mike."

"Hey, I'd be proud to be your first advertiser. Or, rather, my employer would."

I didn't say anything for a moment, and must have looked concerned, for Mike asked "what's wrong?"

"Nothing. Just realized it's getting kinda real."

"How so?"

"Well, I'm not sure what would be more embarrassing—if nobody reads our paper, or if everyone does."

## Seven

I don't think I'd ever seen another kid so impressed with me as when I told Dale about that first ad buy. Student-run papers like the Roeper Free Press were funded by the school, so he hadn't considered the possibility of going after advertisers, but it made practical financial sense. After all, even the xeroxed programs at the yearly New Haven Community Schools Christmas Concert had ads in them from Bawler Towing and Video Scene II. We figured since a quarter page ad had been sold to the foundry for four bucks, an eighth-page ad would be two bucks and a half-page ad would be eight. We decided against running any full-page ads, though, since we weren't sell-outs or anything.

It was a crisp but sunny fall Saturday when we planned to make our pitch to local businesses. To cover more places, we decided to split up on our respective bikes, each armed with business cards and a single copy of the current front page of the in-progress paper. Dale had even made an "ad sheet" which showed the actual sizes of the ads and their associated costs.

"My mom said people will ask about circulation," I told him.

"That's a good point. People will want to know how many eyeballs will be on their ads."

"Uh, yeah."

Dale thought for a moment. "Well, how about we make fifty copies of the first issue?"

"Fifty?" That sounded low. "Why not a hundred?"

"I thought of that, but if we don't sell many, then it will have cost a lot to print, and we'll have a big box of unsold papers. Fifty is safer."

"Wouldn't a hundred sound more impressive to the advertisers?"

"Yeah, but we shouldn't lie."

I thought for a moment. "How about if we print fifty *and* promise businesses their ad will have one hundred eyeballs on them?"

"How?"

"You know, 'cause people have two eyeballs per head."

So that's what we did.

Using graph paper, Dale had drawn two matching street maps of the Village of New Haven, and on each copy he had highlighted Shook Drain, the "river" that divided the square town more-or-less diagonally. He proposed he would take the northeast triangle, and I'd take the southwest triangle. This made me a bit jealous at first, since his triangle included places like Huck's Party Store and Video Scene II, places I knew well, and said so. He insisted he was jealous of my half, too, since my region included the library, one of the places he wanted to pitch having copies of the paper for sale. I stopped complaining when I realized his half also included Centennial Cemetery, with its dirt roads and teetering old tombstones, and in my mind was the scariest place in the world. Not that I thought we'd actually try and get an ad buy from a cemetery, of course, but even riding by the place gave me the creeps.

We had wanted to get an early start, around nine, but by the time we reviewed the street maps and practiced what we wanted to say it was after ten. Riding down Gratiot, my first stop would have been the Dairy Cone soft-serve ice cream shop, but they had already closed for the season. I continued south to Andy's Party Store, which was sort of like Huck's but grimier and smelled of incense. I popped my kickstand, went inside, and smiled at the Middle Eastern dude manning the register.

"Hi, is, uh, Andy around?"

"Andy?"

"You know, the owner."

"Ah. I am owner. There's no Andy."

It had never occurred to me that the owner wasn't named Andy.

"Sorry. I'm, uh, selling advertisements."

"For what? For school paper?"

"Actually, my friend and I are making our own paper."

I showed him the front page. He looked at it for a few moments, turned it to the empty back side, and looked unimpressed.

"That's it?"

"Well, it will be eight pages when we're done. We're still working on it. We're planning to sell it at places like Huck's!"

The man's eyes narrowed to slits. "Oh really. You want me to advertise in a paper sold at Huck's? What would my ad say? You shopped at the wrong store?" He handed me back my paper. "No thanks."

I left disappointed, but saw that the florist across the street was open, and tried there next. The woman I talked to said that the owner only worked Monday through Friday, but politely took my business card and promised they'd get back to me. I thought about stopping in the small diner next door to the florist, but they had a "no solicitors" sign on the door, and since I wasn't 100% sure I wasn't a solicitor, I chickened out.

I got my first positive response at St. Clair Studio, a small portrait photography studio which was famous for doing the senior photos of most graduating students. They weren't open to the public on Saturdays, but I lucked out when I saw the owner entering the front door as I was biking up. A jolly woman with old-fashioned glasses and a kind smile, Jodi Patrick was delighted to hear about our project and committed to a half-page ad before I even showed her the mock-up.

"How are you going to print these?" she asked.

"Uh, well we haven't figured that out yet."

"I think the library has a copy machine and charges five cents a page. How many pages will your paper be?"

"Eight pages for the first issue," I said.

"And you're selling for twenty-five cents?"

I did the math in my head. Like Mom had predicted, we'd lose money on every printing. How many ads would we need to sell to make up for that? Sounded like a Dale question.

"I tell you what," Mrs. Patrick offered. "I'll print the entire run of your first issue for free, in exchange for a half-page ad."

"Wow, really?"

"Yes. I think that's a fair trade."

"Well, I have to check with Dale on that, but it sure sounds great!"

"Here's my card. Just give me a call when you and your friend can talk, and I'll provide the ad I want to run when he says yes." She beamed at my excitement. "Now how about a cookie?"

This morning was going better than I could have expected. Sure, I hadn't technically made a cash sale yet, but St. Clair Studio was donating at least $20 in copying services, which was way more than the half-page ad rate would have brought in. And I got a cookie out of the deal. I was becoming a pro.

I stopped in a few more places and sold two eighth-page ads—one from First Congregational Church who wanted to list worship times, and the other from Happy Times Kiddy Garden, a home-based day care run by a harried woman who reminded me of Mrs. Hannigan from the movie *Annie*. By then, it was getting close to two o'clock, which was the time Dale and I were supposed to meet and share our progress at his house.

"Hey, Mr. Dunkle," I greeted as I rode up. He was raking leaves.

"Hey Jimmy," he said. "Dale's in the garage. I'm impressed with what you two are doing!"

"Thanks!"

It felt good to be included in the praise. Often it still seemed like this was Dale's project that I was just helping with on occasion. Which, if I was being honest with myself, was more or less true, though I at least earned my business cards today.

Dale was sitting on the floor of the garage surrounded by square pieces of thick cardboard he had cut from various boxes. Beside him were two similar cube-like creations he had assembled from the cardboard and joined with silver duct tape.

"Art project?" I asked.

"Newspaper boxes! Huck's agreed to sell them for us at no charge, but said they couldn't put them in inventory or handle the money. We need to come up with something to hold the papers, with a little change slot on top to hold the quarters. It'll be an honor system thing, but they'll put the box by the cash register to discourage anyone stealing them. Cool, huh?"

"Yeah, that's great!"

I told him about my successes with the ads and the printing agreement with St. Clair Studio. In response, Dale made a chittering sound, squinted his eyes, and began clawing at his ears with his fingers. I had never seen anyone do this before and wasn't sure what to say. Eventually he stopped, opened his eyes, and looked at me a little embarrassed.

"Sorry. I do that sometimes."

"Uh, okay." I looked around awkwardly.

"I promise it's nothing! I've done that since I was a little kid. When I'm either stressed or so happy I can't take it."

"Are you happy now?"

"Of course! This is great. Having printing costs covered means we don't have to fill the paper with ads to break even. We can have more quality content! I wrote five more articles this week. And, I sold two ads as well! I think we're only a few articles away from our eight-page goal."

"Wow, so fast?"

"Yeah! Hey, did you finish that article on last Friday's high school game?"

"Almost," I lied. "I can drop it by tomorrow."

"Perfect! How long is it?"

"Uh, I think it will be two panels long." I hedged a bit. "At least, if you find clipart of a football player to fill in any white space."

"Shouldn't be a problem. Football's the one with the goalie, right?"

I stared at him. He cracked up.

"I'm only kidding, Jimmy! Geez I'm not that much of a dork. I do know football."

"You have a football game on your computer, in other words."

"Yep!"

I knew it.

"Where were your ads from?"

"Video Scene II and Larry's Diner," Dale said. "The diner one is supposed to be a coupon you can clip out. 25% off Fish and Chips. He sketched it for me on a napkin. So we'll have to make sure it's placed in a corner of the page, and that whatever's on the back of it isn't too important. I wouldn't want someone cutting out a coupon and then only getting to read the first half of your football article."

"Uh, right."

"Ready to paint this?"

Dale and I took turns using black spray paint on the two cardboard box prototypes, making sure to cover up evidence of appliance logos and bar codes from the recycled packaging. I wondered if it was leftover paint from his bike upgrade.

As the boxes dried, we went inside the house to work on typing up the ads we had collected.

In *The Newsroom*, each page was laid out with either eight panels (two columns of four panels) or a top banner which was double the width of a single panel, leaving six panels below. This allowed you to create a masthead for the entire paper, as well as mastheads for individual sections like "Sports" or "Entertainment." Most pages consisted of random news and opinion blurbs.

Let me give you an example of one of my single panel articles:

```
A SPECIAL VISITOR
By Jimmy Logan
    On Tuesday, October 16 our school had a
```

visitor. He wore black slacks, tinted glasses, and a gray sweater. He also had a seeing problem.

He talked about his seeing eye dog (which he called a "leader dog") and how the dog helped him walk. He also talked about how the dog is smart and well trained. He could tell his right from his left on command. He was also trained to protect his master.

At the end of the show in the gym, he let us pet the dog. Then he passed out braille pads with letters and numbers in braille. It was very interesting. I think being blind would be hard. I wonder how they drive?

And here's one of Dale's:

FRANCHUK RETIRES
By Dale Dunkle

After thirty years of hard work, Walter Franchuk is retiring from public life this December. Those thirty years included four years on the School Board, two terms as County Commissioner, and his current position as Chairman of the County Commission.

We asked Franchuk how it felt to be so important in Macomb County. He laughed and replied: "I never considered myself as being important; I'm just happy that I have helped so many people." When asked about his favorite accomplishment, Mr. Franchuk said the best thing he did for New Haven was helping to bring us Detroit water.

Franchuk, 68, said he would like to thank the people of our community for the opportunity to represent them.

If you needed to write an article or design an ad that was longer than a single panel, you had to load and edit one panel at a time, remember where that panel left off, and then start the next panel even if you were halfway through a sentence. There was no way to view the content of multiple panels at the same time, which meant the only way to see if a multi-panel article flowed the way you thought it did was to print the page on an actual printer. Tedious, for sure, since Dale's Okimate printer took a full twenty minutes to print each page, and you couldn't do anything else on the computer while the printer was in use. Luckily, Mr. Dunkle had rigged up a coaxial switcher box so that we could watch TV while the Commodore ran in the background. I bet that's why we had so many TV and movie reviews in the paper. Well, that and being typical '80s pre-teens.

*The Newsroom* software didn't have spell check, but Dale rarely made mistakes, at least none that I would have noticed. I, of course, submitted my articles handwritten.

"You write your p's weird," he observed.

"I do?"

"Uh huh. How do you make them?"

I drew a lowercase p for him on a scrap of paper.

"Just as I thought. You're starting from the bottom of the letter instead of the top. So it looks more like a hook than a p."

"Is that a problem?"

"Nah, I can read it. It's just strange. Your capital P's are fine."

"Good to know."

Dale would type up my articles as submitted, correcting any bad grammar and misspellings on the fly without comment or critique. For collaborative articles like movie reviews, we would ramble out loud together and he'd type it all up in real time.

After quite a few of these sessions, we had assembled a prototype newspaper that was eight pages long, as planned, with a few blank spaces where we were missing articles, along with some handwritten notes like "word search answers go here". Once the pages were stapled in the upper left corner and folded in half newspaper-style, it looked decently professional.

We took the prototype out to the garage and tested it in Dale's homemade newspaper box. The white paper popped quite well against the black paint, but since the box was designed to stand upright, the single issue flopped forward and drooped over the cardboard strip Dale had added in the front to prevent papers from falling out.

"I'm not worried," Dale said. "When it's filled with papers, they'll stand upright okay."

"What if they sell so well that there's only one or two left?"

Dale grinned. "Wouldn't that be awesome."

I was still a little worried about what this paper would do to my reputation. It was a weird thing to attempt, after all. I hadn't talked about this project at school or to my friends, though once at lunch Dale had brought up an article I had written. The guys probably assumed we were talking about a school assignment or something because they didn't ask any follow-up questions, but I remember being panicked about what I might say if they did. Would I downplay it as no big deal, just something Dale and I were screwing around with? Or would I get excited about it and brag about our progress and how neat it was? At this point, I wasn't even sure what I thought myself.

Biking home, I ran into Marco. He was sitting on the sidewalk in front of his house lighting black snakes with matches. The fireworks, I mean, not the animals. He always had a supply of those little black discs even though most places didn't sell them outside of Fourth of July season.

"Hey dude," I said. "Do you know it's October?"

"Snakes come out in all seasons," he said, lighting three discs at once, and barely glancing up. Two of the resulting snakes joined together to make a double-wide ash tube, while the other went its own way and petered out early. From the looks of the black stains on the rest of the sidewalk, and several ash snakes that hadn't yet blown away and turned into dust, he had been at this a while.

"Ya fighting with your mom?" I guessed. Marco

liked lighting things on fire when he was trying to calm down from a bad day.

"No, she's good. She's pissed about my math grade, though. Really, I'm just bored. Benny's grounded again and you're always with Dale these days."

Shit.

"Naw, dude it's not like that. We're working on something together and it takes forever."

Marco looked up at me.

"Working on something? For a class?"

"Not exactly. We're making, uh, a newspaper."

Marco stared at me like I had sprouted antennae.

"What the hell are you talking about?"

"It's like a school paper," I explained, a bit defensive. "But for the town. We're going to sell it at Huck's."

"Why?"

"I mean, Dale's doing most of it. He's the computer geek. I'm just helping him out, writing reviews on movies and sports articles and stuff. Really, it's cool."

Marco said nothing for several seconds. Then he placed six snake discs on the sidewalk between his legs in a small, tight circle, lighting them all at once so a thick, connected tube of ash appeared to rise out of his lap. It was pretty impressive. And phallic.

"Sorry they don't make short white ones for you," he teased.

# Eight

Mike and my mom were having another rough patch. There was one night where dinner was ready a few minutes early but Mike hadn't arrived yet. Mom kept looking at the clock, irritated, until she gave up and served the two of us. "No reason for you and I to have a cold dinner, just because Mike doesn't care about us enough to show up on time." Mike walked in minutes after we had started, apologizing when he saw we had begun without him, but Mom barely acknowledged his presence at all.

"I had to stay a bit late today," he explained. "I thought I could shower in time if I hurried, but I should have called."

"Well," Mom said icily, "I guess it's all about priorities."

I tried diffusing the tension by telling a funny story from school, but it felt like neither of them was paying attention, so I let my voice sort of fade out.

After the awkward meal, I took Grandma's plate up to her, then went right to my room to do homework. I kept my door open, though, trying to make sense of the raised voices below me. Mike's voice carried louder, as always, and based on snippets like "you're being paranoid" and "how could you think that," I surmised that Mom was accusing him of being unfaithful. It made concentrating on my algebra handout next-to-impossible, so I gave up and tried harder to spy on the fight. After a few more minutes of heated dialogue, I heard the front door slam, followed by Mike's '78 Datsun peeling out of our driveway.

I waited a few minutes before going downstairs. Mom was doing dishes.

"Can I help?"

"You can dry."

We stood beside each other in working silence for a bit, her scrubbing and me drying and stacking the plates and cups on the counter. I knew better than to ask what had happened. I tried my usual technique of shifting the focus to me.

"Dale and I are ready to publish our first issue," I said.

"What?"

"You know, of *The New Haven Herald Jr.* We have all the articles done, I think. We're just trying to get one or two more ads."

"That's nice, Jimmy."

She was washing slowly, distracted, which means I had to dry slowly too to maintain the pace. It would have looked to an outsider like two people who really, really cared about clean dishes.

"I think my favorite article, of mine at least, is a movie review I wrote about *Ghostbusters*, and what I think *Ghostbusters II* is going to be about. Did you know they were making *Ghostbusters II*?"

"No."

"I bet it's going to be great. I wrote about what I think the plot is going to be." I paused, hoping she'd take the hint and ask me to share these thoughts, but she just handed me another dish.

"I think he's cheating on me," she said.

"Mike?" I said, dumbly.

"He gets off at five-thirty. He keeps coming later and later. He didn't make it until nearly seven today."

I tried to wrap my head around this logic. "Wait, you think he gets off work, runs over to some other woman's house for ten minutes, and *then* showers and changes for dinner with us?"

"He's letting you down, too. You'd think he would care about you."

I stiffened. "Mike does care about me."

She turned to me. "Oh, just not *me*, is that it?"

"What? No, I didn't say that at all. I know he likes you a lot, and..."

"Likes! Well, maybe that's the problem right there."

"Mom, he loves you. I've heard him say it."

"Men say a lot of things," she scoffed. She had washed her last dish, and snapped off the light above the sink, even though I was still using the light to dry. For some reason, this irritated me, which made my next words perhaps harsher than I had intended.

"Why are you doing this? Why would you scare him away?"

Mom had been walking out of the kitchen but whirled to face me.

"That's bullshit! I am doing everything I can to keep him happy! *For you!* But he treats me like garbage."

This was simply not true, at least from my point of view. Mike treated my mom better than any guy ever had.

"He's good to you," I countered. "And to me. Don't screw this up, Mom."

"Screw this up? You want a dad so bad you don't care if he's mean to your mother?"

"I have never seen him be mean to you. Not once." I didn't add that I had seen her be mean to *him* many times.

Mom stared me down for what seemed like a full minute.

"You don't understand," she decided. "You're just a kid." Then, as an afterthought: "Maybe I should follow him tomorrow."

I had no response to this, so after a beat, she left me alone in the dark kitchen, holding the final plate. I wanted to throw it across the room.

—

The paper needed one more quarter-page ad to meet Dale's profit goal. So, on the Saturday afternoon a couple days before Halloween, Dale and I set out on our bikes to search for the missing link. As we had before, Dale took his triangle of the map and I took mine, and we made a plan to meet back at his house at three, ad or no ad. After an hour or so of trying to find a single open establishment I hadn't already approached, I was feeling pretty dejected.

I found myself biking up Victoria Street, which housed some of New Haven's industrial businesses, and noticed a young-ish white dude peeking around the old train depot. Since he was the only person I had seen in over an hour, I decided to stop and say hi.

"It's closed," I called to him. "No trains have stopped here since I've been alive."

The man smiled at me. He had too-long hair and two-day stubble; if not for the ironed shirt tucked into his jeans, I'd have wondered if he was homeless.

"Yeah," he agreed. "This is not an active depot."

The way he said it, so matter-of-fact, made me feel defensive of my town.

"We do have trains here. There are active tracks. There's a train that crosses 27 Mile every weeknight at eight."

"That must be irritating for mothers trying to put their children to sleep."

"Uh, I guess. I don't remember the last time I was in bed before eight o'clock. But I'm not a child."

"I didn't mean to imply that you were."

"If you know the building is abandoned, what are you looking for?"

The man wiped his forehead with the sleeve of his right arm. "Hell, I don't know. I love old buildings. Especially old train depots. This was the Grand Trunk line, you know. I bet Tom Edison himself worked out of here."

"The electricity guy?"

The man laughed. "Yeah, the electricity guy. He was what they called a 'news butch.' He sold newspapers to passengers up and down this line, from Port Huron to Detroit. Why, he would have been about your age I gather. What are you, 12? 13?"

"12," I confirmed. "I'm in Junior High. How about you?"

"23. All grown up."

"How do you know so much about our depot? You're not from here, I take it."

"Nope, not here," he agreed. "Michigan, though. I travel all over the state, helping restore old buildings, trying to preserve the past a bit. My grandpa was an archeologist. Do you know what that is?"

"A guy who studies dinosaurs?"

"No, that would be a paleontologist. Archeologists study old human cultures and artifacts, not dinosaurs. Stuff decades or hundreds or maybe thousands of years old, but never millions."

"Because there weren't any people that long ago?"

"That's what they tell me."

I hopped off the bike and engaged the kickstand.

"Have you been inside?" I asked.

"To the depot? Nah, it's locked up."

"There's a window on the track-side that's loose," I said. "I've been in there a few times."

He followed me around to the other side of the structure. It was truly a beautiful old building that just needed some love. Part of me thought it was a bad idea to show this scruffy dude how to break in, but he was gazing at the place with curiosity and wonder, not malice.

"It's a great example of the Italianate style of most Michigan depots," he said, as if to prove my point. "Do you see the transom there?"

I nodded, having no idea what a 'transom' was.

"They don't make structures like this anymore." He grimaced. "Modern construction sucks. Really fucking sucks."

My eyes widened a bit at this. I rarely heard grown-ups swear, not counting my mom's fights with Mike.

"Sorry," he said, observing my reaction. "Fucking *stinks*."

Nice.

I showed him how to pry open the window. "Can I ask why you want to get in there?"

"Oh, like I said, just love these old girls. So much to learn, you know? My grandpa was obsessed with this stuff, too. Guess it runs in the family. I've dedicated my life so far to restoring properties. Learning their secrets, bringing out their best..." He seemed distracted as he poked his head inside.

"Did you see something?"

"Not yet. But I've learned to listen. You ever heard the expression 'good bones'?"

"No."

"People sometimes say a building has 'good bones.' What they mean is that the building doesn't have any major structural problems, is laid out well, that sort of thing. You can make cosmetic renovations and do a bit of strategic restoration and end up with a beautiful place in the end, without tearing down walls or fucking up the original layout too bad."

"Okay."

"Sometimes, when *I* say a building has 'good bones', I mean it literally. People have died in almost any place over twenty years old. Do you know how old your home is?"

I shook my head, uneasy.

"If you're not the first owners, I bet it's seen some death. Or will in the future."

I couldn't help but think of Grandma. I knew she had health problems, and she couldn't even escape in a fire. Had she known, when she agreed to move in with us, that climbing those stairs would be a one-way trip?

"Whether its good bones or bad bones," he continued, "can be up to the building itself. An evil building can corrupt those inside it. It can impart hate, and pain. Did you know the home of a serial killer is four times more likely to be home to a *second* serial killer in the future? All sorts of books have been written on this. I've seen it firsthand as well."

"A specific house can make people evil? Or, are you saying evil people are attracted to certain houses?"

The man smiled. Not the same friendly smile as before, though. It had a more sinister glint this time, a hint of dark amusement, both corners of his mouth glistening slightly with spit. Whether I had impressed or irritated him with my question wasn't clear.

"My job, as a restoration expert, is to help return

properties to whatever their designers intended them to be. To roll back time and undo the mistakes of the well-meaning but incompetent fuck-ups who think they can play God. Respect the property, and you get good bones. Disrespect the property, and good luck."

Not gonna lie, I was creeped out at this point. But I had come this far, and this seemed as good an opening as any.

"Do you offer your services for hire?" I asked.

"Huh?"

"Like, do you fix up people's houses, that sort of thing?"

"Well sure," he said with pride. "That's how I make my living. Ever hear of Albert Kahn?"

I hadn't.

"He was known as the 'Architect of Detroit'. He designed the Fisher Building, the Detroit News and Free Press buildings, the Ford house, *tons* of stuff you've seen. He died forty years ago, but his firm lives on, and they contract me from time to time to help preserve a building some greedy asshole wants to tear down to put in a K-mart."

"Are they going to put a K-mart here?"

"Doubtful, kid. We're in the middle of nowhere."

"This street?"

"This *town*."

I could see he was getting anxious to get inside, and I knew better than to follow a strange older guy into an abandoned building, so I thought I should make my pitch.

"If you offer your services to the public," I said, "you should be advertising in our local paper."

The man cocked his head. "New Haven has a newspaper?"

"Not in years," I admitted. "But we're restarting it."

I pulled out my sales packet. Dale had given me the first four pages of the paper to show off, which was more impressive than just the front page we had used to get our first sales. To my surprise, the stranger took the time to study all four pages, quickly but carefully, as I stood there nervous.

"*Ghostbusters II*, eh?"
I beamed. At least someone was interested.
The man handed me back the sheets.
"Well, kid, I'm not out this way very often, but I'll make an exception for a good restoration job. I honestly do believe some places are special. How about I do a quarter-page advertising my restoration services, and we'll see if I get any nibbles. Sound good?"
"Sounds great!"
He handed me his business card.

*Al Horner | Historical Restoration & General Contracting*

"I'll make sure this gets in the first issue," I said, putting the business card in my pocket. "Now, about that four dollars?"

—

I was feeling good about myself on the bike ride home. Not only had I sold the final ad for the paper, I think I'd sold more ads than Dale altogether. Sure, he was the "brains" behind the thing, and did most of the writing and all that, but I was contributing my fair share. I wasn't just helping him out. I was a full partner. Hell, it was my idea to attempt this project in the first place.
Pax was standing in front of the Black House as I was riding up to the corner. No Derek or T-Too around, only him. Our eyes met, unfortunately, and he called out.
"Jimmy! Stop for a second."
I tried to come up with a lie I could shout back to him without slowing down, something like "I can't I'm late for dinner!" or "my brake lines are cut and I can't stop!" or whatever. But I knew pissing off The Bully wouldn't go over well, and I had instinctively begun slowing down to meet him.
"Yeah, Pax?"
"Hey, I need a couple bucks. Right now."
"Uh, why do you need it?"

"None of your damn business why. I just need to borrow it. I'll pay ya back."

This would never happen, and we both knew it.

"I don't think I have anything," I said.

His face darkened. "Now wait a minute. I know damned well you've got money on you because when I told you I needed money you asked me why. If you hadn't had anything, you would have said so then. But you asked *why*, which means you were trying to decide whether to help me based on my answer. My answer is it's none of your business. So give me the money."

"Pax..."

In an instant, he stepped forward and grabbed the front of my shirt with his left hand, twisting the fabric in a spiral which tightened the collar around my neck.

"I told you," he said through clenched teeth. "I *need* it."

I didn't know what to say. I honestly didn't have any money. Sure, I had the four dollars the restoration guy had given me for the ad, but that wasn't *my* money, it was the paper's. I couldn't let him take that. What would I tell Dale?

"Pax, I don't have anything! I'd help ya if I could, I swear!"

The bully's expression softened for a moment, and I thought he was going to let go of my shirt. But then something happened. His eyes got wide and began flitting back and forth as if he was figuring something out. Pax then glanced over at the Black House, as if someone had called to him from there, though I heard nothing. When his eyes snapped back to mine, they were cold and unyielding.

"Have it your way," he said without emotion. Then he jerked my body violently to the left, lifting me a few inches off my bike seat before I fell to the gravel on the side of the road, my bike crushing my leg at the landing. Before I could register what was happening, I could feel his shoe pressing on the side of my face, pushing the other cheek into the small stones. With the bike still stuck between my legs, and my left arm pinned by my body, I was unable to mount any defense. And it hurt. A lot.

"Stop, please! I have it. I have four dollars. Let me up, I can give you four dollars."

He didn't move his foot. He seemed to be pressing even harder.

"Where is it?"

"In my pocket."

"Which pocket?"

"Uh, my back right pocket, I think."

"Don't move."

He took his foot off my cheek, but I dared not try and stand or crawl away. Instead, I let Pax's hands force their way into the pocket of my jeans, pulling out the dollar bills and Al's business card. I found myself worried that he would steal the card, too, but he paid it no attention, tossing it on the ground beside us and pocketing the singles.

"Thanks, Jimmy," he said casually, and walked away. I extricated myself from the bike, recovered the business card, and stood up to brush the dirt from my jeans.

*You're going to let him walk away?* said a voice in my head. *Tackle him!*

I thought about it. Could I fight an eighth grader? Wouldn't he kick my ass?

*Tackle him now! Beat him up! Choke him!*

My face stung, distracting me. I reached up a hand to touch my cheek and wasn't shocked to see blood on my fingers.

There was only one thing to do. I needed to go home. The dark voice in my head which pleaded for revenge would have to be ignored for now.

—

I called for Mom as I entered the front door, but Grandma shouted down that she had gone out for groceries. She sensed that my voice sounded panicked, though, and insisted I come up and talk with her instead. When she saw my face, she gasped.

"Jimmy! You're bleeding!"

I thought about saying I had fallen off my bike, but I needed someone to know the truth, and it was better that it was Grandma rather than Mom. Mom might have called Pax's parents and made everything worse. Grandma, I knew, could be trusted with a secret. As I let her dab my cheek with a washcloth, I told her all about getting the final ad for the paper, and how the money was stolen.

"Where did this happen?"

"You know the old abandoned house at the end of Chennault?"

"Yes, I know that house."

"That's where Pax and his bully friends hang out. Which sucks because you almost always have to pass them to get anywhere in town, unless you go all the way around to Stevens or out to Gratiot. Maybe I'll have to take the long way more often."

She nodded. "You're going to want to put Mercurochrome on that scrape."

"I know, Grandma."

"I'm upset he took your ad money."

"At least he didn't get the ad! I don't want to tell Dale what happened though. Maybe I can find four bucks in my room instead."

Grandma smiled, and reached down to her purse she kept by the end table. Though she almost never left the house, she somehow kept a fully stocked purse by her bed, containing a long-expired driver's license, lip balm, Tic Tacs, a checkbook, and cash. She handed me a $5 bill.

"Wow, thanks, Grandma."

"I'm proud of you," she said. "Starting a newspaper must be so exciting."

"Yeah, I guess it is." I looked at the cash. "You know, you gave me a dollar more than was stolen."

"Consider it payment for my copy of your first issue."

"They're only 25 cents."

She smiled. "Then I'll take four."

# Nine

Dale and I conducted our final proofing of *The New Haven Herald Jr.*'s premiere issue on Sunday, October 30th, 1988. Because it took so long to print each page, Dale had run some of the spreads the night before, and others were still printing when I arrived at his home around noon. Our job was to use rubber cement to affix physical ads we had been given by our advertisers, and reread each article to look for typos. If we did find a typo, we had to decide whether it was serious enough to fix and reprint the entire section (costing at least twenty minutes of time per page), or to let it go. Sometimes, if it was a simple misspelling that only impacted a single word, Dale came up with a third option of printing just the corrected word on the printer, then carefully cutting out the word and pasting it over the misspelling on the proof. I didn't catch as many problems as Dale did, but I was proud of myself when I pointed out a grammatical mistake that Dale had missed in one of his own articles.

After a few hours of tedious review and unhealthy snack consumption, we laid out all eight final pages of our paper on the coffee table.

"I think it's looking good," Dale said, munching on a Fruit Roll-Up.

"What time do we have to be there?"

Dale glanced at his watch. "It's four o'clock, and she said we could come by any time before six. Think we're ready?"

"Ready as we'll ever be."

Dale took a deep breath. "Okay, let's go."

With genuine care, he placed the eight original pages into a thick binder, then put that binder into his backpack.

As we left the house for our bikes, Dale asked what I was going as for Halloween.

"Tomorrow? Uh, I figured *last* year was my last year. I mean, we're in high school now. Well, the building at least."

Dale's eyes went wide. "You're not going to go trick-or-treating? Are we too old?"

"I think so," I admitted. "Well, I mean, I am. Maybe *you're* not."

"But I don't want to be the only seventh-grader out there."

"I don't think you will be. Besides, if you're in costume, no one will know it's you."

"Well, my costume this year doesn't cover my face. I'm going as an I.R.S. agent."

"A what?"

"You know, the Internal Revenue Service. They collect taxes from grown-ups. I'm going to be wearing a suit and tie and pretend to be all serious, like I need to collect this year's taxes in the form of candy. My dad gave me an old brown briefcase of his, and I've glued big I.R.S. letters to it so people understand the joke."

I had no response to that. It was the dorkiest costume anyone could come up with. Which made it pretty perfect for one Dale Dunkle.

"I guess I get it," I said. "Most kids won't."

"Ah, yes," Dale beamed. "But kids aren't the ones giving out the candy."

We rode up Gratiot to St. Clair Studio. Only one car was there, presumably Mrs. Patrick's, which meant we weren't bothering anyone or interrupting a photo shoot by barging in.

"Hello!" cooed Mrs. Patrick as we entered.

"Hi," said Dale. "I'm Dale."

"Jimmy's told me all about you. I'm happy to help out. What a wonderful thing you're doing. Most kids your age just rot their brains with comic books and video games."

I stiffened a bit at this. I liked comic books and video games. Even Dale liked video games, though he probably read more Shakespeare than Marvel.

"Thank you for printing our first issue," Dale said sincerely. "We didn't want to charge more than a quarter, especially with The Detroit News being so much larger and only fifteen cents. But the printing costs would have been more than a quarter if we did it at the library. I don't know how the big papers print so many pages and charge so little."

"Well, I suppose they lose money on the printing itself, but make up for it in expensive advertising."

"That's what my mom said," I noted.

"She's right."

"Then why charge any money for the paper at all?" asked Dale.

"Because if something costs *nothing*, it ain't worth *anything*."

"Huh."

"Take my portrait packages," she said, gesturing to a sign on the wall. "It doesn't cost me much to blow up a picture to an 8x10, or make some wallet-sized photos for seniors to pass out to each other. But if I only charged the small amount the prints cost *me*, then they wouldn't have any value. A photo that cost you $20 is worth framing. A photo that cost you fifty cents could be thrown away without a second thought."

"Maybe we should raise our newspaper's price to a dollar," I offered.

"No, you can't do that. If it's a dollar, it would need to be as impressive as a magazine. Glossy photos and 100 pages and all that. I think a quarter is exactly where you need to be. Enough of a cost that someone won't grab all the copies to use as toilet paper, but cheap enough to be an impulse buy."

Dale perked up. "An impulse buy?"

"Yeah," said Mrs. Patrick. "Someone buying cigarettes or gum is going to get change back. They'll see your paper there, feel the quarter in their hand, and think 'why not?' They won't miss the quarter even if they don't like your paper. It isn't much risk to them. That's an impulse buy. And that's why I want my studio's ad in your publication. I think a lot of people are going to part with that quarter. Which means a lot of people are going to see my ad and know that St. Clair Studio supported a local kid-run venture. Which makes me the kind of photography studio that they'd want to use for their own kids' pictures when the time is right."

Dale nodded. "You're using our paper to improve your company's reputation in the community."

Mrs. Patrick exploded into a hearty belly laugh. "My boy, of course! That's the only reason any business advertises at all! But it is also true that I think you're doing something cool and want to support it. Consider me a selfish altruist."

That was good enough for Dale. "Let's get printing!"

She took us into the back room which served as her office. On the far wall sat a large Xerox machine, the kind you'd see in the front office of a school. She gingerly took the pages Dale handed her and began to produce our first issue. The machine did not have what I now know is called a "duplexer" capable of printing both sides of a page in a single motion, so once she had printed fifty copies of the front page, she had to place those pages upside down in the feeding tray to print the back side onto them. After these pages were complete, she handed the stack to Dale, and continued onto page three.

This is going to sound weird, but I remember the smell of that copier so vividly. Even today, whenever I'm in a room with a whirring copy machine, I think back to this moment. The excitement and tension was so palpable. Dale seemed to be almost trembling. I could tell he wanted to do his ear-scratching tic but was holding back in public.

Everything went well until page six.

"Oh dear," said Mrs. Patrick. "We're out of ink."

"What do you mean?" Dale looked anxious.

"It's okay, I'm sure I have more in the back."

She didn't.

"Well," Dale said, "I suppose we can pay to have the rest printed at the library. This was still a big help, and saved us a ton of money, and I'm so sorry we used the last of your ink."

"Hold your horses, now." Mrs. Patrick was pressing some buttons on the machine's panel. "I can still print the last pages. They just won't be black."

"Huh?" I asked.

"I'm only out of *black* ink. I'll print the final pages in a different color." Without waiting for our opinion, she fired up the machine again, and pages of blue text started spitting out.

I was disappointed, but kept my mouth shut. Who ever heard of a newspaper having its last few pages in blue ink? But Dale said nothing.

After everything was printed, Dale carefully moved the stacks of papers to his backpack, keeping out one copy of each sheet. We were going to staple and fold all the issues at his house, which would take quite a while, but Dale borrowed Mrs. Patrick's stapler to create a first-ever completed product just for her. We thanked her one final time for her donation of printing services, and she thanked us again for letting her company be a part.

As we hopped on our bikes in the St. Clair Studio parking lot, I had to bring it up.

"I know it's cool that she made all the copies for us, but are you really okay with some of the pages being blue? After all your hard work making everything exactly the way you want it? Doesn't that piss you off?"

Dale shrugged. "You have to look on the bright side, Jimmy. Not even *The Detroit News* is in color."

———

We folded and stapled the forty-nine remaining issues in Dale's garage. We were proud of how good they looked, and we each took a couple copies for ourselves to keep and show off to family.

The painted cardboard box we had made stored about 25 issues at a time, so we loaded it up and stuffed it into a big backpack. Dale put the remaining issues in his computer cabinet for safe keeping, and we checked the time: 7:00 p.m. Huck's would still be open for another hour on Sundays, so we could drop it off and they'd start selling first thing in the morning.

As we hopped on our bikes, Dale's mom stopped us.

"Where do you think you're going?"

"To Huck's," Dale said. "We have to deliver the papers."

"Tonight? After sunset?"

"We'll be back in no time."

"But...it's Devil's Night."

On the off chance you're not from Southeastern Michigan, I should explain. October 30th had been celebrated as Devil's Night in our area for as long as I could remember. Every year in the '80s saw hundreds of fires being set to abandoned homes and businesses in Detroit and the surrounding suburbs. People would save their fireworks from the Fourth of July and make a loud, noisy spectacle of it all. Helicopters would circle overhead the whole night, often into the following day, covering the mischief and vandalism. New Haven was too far from downtown to be considered a "suburb" exactly, but we were still in the Detroit media market, and everyone I knew was glued to the television coverage each year, as networks usually preempted prime-time programming to show a constant live stream of chaos.

Our town saw a bit of Devil's Night excitement some years as well. We didn't have many abandoned buildings to destroy, but you'd hear guns and illegal fireworks going off until early morning, and sometimes mailboxes and other easy targets were blown up by cherry bombs. You'd think the Black House would be a target for arson, but it wasn't. I suppose it's because that's where the three biggest troublemakers hung out, and Pax, Derek, and T-Too weren't about to burn down their home base.

"It's still pretty light out," Dale observed. "I'm sure it's fine. We won't dawdle."

Mrs. Dunkle looked up at the deep blue sky. It wouldn't be truly dark for another twenty minutes at least.

"Okay," she agreed. "But come straight home."

We pedaled down Chennault and up Clark toward the party store. I had forgotten it was Devil's Night, too, so I was now hyper-aware of my surroundings, my eyes darting around the road seeking signs of delinquency. No one seemed to be out. In fact, I don't think we saw a single person or car during the entire quarter-mile trip.

At Huck's, Dale had to explain to the clerk on duty about the arrangement he had made with the owner, Don Huck, to put his homemade paper box on the counter by the register. She was skeptical at first, but ultimately felt it was too weird of a story for us to be making up. She slid a display of Chapstick down a foot or so on the counter and placed our box close to the register.

"Happy?" the clerk asked.

We were.

"I'll be back in a few days to collect the money," Dale said with a smile.

And with that, we were officially in the news game.

Even though we had only been in the store a few minutes, I was surprised how dark it had become as we stepped back into the night. There was blue left in the sky, but a midnight blue at best, with a waning gibbous moon providing the only illumination once we left the plaza. Both our bikes had reflectors, but neither had headlights, and there were no streetlights on Clark between Huck's and Chennault.

As we made our way down the road, I felt a strange electricity in the air. I thought Dale might be feeling it too, as he was uncharacteristically quiet during the ride. I was conscious of the mechanisms of my bike in particular, the derailleur gears and chain, the gentle clicking and whirring of it all. Over that, I could hear my breathing, and Dale's, as we both pedaled just a bit faster than normal.

During the few minutes between Huck's and our street, the sky blackened substantially, and I panicked for a moment, uncertain if I was still on the road. Had we already crossed the bridge, or was it coming up?

An image flashed in my head of hitting the bridge rail and tumbling over my handlebars into the rocky creek below. I didn't dare slow down. The dark was starting to envelop my vision like a blanket, and I had to make it home before I was suffocated forever.

The Black House was coming up on our right. This was both a relief and a terror. It meant we had made it to Chennault, but also that we might be accosted by Pax and his crew if they were out. Tricks in the shadows made me see figures where there were none among the trees and on the side of the Black House itself. I thought I kept seeing someone in the road, too, I was sure of it...and then they were gone, turned into a wisp of dark vapor, either evanescent or unreal.

I could hear something, too. A low moan, a woman's voice, almost certainly from the direction of the house. It had the quality of a wounded animal, not pure in tone but with a gurgle underneath. Soon it blended into the sounds of breeze and rattling leaves as it tapered off, only to return seconds later, louder and more furtive. Neither Dale or I said anything, but I was sure he heard it, as he was ahead of me, and I could see his face turning toward the Black House both times the moaning returned.

As we made the turn onto Chennault, I glanced up and saw a dim, amber light emanating from the west second floor window. Someone was up there, I was certain now, though I couldn't see any form or shadow. Just a touch of light, and that muted moaning.

"Unnghhh.... unnnnghhk-k-kk..."

I began pedaling faster, and as Dale pulled into his house on the left, I didn't say goodbye or good night, but kept moving forward. I remember a sensation of tunnel vision as darkness vignetted my view, black tendrils oozing around my periphery, as if gloved hands were trying to grab my head and yank it backward. I was pumping my legs furiously, yet it felt like I was cycling through tar.

Then...well, imagine listening to a person snoring a room away, and hearing something that sounded like a real word buried in their slow, wheezy intake of breath.

*Jiiiiim.*

Only three houses away now. I could see Mom's ugly blue Chevette in the driveway. The kitchen light was on. I was so close. Yet there was something so seductive about that voice. The urge to slow down and turn back toward the house was beginning to overpower me.

*Jiiiiiimmmmmm—*

A sonic crash and a flash of light knocked me out of my hypnosis. It was a bottle rocket, probably set off from one street over on Stevens. Devil's Night had officially begun.

I left my bike by the side of the house and sprinted through the front door. My heart was beating fast, and I was panting a little, but felt safe.

Mom called down the stairs. "Jimmy? So glad you're home! You shouldn't be out this late, tonight of all nights."

Didn't I know it.

"Sorry, Mom."

"Everything alright?"

"Yep!"

I flashed her a convincing smile. I didn't tell her about the voice.

We watched the news together later that evening. Detroit was ablaze, as usual. 1988 was a bad year for Devil's Night, though nothing came close to 1984, with over 800 documented fires and a city Fire Department begging for help from stations in the surrounding suburbs. It wasn't until the mid-'90s that the city got serious about stopping the destructive tradition, after a one-year-old baby was killed. The city established "Angel's Night" volunteer patrols, with thousands of city residents taking to the streets each October to stop arson before it happened. These patrols continued for the next thirty years.

In the moment, though, I was grateful for Devil's Night, or at least for fireworks snapping me out of the trance of the Black House. For a while.

# Ten

"So, what if nobody buys them?"

"I donno, Zach," I said. "I guess then no one will make fun of me."

"Oh, I'll still make fun of you."

I was having lunch with Zach, Benny, and Marco. I thought Dale might join us, too, but he was eating with some of the nerdy kids I didn't know. After all the time we'd been spending together, and all we had been through to get the paper out, I was surprised that he hadn't joined our table. In a few short months I had gone from being embarrassed if he talked to me in the hallway to being a bit hurt when he ate lunch with someone else.

Marco appeared unimpressed with the discussion. "I'm not gonna buy one of those papers."

"Because he can't read," Zach remarked. Marco punched his arm.

"Why not?" I asked Marco.

"Sorry," Zach interjected. "I meant because he's poor."

Marco punched Zach again, harder this time.

"Really, Marco," I said. "Why are you so pissy about this?"

"Couldn't tell ya. Your newspaper thing is cool, I guess. Just nice to see the original *Ghostbusters* back together."

"Do you have a problem with Dale?"

"Nah."

"He misses you," Benny chimed in. Marco shot him an annoyed look, but Benny didn't mean it in a teasing way. It sounded sympathetic, as if saying "I miss you too."

Changing the subject, I asked Marco how he did on the grammar test they handed back today.

"Eh, not bad. I mean, it was the exact same questions the homework had."

"Then you got an A?"

Marco shrugged. "Something like that. You guys hear about the fire by the cemetery last night?"

We're all good at deflection, I suppose.

I saw Dale had bussed his tray and was heading our way.

"Hey," he said to me. "We did it, huh?"

I smiled. "It's pretty cool."

Dale grabbed an open seat. "Whatcha all talking about? Halloween?"

"The grammar test," explained Zach. "But you're in a higher English class than us so you wouldn't get it."

"I hear in ninth grade English you get books with sex scenes," said Marco. "That's what I'm excited about." (Spoiler alert: This is technically true, but the scenes are *not* sexy.)

Zach continued. "Higher math, too, right? No wonder we don't see you much during the day."

"I see you in band," Dale reminded him.

"Oh yeah. You barely talk in that class."

Dale sighed. "I sort of hate it. I'm the only French horn player so I'm all on my own. I don't even get any attention from the teacher because she doesn't know French horn either."

"At least people can hear you. I'm one of like ten trumpets and we're all playing the same note."

Dale smirked. "I've heard your section. You are most certainly *not* playing the same note."

Zach laughed. He could appreciate a good burn from anyone.

As we were leaving the lunchroom I pulled Dale aside.

"You wanna come over after school? I bought *Super Mario 2*." The game had been released a few weeks earlier, and I was the first of my friends to get it. Not sure why I thought Dale would be impressed by this since he didn't have a Nintendo, or why I was trying to impress him in the first place, but I thought it'd be fun to experience it together.

"Sure," he said. "I'll get off the bus with ya."

And that was that.

—

In Mr. Wright's class, I passed Emilia a coded note. It was a simple shift cipher we had been using in recent weeks, where you'd substitute each letter in the message for something a fixed number of letters up or down the alphabet. They were pretty easy to decode because one of us always started the first message with "hi" or "hey," so if I sent a message that said "khb, zkdwv xs?" it was easy to guess the first word must be "hey" which meant the k was h, the h was e, and the b was y, and you'd deduce all letters in the message were shifted three to the left. It was something Dale had taught me, though I didn't give him the credit because Emilia had been so impressed. I imagine Mr. Wright could have figured out our notes if he caught us, but it was at least harder to decode than pig latin.

Anyway, my translated note said: *Hey, Dale and I put out the paper yesterday.*

After a while, she responded using the same code: *That's cool, where can I get one?*

*Huck's party store.*

*I'm never over there. Can you bring me a copy?*

Mr. Wright was awkwardly using his weird stick-hook to pull down the world map, his back to the class, so I got bold enough to whisper.

"I'll bring you one tomorrow. But I need a quarter."

Her eyes widened in playful shock. "I don't get a friends and family discount?"

I smiled broadly, trying to ignore the butterflies in my stomach at being acknowledged as a friend. "Hey, a guy's gotta make a living!"

Mr. Wright had turned back around and seemed to be glaring in our direction, so we shut up. Later, we shared a guilty glance with each other as he droned on about Pakistan.

I had been thinking about Emilia more than I would admit to anyone. I mean, I had been friends with girls before, but in the way everyone in grade school is sort of friends with everyone else. This was different. I had fantasies about running into her at the movies with our respective cliques, and then all deciding to go into the theatre in a big group, but with her and I ending up side-by-side, by chance, whispering our own private jokes to each other as our elbows touched on the armrest. Or maybe being assigned some school project together which might require late night phone calls, all business at first, but then sharing stories and laughter and favorite songs until one of our parents yelled for us to hang up and go to sleep.

I also thought about what it would be like to kiss her. I had decided I wouldn't go for the lips or anything, but her upper cheek, just below her eye, in a way I could play off as a friend-kiss if I needed to, but that would feel more intimate than that, if I did it right. I would look at her surprised expression and say something sweet but not too romantic by way of explanation. Maybe "you're neat." And if she blushed and complimented me back, perhaps I'd try and hold her hand, and we'd simply walk somewhere together, enjoying each other's company.

If this sounds like a sentimental, sanitized downplaying of the "real" thoughts of a 12-year-old boy, let me assure you that I was more than capable of grown-up fantasies back then as well. But such thoughts would be of people who weren't "real" to me, like Paula Abdul or Cindy Crawford or that girl from the Whitesnake video. The crush I had on Emilia wasn't *platonic* exactly, but at this point it was more sweet than naughty. The only other time I had felt these kinds of butterflies for someone, or imagined what it would be like to feel their skin against mine, or their kisses on my neck, was...well, I just had learned not to think about that.

—

Dale and I sat together on the bus ride home, which was pretty rare. I probably should have sat with Marco, given his sulking, but oh well. It's not like Dale was replacing my closest friends. We just had a connection on this one thing.

At my house, we ate Cheetos and played *Super Mario 2* and talked about possible article ideas for the second issue. Dale was still pretty bad at Nintendo games, but he got the hang of this one okay, and it helped that neither of us knew the levels yet so I wasn't much better than he was. The article ideas we had were nothing special, mostly variations on stuff we'd already done, though Dale liked my pitch of a "gift ideas" column where the two of us would debate Christmas present possibilities for different age groups. ("The best gift for an 18 to 21-year-old would be a new Porsche," I suggested.)

"Don't eat too much junk food," Mom chided. "You'll spoil your appetite."

"What's for dinner?" I asked.

"Mike's picking up pizza for us and will be here in an hour."

"Can Dale stay?"

"Of course, if he calls his parents."

Trick-or-treating began at 6:00 p.m. Mom had put on a witch costume and was passing out Hershey's Miniatures whenever kids came to the door. She let us each take two chocolates for ourselves; I picked Krackel because those were the best, and Dale picked Mr. Goodbar because of course he would. Mom's favorites were the Special Darks, and she always set some aside for herself every Halloween "since kids don't like them anyway."

After hearing the tenth "trick-or-treat!" chorus from neighborhood kids, it dawned on me that Dale was missing his plans.

"Dude! I forgot you were going to go out tonight. I'm so sorry. Do you want to leave and get your IRS costume on?"

"Nah," he said. "I chose to stay. I'm too old to go out. Besides, I'm having a great time with you!"

By the time Mike arrived, we were starving. Mike always ordered a comical amount of food, so I had no doubt there would be enough for company. Sure enough, he walked in with three Huck's pizzas and a big smile.

"Hey, champ," he said to me. "And who's this, then?"

I was surprised to realize Mike had never met Dale.

"I'm Dale," said Dale. "Nice to make your acquaintance."

"Ah, yes! I've heard so much about you. In fact, I tried to buy your paper just now while picking up dinner, but I didn't see any. Maybe they sold out!"

Dale and I looked at each other. Was it possible?

"You two can bike up there and check after dinner," Mom said, reading our minds. "For now, let's eat."

We scarfed down our food faster than normal, then raced outside the second we were excused from the table. I jumped on my bike and Dale jogged beside me on the way to his house, dodging miniature werewolves and spider-men and storm troopers.

"They're selling like hot cakes!" he beamed.

"I guess we should have printed more than fifty."

"Yeah, but who knows what color ink we would have had to settle for then?"

I laughed. "I guess it was wishful thinking that no one would read it."

Dale was surprised. "Why would you say that? After all that work!"

"I donno," I admitted. "It's weird to think of someone paying for our ramblings. But hey, if that's what people want, I'm okay with being famous. Unless everyone who bought it returns it. Ya think Huck's has a return policy?"

Dale shook his head. "No one's going to return it. It's the hottest paper in town!"

"What are you going to do with the money?"

"Well, like we said. We'll split it 50-50. If we sold

all 25 papers in the box, it's over six bucks."

"That'll buy a lot of Garbage Pail Kids," I said.

"Twelve packs a piece," he agreed. I tried not to be annoyed at his math speed.

When we got to Dale's, he ran in to grab a stack of replacement newspapers from our stock. He came out wearing a backpack, and smiled broadly at me before racing to his garage to grab his ride. I noticed a sort of giddiness in Dale I had only seen a few times before, and hoped he wasn't going to do that weird ear-scratching tic of his, since he'd probably crash his bike if he tried.

At Huck's, we looked by the counter where we had left our box. Mike was right that there were no papers, but also, no box. Something was wrong.

Dale approached the cashier.

"Excuse me, but what happened to the newspaper box for *The New Haven Herald Jr*? If you sold out, we'd be happy to refill it for you!"

The cashier, a teenage boy who probably went to our high school, looked dumbfounded for a bit. Finally, it clicked.

"Oh! Oh yeah, sorry. No, we didn't sell out. I had to put the box up there." He gestured to a high shelf behind him. There was our newspaper box, filled with unsold papers. All of them.

Dale looked crestfallen. "But, Mr. Huck said they could be right here, by the gum!"

"Sorry kid," the cashier said with a shrug. "The box kept falling over every time I closed the cash register. It was getting annoying. I had to move it."

Dale turned to me. "Guess you got your wish," he observed, bitterly.

I thought of something.

"Hey," I offered, "if we come back with a new box, something well-built that won't fall over, will you put it back where it's supposed to be?"

To his credit, the cashier seemed to understand how much this meant to us and handed Dale our inadequate carboard container.

"Sure, kids," he said. "I promise, if you make something that won't keep falling over, I'll put it right back in front of the register."

We biked back to Dale's house and explained the situation to Mr. Dunkle. He thought about the problem for a moment, then said he might have something. After a few minutes of searching his workshop, he came back a 10-inch metal box with a hinged lid.

"I think this will work," said Mr. Dunkle. "You can put the papers in this part here, and then maybe tape a copy of the current issue to the open lid, like professional news boxes have one copy of the paper affixed to the glass door."

Dale fished our original paper receptacle from his backpack. He counted out the papers inside, sighing as he confirmed that not a single one had been sold. He handed his father the full stack, and Mr. Dunkle showed us how the papers would fit. His solution was sturdier and more professional than our cardboard prototype.

"But where will people put the money?" Dale asked.

Mr. Dunkle fished a blue plastic case from his jacket pocket, about the size of a pack of cigarettes.

"What's that?" I asked.

"It's where I keep my cigarettes."

He disassembled the case and showed how the top half could be mounted to the lid in a way that could collect quarters, but not allow people to easily take them. We agreed it would work well, so he got out a tube of super glue and adhered it in place. Dale grabbed a permanent marker and wrote 25¢ on the case. Then, because we were now paranoid, we set it up on a card table in the garage and bumped the edges, trying to simulate the closing of a cash register. The box never fell over, and the papers stayed put. The whole build and testing process didn't take long at all, even with Dale's little sister bouncing about and peppering us with a thousand questions.

"What time is it?" I asked.

"8:20," said Mr. Dunkle.

Huck's was still open. But, it was dark, and I shuddered at the thought of another nighttime ride. Dale must have seen the worry on my face.

"Can you drive us there, Dad?"

"Alright."

To be honest, I didn't love getting help from a grown-up at this moment, not even for a ride. The coolest thing about this whole paper was that there was no adult involvement at all. No parents spell-checked our articles, or asked their friends to place ads, none of that. It was all ours. Mine and Dale's. Okay, mostly Dale's. But no grown-ups. Accepting help from Dale's dad on assembling a sturdy newspaper box and, now, the ride to Huck's, bothered me in a way I couldn't quite articulate.

Dale must have had something of the same thought as we pulled up.

"Hey Dad, can you wait in the car?"

"Sure."

We went in.

The cashier looked surprised to see us back so soon.

"We fixed it!" said Dale confidently. "This one won't fall over, we promise." Without asking for permission, Dale pushed some gum and candy bars aside and set up the box in its proper place. Knowing the cashier must be skeptical, Dale made a point to jiggle the metal box back and forth to demonstrate its stability, then turned to look the guy straight on, defiant, daring him to find fault with the thing. It was the very first time I ever thought that Dale Dunkle, age 11, was cool.

"Uh, yeah, that'll work," the teenager admitted. "Thanks."

"Thank *you*," Dale said.

Dale motioned for me to follow him to the back of the store where they kept the refrigerated drinks. I picked out an orange pop. He grabbed a Minute Maid lemonade.

"Still don't drink pop, eh?"

Dale shrugged. "I'm allergic."

Not so cool after all.

We made our way back to the front of the store and paid for our celebratory beverages. A middle-aged woman was behind us in the checkout line with a six-pack of Vernor's ginger ale. She was wearing a tiara and her cheeks were glittered, and I couldn't help but notice she had picked up a copy of *The New Haven Herald Jr.* from the box. She was still looking at it as we made it to the exit. Dale was pushing the door open, but I stopped him.

"Hey, wait. Don't you want to see if Tinkerbelle buys a copy?"

"Nah," said Dale. "I don't want to jinx it."

# II

THE PAPER

# One

*The New Haven Herald Jr.* sold every copy of its inaugural issue. Dale and I spent a decent amount of Christmas break working on the second issue, which we printed 100 copies of and distributed the first week of January. We had expanded our distribution to include Video Scene II and the local diner near St. Clair Studio. Dale had tried talking the librarian Mrs. Waterloo into selling papers as well, but she explained that libraries don't sell things. However, she did agree to *buy* a copy of the newest issue for visitors to peruse, adding the same "reference material: do not borrow" sticker to it as other area newspapers. I was disappointed at first, but Dale was overjoyed.

"It means they're taking us seriously!" he insisted.

Now winter, it was sometimes hard to bike everywhere we wanted to go. The main streets were plowed when the village got more than a couple of inches, but side streets stayed unplowed for days, and few residents kept their sidewalks shoveled either. I'm not saying I didn't enjoy a good snowball fight now and then, or bundling up and sledding down by the creek with Benny and Marco, but I hated being unable to travel whenever and wherever I wanted. I could tell that Dale, too, resented having to get rides from his parents. It's hard to get spoiled by that sweet, sweet freedom just to have it yanked away for a couple months each year.

We weren't bored, though. Dale had received a particularly cool Christmas gift.

"It's a PXL 2000!"

"A what?"

"It's a portable video camera," he explained. "But

it's light and durable, and takes videos on regular audio cassette tapes instead of VHS or Beta. We can use it to film interviews for the paper!"

I was impressed. I knew camcorders existed but didn't know anyone rich enough to own one. *America's Funniest Home Videos* was still a year away at this point.

"Your parents bought you a video camera?"

"It was from Santa!"

Holy shit.

My face must have gone pale because Dale hastily added: "I know my parents pretend to be Santa, but the big gifts still say they're from Santa on the tag. Keeps the magic alive, ya know?"

"Uh, sure."

"But it's not like an *adult* video camera," he explained. "It's for kids like us. I mean, it's made by Fisher Price!"

It's hard to imagine in the current age of ultra-high-resolution video cameras built into the cheapest cell phones, but in the '80s, few people were able to record video of themselves on a regular basis. Sure, there was always a rich uncle with a Sony Handycam filming a kid's school recital or something, but even that was rare to see, at least in New Haven. Certainly no kid would have had their *own* camcorder until the PXL came along. At only $100, the PXL 2000 was a fraction of the cost of a "real" video camera, though still pricey for a kid's product. I mean, that was more than my Nintendo!

The PXL was a fraction of the quality of a real video camera, too. Filming on audio cassette tapes provided little recordable bandwidth, so the video had to be very low-resolution and in black and white. The tape mechanism was incredibly loud as well, leading to a projector-like whirring sound over the top of everything you tried to film. Dale realized early on that you could eliminate this loud whir by plugging the PXL into a VCR instead, and recording directly onto VHS tapes instead of audio cassettes. Naturally, that only worked when you wanted to film something inside the house within a cable's length of a VCR, but in the winter, when we were stuck inside anyway, that didn't end up being much of a restriction.

"Let's make another sci-fi movie," Dale would say.

"No, let's make another horror movie," I would counter. "But this time we need to use heavy metal music as the soundtrack!"

"Ugh, I hate heavy metal. Can't we use the scary music I chose last time?"

"*Nature Trail to Hell* by Weird Al Yankovic is *not* scary!"

And we'd end up creating some weird *Star Trek* rip-off with a Freddy Krueger-style bad guy as a compromise. All improvised, of course, and barely watchable in the end, but a fun way to spend an afternoon when we were procrastinating from writing articles.

At school, Zach did indeed make fun of me for the paper, but not harshly. He'd just say things like "hey, this is off the record, but can you pass the ketchup?" On the other hand, Marco was noticeably irritated about the whole thing and changed the subject when it came up. Only Benny went out of his way to tell me he liked something I had written: a review of the movie *Scrooged*. No one else ever mentioned the paper to me, so I didn't bring it up to them. Even Emilia, who had claimed to like the first issue, never asked about the second, and so I didn't tell her when it came out. I was proud of what we had made, but also a little embarrassed.

I was at Huck's after school one not-too-snowy day and noticed our box was empty. Only Dale had replacement issues, so I rode to his place to let him know it was time for a refill.

"Oh good," he beamed. "It looks like the ad worked!"

"What ad?"

"Check it out." He grabbed a copy of *The Lenox Observer*, a small weekly newspaper out of nearby New Baltimore which sometimes covered New Haven news. Turning to one of the back pages, he pointed to a small ad he had circled with a red marker:

> Extra! Extra! Read all about it!
> THE NEW HAVEN HERALD JR.
> New Haven's first newspaper in over 20 years!
> Now available for sale at Huck's Party Store, Video Scene II, and Haven Place Diner. January's issue is out now.
> Just 25 cents!

"Whoa," I said. "How'd you get us in the *real* paper?"

"It's a classified ad. My mom placed it for us."

"Was it expensive?"

"Nah. People place classified ads all the time for their garage sales or looking for babysitters, that sort of thing. I said I could pay for it out of our sales so far, but she said it was her treat. Isn't that neat?"

"Yeah, it's cool. You think that's why Huck's is sold out?"

"Might be. This issue came out yesterday so a lot of people have probably seen it by now."

"Well, let's go fill those boxes!"

In warmer months, Dale and I could have each grabbed a stack of papers and split up to deliver them. But in winter, when it was slippery and cold and got dark early, Dale's parents wouldn't let him bike anywhere by himself. I'm not sure how having another person around made travel safer, and joked that his folks just wanted a witness if he got hit by a truck. Then again, the kid was only eleven. He *should* have more restrictions than me.

We hit Haven Place Diner first. They still had a couple copies left, but we restocked them anyway, and the owner thanked us for mentioning their restaurant by name in the classified ad. He even offered to pay for a quarter-page ad in the next issue.

"What do you want it to say?" asked Dale.

"Well," the man said, "I see you run ads for Larry's Diner, too. With a coupon, yes?"

"That's right. 25% off Fish & Chips."

"And he runs this ad every issue?"
"So far, yeah."
"Perfect. Make my ad for 30% off Fish & Chips."
Both Video Scene II and Huck's were out of issues completely, so Dale filled them back up and thanked the owners for their support.
While leaving Huck's Plaza, I noticed a plume of gray smoke rising from the east.
"Hey Dale, look at that!"
"A fire?"
"Appears so!"
Dale and I grinned at each other. Breaking news!
We pedaled as quick as conditions would allow, since 27 Mile Road was gravel east of Gratiot and not well-plowed. There was indeed a small house on fire, with two fire trucks parked out front, and firefighters were using a large hose to control the blaze. Several other uniformed men were standing close to the road, surveying the scene.
Dale hopped off his bike first and unzipped his backpack. He pulled out his PXL 2000.
"You brought that with you?"
"A journalist is always prepared," he said, handing me the camcorder. "Can you videotape me talking to the firemen?"
"Uh, sure. What are you going to say?"
"I'm going to ask questions."
He approached the nearest man with a confidence he rarely had around kids. Grown-ups were his comfort zone.
"Dale Dunkle, *The New Haven Herald Jr.*," he said by way of introduction. "Do you have a moment?"
"Uh, sure, kid," the man replied. "How can I help you?"
"Well, for starters, do you know who caused this fire?"
The man smiled. "Yeah. We did."
The fireman, who it turns out was the Fire Chief, explained that the New Haven Fire Department was an all-volunteer force which conducted live trainings once or twice a year in real-world environments. When an

old structure was deemed unsalvageable, the property owner might be forced to spend thousands of dollars to have it safely demolished. Or, they could donate the home to their local fire department, saving demolition costs and earning a tax deduction as well. The arrangement was in everyone's best interests, from the firemen who got invaluable training, to the homeowner who saved money, to the community rid of an eyesore.

After the interview was complete, I got extra footage of the fire itself, including the moment where the roof of the home collapsed spectacularly into the inferno below. It was exciting to watch men brave the dangerous building, once returning with large sacks across their shoulders, which I assumed represented unconscious rescued people.

"This is going to be a great story," Dale said.

"It's also going to be great stock footage for our future movies!"

Dale giggled. "It's like we have a special effects budget!"

"Hollywood here we come!"

"Let's go back to my place and see what we got."

We hadn't realized how dark it had become while staring into the burning flames of the old house, so the ride down Clark was a little scary. My eyes adjusted eventually, in time to see the gloom of the Black House on my right as we turned onto Chennault. I wondered why the Fire Department hadn't gotten around to burning that eyesore down, too.

When we got to Dale's house, Mrs. Dunkle was waiting for us.

"Jimmy, your mom called. She's worried about you being out so late."

"I'll go home in a few minutes," I promised. "Dale and I got footage of a fire that we want to watch first!"

"A fire?"

"Yeah," Dale said. "The fire department was practicing on an abandoned house. Can we please watch the tape before Jimmy leaves?"

"Oh, alright," she agreed. "Dale, you also missed a call from a reporter at *The Anchor Bay Bulletin*. She's

going to call back in about a half hour."
"*The Anchor Bay Bulletin?*" he asked, puzzled.
"Why are they calling me?"
Mrs. Dunkle smiled. "They want to do a story on your paper, of course!"
Dale and I looked at each other. I didn't know any details about circulation or whatnot, but *The Anchor Bay Bulletin* was a bigger paper than *The Lenox Observer*. They had actual coin-operated paper boxes and everything. I'd later learn they were almost as large as *The Chronicle* in terms of distribution in our area.
"That's really neat," I said. "Want me to stick around for the call?"
Mrs. Dunkle shook her head. "I promised your mom I'd send you home."
"Alright," I acquiesced. "But Dale, don't forget to say how awesome I am!"
Dale laughed. "I won't!"
The fire footage was indeed dazzling, albeit fuzzy and black and white. It was hard to hear the audio in Dale's interview, but if you turned the volume up all the way, you could create a decent transcription. The best part of the video was the fire itself, and there was no question we'd cut it into homemade movies later. At one point, the whiteness of the flames against the night sky looked like an explosion in space; later, Dale would use that clip to depict a space station blowing up in *Star Voyage VII: Revenge of the Monster*.
The whole time we were watching, though, I suspected we were thinking about being written up in a "real" paper. I daydreamed about it on my ride home, too. You'd think I'd have been nervous or embarrassed to have an article written about Dale and I. Hell, at school, I'd done a decent job at not linking myself too tightly to Dale at all. People knew we were friendly, sure, but few students knew we had this side project together. A newspaper article about us would cement the obvious: Jimmy Logan was *friends* with Dale Dunkle. *Close* friends. Close enough to spend a lot of time together making something dorky. No getting around it. Yet all I felt was excitement. And, more importantly,

an intoxicating sense of pride about the whole endeavor.

Mom was irritated when I came in, but softened as I told her the news.

"My boy's going to be in the paper? That calls for a celebration!" She poured a glass of wine for herself and a chocolate milk for me.

"It's no big deal," I lied.

"Do they need your photo? I could send them your last school picture."

"I don't think they're going to have pictures. It's an article about two boys making a newspaper."

"Did they interview you?"

"Nah, they're talking to Dale now. Mrs. Dunkle said you wanted me home."

"Well, that's true," Mom admitted. "I hate when you're out past dark."

"It's not late. It just looks late."

"Daylight Savings Time," she said.

"Actually, Daylight Savings Time ended in October. We're now on regular time. It gets dark faster because the Earth is tilted away from the Sun this time of year."

Mom took a long sip from her wine glass. "Is that so?"

"Yeah, I think so."

"Did you learn that at school?"

"Dale explained it to me. I was asking why it was so dark and he went into one of his little teaching spells."

"That must be irritating."

"Nah, it's alright," I said. "He's not trying to show off or anything. I think he just loves talking about nerdy stuff."

Mom took another sip, then eyed me carefully. "Jimmy, does he think you're dumb? Does he ever try and make you feel like you're not as educated as he is?"

"No, I don't think so."

"I mean, it's good that you have a smart friend who can teach you things. But, what is he getting out of it?"

"What do you mean?"

"What is Dale getting out of your relationship?"

I had no answer to this. I had never thought about it that way. I didn't think adolescent friendships had to be transactional. We had fun together. Wasn't that enough?

"Uh," I stalled. "I guess maybe I make him seem cooler?"

Mom downed the last liquid in her glass. I had barely touched my Nestle Quik.

"You just make sure it's an evenly-matched friendship," she said. "Don't let him take advantage of you. You're a special boy. Just as special as Dale Dunkle. I don't want you to feel like you're lucky to be around him. I want him to feel he's lucky to be around you."

"We're friends, Mom."

"If only life was that simple, Jimmy."

# Two

Dale wrote an article about the fire that night. He placed it on the front page of the third issue, and brought me the first two pages to review at lunch while we were eating with Zach, Marco, and Benny. He explained there was no way to extract a picture of the actual fire from the PXL footage, but a friendly clipart graphic of a burning house got the point across. The article spanned two panels, and read like this:

```
FRIENDLY FIRE
By Dale Dunkle
     On January 30, 1989, the New Haven Fire
Department intentionally burned down a nice
little house at 32140 27 Mile Road. Why?
Because they were in training, that's why!
     It was amazing. A wall fell here, a
window frame melted there...weird.
     I was a little disappointed because the
firemen didn't do as much as they do in the
movies, but Fire Chief Keys explained that
there was no need for heroics when a
property was empty. There were no people
inside, or even furniture that would need
to be saved. The owners of the property had
donated the vacant home to be used for
firefighter training, and because New Haven
has an all-volunteer Fire Department, it
was more important that they learn to use
the hoses and other equipment. For some of
the firemen present, it was the first time
they had been wearing their gear.
     It's strange how something like wood
and metal and brick can burn up without a
trace, and I started to imagine my own home
```

burning up in flames. It made me think about escape routes and smoke detectors. Maybe you should make a plan, too.

"Hey, that's pretty good," I said. "But, where'd my article about the potholes go?"

"I moved that to page two," Dale explained. "I figured a fire would be a better lead story."

"That might be true, but look." I pointed to each byline on the new front page. "Every article on page one is yours. Someone reading the paper will think it's a one-man show."

Dale was nonplussed. He either hadn't noticed or didn't care. "Well," he said, "the Editor's Welcome and the Quick Comments sections always go on the front, and we can't move the Index. I'm sure it's fine. They'll see your articles as soon as they open it, including that Red Wings breakdown you wrote. I pasted their actual logo onto that one."

He handed me the second page. The Detroit Red Wings logo did indeed look cool next to my column. I guessed it was all okay.

Zach reached out a hand. "Mind if I take a look?"

"Sure," said Dale, passing over the pages. "But don't get any ketchup on them. They're originals."

Zach looked down at his plate to confirm it contained no ketchup, then read over the first page. Within moments, his eyebrows furrowed. "You spelled the chief's name wrong," he said.

Dale perked up. "What? Are you sure?"

"Pretty sure. He's my dad."

I was shocked by this. "No way, dude! Your dad's the Fire Chief? I thought he worked at Bawler Towing."

"He does. The fire gig isn't full time. But I promise I know how to spell his name because it's my name too. K-E-Y-E-S."

"Sorry about that," said Dale. "I didn't ask him how to spell it. And I didn't know he was your dad. I don't think I knew your last name, to be honest."

"Well, I'm sorry you don't know much about me. And I'm sorry that my dad risking his life for the people of New Haven isn't as impressive as actors in the movies." He handed Dale the papers. He hadn't even glanced at page two.

Dale took them but said nothing. I could tell he was hurt, and in his silence I began to worry he might actually cry. There's no way that would make anything better, so I stepped in.

"It's all good," I said cheerily. "We'll fix the article tonight. Did you hear Dale and I are going to be in *The Anchor Bay Bulletin?* They're writing about the paper."

Marco chuckled without looking up. "I bet they'll spell *your* names right."

Dale stuffed the papers in his folder and walked off without saying a word.

"Come on guys," I admonished my friends. "You made him sad."

"Dude," said Zach, shoving fries into his mouth. "You were ragging on that nerd a couple months ago with the rest of us. Now you're his big brother?"

"I just miss clubhouse time," grumbled Benny.

"Shit, I'll write an article for ya if it means we get to hang again," said Marco. "Not that you bothered to ask."

This caught me off guard. It seemed to surprise Zach and Benny, too. They weren't complaining about being left out of the paper. Only Marco was.

"You want to work on the paper?" I asked.

"Naw. But what, you think because I was held back that I'm slow or something? I can write. I've had to listen to the two of you brag about this thing for months like it was some cool little side club for just you white boys and even when you saw I didn't have shit to do..." Marco trailed off. "Whatever, man, it's fine."

He was right. It never occurred to me to ask Marco, or anyone else for that matter, if they wanted to be involved. It was Dale and my thing. Separate from everyone else. Which I guess, even if they didn't want to be on the paper necessarily, was Zach and Benny's complaint, too.

"Marco, I'm sure Dale would let you on the paper if you asked."

## THE PAPER

"I'm not going to kiss up to some 11-year-old kid and beg his ass if I could pretty please hang out with him. Screw that." Marco shook his head. "They probably didn't have Black kids at his fancy smart-kid school. He barely even looks at me."

"You never say a word to him."

"Hang on," Zach interjected. "How the hell did this become a debate on whether Marco is cool enough to hang with *Dale Dunkle?* I thought the reason we were mad is because Dale Dunkle isn't cool enough to hang with *us!*"

I stood up.

"Look, I'm going to find Dale, let him know that you, Marco, want to write articles, and that you, Zach, are just a dick."

"That's fair," said Zach. "Maybe Marco can write about how these school fries are too damn salty."

"What about me?" asked Benny.

"You want to write articles?"

"Not really."

"How about making a word search?"

"Okay."

"Great. Zach? Sure you don't wanna be involved?"

"Just spell my dad's name right and I'm good."

"Fine. This is easy. Marco, write something for the next issue. Doesn't matter what about. Benny, start thinking of how to make a word search or crossword puzzle or something fun. And Zach, try and be nice to the kid. I know he's a nerd. But it's not like the rest of us are running the school either, ya know?"

Everyone was silent, which I took as agreement.

"Well good," I said, still standing. "The article about Dale and I will come out next week I'm sure, so we need the next issue done as soon as possible to take advantage of the publicity."

Zach smirked. "Did you talk to a reporter?"

"What? No, Dale did."

"Uh huh."

"Dale promised he'd talk about me, though." This sounded lamer out loud than it did in my head.

Zach threw his hands up in defeat. "Look, you all

can help Dale with his little project all you want and I won't bust your chops too much. I live on the other side of town so I never see any of you assholes outside of this place anyway. I'm just pointing out this is Dale's baby, not yours. And whether he lets Marco write shit, or Benny play delivery boy, or Jimmy be Executive Vice President of Operations or whatever, *he's* getting the credit. That's all I'm saying. Now pass me the goddamned ketchup before I become a freakin' mummy."

—

The friend skirmish happened on a Thursday. *The Anchor Bay Bulletin* came out on Tuesdays, and we assumed the article about our paper would be in it. We were almost sold out of our second issue, which means we needed to get the third issue complete over the weekend in time to have it copied and distributed Monday night.

We still had a bit of space to fill, so Dale and I wrote our first horoscope section that Saturday. It was nonsense, of course, ad-libbed and typed up in real time. It included such wisdom as:

```
     PISCES: If you are living in a two-
story house, you will have fun tomorrow. If
you aren't, you won't.
     LEO: Your money will vanish when you go
to the store if you aren't careful. Only
buy things you truly need.
     SCORPIO: If the next person you see is
related to you, you might win the lottery.
     CAPRICORN: Read Pisces instead. We
don't have time to write all twelve!
```

Damn, we were funny.

Printing took hours, as always, so Dale dropped the final pages off to Mrs. Patrick Sunday night. Given how much she was donating, we upped her "free" ad to a half-page. We had increased our printing target to 200 copies, and like the previous installments, the third issue was eight pages (four double-sided sheets.) Mrs. Patrick delivered the stack of papers to Dale's house Monday afternoon, and we spent over an hour stapling and folding them after school. Although it broke our informal independence rule, Dale's dad had offered to drive Dale around to deliver the new issues that night. I got to go home for dinner instead of making Mom nervous.

I showed my copy to Mom and Mike over pork chops and potatoes, and to Grandma when I brought up her meal. Each of them had a different favorite article of mine. Mike liked the Red Wings piece, Mom liked my rant about the potholes, and Grandma liked my review of *Batteries Not Included*, a movie she and I had watched together on the small TV and VCR in her bedroom over Christmas break. All three said how proud they were of me. To her credit, Mom didn't even complain that I wasn't on the front page.

I read the issue cover to cover one last time before going to bed. It was our best yet, by a mile.

—

Mom showed me *The Anchor Bay Bulletin* when I got home from school the next day. The article was on Page 5.

> YOUNG ENTREPRENEUR LAUNCHES LOCAL PAPER
> By Jennifer Burton
>     NEW HAVEN – At an age when most children are focused on cartoons and little league, 11-year-old Dale Dunkle is making headlines by creating them. Demonstrating remarkable talent and initiative, Dunkle has launched his own newspaper, *The New Haven Herald Jr.*, which is quickly gaining attention in the community.
>     From a young age, Dunkle showed a passion for storytelling. Now, he's channeling his writing talents into a new venture, learning layout and printing skills as well to produce his bi-monthly

publication. He may be too young to write for his school newspaper, but isn't too young to create competition.

Alongside his friend Jimmy Logan, Dunkle covers everything from news and entertainment to sports and the weather. Showing an entrepreneurial spirit far exceeding a child's lemonade stand, Dunkle even secures advertisements for the paper from local businesses using a professional ad rate sheet he also designed himself...

The article went on for several more paragraphs, describing Dale's energy and "quick mind", his thoughts on what it's like to be a gifted child, and how Dale's parents were supportive of the paper but did not assist him. The only mention of my involvement was "alongside his friend Jimmy Logan." By the end, I realized the piece wasn't about the paper at all. It was about Dale.

"Well," I said. "At least they printed my name."

"Uh huh," Mom responded.

I silently reread the piece.

"You know," I grumbled, "this whole thing was my idea. Dale was showing me the computer program, *The Newsroom*, and talking about how he missed working on the paper back at his old school. I'm the one who told him to start his own."

"Are you really writing your articles, or does Dale do everything?"

"What? No, I write mine. I mean, he types them up and edits them, but they're my ideas."

"But the paper would be more or less the same if you were involved or not, right?"

This stung, even though I still couldn't see what she was getting at.

"Well, maybe Dale doesn't *need* me but I make the paper so much better," I insisted. "Dale doesn't know anything about sports. And he hasn't lived here in years so he doesn't know much about how New Haven works either. I help him a lot there. And the part about him getting ads...it was *your* suggestion that we go out and get ads, and *both* Dale and I talked businesses into supporting us! Heck, I've brought in more money than he has. It's not fair that they made it out to be just him."

Mom said nothing and lit a cigarette.

"Wait, don't you believe me?"

"I'm sure you helped, Jimmy. It's nice of you to help your friend with his project, and I hope he appreciates it."

Before I could answer, there was an excited knock at the door. It was the gifted boy genius himself, Dale Dunkle.

"Hey," I said. I tried to sound irritated because I was. Dale didn't seem to pick up on it.

"Did you read it?" he beamed.

"Yeah."

"Isn't it exciting? I've never been in the paper before. I mean, not counting ours. I thought it was so nice! She talked to me for like a half hour that night and then came by in person the next day after school. That's when I got to show her how we make the paper and some of our PXL movies and stuff. She was interested in it all!"

"You didn't tell me she came by in person."

"Didn't I? I was sure I told you about it, the questions she asked me and everything."

"I thought that was just the phone call."

"What difference does it make?"

"Because maybe if I had been there in person with you, she would have realized it wasn't a single person doing all the work!"

For the first time, it clicked with the bowl-cutted doofus that I was unhappy. His eyes widened.

"You're mad that the article's mostly about me and not you?"

"A little, yeah!"

Dale looked away for a moment, lost in thought. I sensed he was rereading the article in his mind, from memory, like a goddamned savant. When he apparently got to the end, he looked back at me.

"Gee Jimmy," he said. "I'm really sorry. I didn't tell her what to write. I talked about both of us, I did. I wish the article had been more about the paper than about me. Some of it was a little embarrassing, to be honest. I don't like to remind people that I'm a year younger, or that I went to that fancy school. It was fun to be asked about what I'm like by someone who was interested in what I had to say. I suppose I did talk about myself a lot. But I was just answering questions, you know?"

"I guess so."

"And after all, it doesn't matter which of us the article was about. The fact is that more people will know about our paper now and buy it! Who cares if they just wanna see what the nerdy kid was up to? They'll read all your stuff too. And buy more ads. This is a good thing!"

I knew he was right, of course. And nothing in the article was wrong exactly. Dale had the experience and knew the software. He did do all the typing, picture placement, layout, all of it. Like Zach said, the paper was Dale's baby. It wasn't something I could have done. I didn't have a computer. All I had was a Nintendo.

Dale stayed at my place until he left for dinner, and during that time I absolutely kicked his ass at both *Double Dribble* and *Karate Champ*. Like, it wasn't even close. I was merciless. It couldn't have been much fun from his perspective. At one point I shouted at him, rather nastily, "I guess you can't do everything after all!" But somehow he was a good sport about it. Better than I would have been had the situation been reversed, for sure.

Mike arrived as Dale was leaving. I helped Mom set the table and Mike cracked open a beer. I didn't say much over the meal, and nobody mentioned *The Anchor Bay Bulletin*. I had seen Mom whispering to Mike before we sat down and guessed she had brought him up to speed. They barely talked to each other either, except for Mom complaining that Mike forgot to bring her aspirin like he had "promised."

# THE PAPER

After the dishes were done, Mike asked if I wanted to play chess.

"One game, Jimmy?"

"Sure, Mike."

As we set up the board, he brought up the article.

"I just wanted to say that I think it's quite cool you guys are being noticed," Mike said. "I'm proud of you."

"Yeah. People will know more about us now. Dale, anyway."

Mike played his standard opening move with the King's pawn and waited for my typical response. I gave it.

"You like Elton John, right?" Mike asked.

"Sure, I guess." He wasn't my favorite, but Mike and my mom played his albums a lot, and some songs, well, everybody knows.

"I saw you air drumming to *Tiny Dancer* last week. Do you want to learn to play drums?"

"I played drums in band last semester," I reminded him. "But just snare, or bass drum sometimes."

"I bet I can get you a used drum set to play on, if you're interested."

"Not sure mom would love that."

"I'll convince her. But that's not why I brought up Elton John. You've heard a lot of his music, I'm sure, like *Rocket Man, Bennie and the Jets, Crocodile Rock, I'm Still Standing...*"

"*Movin' Out*?" I offered.

"No, that's Billy Joel."

"Oh."

"My point is, Elton John has had tons of hits and he's a household name. He gets to be on TV whenever he wants, plays packed stadiums, all of that. Even if not everyone loves him, everyone knows who he his. And I bet you know more lyrics by heart than you think."

"Yeah, probably." I would never admit it at the time, but I did have a soft spot for *Don't Let the Sun Go Down on Me* and could sing every word.

"What do you think of Bernie Taupin?" Mike asked, capturing my knight.

"Who?"

"Bernie Taupin wrote the lyrics to all the songs I mentioned. Every one of them. Elton John writes the melodies and Bernie writes the words."

I was shocked by this. "The lyrics *are* the song! You wouldn't even know what a song was called without lyrics."

Mike nodded. "I agree. But music is a collaboration, right? I mean, Elton John doesn't play his own drums or bass guitar or anything either. He's the face of the band, and there's no Elton John without, well, Elton John. But so many people are behind the scenes to make it all happen. And yeah, some of those guys, like Bernie Taupin, deserve a big chunk of the credit."

"No one's heard of that dude!"

"Music lovers have. It's not a secret or anything. Bernie's half the reason Elton John is famous. He just doesn't get articles written about him, ya know?"

"I didn't know that." My king was in trouble now. I tried to escape.

"I bet as long as Elton treats Bernie well, and they make good songs together, I'm sure Bernie's cool with the whole thing. But, if Elton started taking credit for Bernie's lyrics, too, well at that point Bernie would tell him to fuck off. You get what I mean?"

I did.

Mike smiled, knocking over my queen. "Checkmate."

"Huh."

Guess I wasn't going to become a man today.

# Three

Marco submitted his first article the following Friday. He just handed it to Dale in the hallway without a word. Dale showed it to me after school.

"It's good," I admitted.

"I think so too. Not very timely, though."

Marco's article was about Christmas, which was nearly two months ago. But it had an interesting angle. Like me, Marco was being raised by a single mom, and finances were tight. Here's what he wrote:

```
STOP GIVING SANTA THE CREDIT
By Marco Parnell
     Every Christmas it seems like the
biggest gifts come from Santa. Most of my
friends have gotten new Nintendos,
Ghostbusters Firehouses, Laser Tag kits,
and other expensive toys.
     But if Santa is real, why does he give
some kids toys that cost a hundred bucks,
and other kids get a single G.I. Joe?
     Is it because some kids have been
"naughty" and don't deserve the best toys?
That's what I believed growing up. I didn't
understand how Santa could give my cousin
the Barbie Dreamhouse she wanted but Santa
only gave me a sweater. I never got any of
the big items on my Christmas list. I was
10 years old when I found out the truth.
     Maybe parents should stop pretending
big expensive things are from Santa, so
kids like me stop wondering what they did
wrong.
```

"We have to put it in," I said. "We don't have much for the next issue yet, and it's sorta ballsy of him that he gave it to you at all."

Dale nodded. "Yeah, I know. Brave to admit to the world that your mom doesn't have much money."

"His mom does okay, but his dad isn't around, like mine. It's hard for one parent to afford the same things as two parents."

"You're the one with a Nintendo."

"You know damned well your computer cost more than a Nintendo, Dale."

The article went in. Dale even added a "welcome to Marco, our newest writer" blurb in the Quick Comments section on the front page.

"So, why do you think Marco *wanted* to get involved?" asked Dale. "Do you think his mom made him do it? Maybe she saw the article in the *Bulletin*?"

I cringed. If anything, I thought that article would have made him *less* likely to help, since it proved Zach had a point.

"Nah," I said. "He mentioned that he wanted to last week. I think he had been a little jealous of our project. Or at least jealous of all the time it takes. I used to hang out with Marco and Benny most days after school. Now a lot of the time I'm with you."

"They've never been to my house," Dale realized.

"Have you asked them over?"

"No."

I had mixed feelings about my friends possibly hanging out with Dale, but I wasn't sure why. I didn't think it was jealousy, exactly. Perhaps I didn't want my two worlds colliding. I mean, I didn't want Dale playing chess with Mike either.

But since we were mixing things up, I decided to ask Emilia if she wanted to write something for the paper too.

We were in Mr. Wright's class and she had already sent me a coded note. It read "U'y ea nadqp," which was easy to figure out since the apostrophe gave away the first word: I'm. If V was I and z was m, that meant the rest of the message was "so bored."

I flashed her a sympathetic smile. She smiled back, perfectly. She had this strand of hair across her cheek that had fallen out of her ponytail and, oh my God, every time she looked up or down or at me or anywhere, the maverick hair caressed her skin. "I can touch her but you can't," it teased.

I started writing the note, and got as far as coding "Maybe you should" when Mr. Wright called on me.

"Yes sir?"

He asked some sort of question.

"Uh, the Mongols, sir?" I answered.

I must have been right, for he moved on. Where was I. Ah, yes. I coded "write an article for my paper!" and passed it over.

I kept stealing glances at Emilia as she worked through the message. I had used the same 12-character shift as she had, so it would be easy, and she seemed to make short work of it. But by the end, she shot me a confused look.

*Oh no*, I thought. She had no idea what I was talking about. Did she forget that I was writing the paper with Dale? Or maybe she had read that *Anchor Bay Bulletin* article and her look meant "but I thought you had nothing to do with that thing after all." Or maybe her expression meant that I was foolish for asking, like "you think I'm dorky enough to play newspaper with you and your dweeb friends?" I couldn't read her, but knew I had said something wrong.

Hastily, I sent a short apology message, also coded in the same 12-character character shift: "sorry, just kidding!" She seemed to translate this one okay, but gave me a confused shrug as if she didn't know what I was kidding about.

I was thinking about it later that night when it hit me I may have mistranslated part of the message. Perhaps after Mr. Wright had interrupted me I had reversed the character switch, so that my first three words were 12 characters ahead in the alphabet, but then the last few words were 12 characters behind. I had done this by accident before and it had led to an early message of mine being half-gibberish. So perhaps the message she had translated wasn't "maybe you should write an article for my paper" but rather "maybe you should idufq mz mdfuoxq rad yk bmbqd." That would explain her confusion, though I supposed the "what are you talking about, loser?" hypothesis was still the simplest solution.

Gah. I needed to stop obsessing over this. I thought I should go back to thinking about Emilia's lips instead of her mind. Safer that way, for my ego and all.

Anyway, Marco was a great addition to the team. One snowy day at Dale's after school I showed Marco the PXL footage we got of the fire and man was he jealous, of both the fire and the camcorder. He insisted we make a horror movie together, but since he had to go home earlier than I did, he asked to be killed off first.

"That works out, though," Marco said. "The brother always dies first in a scary movie."

"The brother?" asked Dale.

"He means the Black guy," I explained.

"Oh. I never noticed that!"

"You wouldn't," said Marco. "But I sure as hell do."

Dale smiled. "So you're saying this movie will be in the modern film tradition!"

"Something like that," he shrugged.

"I promise you'd make it to the end of our movie if your mom didn't have dinner so early," I said.

One thing we learned by playing around with Marco and the PXL 2000 was how much the camera struggled to show Black skin, and dark scenes and objects in general. Even if we had all the lights turned on in Dale's basement while filming, it was hard to make out anything shot in shadow without cranking the brightness knob on the television on playback, which turned all the blacks into greys. I knew the PXL was only a toy and all, but it was still disappointing that the fake blood we had added to Marco's face for his final shot was invisible on the screen. Blood was hard enough to capture with a black-and-white camcorder against *white* skin. Against Marco's skin it didn't register at all.

Mrs. Dunkle overheard our complaining and offered a suggestion.

"Have you tried chocolate syrup?"

"For what?" I asked.

"For the blood," she said. "Alfred Hitchcock shot most of his films in black and white, too, and used chocolate syrup instead of fake blood. It shows up better on camera. And it's cheaper."

Dale grinned. "And clean-up will be delicious!"

Marco had already left, but we decided to test it for the next scene, in which Dale himself would be the final victim. He ran upstairs to the kitchen and returned with a plastic bottle of Hershey's syrup.

"Squeeze some on my face," Dale encouraged.

I took the syrup. I hadn't ever seen Hershey's come in a bottle like this, as my mom always bought the traditional Hershey's tins that you had to puncture with a can opener. Being unfamiliar with this modern advancement in packaging, I squeezed way too hard and exploded a quarter cup of chocolate goop all over Dale's face and up his nose. If he hadn't been wearing his glasses, he might have gone blind.

Dale sneezed out chocolate, startled. Then he removed his Hershey's-splattered glasses as I tried not to laugh.

"Can I see that bottle?"

I handed it to him.

He spun it around and squeezed an equal or greater amount of syrup on my own face and hair. I don't know why I was so shocked, but I was. Retaliation was something Marco would do, but not something Dale Dunkle would do.

Dale didn't try to suppress his laughter as I had. It came freely, loud and clear, like he was having the time of his life.

"Give me that!" I squealed, lurching for the bottle.

"Not in the house," he laughed, and raced for the back door. He had gotten all the way outside and halfway into the backyard, squirting me with syrup from a distance to try and slow me down. I tackled him in the snow and the bottle went flying out of his hand. It was the first time we had been physical with each other since we were little kids.

Dale and I were roaring hysterically at this point, our faces and shirts covered in smeared chocolate and snow.

After a bit more playful wrestling, I sat up, panting. Looking down at my body, I could tell I was a mess. Plus, I needed to stop, because all that touching and rubbing syrup on each other was causing an unwanted physical reaction, and that would have been embarrassing, to say the least.

"I shouldn't go back in your house like this," I said.

"But look!" Dale pointed to the dramatic splattered "blood" trail in the snow illuminated by his back porch light. "Doesn't that look awesome?"

"You're right," I agreed. "Can you get the PXL? We'll shoot the final death scene out here."

Even in the dim ambient light of a winter dusk, the contrast between the black syrup and the white snow looked great on camera. Dale's mom had been right. Though, I doubted she would have approved of the way we found out. And my own mom was going to kill me. Chocolate didn't wash out well, at least not with that white box generic laundry detergent she bought.

The final shot of the film was pretty epic, though. Over the summer, Dale and his dad had built a rudimentary treehouse in his backyard—barely more than a small bench to sit on—but it gave Dale the idea to have me climb up the ten feet and shoot downward, film crane style, so all you saw was a small, splayed body and a blood trail in a sea of white snow. Hollywood, here we come.

After I climbed back down, a faint chirping sound from Dale's calculator watch alerted us that it was time for me to go home. (Have I mentioned before that Dale had a calculator watch? Because of course he had a calculator watch.)

"I'll see you tomorrow in school," I called out as I was leaving.

"Alright, love you!" he called back.
"What?"

Dale went white. "Oh my God! Sorry about that! That's what I say to family!"

I was weirded out, but tried to play it off like it was nothing. "Man, you're lucky no one was around to hear that. I'd have to kick your ass to keep my rep."

"Really, I *promise* I don't love you," he said, looking miserable. Then he thought of a way out. "I mean, I don't even like you! You kind of suck."

I laughed. "You suck too, nerd!"

Now he just smiled. "Go to hell, Jimmy Logan!"

"Fuck off, Dale Dunkle!"

I grinned, turned, and headed toward home. Crisis averted.

But I thought about it, a bit, as I walked alone down the dark street. I'm sure it was an accident, like he said. Dale didn't *love* me. But how did I feel about him? Or any of my friends, for that matter? Did I *love* any of them, or just *like* them? And if a friend did graduate to the level of "love," when, if ever, would it be appropriate to say so?

After Dale had left New Haven the first time, when we were little, I had gotten quite close with Benny. We used to hold hands while walking on the sidewalk together, though that stopped when some of the older kids started calling us "fags." Benny was the only friend I could remember ever saying "I love you" to, and not by accident. In general I wouldn't say it to anyone, not even to Mom or Grandma. I'd heard Mom and Mike say "I love you" to each other, though not as much as you'd think. Usually only after a fight, assuming Mike didn't storm out first.

As if these memories had willed it into being, I saw Mike storming out of the front door as I approached.

"Mike?"

He didn't seem to notice me. He was already in his car and backing out of the driveway when I got close enough to make eye contact. I thought about calling out his name again, but if the two of them did indeed have a fight, it was best not to get involved. Mom could push Mike's buttons in a way that made him a completely different person. I'd wait until the Mike I knew was back.

As I entered the front door, I heard Mom crying down in the den. I considered going straight up to my room, but was frankly hungry for dinner and figured I shouldn't have to starve due to a lover's spat that I wasn't a part of.

"Hi Mom," I said when I reached the bottom of the stairs.

She stopped crying. "Dinner's on the table," she said. "It's just Kraft mac and cheese."

"Sounds good to me."

I sat down and scooped myself a helping. After a moment, Mom sat down too. Her straight brown hair was pulled back in a ponytail, but quite a few strands had made their way free and danced frantically beside her puffy face as she turned to me. What had been endearing on Emilia seemed wretched on Mom. Her right hand held a cigarette which needed to be ashed.

"I don't think Mike's going to come around anymore," she said.

This wasn't the first time she had said this. If this was love, maybe I was right not to want any part of it.

"Oh?" I said, trying to keep the bitterness at bay.

"He's just not a mature enough person for us. For *you*. I want you to have a good role model, and he's not ready."

*You're the one who's a shitty role model.*

"He was so mean to me today," she continued. "He said he didn't believe me about something. I deserve a man who will always believe me."

"Have you ever lied to him?" I asked, a bit too sharply.

Her eyes narrowed. "Why, what has he told you?"

"Nothing," I said, and it was true. I could think of only one or two times Mike had even mentioned Mom. Our conversations were all sports and chess and Bernie Taupin.

"You're lying to me," she said.

"I'm not!"

"*Yes you are.* I know he badmouths me to you. He's

trying to turn you against me. It's called *parental alienation*. I read about it in Good Housekeeping. But it's not going to work because he's out of our lives now. You don't have to lie to defend him. He can't hurt you anymore."

I threw down my fork.

"What the hell are you talking about, Mom? He's never hurt me, not once! He's trying to be a nice guy and all you do is criticize him and pick fights! And now you kick him out again and I don't get a say at all!"

"How dare you talk to me like that! *I am your mother!*"

"Yeah, and you just called me a liar! Maybe I deserve a mom *who will always believe me!*" I kicked my chair back and stood up. Mom stood up, too.

"Where do you think you're going?"

"To my room."

"You're going to sit down and eat your dinner until you're excused."

I shook my head, exasperated. "You claim to love me, but you don't trust me. You claim to love Mike, but you don't trust him either. You don't talk to Aunt Sharon anymore, because of God knows why. You never mention any of your other friends. Do you even have friends?"

Mom's face was so red I thought she might explode. "You are never seeing Mike again! Never! *Do you understand me?*"

"No! What gives you the right to cut someone out of my life? I love him!"

A beat passed between us. I'm not sure which of us was more startled at this admission. I certainly hadn't been planning to say that. I had never even thought about it before now.

For the briefest of moments, it seemed our joint shock would be enough to diffuse the tension. But then Mom's face began to contort once again into a familiar skin-flushed, creased-forehead fury. She looked as if she was going to spit in my face.

"Maybe so," she hissed, "but *I'm* the one who's *pregnant.*"

# Four

I wish I could report that Mom came to my bedroom later to apologize, or made a peace offering of cookies or something, which would have allowed me to apologize too, and we'd have hugged and everything would have been okay. That's what other moms might have done, so I hear. But not my mom. She felt disrespected by me, and it would be several days before she could let that go. I remember fearing she would never fully forgive the blow-up and would probably bring it up months or even years later. The time I threw down my fork and raised my voice to *my own pregnant mother.* But maybe I was becoming more like her than I realized, because I fell asleep that night thinking I'd never forgive her, either, if she had really kicked Mike out of our lives forever.

I know what you're thinking. What if Mike *had* doubted whether she was pregnant? Wouldn't that be reason enough to kick him out? Why was I so quick to side with Mike over my mom? A gut feeling, I suppose. And experience. I knew that she had lied to Mike at least once before, and it wasn't Mike who told me about it. I had overheard her talking to him on the phone asking if she could borrow money because she had been too sick to work at the restaurant that week. But she hadn't been sick. She had just gotten home, and she was still wearing her waitress polo while she was on the phone with him. I never brought it up, but it bothered me.

There was another time, too, when they broke up after dating for a month or two, and then she apparently said something that got them back together, and

Mike was super sweet and doting for a while. I remember thinking that maybe she had told him she was pregnant then, the way he was acting around her, ya know? I had wondered if I was going to have a baby brother. But the subject never came up and no baby ever appeared, so I assumed I had misread the situation. Now I couldn't help but wonder if I had been right, which means she either lost the baby the first time, or had just claimed to be pregnant to get him back.

Anyway, those were the thoughts I was having during the next few days of Mom hardly speaking to me and no Mike around. She was pregnant for sure, though, because Grandma talked to me about it later that week.

"Your mom told me she told you," Grandma said, a note of empathy in her voice.

"Yeah," I said.

"Do you want to talk about it?"

"Not really. I mean, I always wanted a kid brother, at least when I was younger. But now I'm 12. Having a baby around would make me more like a dad, not a big brother. I'll graduate high school before he's in kindergarten."

"It's going to be hard on your mom raising a baby alone. You might need to help."

"Why? She raised *me* alone."

"No, *I* helped her. A lot. But I'm not going to be able to help this time. With my arthritis I think my days of changing diapers are over."

My eyes went wide. "She's going to make me change diapers?"

"Probably, yes."

"This sucks. I have a life too! I didn't ask to be a dad. She needs to get Mike back. He'd be a great dad." I didn't add that I knew this from personal experience.

"Maybe he'll come back," said Grandma. "Maybe he won't. The baby's due at the end of August. There's time. But they both have to want to make it work."

"Sex sure makes things complicated," I said. Then my cheeks flushed as I realized I just said the word "sex" to my grandmother. She laughed.

"That's why I'd advise against it," she teased.

I responded something like "don't worry, I'm not interested in sex" and felt a bit guilty for saying so, because it wasn't true. I mean, I wasn't fantasizing about full-on intercourse or anything at this point in my puberty journey, but I was certainly noticing a strong physical response down there when I thought about kissing or holding Emilia.

Not everyone thought Emilia was as special as I did, though. Around this time is when I saw her getting bullied by a couple guys and an older girl in the hallway. They were being quite aggressive, backing her into the row of lockers while telling Polish jokes.

"Did you hear about the Polack who won a beauty contest? *Neither did I!*"

"She's not laughing! She's probably *too stupid to get it!*"

At this point, the older girl knocked Emilia's history book out of her hand. It landed on the tile floor with an echoing thud.

I thought about turning around and avoiding conflict, but Emilia's sad eyes found mine and I froze. The coward's way out had closed. I took a quick breath and found the courage to march up to them.

"Hey, you dropped your book," I said to Emilia, retrieving it for her like it was a normal interaction. "Come on, we're going to be late."

One of the bullies put his hand on my shoulder. All three of them were taller than me.

"Don't interrupt us, punk," he said.

I swallowed hard, realizing I may have bitten off more than I could chew. But I had an idea.

"Come on, guys," I said. "She's Polish. If I don't show her to class she might end up in a janitor's closet or something."

The bullies chuckled. I took Emilia's hand. It was warm and soft and just a bit sweaty. It sent tingles through my arm. It occurred to me later that it was the first time I had ever held a girl's hand, outside of family.

"It's this way," I said, gently pulling Emilia away from them. The punks didn't pursue us. My plan had worked.

When we got closer to class, she pulled her hand away.

"Hey, Jimmy?"

"Yeah?"

"I know why you said what you did, to get me away from them, but it still hurt my feelings." She looked down at her shoes. "You know Polish people aren't ugly and stupid, right?"

I'm not going to pretend I haven't told my fair share of Polish jokes. This was the late '80s. The only thing more prevalent than Polish jokes were dead baby jokes. But I was stunned that she asked me this. Obviously I knew Polish people weren't stupid. More importantly, I knew Emilia wasn't stupid. And she certainly wasn't ugly. I thought she was the most beautiful girl I had ever seen.

I wish I could have told her that. Instead, I said "of course."

She nodded. "Well, thanks for helping me."

"Who were those guys?"

"I dunno," she admitted. "They bully the other Polish kids too, especially Magda. I think the one guy and the older girl are related. Pretty sure they're German."

"Do you know any German jokes?" I asked.

She thought for a moment, then said: "What do you call a blind German?"

"What?"

"A not-see."

It took me a second, but I laughed. "Okay, next time, we'll tell German jokes back, deal?"

"Well, no," she said. "I think that's mean. I don't want to be mean."

"But they were mean to you first."

"I know," she admitted. "But bullies are the bad guys. I don't want to be the bad guy. Otherwise I'm no better than them."

"Emilia, I promise you are *so* much better than

them. You're amazing."

She blushed. It was so adorable my heart skipped a beat.

"Thanks, Jimmy. You're pretty cool yourself."

You could have knocked me over with a feather after that.

The bell rang, and that was it. The first time I ever said something romantic to a person of the opposite sex. The first time I made a girl blush. I still think about it today, over thirty years later.

If this was *completely* a work of fiction, I could say something here like "and that's when I knew we were falling in love, and today we have two children together and a house in the Hamptons" or whatever. But, spoiler alert, I didn't end up marrying the first girl I had a crush on. Does anyone?

Still a sweet memory.

At the time, though, it got me mad thinking of someone I liked getting made fun of. It made me feel angry about the times I had seen people like Benny and Dale get bullied too. And me, for that matter. If I had a nickel for every time I or someone I cared about had been bullied...well, I'd be broke because the bullies would have beaten me up and taken it all. But still.

The more I thought about it, the more I realized how prevalent bullying was in my school. Openly, even in front of teachers. Hell, sometimes the bullying came *from* teachers. Mr. Gilbert called the struggling kids "retards" in front of everyone. Our gym teacher, Coach Ducker, called boys "fairies" when they were weaker or slower than the rest. We all laughed, even the weak kids. And that was just the verbal stuff. Kids really *were* beat up for their lunch money at New Haven. They got tripped in hallways. I had even seen a real-world "kick me" sign placed on a nerdy kid at recess, and people didn't stop kicking even after the boy was sobbing. They just called him a baby. And no one stopped it.

"I think we need to publish a real article about bullying at New Haven," I told Dale after school.

"Like the first fake article you wrote?"

"Yeah, but serious. And you should write it."
"Me? Why me?"
"Well, because you've been bullied a lot this year. I've seen it."
Dale nodded. "That's true, but I don't think writing an article about it is going to make me get bullied less. I would sound pretty weak."
He was right. I imagined Pax doing his damned sing-songy voice. "What, did the crybaby get his feewings hurt?"
"Seems like an important topic, though," I said. "I don't know if grown-ups realize how bad it is in school."
"And out of school," Dale added. I wondered if he was thinking about his orange bike. Then I wondered if he was thinking about me piling on, too.
I decided to change the subject.
"My mom's pregnant," I admitted to someone for the first time.
"Whoa! Congratulations!"
"It isn't mine," I deadpanned.
Dale laughed. "Well, but it will be, kind of! Besides, having a kid sister isn't terrible. Debbie's even co-starred in a couple of my *Star Voyage* movies."
"I guess I thought my mom only wanted me."
"Are she and Mike going to get married?"
I looked away. "I don't think so."
"Oh. That's too bad."
Yeah, I thought. It was.
"Do you want to write an article about it?" he asked.
"Not really. It's kind of personal."
"So is writing an article about being bullied."
"I guess. What are you writing about instead?"
"Ah, check this out!" He retrieved a graph paper notebook and opened to a page where he had drawn a large square with a large, pencil-shaded circle inside it. "I discovered an alternative to pi!"
"You mean...cake?"
He laughed as if I had said the funniest thing in the world.

"I mean 3.14," he explained. "You know, that number that lets you find the circumference and area of a circle?"

"Uh, sure." We had covered it in math, but I hadn't thought a lot about it to be honest.

"We know the way to solve the area of a square is to multiply one of the side lengths by itself. You square it, literally. So, the area of a 10 by 10 square is 100."

"Following so far."

"So, if you were trying to find the area of a circle, then wouldn't the easiest way be to know what *percentage* a circle takes up of a similar square, then multiplying that percentage by the area of the square?"

"Makes sense," I lied.

"That's what I figured out! I added up the shaded part, and determined a circle takes up 78.5% of its surrounding square. So if you know the diameter of a circle, you just multiply it by itself, like you would with a square, then times that by 78.5% to get the area. Makes way more sense than cutting the diameter in half, squaring it, and multiplying by some abstract number."

I stared at the graph paper, trying to comprehend.

"The percentage works for the circumference too. The circumference of a square is adding up its four sides, right? If the circumference of our square is 40, then the circumference of our 10-diameter circle would be 40 times 78.5%. And if you're just trying to get an approximate answer you can do in your head, just round up to 80%!"

This was the nerdiest thing I had ever heard come out of the mouth of an 11-year-old. But my face must have looked more impressed than horrified, because Dale beamed.

"I call it a Dunkle!"

Dale turned the page of the notebook and pointed to a symbol he had drawn, which was a lowercase 'd' and a lowercase 'b' next to each other with the stems connected on top. After a moment I got what he was going for, as the symbol looked like a 'd' mirrored back on itself, presumably to represent his first and last initials. But I couldn't unsee my first reaction, either.

"It looks like a cock and balls, Dale."

Dale's smile faltered. He stepped away with the notebook, studying the page, then turned back to me.

"Well, darn," he said. "I guess I can tweak it a bit."

"You think our readers are going to be interested in this?"

"I hope so! I mean, some of them will." His voice got a little soft. "I find it pretty interesting."

Now I felt bad. Though, not bad enough not to tease him.

"Dale's dick equation on page 4!"

"Stop it," he said, though he was suppressing a smile.

"The Pythagorean penis!" I continued.

That got an actual laugh.

"Okay, Jimmy, *that* was funny."

I smiled, proud of myself. "Guess your nerdiness is rubbing off on me."

"Well, that's good," Dale beamed. "Because I have a surprise for you." He picked up a couple papers from the nearby desk. He handed me a printed draft of the front page of our current in-progress issue. It took me a second to notice.

"You changed the masthead?"

"I did."

Below the name of the paper in small, bold print were these new words:

*Founded by Dale Dunkle and Jimmy Logan.*

—

I couldn't sleep. I felt hot. My bed was against an exterior wall which was always cool, especially in the winter, so I pressed my forehead against it. It soothed, as usual. But the paint didn't feel as smooth as it should have. There was a bump in the wall, very slightly raised, a half-inch wide. I picked at the circular spot until the paint flecked off, revealing the head of a stud nail. I pressed my head against the nail, which was colder than the painted drywall had been. I imagined it leaving a circular indentation in my forehead which might look as if I slept on an M&M.

For some reason, my thoughts turned to the Black House, and all its chipped black paint, exposing hundreds of exterior nails. I wondered why abandoned houses always looked like that. Our house had hardly any chipped paint, but it's not like we ever repainted it or touched it up. What is it about being abandoned that causes color to flake off? Or were Pax and his crew doing the same thing I did, picking and picking until they found something hard, day after day?

I bet the inside of the Black House looked even worse. You could see in a bit through the upper windows if the light was right. Not clearly or anything, but enough to notice the walls were in bad shape. I saw a scary movie once about a mental hospital where all the rooms had cracked, peeling paint, and no one seemed to care, but it made the shots of crazy people bashing their heads into the walls more unsettling.

They taught us in Mr. Archie's science class that paint used to be made with lead, but they found out in the late '70s that it was bad for kids if they ate the paint chips, or even breathed in paint dust, so now it was illegal. I thought about the paint I had chipped off and wondered if it was lead. Not the blue paint color of my room, since that was new-ish, but the layers underneath that I had exposed by revealing the nail. It was too dark to see, of course, but I imagined the little chips were on my bed. Maybe on my pillow. I would probably inhale them in the middle of the night. That could lower my I.Q., Mr. Archie had warned. And still I kept picking.

# Five

In the Spring of 1989, I began to notice collarbones. I don't think I had ever paid much attention to them before, on myself or anyone else. But warm weather brought lower cut t-shirts and tank tops back into the school hallway fashion show, and it was like I was seeing this body part for the first time. They were a perfect blend of definition and delicacy, strength and grace.

On Emilia Jankowski, I loved the way hers complimented the contour of her neck, especially when she laughed, tightening the skin and accentuating the shadows caught by the cavity. It created a sort of frame to her face that underlined her beauty. Luckily, she almost always wore a small crucifix around her neck, so if she ever caught me staring, I could claim to be admiring the jewelry.

One thing that sucked about being a 12-year-old boy in the late '80s was that there was no one who I could talk to about these feelings. Sure, 12-year-old girls could babble to each other about cute boys and crushes all the time. Everything from *Babysitters Club* books to New Kids fan magazines to board games like *Girl Talk* encouraged girls to dish about their deepest desires. But boys had none of that. Our media and magazines never mentioned girls at all. It was all guns and explosions and action figures. And you sure as hell weren't going to bring up girls to your friends. If I had mentioned to Zach or Marco that I was daydreaming about Emilia, or pointed out the attractiveness of her clavicle, I'd never live it down.

So, I suffered in private.

Emilia wasn't my only distraction, though. I was

distracted a lot at school these days, and it was starting to affect my grades. I had never been an A-student, but usually got B's and an occasional C. The last month had been much worse. My mind was filled with too many things, including bullies, the pregnancy, Mike, articles for the paper, the Black House, lead paint, and now the female clavicle and the subsequent fear of getting an erection during the school day.

"I think I bombed that math test," I admitted to the guys at lunch.

"With all the circles?" asked Benny.

"Yeah. I think I was doing $2\pi r$ instead of $\pi r^2$."

I was glad Dale wasn't with us. He would have whipped out his notebook and Dunkled us to death.

"Didn't you fail that history quiz too?" Zach asked. "Guess that means you'll be doomed to repeat it, right?"

"I'll be fine."

"It ain't so bad to repeat a grade," offered Marco. "I'll be the first in our class to drive a car. You'll all be asking me for rides by the end of freshman year."

"Your mom gonna buy you a car?" I asked, cocking my head.

"She better!" Then he thought about it. "Well, I mean, I'll find a way to get one."

Zach scoffed. "With what, your bar mitzvah money?"

"What the hell's a bar mitzvah?" Marco looked at me. I also didn't know.

"Do you need a study buddy, Jimmy?" asked Benny. "I don't have all A's or nothin' but I think I understand social studies and math pretty good."

"Eh, maybe. I'm just not concentrating well."

"It's understandable," said Zach. "I mean, you're going to be a daddy and all."

At this point, my friends all knew that my mom was due in August. I didn't share much about the on-again, off-again Mike drama, but no one ever asked, either. Still, Zach's comment pissed me off. I tried not to show it, but I did change the subject, kind of.

"Any of you guys see the movie *Child's Play*?"

# THE PAPER

I couldn't distract Mom so easily. The school had called her down to the office during the school day to discuss my failing grades. I wasn't even there. I found out about it that night over dinner, just the two of us. She had bought a bucket of Kentucky Fried Chicken, my favorite, and was being uncharacteristically sweet to me when she dropped the bomb.

"We need to talk about your marks, Jimmy."

"I'll be fine." It was becoming a mantra.

"You're not fine. Principal Bartlet said you may have to go to summer school if you can't get math and social studies back up to C's."

I stopped eating.

"Summer school?"

"It's what they're doing now so kids don't have to repeat grades when they've fallen behind. You don't want to have to do seventh grade *again*, do you?"

I most certainly did not. That was a fate worse than death. But summer school didn't sound much better.

"You mean, instead of summer vacation, I'd have school days? With the other dumb kids?"

"You're not dumb, Jimmy. You're just not applying yourself. Do you think you're spending too much time on Dale's paper?"

What the hell.

"No," I snapped. "Dale spends way more time on *our* paper than I do and he's all A's for sure. I'm just having a rough patch. It's fine."

"Well, perhaps I should call Dale's mom and see if Dale might be willing to tutor you. You said he was in advanced classes, right?"

This was too much. I leapt to my feet.

"I don't need some 11-year-old to teach me math!" I said, even more defensive now. "Maybe I'm stressed about a lot of stuff, okay? You're having a baby and I haven't seen Mike in weeks. Is he going to be around, or am I going to be expected to do everything? You know, I didn't ask for any of this!"

It wasn't fair to blame my bad grades all on the baby. I knew that. So did Mom. She stood up, too.

"I think you're being awfully selfish. You think I

want to raise another kid on my own?"

"Then don't raise it on your own! Get Mike back!"

"It's not an *it*, it's your sister!"

This was news.

"How do you know it's a sister?"

"I had my check-up today. They did an ultrasound. We're having a girl!"

She misread my expression as an invitation to hug me. I stepped back.

"Wait a minute. *We're* not having anything. *You're* having a girl."

"Now you listen to me, Jimmy. You are going to fix your grades, whether I need to hire Dale as a tutor or not. Then you're going to be respectful to your mother. And you're going to help when this baby comes, because that's what a man does and I need you to be a man right now. I'm sorry if you have to grow up a little faster than you wanted to but that's just the way it is. I had to grow up faster than I wanted when I had you, too."

Was she blaming me for *both* her mistakes?

"This isn't fair," I seethed.

"Life isn't fair."

I tried to calm down, I really did. Mom wasn't being awful today. She brought home my favorite meal and she wasn't yelling. And I'm certain she was scared about raising another kid by herself, even if it was her fault for driving Mike away.

We stared at each other in silence for a moment. Then she started piling an empty plate with chicken and mashed potatoes.

"Take this to your grandmother, please."

I took the plate and regarded the lukewarm food. Not for the first time, I thought it was unfair that we ate when everything was hot and fresh, and Grandma waited for a plate to be brought up to her after we had finished. It made no sense. Even if she couldn't make it down the stairs, surely we could bring a plate to her at the start of the meal, not the end. For that matter, couldn't we have dinner upstairs a couple times a week? I mean, we could set up a card table in her room or something. Or in the hallway. Grandma wasn't bedridden.

"Is something wrong?" Mom asked.

I looked up at her. I wasn't sure what to say. And then there was a voice in my head.

*Tell her she's being mean to Grandma.*

I resisted.

*Tell her she's a bad mom and a bad daughter.*

"No," I whispered to the voice.

"Then go on," Mom said.

*Tell her!*

"Mom," I said, carefully. "I think you're not very respectful to your own mother. Why do we always wait until after dinner to give her cold food? Why can't I bring her food when it's hot? Or even eat upstairs with her once in a while?"

Mom was taken aback. "What in the hell are you talking about?"

*Tell her she's selfish and you hate her.*

"I just think you're selfish sometimes."

The look on her face. Oh my God. I thought she was going to hit me. I imagined the plate of fast food flying across the room. At least she was sure to launch into one of her long diatribes about all she's sacrificed as a single mom, what an ungrateful brat I was, and all that.

But she didn't do anything. She only turned her back to me and started tidying up the table as if I wasn't there.

I went to give Grandma her dinner.

—

That night, when I got up to use the bathroom, I heard Mom's voice downstairs. She was sort of whisper-yelling to someone, and I realized she must be on the phone with Mike. She had a phone in her bedroom, but chose to go downstairs to the kitchen instead, I'm guessing so I couldn't hear.

I leaned against the railing to listen. At first I thought she might be apologizing, but it wasn't like that, really. Instead of saying things like "I'm sorry I got angry" like you would in a normal post-fight conversation, she was berating Mike for "abandoning his responsibilities" and calling him "weak." Yet she was crying, too.

Part of me wanted to go down there and beg her to just suck it up and say she was sorry, even if she wasn't. That's what you're supposed to do, and then Mike would come back. But she couldn't do it. Instead, she doubled down on bullying. She was bringing up every minor mistake Mike had ever made in their relationship, from forgetting to buy an ingredient on a shopping list one time, to not properly fixing the kitchen sink six months ago.

I wish I could say I felt empathy for Mom in these moments. Like Grandma told me, Mom just couldn't get past things, and it really is hard to live that way. The more I eavesdropped, though, the angrier I became. You'd think some familial instinct would kick in and I'd want to hug her and tell her I loved her. She was in pain, after all. But I didn't feel anything like that. I didn't feel any love at all.

When I finally heard her slam down the phone, I stormed to my room, got in bed, and covered my head with my blanket. I remember thinking it was a good thing she hadn't caught me listening and confronted me. I might have pushed her down the stairs.

—

Over the next few days, I self-medicated my anger with heavy metal music. I nearly wore out Metallica's *Master of Puppets* cassette in my Sony Walkman. Sometimes I tried drumming along to the simpler songs on my practice drum pad or, if I needed to vent, on my pillow where I could hit harder. I couldn't figure out complex songs like *Battery*, but I had totally mastered the rat-a-tat rhythm from *One*, the newer single from *...And Justice for All*. Even all these years later I catch myself tapping that particular rhythm on something at least once a day.

Anyway, I was walking home from Huck's one Saturday when the song *Welcome Home (Sanitarium)* began blaring through my headphones as I was approaching the Black House.

*Welcome to where time stands still*
*No one leaves and no one will...*

It was hard not to imagine the Black House as a fitting home for psychopaths. Hell, as often as Pax hung out there, perhaps it already was.

No one was around today, so I slowed my pace and stared up at the dismal structure. Something was different. Maybe a bit more paint was peeling from the soffits, or another shingle was missing. I couldn't figure it out. But I couldn't look away. I felt like if I just stared more intently the mystery would present itself. Then I forgot what I was trying to figure out and continued gazing at it for no reason at all.

*Keep him tied, it makes him well*
*He's getting better, can't you tell?*

A great idea popped into my head, and I laughed out loud. It was perfect.

I walked over and knocked on Dale's front door. (Yes, using the rhythm from *One*.)

"Hey Jimmy!" he answered. "Wanna work on the paper?"

"Yeah sure," I said. "I've been actually writing a lot lately."

"Oh? Do you have the articles with you?"

"Not like that. I've been writing songs. Or, at least trying to."

"Can I help?"

I was so hoping he would offer.

Over the next twenty minutes, Dale "helped" me "write" Metallica's *Sanitarium*. I would recite lines from memory, but leave words out, as if I wasn't quite finished. Nine times out of ten, Dale would suggest the actual word missing from the line. He had never heard any Metallica, but the lyrics aren't that complicated, so rhyming "brain" and "insane" isn't much of a stretch. Only once did I have to excuse myself to double-check the cassette liner notes for a forgotten phrase, and then I shouted it from the bathroom as if I had had an epiphany on the toilet.

"It's really good," Dale insisted. "I'm impressed!"

"Thanks."

"Can we publish it in the paper as a poem? I mean, I'll give you first writer credit of course! It's mostly your baby! I just made the rhymes work and polished it up, you know?"

"Yeah, I don't think we should publish it."

"Why not? It's great!"

I almost admitted the prank at this point, but another idea snuck in.

"Because I want to hear what it's like with music first. I bet I can get my cousin's band to try running through it this weekend. I'll make a recording if I can and play it for you!"

"Wow!"

That night, I recorded my own voice on a cassette saying "okay guys, quiet down! I'm about to record. 3... 2... 1..." and then played the real track from my stereo. The lowered fidelity from holding a microphone up to a stereo speaker made it sound like a garage band running practice. I even threw in a couple "yeah!" and "woo hoo!" sounds to add realism.

I waited until Monday to share it. Dale was joining Zach, Marco, Benny and I for lunch, and he brought up the song.

"It's really exciting," Dale said. "Jimmy came up with a great song idea and we wrote it together. He's going to have his cousin's band sing it!"

This was my cue.

"Hey, they tried it out on Sunday. I brought the tape. Do you wanna hear?"

"Of course!"

"I can't play it loud enough for the whole table. We'd get in trouble. But I have my headphones. You can listen to it first, Dale."

I passed him the Walkman.

For the next several minutes, we watched Dale in silence as he grinned and bobbed his head to the mighty Metallica. I hadn't told anyone else about my little prank, so they just gazed at me quizzically. Had I really written a song?

When it was done, Dale was glowing.

"It worked! Something we wrote! I mean, I still might tweak a line or two, but this is awesome, Jimmy! Wow, I guess I like heavy metal now after all!"

Zach, predictably, was skeptical.

"Mind if I listen next?"

He took the headphones. Within seconds he was smiling.

"Alright, assholes. Are you both punking me, or is Jimmy punking Dale?"

"What do you mean?" Dale asked.

"This is Metallica," Zach explained, stopping the tape. "I own this album."

Dale shook his head. "No, no that's impossible! We wrote it together!" But when he looked over at me, I couldn't hold it in. As I cracked up, his jaw dropped.

"I'm sorry, dude," I said, wheezing. "I don't know what came over me. You were so excited!"

Dale was flabbergasted. "But...that's a terrible prank! I was impressed by your songwriting and told you so! The prank is that I was wrong to think you were a good writer?"

I had tears in my eyes from laughing. "The best part is when you were trying to take credit for some of my writing and it wasn't even mine!"

Zach and Benny exchanged a glance but kept quiet. Only Marco spoke up, when it appeared Dale was about to cry.

"Alright, Jimmy. You can stop now."

"It's just so fucking funny, dude!"

*It was funny.*

Then I looked back at Dale. Really looked at him. He did seem hurt. Humiliated, even. But he also wasn't going anywhere. He didn't stand up and storm off with his tray of half-eaten food, like I probably would have. He eyes just sort of bore into me, searching for answers, trying to understand. I wasn't sure I fully understood myself.

I decided to throw him a bone.

"You're a good sport, Dale. Sorry I teased you."

After a beat, he smiled.

"It was pretty clever the way you pretended to talk to your cousins on the tape."

"Thanks, I thought so."

"I'll try and think of a way to get you back."

I chuckled. "Bring it, paperboy."

The tension at the table had eased. I hoped Dale understood that it wasn't some grand plan to take him down a few pegs or anything. It was only a prank. An idea that popped in my head. Sure, I saw a vulnerability and exploited it. But I wasn't trying to be mean. At least, I didn't think I was.

# Six

In April I turned 13, and so for a couple weeks I was the same age as Marco, whose 14th birthday would be in early May. Zach and Benny didn't turn 13 until the summer, and I was temporarily two years older than Dale, who would turn 12 in August. Sure, there were a bunch of other kids in my class who had turned 13 earlier in the school year, but among my circle of friends I was the oldest, if you didn't count Marco's unfair advantage.

Becoming a teenager felt like a real milestone. On the day of honor I got to have a Friday night party at my house with six friends, including Dale, Marco and Benny, and three others I won't mention by name since they don't factor into this story.

Zach couldn't make it due to a family thing, but he sent ten bucks in a birthday card. I had thought about inviting Emilia too, but chickened out, since it'd be way too weird for her to be the only girl there, and the guys didn't know anything about my obsession with her or even that we were friends. Plus, it was hard to imagine Emilia would have enjoyed a bunch of smelly sugar-hyper boys laughing and yelling at the TV all night. Her parents might not have let her come to a late-night boy-girl party in the first place.

Since it was a 13th birthday party, I picked two PG-13 movies: *Critters* and *Weird Science*. Both were awesome, as I recall. (I haven't seen them since so don't take either as a recommendation.) Mom ordered the pizzas and made several batches of popcorn for us with the Whirley-Pop, but otherwise stayed out of our hair.

The next day, Mom, Grandma and I had a private

birthday celebration for me as well, with gifts from family and a Duncan Hines chocolate cake. I was happy that Mom thought to do it in Grandma's room, and supposed I could take a little credit for that idea, though I didn't rub it in.

Mom and Mike still weren't getting along, but he had sent a birthday gift: a computerized chess game from Radio Shack. It had small physical chess pieces you would push into the board to tell the computer what you were doing, and then LED lights to indicate which of the computer's pieces you'd have to move on its behalf. Unlike Mike, the computer had ten skill levels to choose from. On level one, I could beat it every time, but levels three and up were always won by the computer. Guess I still had a lot to learn.

The best part about April in Michigan is that the snow melts and usually doesn't come back. Warmer weather meant more freedom, and once again my bike and I were attached at the hip, so to speak. The days were longer, too, so I could stay out later and hang with friends after dinner without freaking anyone out.

I was working to get my grades up as well. Anything to avoid summer school, and without Mom calling Mrs. Dunkle and hiring Dale as my tutor. It helped that Mr. Wright's class had gotten a little interesting with all the Tiananmen Square stuff going on, and I had taken Benny up on his offer to study together. He wasn't a great student either, but we filled in each other's knowledge gaps. And it was nice to spend time one-on-one, though it was sometimes a little awkward. I tried to talk to him a bit about my crush on Emilia, but that just made him get quiet. I didn't think he'd ever had a crush on a girl. Maybe he never would.

On paper, as they say, everything seemed fine. But there was something gnawing at me. At night, I had taken to rubbing that exposed stud nail in the wall by my pillow. It felt comforting somehow. Evidence of the real world peeking through the window dressing of blue paint. I had found another hidden nail head about where my navel would be while I was in bed. I had picked at this one, too, like you'd pick at an old scab, finding enormous satisfaction in exposing the metal. I wondered how many other nail scabs I'd find if I put my mind to it.

I was having darker thoughts in general. Dale noticed my articles for our sixth issue had taken on a more sarcastic tone that bordered on disrespect. Whereas a few months ago I might have written "New Haven baseball team sadly loses close game to rival," now I was writing "pathetic New Haven baseball team crushed as usual." For his part, Dale would tone these down as to not sound so bitter and insulting, but the published product was still negative. Even my movie reviews sounded angry in a way they never had before.

"Is anything wrong, Jimmy?" Mom or Grandma would ask with frustrating regularity.

"No," I would say, believing it to be true. I was just growing up, after all. Grown-ups didn't have to like everything all the time, so neither did I.

One day I was riding to Huck's by myself when I saw Pax and the usual suspects sitting on the front step of the Black House sharing a magazine. This was a bit outside the norm, as they usually hung out along the side or rear of the house so they couldn't be seen. In this case, it was as if they wanted to be seen. Like I explained earlier, the Black House sort of overlooked all of Chennault, so anyone driving down my street toward Clark would be looking right at them.

"Yo, Jimmy," Pax called.

I thought about passing them, but decided against it, as always.

"Just running to Huck's for a pop," I said, knowing he'd probably demand I get him one as well. Instead he did something unexpected.

"Come over here and check this out."

I hopped off my bike and walked toward them. It became clear that the magazine they were brazenly reading for all to see was a *Hustler*.

Pax exchanged conspiratorial glances with T-Too and Derek before he turned the magazine around to me. It was a full-page photo of a nude brunette on a bed pinching her nipples with her fingers.

"Isn't she hot?" Derek prodded.

I took a step forward and leaned in to see the image better. Marco had shown me a *Playboy* or two in the past, but this was different. *Playboy* was fully nude too, but in a more tasteful, glamorous way, with the models' legs always closed. This *Hustler* subject had her legs spread wide, her hair was tousled and her skin glistened with perspiration. It was my first exposure to raw pornography, and, if I'm being honest, I liked it. I could feel my body reacting to it, too. I think I audibly gasped.

"Uh, yeah," I answered belatedly. "She's beautiful."

There was a beat before Pax, Derek, and T-Too burst out laughing.

"What?" I asked.

"Dude," laughed T-Too, "d-don't you think she looks like your mom?"

Horrified, I looked at the face in the photo for the first time. She didn't really look like my Mom, but her straight brown hair was similar, and I guess the nose was pretty close.

"Shut up," I said. "She does not."

Pax turned the magazine back around and studied it. "I think you've got the hots for your mom, Jimmy."

"Whatever," I nearly whispered. "Besides, my mom's pregnant."

Another beat before a second round of laughter.

"Now we know she fucks!" Pax howled.

"You gonna be a daddy!" added Derek.

All the blood that had rushed to my groin seconds earlier was now pooling behind my eyeballs.

*Punch them in the face.*

Obviously, I couldn't do that. Hell, I couldn't take on Pax one-on-one. The three of them would murder me in seconds. Yet the voice in my head was insistent.

*Bite them. Bite them until you taste their blood.*

I tried to calm myself but I was trembling. I backed away from the howling goons and got back onto my bike. They didn't call out to me or anything as I left. They just kept laughing.

## THE PAPER

*You should have fought them all. You coward.*

Bullshit. I had been playing my electronic chess game and knew damned well that when you were down to a single piece it was impossible to win. A bare king can't even put his opponent in check. The best you can hope for is a draw—but if you're up against three pieces, a draw's pretty damned unlikely.

By the time I got to Huck's, I wasn't in the mood for shopping. I rode my bike around for a while to blow off steam. It didn't work. If anything, the hour I rode in circles generated so much new steam I could feel it coming out of my ears like in an old cartoon.

*You let them say that shit? Just rode away in silence? So pathetic. You're pathetic.*

I decided I had to face them. To defend my honor. And my mom's for that matter. Maybe I'd get my ass kicked, but I was 13, damnit. I had to learn to be a man, not a joke.

It was dusk now, but I rode down Clark toward the Black House with reckless abandon, channeling all my rage into my pedaling legs. When they saw me coming, they'd know I was a serious threat for the first time. They'd be scared. Maybe they'd even run.

They were still there, alright. At least two of them, standing out front. And I had called it. When they saw me, they reacted with shock. They stepped back. They almost stumbled into the ditch with fear.

*Kick their asses. Show no mercy.*

I leapt off my bike and started toward them, fists clenched. Only then did I see it wasn't Pax's goons, but two random white kids, both maybe 9 or 10. I had no idea who they were.

I glanced around, surprised. Was this a trap? Where was Pax? Where were Derek and T-Too? Were they hiding behind the house?

"Pax?" I shouted into the air. No reply.

I turned to the randoms.

"Who the hell are you," I barked, an order instead of a question.

"Uh, I'm Tony," said the taller one. "This is Jason, my little brother. We moved in on Stevens last month, and we're exploring the neighborhood."

Tony was trying to look brave, but sounded nervous, and Jason was visibly trembling. I turned to the brother.

"Is that true?"

Jason glanced down and fidgeted with his fingers.

"Answer the question. Is your name Jason? Did you move here last month?"

"I... don't know..." he answered, miserably.

*Worthless little shit.*

My eyes darted back to Tony. He no longer looked brave. He looked like he wanted to vomit.

I studied him for a moment. He was wearing a stained button-down shirt tucked into a pair of faded jeans. One of his shoes was untied.

"Seems your little brother is confused, Tony."

Tony said nothing.

"Did you see any other guys around here? Older kids?"

Tony shook his head.

"If you're lying to me, I swear to God..."

"There was no one here, sir!" Tony answered. "Can we go home now?"

My heart was still beating so hard I could feel it in my fingertips. But the adrenaline that had been building the last hour, which had been trying to turn me into a murderous madman capable of attacking three older, stronger kids, was starting to recede.

"Beat it," I said with a regal wave of my right hand. The brothers turned and ran toward Stevens.

*Let them know who's boss,* the voice reminded.

"And I don't want to see you in front of this house again!"

They didn't reply.

I peered up at the house, wondering why I had said that. Was I trying to protect them from bullies? Or was I being protective of the house? Maybe I was trying to assert some authority on behalf of the entrance to Chennault Drive? I had no idea.

The first story windows of the Black House had been boarded up as long as I could remember, and the second story windows were a mix of boards and half-intact glass panes, a few shot out by small guns or fireworks. I wasn't sure I had ever tried to look into the upstairs rooms before. Though the ambient light was dim, I thought I could make out writing on one of the walls. Spraypainted, maybe. What did it say? The harder I looked, the more the words seemed to fade in and out of the darkness. For a moment, I thought the letters were even rearranging themselves in front of my eyes. I'd blink, and it was a new word. But I couldn't read a thing. Not at this distance, in this light.

I walked back to retrieve my bike. As I mounted it, I noticed the little girl at the corner house staring at me from her front lawn. Had she been there the whole time?

"What?" I asked.

She frowned.

I decided she had probably seen my interactions with the Stevens brothers. She was likely judging me for being mean.

"Look, if you saw me giving those kids a hard time, I'm sorry. I was in a bad mood and thought I was coming back to talk to Pax."

She remained frustratingly mute, but glanced up and to the left, and I followed her gaze to the second story of the Black House across the street. Perhaps she had been examining the windows the same time I had been.

"Have you ever seen anyone up there?" I asked. "Do Pax and his friends ever break in and hang out inside?"

After a few silent seconds, it occurred to me that I was trying to ask serious questions of a child, and had even apologized to her for my behavior for some reason. As if I had to justify my actions to a random kid I didn't even know. What the hell was the matter with me.

"Whatever, retard," I spat, and began riding toward home.

—

That night, I found another nail scab to pick at, on the wall near my light switch. But this one was different. As I chipped the paint with my fingernail, I felt the same familiar satisfaction, but it was accompanied by a touch of physical pain. When I studied the exposed nail head, it appeared to be bleeding, like a proper scab would bleed. But that wouldn't make sense. The walls of my bedroom weren't made of flesh. They couldn't bleed if they were picked. It had to be blood from my finger. Maybe a sharp bit of dried paint had sliced my skin in just the right way to have transferred blood onto the wall. Or maybe the old nail head itself was sharper than expected. I knew the injury had to be mine. Yet when I examined my finger, the skin was intact.

# Seven

I completed seventh grade (yes, I passed) on a sunny Friday afternoon in June of '89. Last days of school were always half-days, and since most of our parents were working, a bunch of us walked across Gratiot to Dairy Cone after the final bell to stuff ourselves with soft-serve ice cream. Back when some of us used to do Little League we'd go there after every official game. The coaches would buy small cones for the kids who hit singles, medium cones for the doubles, and large cones for the triples. The rare home runs got triples dipped in chocolate shell coating. Zach and Marco were on the team with me each year, but the only sport Benny did was youth wrestling, which he was allegedly good at despite his size.

 Dairy Cone only had a couple of picnic tables, so Zach, Benny, Marco, Dale and I sat on the grass together beside the parking lot. Emilia was there too, though she stayed talking with her girlfriends, only exchanging a few smiles with me when no one was looking.

 "Going anywhere fun for the summer?" Zach asked us all.

 No one was.

 "Aw, that's too bad," he said. "We're going to Florida. My Dad got us tickets to Disney World."

 "That's awesome!" I said, jealous.

 "I mean, I'm a little old for Disney," Zach lied, "but my lil' sis is so excited she's been sleeping with a Mickey Mouse doll every night."

 "I hear Epcot's amazing," Dale said. "I want to go to Spaceship Earth so bad."

 "You should check out the new MGM Studios too,"

I added. "They showed some of the Great Movie Tour animatronics on TV a few weeks ago. Way cooler than Major Magics or Chuck-E-Cheese."

"We'll apparently see it all," Zach grinned. "Dad got one of those weeklong everything passes."

"They got any roller coasters?" asked Marco.

"I don't know," Zach said. "I know they have rides, but they're family-based, so nothing too scary."

Marco rolled his eyes. "Rides *need* to be scary, man. That's why I'm gonna beg my mom to take me to Cedar Point this summer. The Magnum XL 200 opened a few weeks ago, and it's the tallest, fastest, steepest, most bad-ass coaster ever made. It's twice as high as the Gemini!"

"I would never go on that in a million years," admitted Benny. "I don't even care if you make fun of me for it."

"All of us should go," Marco said. "Benny can hold our Cokes while the rest of us become legends."

We all laughed, even Benny. Nothing wrong with being a wimp if you admitted it.

New Haven was two-and-a-half hours from Sandusky, Ohio, which meant Cedar Point was our closest major theme park. Boasting the most roller coasters of any park in the country, Cedar Point remains the pinnacle of the summer experience for many Midwestern kids.

Marco turned to Dale. "What about you, dude? Ever been to the Point?"

"Yeah, last summer," he said. "That new Iron Dragon was awesome. The trip was a consolation prize for telling me I had to leave Roeper and come back to New Haven."

I was sort of impressed. I wouldn't have thought Dale would be interested in coasters. Perhaps he enjoyed the physics of it all.

Marco frowned. "You needed a consolation prize to slum it with us here, huh?"

"I didn't mean it like that," Dale said. "I just didn't want to leave Roeper is all."

"Oh, knock it off, Marco," Zach butted in. "Don't

make Dale feel guilty for insulting New Haven when you hate it here more than all of us put together."

Marco ignored him. "Were they any Black students at that fancy rich kid school of yours, Dale?"

"Well, sure!" Dale said. "There were plenty of kids on scholarships!"

That was not the right thing to say. The look on Marco's face must have sent a chill down Dale's spine.

"I mean, I didn't..." Dale stammered. His eyed darted to me for help, but I had nothing.

"You think all Black kids like me must be poor and need scholarships? Is that it?"

"Hey, I was on a scholarship too! I'm not a rich kid. We live in the same neighborhood in nearly identical houses. I was trying to explain that it wasn't a white kid school."

"No," Marco deadpanned. "Just a smart kid school, right?"

"Exactly!"

"Then why are you back here? Did you fall out of a tree and get dumber?"

I smiled but tried to hide it.

"No, my parents didn't have enough money to send both me *and* my little sister there, so it seemed fairer for us to come back to New Haven."

Marco threw his hands up. "But it wasn't a school for rich kids. Okay."

Dale looked at me again, but I wasn't sure what to say. Or maybe this new cynical, bitter version of me enjoyed a touch of drama from time to time.

Benny stepped in instead.

"Zach's right, Marco. Stop giving Dale a hard time. It doesn't matter what he did in his past, or that he's a year younger, or that you're a year older, or who's smart and who's average, or who's Black and who's white. We're all here in the same boat. That makes us equal, right?"

We sat silent for a moment, until I decided to break the tension with a smart-ass remark.

"If we were equal," I said, "Zach's rich-ass parents would be taking us *all* to Disney World."

Zach threw the last bite of his cone at my head.

I found out later Marco was upset because, despite high-enough grades, he had been denied a spot on the year-end honor roll, on the technicality that students who repeated a grade were ineligible for that sort of academic recognition. But Marco didn't repeat *this* grade, he had repeated *first* grade. He was experiencing the seventh-grade curriculum for the first time, same as the rest of us. And he had worked hard this year. He deserved a spot on the honor roll as much as Dale deserved his.

"That's bullshit," I said when he told me.

"Yeah, well, I'm used to that sort of stuff."

"You should write an article about it in the paper! Make people aware at how unfair they're treating you and others."

Marco laughed. "Dude, the last thing I need is to piss off the school. They held me back before. You don't think they could do it again?"

"You think the school administrators read our paper?"

"Oh, I *guarantee* they do."

"What if I write the article myself, but talk in general terms, and not use your name at all?"

"Then I reckon I'll set your house on fire, Jimmy."

I dropped it.

It wasn't just a sense of civic justice that compelled me to suggest an article, though. With exams and other academic responsibilities taking priority in late May, Dale and I had agreed not to release a June issue of *The New Haven Herald Jr.*, instead promising readers of the early May release that July would be a "double issue" to make up for the missing month. A week after school ended, we were still very light on articles, and running out of ideas.

"We could probably get more ads," I suggested.

"Nah, we're already half advertisements as it is," Dale said. "If we have too many ads, people might get upset."

"Really? I didn't realize it was that many. Did we get new companies I don't know about?"

"A couple, but it's more that our current advertisers keep asking to increase their ad sizes so they're taking up more space."

"Can I see?"

Dale handed me the in-progress layouts for the upcoming double issue. Many of the pages were ads next to "article goes here" sticky notes. I saw only one ad I didn't remember seeing before, for an in-home childcare.

"Is that Marco's cousin?" I asked, recognizing the name.

"Yep! Marco brought that ad in the same time he wrote that funny article about falling into the creek."

"It looks like Al Horner's still advertising, too. He doesn't even live around here. Thinks he gets any calls?"

"I assume so," Dale said. "He mails a five-dollar bill in cash every month and tells me to keep the change. I mail him a copy of each paper to his address in Detroit as a thank you."

I nodded, thinking of the brief conversation we had had by the old New Haven Depot about restoration and "evil" houses. It gave me an idea.

"I think we should do a piece about the Black House on the corner," I said.

"Because people think it's haunted?"

"Because it *is* haunted."

"Why don't you write it?"

"You're a better writer than me," I admitted.

"Nonsense. You wrote my favorite heavy metal song!"

I laughed.

"Really, though," Dale continued, "I think you should give it a shot since it was your idea. Everyone likes a good haunted house story, even in the summer."

"My mom knows come of the history. She said it was owned by the first Black farmer in Macomb County."

"Is that why they call it the Black House?"

"No." Although now I was starting to wonder.

"Want to go over there now and check it out?" Dale asked.

"Sure, as long as Pax and his friends aren't there."

"Can I bring the PXL? Might be useful to get some images of it so you can describe it perfectly later, and I can also get some creepy footage for our next horror movie."

It was still light out, so it didn't feel like a scary time to be exploring the place. No one else was around so we had the property to ourselves. Dale got footage of the front and the sides of the old house, including the broken upstairs windows.

"Can you zoom in to read the writing on the wall up there?" I asked.

"Nope, no zoom feature. Are you sure its writing?"

"I think so," I said. But it was a little too bright at the moment to see very well. You needed just the right dusk light to make out anything inside.

"Let's go around back," suggested Dale.

For as many times as I had passed by this place, I had never walked around the building. After all, the back of the house butted up against unruly and unused fields. Plus, the "No Trespassing" sign on the side of the house had scared me away from exploring too much. I was a little surprised that my goodie two-shoes young friend didn't seem bothered by the warning.

Unlike the front door, the back door wasn't boarded up. It exited out onto a few wooden stairs and a small concrete patio. The window in the back was boarded up, like all the first-floor windows, but not the door.

"Want to try it?" asked Dale.

I couldn't believe it. Was this 11-year-old braver than me?

"I don't want to get in trouble," I said, lamely.

"Just see if it opens," he insisted, filming the whole time. "We don't have to go in. Just see if we *can* go in."

I nodded. But even on this calm, sunny day, I felt goosebumps rise from my wrists to my upper arms, and the hairs on the back of my neck began to tingle with an electric charge. As I ascended the two steps and reached my hand toward the knob, I could hear—no, *see*—my heart beating in my chest, straining to break free. Only knowing I was on camera, and not wanting to chicken out in front of Dale, gave me the strength to continue.

The knob was cold. Too cold, I thought, for a metal object on a warm afternoon.

*Nothing wrong with cold, Jimmy.*

I attempted a quarter turn. Mercifully, the door was locked.

"No dice," I said, trying not to sound as relieved as I felt.

"Worth a shot," Dale replied chipperly.

And that was my first official attempt at breaking and entering. Well, except I didn't break anything and didn't enter. Trespassing, then. *Attempted* trespassing. Was that even a crime? I wasn't sure.

"Are you still filming?"

It was a silly question, since I could hear the faint hum of the motor running and Dale still had his left eye glued to the eyepiece, but he responded in the affirmative anyway.

I smiled, putting on my best newscaster voice.

"Folks, we're standing here in the back yard of what neighborhood kids call the Black House, at...well, I don't know the address because there are no house numbers in the front and no one has lived here since I've been alive. But you'd know it if you saw it. Anyway, *The New Haven Herald Jr.* has decided to do an exposé on this place, to see if the stories are true: is it haunted, or just a convenient place for the town delinquents to smoke cigarettes and read Hustler magazines? Stay tuned for the full story...at eleven."

Dale chuckled and turned off the camera. "That was pretty good. Maybe someday we'll turn the paper into a public access TV show instead."

"What's public access?"

"It's that channel on cable that shows announcements and village council meetings and stuff. My dad was telling me that anyone can be on it if you have the right equipment." He glanced down at the PXL disapprovingly. "Probably needs to be in color, though."

"*The New Haven Herald Jr. Show?*"

"Nah, we'd need a different name for TV."

"*Herald Tonight?*" I suggested.

"Better," Dale agreed.

We were going to go back to his place to watch the footage, but Dale noticed he was late for dinner so we agreed to hang out later in the week instead.

"You go on," I said. "I'm going to stare at the place for a while and look for ghosts."

He left, and I did stare. Something about the daylight and the lack of bullies made the old house seem more approachable than before. I mean hell, I had almost gone inside. This is the place I had begun to fear was calling out to me? It was just an old building. In need of some of Al Horner's "adaptive reuse" was all. If anything, it was sort of beautiful as-is. There's something about the way neglected paint buckles and peels that looks like alligator skin. If I stared hard enough, would I uncover a code in those cracks? Maybe my next message to Emilia could be coded in a drawing of reptile scales.

"Yo," said a voice.

I spun around. It was Pax. He seemed to be alone. I'm not sure how long he had been standing there, as I hadn't heard anyone approach me.

"Oh, hey," I stammered.

Pax didn't say anything. He just sort-of studied me for a few moments. Then he reached into the back pocket of his jeans to retrieve a crumpled pack of Marlboros and a Bic lighter. He put a cig in his mouth, then asked if I wanted one as well. He shook the pack so that a single offering rose up above the others. For some reason, I took it.

I had never tried a cigarette since I had never been offered one before, but I had a general idea of the mechanics of the activity. It was the '80s and most adults smoked, including my pregnant mom, who smoked Kools, and Mike, who rolled his own using Zig Zag papers and a tin of Bugler tobacco. I think all my teachers smoked, too, given the permanent cloud hovering around the door to the teacher's lounge.

Pax lit his own cigarette first, then tossed me the lighter. I caught it awkwardly.

"Suck in a bit while lighting it," he said, suspecting my inexperience. I did as he advised, and the tip glowed red. A pretty even light, too, all things considered. I didn't cough, which I was proud of, though later I learned that was because I was only sucking the smoke into my mouth and not actually inhaling.

"Thanks," I said. I lifted the lighter for him to take back, but he shook his head.

"Keep it," he said. "Every man needs a lighter."

I wanted to ask why he was being nice to me, but couldn't think of a way of phrasing the question that didn't sound tragic.

"Thanks," I eventually mumbled, tucking the Bic in the front pocket of my jeans.

Pax nodded, looking back to the house. I looked, too. We stood there for a few minutes in silence, smoking our cigarettes, staring at the ugly beauty of it all. Me and the bully I hated, who had hated me first and made my life hell for as long as I could remember. Why was he treating me as an equal for once? And, why was I letting him?

"Ya know," he said, "your friends are fucking lame-os."

"I know," I agreed, though I didn't really think this. I thought *his* friends were the lame ones.

There was another pause as Pax took a long drag. I noticed he appeared quite a bit older than your standard eighth grader. I thought it was the cigarette at first, or perhaps the way the skin on his face was pock-marked. Or maybe it was something else. Something in his eyes.

"I've been inside a few times," Pax said.

"Yeah?"

He nodded. "Yeah. It ain't much in there. It's just forgotten."

"How do you get in?"

He took another drag, so I took one, too. This time,

though, some of the smoke snuck into my lungs, and I coughed.

Pax laughed, but without his usual malice. More of a brotherly chuckle.

"You ain't ready for that, kid."

*It ain't Cedar Point.*

I forced a smile. "Hey, I know it's not Cedar Point or nothin', but we don't have that much to do around here..."

"What'd you say to me?"

Pax's eyes were cold now. The change was instant, like someone flipped a switch.

"Uh," I stammered. "Just that there's not much to..."

"Who told you I couldn't go to Cedar Point?"

"What? I didn't..."

In one lightning-quick motion, Pax threw down his cigarette, took two big steps forward, and grabbed my neck with his right hand.

"*Who. Told. You.*"

I honestly had no idea what he was talking about. I tried to say as much, but his fingers on my throat were too tight.

*Kick him in the nuts*, said the voice in my head.

I couldn't do that. Pax would kill me.

*Kick him or you're dead.*

His face was inches from mine. I could smell the smoke and feel the hit of his breath on my skin. My peripheral vision began to darken, and I worried I would pass out. I had to do something. But before I could act, his dark eyes opened a bit wider and his grip lessened. Perhaps a voice in his own head had told him to lay off.

He tossed me to the ground. I stayed down, choking and panting. When I dared to look up, Pax was gone.

Later I heard from Marco that the school hadn't allowed Pax to go on the traditional year-end eighth grade class trip to Cedar Point. Not sure if it was grades or disciplinary issues or what, but he was the only one denied the opportunity. And Pax hadn't even known he couldn't go until they stopped him from entering the bus in the school parking lot, and he had to walk back to The Heights in shame as all his friends went to Ohio.

I guess he thought I was making fun of him, which would explain his anger.

But his offering me a cigarette, being nice to me at first? That was a mystery.

# Eight

We got the July issue out in time, though without an article about the Black House. I wasn't in the mood to write one after what had happened with Pax, and Dale said something went wrong with the PXL tape, too, so we didn't even get usable footage for our horror movies. Instead, Dale came up with two more articles on random topics to fill the unused space. It was the most Dale-heavy paper we had put out so far, though Marco and I still had a couple good submissions each. I was especially proud of my Tigers piece:

    CAN TIGERS TURN IT AROUND?
    By Jimmy Logan
        Well, it's been a wild season for the
    Detroit Tigers so far. Our beloved Sparky
    Anderson went into the hospital with
    exhaustion, Jack Morris was placed on the
    disabled list for the first time ever, and
    the Tigers are in the last place in the
    league. Can Lou Whitaker and Alan Trammell
    save the season? I believe they can!
        Recent wins against Boston and Oakland
    prove that the team hasn't given up just
    yet. Sweet Lou is totally on track to have
    another year of 20 home runs! He looks
    amazing out there. And remember last year
    when Tigers were in fourth place forever
    and finished only one game behind first at
    the end of the season? Maybe they're saving
    their best for last!

In case you're wondering, the Tigers had their

worst season ever and never left last place for the remainder of 1989. But, Lou Whitaker did earn 28 home runs, a career high.

Summers in Michigan are fun because we're on the far west side of the Eastern Time Zone, so the sun doesn't set until well after 9:00 p.m. This meant I could stay out late without express permission, since like many kids, my curfew was "when the streetlights came on." Bad for drive-in movie theater start times, but good for us. Dale's curfew was a little earlier than that (he was just a kid after all), so Marco and I would sometimes hang out for the final hour or two even if I had been with Dale during the afternoon.

"Got any quarters?" Marco asked one evening.

"A few. And some nickels I think."

He checked the clock. "7:45. We can make it."

I followed him outside and we hopped on our bikes. Within ten minutes we were at the train tracks on Clark a hair past Victoria Street.

"A train comes by every weeknight," he reminded me. "Put some change on the track like this." Marco reached into a pocket and placed a couple pennies on the steel.

"Won't that make the train derail?" I asked.

Marco laughed. "Come on, man. Do you know how much a train weighs?"

I placed a quarter and two nickels a few feet down from his pennies.

"Now what?" I asked.

"We wait."

The crossing only had a stop sign and simple flashing red lights which were hard to see during sunrise (traveling west) or sunset (traveling east), so you really had to listen for the alarm. They didn't add a modern descending barrier system until the mid-'90s, after a young man named John Lockerbee was driving with the radio too loud, didn't see the lights and got sideswiped by a fast-moving southbound freight train. We stepped back to the safe side of the stop sign just two minutes before hearing the whistle and having our hair blown back.

After the caboose had passed, we walked over the find our coins. It took a while, as they had moved quite a few feet from where we had left them. Two of Marco's pennies were untouched, having been blown or vibrated off the track, but a third had been flattened into a thin copper pancake. My quarter and one of the nickels had been similarly flattened, with the quarter in particular seeming almost twice its original size. The only way you could tell it had once been a quarter was the faint outline of the eagle's wings on one side. We couldn't find my last nickel at all.

"Think Huck's will still accept these, Marco?"

"Probably not. That's why I prefer to waste pennies."

We tried a few more coins over the coming days, and a few other coin-sized items like metal washers. Eventually, we got yelled at by a passing cop for being near the unsafe tracks.

"Haven't you ever seen *Stand by Me?*" the cop growled.

We hadn't. So that night, we asked Marco's mom to rent it for us. Kinda freaked us out about train tracks for a while.

At the end of the month, Mom signed me up for a week-long Parks & Rec summer day camp. I wasn't thrilled with the idea, since I felt I was a little old for summer camps and would have rather stayed home and played video games. Mom, however, was putting in extra hours at the restaurant saving up for when the baby came, and she was getting wary of my being left to my own devices for twelve hours or more each day. She'd drop me off at the center early in the morning, I'd do the camp stuff, then I'd walk back around 5:00 p.m. and wait for her to get home.

The New Haven Parks & Rec people divided the camps into three different specialties: science & technology, arts & crafts, and sports & leisure. Mom wanted me to do the science one, but I convinced her to let me do the sports program instead, on the grounds that I had gotten my grades up to avoid summer school and I didn't want to learn anything I didn't have to. A bad attitude, I suppose, but she also knew I didn't want to do camp at all, so it seemed a fair compromise.

The only person there who I knew was Emilia. But she was in the arts camp, so I only ran into her during lunches when all the divisions ate together, and I didn't sit with her or anything.

Actually, the first lunch was kind of embarrassing. I must have been absently looking in her direction a little too much because she came up to me while I was clearing my tray.

"Hey, Jimmy!"

"Oh, hey Emilia!"

"Did you hurt yourself in your sports camp?"

"Huh?"

"I saw you kept nibbling on your knuckle."

I looked down at my right hand.

"To be honest, I had been imagining I was kissing your collarbone," I most decidedly did not say.

I claimed I had taken a hardball to the hand.

"Aw, well feel better Jimmy!" Then she smiled gorgeously and returned to her friends.

Perhaps I also didn't talk to Emilia much because I was distracted by a girl in my own camp. Her name was Kat and she was the first tomboy I'd ever had a crush on. Her auburn hair was short and tight against her face and tapered in the back, which exposed red freckles on her neck matching the ones on her cheeks. She was spunky and feisty and kept up with the boys in all the sports we tried. And I was pretty sure she liked me, too, because she laughed way too hard at my jokes and silly asides.

On Wednesday that week I was in my bed thinking about those freckles and, well, let's just say I was doing something that all 13-year-old boys do more often than any of us would ever admit. We hadn't had sex ed in school yet and my mom hadn't had "the talk" with me (thank God) so I didn't know if I was doing it right or how normal it all was. Apparently that night I had been careless and forgotten to close my door all the way, and I wasn't even under the covers when Mom walked in. She gasped and dropped a laundry basket before I noticed her arrival, and I screamed "get out!" as I frantically covered myself with a blanket.

To add to the horror, I heard Grandma call out "is everything okay?" which meant Mom would have to tell her about it, too.

Mortified beyond belief, I lay there for a long time, strategizing ways I could avoid running into either of them for the next few days. After about a half hour of this I heard the front door open. Maybe Mom had decided she couldn't face me either and was going to check into a hotel for the night.

To my surprise and further humiliation, there was a knock on my bedroom door.

"Hey, champ, are you decent?"

Holy shit. She had called Mike to give me the talk. I couldn't believe it. He hadn't been around in ages and I wasn't sure they were on speaking terms.

"Uh, give me a minute!"

I threw on my shorts and a t-shirt and opened the door. Mike looked miserable. It helped diffuse the tension, and I laughed.

"Oh good," I said. "I'm glad you're as unhappy about this as I am."

He smiled. "Yeah, I'm sorry. Your mom felt that you needed a man to talk to."

"Do I really?"

"It's okay. Let's just get through this as fast as possible and we never have to speak of it again."

"Deal."

He glanced at my bed and suggested we go to living room. I don't think he wanted to sit next to me on my shame-filled comforter. Mom was in the kitchen when we came down, but she gracefully avoided eye contact and snuck up the stairs.

"So," Mike began, but I stopped him.

"I already know about some of this stuff. I know where babies come from and all that, and what sex is."

"Well, that's a good start," Mike said. "But it's possible some of what you learned from boys on the schoolyard isn't accurate."

"And you're the expert?"

"Your mom's pregnant, ain't she?"

He was momentarily rattled, perhaps realizing that wasn't a very appropriate thing to say. Then we both laughed out loud.

Over the next few minutes, Mike gave me a frank breakdown on sex and safety and all of that, even explaining how "clearly" the pill wasn't 100% effective, given my sister's coming arrival next month.

But when he awkwardly asked if I had ejaculated yet during my "me time," I didn't know how to answer.

"I think so," I said. "Is that when it feels good when you do it enough?"

"No," he said. "That's an orgasm. An ejaculation is when something comes out."

"You mean sperm? How could you tell? I thought it was microscopic."

"Sperm is, but it's, uh, inside a sort of gooey substance to make it safe for...travel."

"You mean I'm going to *see* it come out someday?" I was horrified.

"Yeah," Mike explained. "It looks a lot like the liquid hand soap that your mom has in the bathroom."

"The white stuff?"

"Yep."

"How much comes out?"

"Uh, maybe a tablespoon or so?"

"Oh my God." This was the worst thing I had ever heard. And I was embarrassed that I knew nothing about it. It was like back in fifth grade when I was joking how awkward it would be if you got a boner while having sex with someone, and Marco thought it was the funniest thing in the world that I didn't know that's what boners were *for*.

"Yeah. It's why I agreed to come and talk to you about it. Because no one told me about that part when I was your age, either. I was a church-going lad, and the first time it happened I thought God was punishing me. I assumed I had committed a deadly sin. I prayed and prayed and vowed not to touch myself there ever again, not even to use the bathroom."

I let this sink in. I wondered what I would have done had it happened to me without knowing what was coming. Would I have asked my mom about it? Or Marco? I had no idea.

"But," Mike insisted, "it *is* perfectly normal. Every guy masturbates. Every guy orgasms. Every guy ejaculates, when he's old enough. When you do it by yourself, it just makes a mess. But if you do it inside a woman, it makes a baby. Do you understand?"

I did. It was scary, but I was glad for the heads up. I had a thought.

"So, if a woman lets you do that inside her, it means she wants to be a mom?"

"Oh, no, not necessarily," Mike said. "Men and women both like sex even when it's not to make a baby. That's why you need to use protection."

"You mean rubbers?"

"You know about those?"

"They sell them at Huck's."

"Well, yep. That's what they're for. To have sex with less of a risk. But again, I want you to understand that contraception isn't foolproof. Having sex always means there's a risk of making a baby. So, don't have sex until you're willing to take that risk."

I thought about asking Mike why he had been willing to take that risk with my mom, but didn't.

"What about...when men have sex with other men?"

"You're familiar with that?" Mike asked.

"Well, I know about Elton John."

"Isn't he married to a woman?"

"They got divorced last year. But he's admitted to having sex with guys, and I read he's with a guy now."

Mike was surprised, more at my knowledge of it than the fact itself. "Where did you read that?"

"Uh, a magazine Marco had." I didn't mention the name of the magazine, as it wasn't age-appropriate.

Mike nodded. "Well, yeah, I suppose there are some people who prefer having sex with their own gender."

"Is it because that way they don't have to worry

about making babies?"

"Maybe." Mike was eyeing me with a weird expression now. I felt compelled to set the record straight, so to speak.

"I'm fantasizing about girls, I promise!"

"Uh, I believe you. Anyone in particular? Actually, don't answer that. I don't think I want to know."

Probably for the best.

Even under these unusual circumstances, it was good to see Mike again. I had missed him joining us for dinners. I missed our chess games.

"I hope we can talk about something else next time," I said.

"Me too," he chuckled. "But for now, I gotta run. I promised your mom I wouldn't be long."

"Oh. Alright."

"I did tell her I'd install a lock on your door, though. Just in case."

I was thrilled at this but tried not to show it.

"Thanks."

We stood up together.

"I suppose this concludes your first talk from Mike Healy's School of Awkward Topics," he said, beaming. "Congratulations, graduate."

He started to hold his palm out for a handshake, but thought better of it.

---

I arrived home the next day to find Mike's car on the street and the garage door wide open. This was a surprise because we barely used the detached garage at all. It was only a one-car unit filled with old junk, and Mom didn't park in it because it didn't have an automatic door or anything and she didn't want to have to leave her car to open and close it. When I walked up, I saw Mike had cleaned half of the garage, put down an old scrap of carpet, and assembled a small, used drum set.

"Hey, sport," he beamed. "Check it out."

"For me?"

"Yep! I had the day off today and I picked this up from a buddy of mine. It's not much to look at, but he tuned it up for me so it'll probably sound alright. Your mom said it was okay as long as it wasn't in the house and you didn't play it after dark."

The kit had a bass drum with a tom attached, a snare drum, and three cymbal stands, though I noticed only one of these stands, the hi-hats, had real brass-colored cymbals. The other two "cymbals" were hubcaps. Mike noticed me noticing.

"Yeah, sorry about that. You're short a ride and a crash. Jerry didn't have any more that I could afford, but if you really take to it, I'm sure we can get you some."

"It's so cool, Mike!" And it was.

"Go on, try it out."

I sat down on the stool and picked up the drumsticks that were resting on the snare. I used my right foot to hit the bass drum pedal first. It made a thundering sound in the old garage that startled Mike but not me. I then tried hitting the snare, but it didn't sound right.

"Oh, hang on," Mike said. "Jerry showed me what to do here." He leaned over and flipped up a metal switch which activated the snares. I should have remembered that from band class. When I tried again, it had that bright, agreeable buzz sound I was expecting. It was much more satisfying than my rubber drum pad I practiced on during the school year.

For the next few minutes, I tried figuring out a simple beat, settling on Queen's *We Will Rock You* boom-boom-clap on the bass and snare. Mike looked as proud of me as he did when I captured an important chess piece.

"You're a natural!" he insisted.

Things got more complicated when I tried adding cymbals and hubcaps. It's one thing to drum simple patterns on a snare like in school band. It's a whole other thing to work a kit with your feet involved. Eventually, though, I was able to get a decent riff going by hitting hi-hat eighth notes with a kick on one and a snare on three. I wasn't thinking of any particular song, but Mike's eyes lit up as if he recognized what I was playing.

"*Tiny Dancer!*" he exclaimed, and began to sing along with a big booming off-key voice that made me laugh out loud. But I didn't lose the beat, even when I joined him in the next line.

We sang the chorus twice, and I ended with a dramatic and I'm sure unlistenable hubcap and tom solo. Mike laughed and patted me on the back.

"Sounded good, kid."

It didn't, but I appreciated the compliment.

"I think Metallica might be out of the question for a while," I said.

"With enough practice, anything is possible."

I hadn't noticed Mom standing there outside the garage, holding her belly with one hand.

"Jimmy, it's time to come in for dinner."

She hadn't said Mike and I, or "boys", only me. I turned to Mike, disappointed. He just shrugged.

I put the sticks down, stood up, and made a point of giving him a big hug.

"Thanks for everything, Mike."

"Of course."

I was feeling great about my first time behind the kit. As Mike walked to his car alone and Mom and I walked inside, she tried her best to dampen my enthusiasm.

"You might not want to show your friends that drum set just yet."

"Why not?"

"The pieces don't match. And even I know those are fake cymbals."

"Come on, Mom. It's great."

"Well, I told Mike that if it gives you something else to do with your hands, I didn't have a problem with it anymore."

Wait, is that what this was? Had Mike tried to get me these drums weeks or months ago, and Mom grudgingly allowed it now as an alternative to masturbation? I was so irritated I couldn't look at her during dinner. Thankfully, she didn't seem to want to talk to me either, and did not complain when I went back out to the garage to play on them the rest of the night, and the next.

—

The final day of the week-long camp was really fun. The weather was perfect and we devoted the whole afternoon to softball. I hadn't held a bat since I stopped doing Little League the previous year, but I was still pretty good, hitting two triples which earned us three runs. Kat was on my team and gave me a big hug when we won at the end.

"You were great!" she declared.

"You too!"

Then she gave me a wink and bounced away to congratulate someone else. I was on cloud nine.

Like me, Kat walked home after camp each day, though in the opposite direction. After the final goodbyes with the kids and camp staff, I offered to walk her home, because I had to "go that way anyway" to talk to a "potential advertiser" for the paper. This wasn't true, of course—I actually hadn't talked to Dale the entire week and didn't know our current needs—but it was a plausible enough excuse, and gave me a chance to talk about *The New Haven Herald Jr.* organically without it feeling like a brag.

"Have you seen our paper?" I asked.

"Nah, but I don't live in New Haven during the school year."

"I wondered why I hadn't seen you around."

"Oh?" she said, with a hint of a smirk. "Are you saying you would have found me memorable?"

I could feel my face flush. "No! Well, I mean, maybe..."

Her smirk melted into a grin.

"You're cute when you're flustered, Jimmy."

"Thanks, you too."

"When I'm flustered?"

"I've never seen you flustered."

She laughed. "Yeah, I'm unflappable."

"Where do you live during the school year?"

"Detroit, with my mom. I spend summers here with my dad."

"You go to Detroit Public Schools, then?"

"Not yet. I go to a little Catholic school called St. Brendan's. Been there since third grade. But it only goes up to eighth, so next year will be my last."

"Do you like it?"

"I like English," she said. "We're reading adult novels already, while most of my friends in other schools are still reading short stories in old textbooks. And the nuns are kinda cool."

"Are there uniforms?"

She beamed. "Picturing in me in a little plaid skirt, are ya?"

When we arrived at her place, a tiny ranch home with an overgrown front yard, Kat invited me inside. Her dad was still at work so we had the place to ourselves, and we ended up sitting together on her living room couch. We were both wearing an orange Parks & Rec shirt and jean shorts, and as we sat the bare skin of our knees kept touching. We talked a bit more about our different schools and music tastes, but she started giving shorter answers to my questions, and licked her lips and peered at me expectantly.

*Kiss her already.*

But I was nervous. My palms were damp and I could feel my heart beating in my head. I had never kissed a girl, and I wasn't sure if I was reading the signals right. I thought I should do the gentlemanly thing.

"Can I kiss you?" I asked.

Kat's eyes widened a bit, and then she burst out laughing.

"Well not *now*," she said.

"I'm sorry. I thought..."

She cut me off. "Jimmy, you don't *ask* a girl if you can kiss her. You just should know she wants to be kissed, and kiss her! A man *takes* what he wants. Would this have been your first time?"

I nodded pathetically.

She sighed. "Well, haven't you ever seen a movie?"

"Okay, let me try that," I said, leaning in for a kiss, but she stopped me with the palm of her hand.

"Jimmy, the moment has passed. I'm sorry. You're a nice kid and all but you should probably go home. My dad will be back soon anyway."

I must have looked crushed, because she took pity on me ever so slightly.

"It's all good, I promise," she said. "Thanks for the talk!"

I began the long walk home in shame, the voice in my head berating me the whole way.

*Loser. Failure. What a joke.*

At first I wished I had my bike. Biking a mile takes no time at all, but walking a mile on your own takes an eternity. After twenty minutes, though, I was no longer in a hurry to get home. I just wanted to wander around aimlessly and listen to the self-hating voice in my head. Even when I made it to Chennault, I walked right past the street without stopping. I wanted to get to Huck's and drown my shame in Hostess cupcakes and Redpop.

As I reached the parking lot, I started to feel a little better about myself. I knew I might never see Kat again, but there would be other girls. There would be Emilia. All this showed was that I was cute and likeable enough for girls to be interested in me. Not sticking the landing didn't make me a loser. I'd know better next time.

I walked past the newspaper boxes and reached for Huck's front door. But I stopped. I had noticed something.

I retraced my steps and peered into the blue *Macomb County Chronicle* newspaper box. On the top of the current issue, where it showcased "top stories" you'd get to read inside if you bought a copy, was a picture of Dale Dunkle. The caption beside the photo read:

"Boy Publisher Not Yet 12 Years Old. Page 3."

I fished out a dime and a quarter from my jeans

and bought a copy. The full article was indeed on page 3, and featured a large black and white image of Dale sitting beside his computer with *The Newsroom* software open on the TV behind him.

The article began as follows:

```
11-YEAR-OLD PRODIGY IS PAPER PUBLISHER
By Susan McCallister
    NEW HAVEN - There's a new kind of
paperboy in town.
    Armed with just a Commodore home
computer and knowledge gained from a
journalism class at his former grade
school, 11-year-old Dale Dunkle decided to
publish his own newspaper rather than
delivering the work of others.
    "I do it all myself," Dunkle explained
with considerable pride. "Writing, editing,
puzzles and cartoons--without any help from
my parents."
    First launched in October of 1988, The
New Haven Herald Jr. began with a small
circulation of 50 copies sold at a single
location. Today, the kid-run publication
has expanded to 250 copies per issue, sold
throughout the village and even by mail.
Dunkle says he's just getting started...
```

The article went on for a dozen additional paragraphs, detailing Dale's writing process, how he solicits ads from local merchants, his love of science fiction, and all the locations in town someone can pick up a copy of the paper.

The article was well-written, flattering, and informative.

It didn't mention me at all.

# Nine

I showed up at Dale's house minutes later. I don't remember walking there. I just remember the anger. And how hard I pounded on his front door.

Dale answered. But unlike last time, when he didn't understand why I wasn't excited about the piece in *The Anchor Bay Bulletin*, he knew why I was upset.

"You saw the article," he said, flatly.

"Yeah, I saw it."

"Jimmy, I don't know why she didn't write about you too. I told her all about our partnership and all you do for the paper…"

"You didn't say 'I do it all myself'?"

"Well, if I did, I only meant I don't have any help from my parents."

"*We*," I corrected. "*We* don't have any help from *our* parents."

"Look, I worked really hard for this. I write most of the articles and lay it out on the computer and everything. I won't let you make me feel bad about me being proud of my paper."

"It's *our* paper, you fucking dick!"

I was shaking now. I wasn't sure whether I was about to cry or knock his ugly green glasses off his face.

"Jimmy…"

"You don't get it, do you. When that last article came out, the one that at least mentioned my name, it made my own mom think that the paper was your project alone. That you wrote my articles, too. That you didn't need me at all. And why wouldn't she think that? You're Dale Dunkle, boy genius, and I'm just Jimmy, who never impressed anyone in my whole life.

Not a single teacher, not anyone in my family, not any girls, no one. Just another fucking loser kid from a loser town."

"I'm from this same town, Jimmy. And at least people *like* you! I'm the geek everyone makes fun of all the time. You'd really trade places with me?"

"That's not the goddamned point."

Dale pressed further. "Sure it is. That's exactly the point. The only thing I have that makes me special is my brain. Why shouldn't I be excited when people want to talk about it?"

"Because it wasn't just your brain! You needed me, too! And Marco! And your teachers at that fancy school to show you the software! And your parents for sending you to that school in the first place! And Mrs. Patrick to print the issues for free!"

Dale didn't interrupt, so I continued.

"Let's say I agree you have a super special brain. It's highly impressive. One in a million. Fine. But I've seen you write your articles, Dale. I've seen how easy it comes to you. The ideas, the spelling, grammar, typing, all of that. It flows out of you fully-formed like you had everything memorized already. It's a fucking magic trick. Yeah, you can write an article in minutes and it's better than I could do in hours. But you know what? *I spend the hours.* So, who should be prouder between you and me? The person who whipped out impressive shit without effort, or the person working their ass off to do something that's really, really hard for them?"

Before Dale could respond, we heard a voice calling from the kitchen.

"Everything alright down there?"

"I'm fine, Mom," Dale shouted back.

But his voice cracked a bit on "fine." He wasn't fine. I had hurt his feelings.

*Good.*

"It's like the honor roll," I said, more measured. "It's not a reward for hard work. It's rewarding the kids that everything already comes easy to. The ones who were born to a good family, with two parents at home, who were told how brilliant they were every day of their lives and never had reason to doubt it. I almost failed seventh grade, did you know that? But I didn't. I got my grades up. I bet I worked harder that last month of school than you've ever worked at anything in your life. Yet you won't see my name on a list, will you."

"Jimmy, I am so sorry." His voice was weak. "I promise. I couldn't do the paper without you. And...you're my best friend."

I had made my point. He had listened. And he was holding back tears, I could tell. It was time for me to give a peace offering. Maybe "I'm sorry too," or a sincere compliment that would repair the crack in our relationship.

But the voice in my head wouldn't let me. It whispered dark things into my brain, words of hate and malice that would crush Dale's spirit and leave him sobbing in his bedroom for hours. I knew his most vulnerable spots, after all. His insecurities about being an outcast. Of being liked only by grown-ups and not other kids. And he'd given me all the ammunition I needed, just now, to end this charade once and for all.

"Well, you're not my best friend, Dale. Because you don't have any friends. Nobody likes you. We all think you're a freak. So go fuck yourself and your paper, and take my name off your shitty masthead."

With that, I spun around, and began toward home.

—

It seemed a longer walk than normal, but I wasn't alone. The voice was with me. Congratulating me. Telling me what a loser Dale was, and how I was better off without him.

*Maybe you should make your own paper. Then he'll see he's not so special.*

I don't know how to do that.

*Sure you do. You've watched Dale do it dozens of times.*

I don't have a computer.

*Tell your mom you need one. For school. Tell her*

*you'll even sell your Nintendo to pay for it. She'll be so impressed she won't actually make you sell it. Then you'll have both.*

She needs the money for the baby.

*Fuck that baby. You were here first.*

I thought about stopping by Benny's on the way home, but I was already late for dinner. Besides, there was a bit of wetness on my cheeks and I didn't want to admit, not even to myself, that I had been crying. Yeah, Benny would have been sweet about it, would have given me a hug and told me how much I meant to him or whatever. But did I really want to acknowledge that I was in mourning over Dale fucking Dunkle? No way.

And stopping by Marco's would have been worse. He'd been jealous I had hung out with him less and was spending time with an 11-year-old in the first place. He might have cheered me up with fireworks or something—hell, he would probably have taken a copy of *The New Haven Herald Jr.* and had me set it on fire. But what if he still wanted to write for the paper and chose Dale over me? I couldn't take that chance.

As much as I hated to think it, I needed my mom.

*No you don't.*

I opened the door and shouted "I'm home!"

"Hi Jimmy," came Grandma's voice from upstairs.

"Hey, Grandma!"

I walked down to the kitchen expecting to see food on the table. But it was empty, and nothing was ready to cook.

I looked over at the clock. 6:45 p.m. Had I missed dinner altogether? A check of the fridge revealed no leftovers.

"Mom?" I called. Nothing.

She wasn't on the lower level at all. Perhaps she was lying down. I walked upstairs and checked her bedroom, but it too was empty. No one was in the bathroom, either.

"Grandma, do you know where Mom is?"

"I haven't seen her since she got home."

"She didn't make dinner."

"Huh. Is her car here?"

"Yeah, I think I saw it when I was walking up."

I went back out the front door to check that I hadn't imagined it, and there it was, ugly as ever. So, what the hell? I wasn't sure whether to be angry or concerned.

I walked around the side of the house to the backyard. There she was, sitting on the back patio with a glass of wine in her hand and a half-empty bottle beside her.

"Hey Mom. Didn't you hear me calling?"

She said nothing. She was looking in my direction, but not exactly at me.

"You forgot to make dinner," I added.

"Mike and I are through," she said, still not meeting my eyes. "For good this time."

"Okay."

"I deserve someone who always puts me first, don't you think? I'm almost certain he's seeing someone else."

"You already broke up with him. Wouldn't he be allowed to date?"

Mom scoffed at this. "We have a child coming. *His* child. How can he prove he's worthy if he's not trying to win me back? You think he's allowed to put his dick wherever he wants?"

I must have looked stunned, for she laughed at me.

"Oh, don't act like it's such a crime for your mother to swear. You're a man now." Then, with a slight look of disgust: "I've *seen* it."

"I quit the paper," I said, trying to change the subject to the thing I needed her for. "I told Dale I wasn't going to hang out anymore either."

Mom took a drink but didn't say anything. I noticed a fresh red wine stain on her belly-stretched t-shirt.

"Did you see there was a big article about him in the *Chronicle*?" I continued. "Said he did everything himself. Didn't mention my name at all this time. Not once!" My voice was trembling but I didn't care. "I've done so much for him and when I'm not around, I guess I don't exist!"

"I would have married him, you know that?"
"What?"
"Not now, though. He had his chance and he blew it."

I felt my face flush. She wasn't listening to me at all.

I stood there for a few moments, hoping she would acknowledge my story. But she didn't. If I walked back in the house she might not even have noticed.

"What's for dinner?" I asked, coolly.

Mom seemed annoyed at this question.

"I don't know, Jimmy. I can't deal with that right now. Do you know I saw a mouse in the kitchen? That was the last straw. Mike wouldn't even come over to catch it. Can you imagine? The pregnant mother of your child having to live in a rodent-infested house. He's like you. Only cares about the now. Never the future."

"But I'm hungry."

"Just have some cereal or something." Then she poured herself another glass of wine.

*You don't need her.*

"Mom…"

*You don't need her.*

I walked to the side of the house, grabbed my bike, and took off.

—

In my memory of this evening, it began to rain as I made it to the street. I actually don't think it was raining, though. Not that it couldn't have been; unexpected showers and storms show up all the time in a Michigan summer. I just don't think it was, because I don't recall my clothes getting wet or cycling through puddles or anything. Maybe it *felt* like it was raining. Or I'm just conflating this memory with a different emotional bike ride a couple weeks later.

Memory is a fickle thing. It's why two people can never remember the same event the same way. I bet if I asked my mom about that night, she'd recall it as a time I didn't show any empathy for *her*, trying to make the conversation about my own problems rather than acknowledge she was in pain. And hell, perhaps she'd have a point. But it'd depend on how many times she had thought about it since then. Did you know that the more often someone recalls a memory, the less accurate the memory becomes? Every time we pluck something from our past and think about it, our brain changes it, and adds details that may or may not have been there, like a giant game of 'telephone' with our own subconscious. Whenever we think of a memory, we rewrite the memory, subtly or even dramatically, whether we want to or not. For most people, the details we're adding make ourselves more heroic, or at least more sympathetic. And then we believe this version of the truth is the only truth. Everyone's a victim in their own story.

Grandma said my mom is a past-oriented person. She brings up memories and thinks about them often, each time rewriting them just a bit, to the point where she now thinks everyone in her past has been out to get her from day one. But as a present-oriented person, I don't think about the past much. Except, of course, to write this book.

Let me tell you what I remember from that night.

I started by furiously pedaling down Chennault, toward the Black House, thinking I would crash right into it. Then I remember my anger growing, and I turned left on Clark toward the center of town. At one point, I made a hard right into Centennial Cemetery, and rode up and down the rows of creepy headstones, wondering whether my mom would care if they found me dead in the morning. I abandoned the cemetery and rode past the library, and thought about making the sharp left down Main St. toward the old train depot, but realized I didn't want anything else to remind me of *The New Haven Herald Jr.* Instead, I kept heading west, straight into the slowly setting sun (see? told you it wasn't raining), all the way to the edge of town, where Clark turns into a dirt road and is called 27 Mile again.

At this point, I thought about turning around. I didn't like riding on gravel roads. Sometimes you'd slip a bit, especially at high speeds, and I had taken a pretty nasty fall a few years back and gotten a few small rocks stuck beneath the skin of my right knee. But I wanted to press on, too, to see where I would end up. How far did the mile roads go, anyway?

I crossed Bates, a road at least I had heard of, and then Place Rd., which I hadn't. The houses were becoming more spaced apart the further I got from the village limits. Some of the homes were quite nice, as I recall. Others were old and crumbling, with dilapidated chain link fencing boasting an ominous "Beware of Dog" sign or two.

After a while, most of my view was nothing but farmland. The road began to narrow, and there weren't even ditches anymore, just close trees on either side of me. The mighty mile road constricted to more of a driveway. Finally, it stopped.

I got off my bike and, guessing the rough gravel wouldn't support a kickstand, let it fall to the ground.

There was no signage to indicate the end of the road. Only a thin, short metal guardrail overgrown with vegetation. I walked right up to it, put my hands upon it, and surveyed what lay beyond.

There wasn't a house in sight now. Not even a single plowed field. There was only grass, trees, and swampy marsh as far as my eyes could see. It was undeveloped land, probably untouched since Michigan became a state. Clark, 27 Mile Road, my whole world, ended in nothing.

I stood there for a long time.

You'd think watching a sunset over uninhabited acreage would be calming and peaceful. But it wasn't. It was ugly, the oranges brown and lifeless. The dimming light cast unappealing shadows across the unkempt vegetation and twisted, lifeless trees. Any perspective I hoped to gain from the experience of solitude was marred by the increasing realization that I needed to leave. The anger that had consumed me an hour ago had mellowed, replaced with a sort of self-pitying melancholy, which was more miserable than insightful.

As the sun fell below the horizon, mosquitoes started to smell me. I caught one attacking my neck and slapped an already-engorged one from my arm. Within seconds they were everywhere.

I mounted the bike, with vicious, hungry bugs swarming around my ears, and began my trek back east. The sky in this direction, away from the sunset, was already midnight blue. It occurred to me that my lack of a headlight could prove even more treacherous on a dirt road than in my neighborhood. It wasn't dark yet, of course—Michigan summer nights stay light longer than you'd expect—but time was running short.

I still wasn't sure where to go. I knew I didn't want to go home. I thought about trying Marco or Benny, but either of their moms would call my mom for sure, especially if mine had already called looking for me, which was likely. Or maybe not, since she didn't seem to give a crap about me these days, but it still wasn't worth the risk. Dale, obviously, was out of the question. I wish I knew where Mike lived. I'd never been to his place and wasn't sure it was in New Haven at all.

I even thought about trying Kat's house. I could make a grand romantic movie-style gesture like that dude with a boombox in *Say Anything*, which I had seen in June at a double feature at the Mt. Clemens Drive-In. It played as the second film after *Indiana Jones and the Last Crusade*, which was awesome (I wrote a great review on it for the paper). Marco's mom had driven us on the condition that we'd stay for the rom-com too, and we had agreed. It was a decent comedy, I guess, though we wouldn't have admitted that to anyone.

Of course I didn't go to Kat's.

There was only a touch of twilight left as I arrived back at Chennault. I stopped at the junction, still uncertain what to do. To the right was home. Or I could keep going straight, if Huck's was still open. I might at least get cupcakes and put off the inevitable a bit longer. It was like being down to your last piece in chess. There's no way to win at that point. You can only kill time. I needed somewhere to sleep. Checkmate.

Instead, I was compelled to look to my left, to the Black House. Something had changed.

For as long as I could remember, the entrance to the front door had been blocked by two large boards. Indeed, the two boards that had always been there, angled into a sideways V-shape, were still intact and in place.

But *behind* those boards, the front door was open.

# Ten

I knew I would have to be crazy to enter the building at night, without so much as a flashlight. Maybe I could go home and get one. I could sneak into the garage without being noticed. There was bound to be a flashlight in the workshop area. But what if Mom heard me rifling around? Hell, what if she was waiting on the front porch for me and saw me ride up? Too risky.

Then I remembered Pax's lighter.

I hadn't smoked since then, but I had taken to carrying the Bic in my jeans pocket anyway. I thought it was safer to have it on me than in my room somewhere. How would I explain to Mom why I owned one? Besides, I thought it'd be cool the next time someone offered me a cigarette; they'd ask if I needed a lighter and I'd say "nah, I got it" and casually whip out my own. The way guys in the movies have bottle openers attached to their keys in case someone offers them a cold one. Always be prepared, as they say. Today, I was.

On the off chance someone came looking for me, I decided to stow the bike in the back of the old house where it couldn't be seen from the road. Then I walked back around to the front, took a breath, and ascended the porch steps.

The front door was indeed open. The two boards were still blocking the entrance, but I realized I wouldn't even have to try and pull one of them down. I could shimmy between the open arms of the V and walk right in. So, I did.

I couldn't see a thing. The twilight didn't penetrate past the door frame at all, as if blocked by an invisible shield. I might as well have been standing in a cosmic void. I momentarily closed my eyes for strength and couldn't tell my eyes were shut.

Holding the Bic two feet in front of my face, I dragged my thumb across the spark wheel. The fork caught, the gas released, and a flame appeared on my first attempt.

Have you lit a lighter in a dark room recently? It's sort of magical. Way better than a flashlight. Rather than a single bright circle of illumination creating shadows everywhere else, a flame creates soft, uniform light across every surface within a good twenty feet. A flashlight in an unknown space can be terrifying. A flame is warm and pleasant. Even if all it revealed in this case was a sea of human bones.

I'm just fucking with you. There weren't any bones.

No, it was exactly what you might imagine an abandoned home would be like. It was in poor shape, with peeling paint and holes in the plaster walls and all that, but it wasn't scary. It was just *empty*, and a little sad. This was what I had spent years of my life afraid of? It was so underwhelming I almost laughed.

I was standing in a small entrance foyer. To my left was a living room with a brick fireplace. To my right was, I assumed, the formal dining room. There was no furniture present, but a low-hanging chandelier in the center of the room implied a table should be beneath it. Plus, there were drawers built into the outside wall with a sideboard on top. When I explored further, the flamelight revealed a door which I imagined would lead to the kitchen. This turned out to be a rather ornate double-hinged door and, as I suspected, a kitchen was on the other side. An old white fridge and matching gas stove were still in place, though both were covered in dirt and fallen ceiling paint. At the far end of the kitchen was a small window and another door, which was boarded up from the inside. Since there was only one door on the back of the house, I knew I had found the door I had attempted with Dale weeks prior. I guessed no one had come through that door in many, many years.

I walked back through the dining room and into the empty living room. This space connected to another area which appeared to be some sort of study. Three of the four walls boasted built-in wooden bookshelves. There was space for a pretty impressive collection, I imagined. In addition to being Macomb County's first Black farmer, Jerome White must have been an educated man. Even if all that was left as proof were these shelves, empty except for dust.

The lighter was getting hot, so I released the fork and blew on the metal spark wheel to allow it to cool. It's amazing how fast an extinguished flame plummets you into darkness. Especially in this study, without a single window to the outside. In such complete blackness you become distinctly aware of the sounds of your own body. Your breath, your heartbeat, the saliva in your mouth, all of it. For the first time since crossing the threshold, I was getting creeped out.

I had to get the light back on. But when I tried to make a spark, the metal wheel burned my thumb, and I dropped the Bic. I felt but did not see it hit my right foot and bounce off somewhere. In the dark, I squatted down, feeling around for it on the floor. The fingers of my right hand found something, but it wasn't a lighter. The object was small, cold, and wet. I recoiled.

My heartbeat was louder than I expected. Faster, too, as was my breathing.

I was on my knees now, arched forward, feeling for the lighter with both hands, hoping not to encounter the wet thing again. Why couldn't I find it? It had to be here somewhere.

*It's going to be okay,* said the familiar dark voice inside my head. Usually this voice would pressure me or berate me. But today it was supportive, even encouraging. *Stay calm. You'll find it.*

And I did. My left hand almost batted the lighter away at first, but I steadied myself and recovered it. The Bic was still warm, and I held it for a bit.

The dark was scary, but so was the light. At least in the dark I couldn't see if there were monsters in the room with me. In the dark I never had to discover what the wet thing was.

Could I make it back to the front door without the light? I wasn't sure. I kept blinking, wanting my eyes to adjust. Surely there should be some ambient streetlight flowing through the open front door. I should be able to make out the shape of the exit. But I couldn't. Before me and around me was nothing but pitch.

I lit the flame.

The reason I couldn't see the front door was because there was now a wooden bookshelf in front of me. And to the left and right. Had the room closed in on itself? No. I had gotten turned around somehow. The living room and foyer were now *behind* me. I spun around and made a break for the exit.

But when I got to the front door, I stopped. Something wasn't right. Something should have been there that I didn't see. What was it?

Right, the stairs. There should be stairs somewhere leading to the second level. To the bedrooms.

I walked around again through the dining room and kitchen. Nothing. Then back to living room and study. It was maddening. There had to be a way up.

*Jiiiiiiim.*

At least that's what it sounded like to me, at first. But it was the sound of a creaking door.

I went back to the small foyer. There, facing the front door, was a staircase. It had been there the whole time. How had I missed it? I must have been staring right at it when I entered. And yet it didn't reveal itself to me until I was about to take off.

I felt a soft breeze on the back of my neck. Behind me was the door the outside world. Back to my mom and the so-called comforts of home. Before me lay a narrow, wooden staircase missing its handrail, going up, where I might finally read the mysterious words painted on one of the bedroom walls.

I think you can guess what I decided.

The first wooden stair groaned so loudly I thought I might drop the lighter again. But I didn't. I kept going. Even after three steps the darkness was impenetrable before me. I began to wonder if the stairs went anywhere at all. They just faded to black. Maybe at the top I'd fall into a pit. But eventually I could see the end, and I found myself in a simple hallway, with an open door before me, an open door to the right, and a closed door to the left.

The lighter began to feel warm against my thumb, but I didn't dare let the flame go out. I thought I'd keep the light on until it burned the flesh of my hand clean off. I was on a mission.

I entered the door on my right. It was a small, empty bedroom with windows on the south and east walls. Like everywhere else, the paint was peeling, and the flooring was in disrepair. One corner in particular was in rougher shape than the rest, with several floorboards looking curved and mangled like cardboard left out in rain. I looked up and saw large cracks in the ceiling above the damage, and imagined sunlight might stream through these cracks during the day. A small closet was nearby, its door twisted inward somehow and hanging from a single hinge. There was nothing more to see.

Back in the hallway, I went right, accessing what seemed to be the home's only bathroom. The floor was tiled in small, white hexagons, and the walls were large green squares up to chest level.

The toilet was missing, but a clawfoot tub was intact, as was the sink. Above the sink was a mirror with a deep, vertical crack running down its center. It revealed an adult-looking young man holding a lighter. I was not scared of this figure but did not immediately recognize him either. As I moved the flame closer to the mirror to get a better look at myself, the largest crack divided the light in two, with only one of the reflections showing a flickering flame, and the other reflection showing a solid, steady flame. My face was visible on both sides of the crack, but in only one side of the mirror did I seem to be smiling.

I was vaguely aware of the smell of butane mixed with burning plastic. I had to give the lighter a break after all or I feared it would explode in my hand. My thumb eased up on the lever and the room went dark.

# THE PAPER

As I had downstairs, I held the extinguished lighter close to my face and blew in its general direction to cool it down. I kept waiting for my eyes to adjust to the blackness but they never did. My breathing became rhythmic, soothing even, inhaling through my nose and blowing cool air out of my mouth over and over again. After several minutes of this hypnotic pattern, I tapped my thumb to the metal sparkwheel to test its heat. It was still warm but wouldn't burn me. I lit the Bic once more.

I seemed to have again shifted my position. While I was certain I had been facing the mirror when plunged into darkness, I had rotated somehow and was facing the hallway. Something else had changed, too, and it took me a moment to realize what it was. The door to the bedroom I had already explored was now closed, and the previously-closed door, to the only room I had not yet entered, was ajar.

Had I been mistaken earlier? Had the last door been open this whole time? Was the house just drafty? Or was someone here with me?

I called out a weak "hello?" but heard nothing in response. The hallway was still.

Now, I know what you're thinking. You're thinking I should have hightailed it out of there at this point. This would be the part of a movie where people yell "don't go in there!" at the screen. But I wasn't scared. Not really. Not as much as I should have been.

Brandishing the flame in front of me, I made it to my final destination. To my great surprise, the room wasn't empty. There was a wooden rocking chair to the left of the door, a modest bed against the far wall, and an end table beside it that contained several white pillar candles. I couldn't believe my luck, and lit all three candles, finally being able to give the poor lighter a break. In the warm light, I could see the entire room clearly, and was surprised to find it in decent shape. I mean, it was still barren and all, but there was a blanket on the bed, and even a pillow! There was some peeling paint on the walls and ceiling, but nothing like the previous rooms. This space felt like it had been abandoned for mere months, not decades. It made no sense, yet here I was.

It occurred to me that this should have been the room with the red writing on the inside wall. But no such writing existed. The wall in question merely had a geometric red pattern painted on it. No wonder we couldn't make out actual words from the street. There weren't any words. It was an optical illusion.

I sat on the edge of the bed and stared at the pattern for a bit. I recognized it somehow. Was it the same pattern as the hallway tile in the high school? Or in the bathroom at the diner? I couldn't place it. But it was comforting. Familiar.

The bed was soft underneath me. The flickering candlelight dimmed a bit as I yawned. All the adrenaline from earlier was gone now. I just wanted to sleep. *Needed* to sleep.

*Sleeeep.*

Somewhere in the back of my mind I knew I had to go home. It had been fun exploring the old haunted house, but I wasn't going to spend the night here. That would be insane. It wasn't safe. What if the ceiling collapsed? Hell, what if I had to use the bathroom?

Besides, I wasn't a runaway. Not that I hadn't tried running away before, as all kids have. You get in a fight with your mom and feel unappreciated or whatever, so you pack some Slim Jims and Cheez-Its and your favorite baseball cards into a bag and you take off down the street, only to realize how ridiculous you're being before you even get a block away. No matter how mad you might get at your situation as a kid, how unfair life seems in the moment, home is home. Sure, I was going to be in trouble for storming off. But it was time to go.

I looked over at the bedroom door. It was closed now. Had I closed it?

*Staaay.*

The bed seemed to get less tangible by the second. I could feel my body lilting, sinking into it, the softness enveloping me, first my hips, then my lower back, then my arms. I imagined myself floating on an inflatable raft on a sunny day, not caring that the raft had a leak and was slowly capsizing, because the warm water would feel so good against my skin when I fell. My eyelids became heavy, and the will to return home melted away.

*Sleeeeeep.*

My head hit the pillow, and I was gone.

# III

# One

I awoke to the smell of urine.

"Mom?" I called out, for some reason.

It was early morning. There was sunlight coming in through the window, but it wasn't bright yet. Just light enough to see that I wasn't in my own bedroom.

I sat up, panicked. And then I remembered.

I was in the Black House. But it was different. I was still on a mattress, but it was on the floor, not a bedframe. There was no end table. No candles, either.

I realized my pants were damp. Had I had an accident overnight? Maybe the stench was my own.

I stood up and looked around. The room was filthy. I never would have chosen to sleep here. The mattress was bare and covered in brown stains. There was garbage strewn across the floor, everything from beer cans to what I thought might be used condoms.

The far wall had red writing on it after all: the word "sleep" repeated at least a dozen times, each in a different handwriting. One of the words stood out as redder, fresher. There was something familiar about the shape of the letter p.

I studied my hands. The index and middle fingers of my right hand were stained with dried blood. When I touched them with my thumb, I found they were sore, too. Stepping closer to the wall, I noticed several exposed nails, also stained. I realized the whole wall was dotted with a grid of nail heads. How many of them had been bloodied by the fingers of others?

I had to get home. But I wasn't scared, exactly. I was angry. I felt abandoned. Betrayed, even. It was Mom's fault I had spent the night in this shithole. Or Dale's. Anyone's fault but mine.

My Bic lighter was on the floor next to the bed, so I grabbed it. Beside it was a small pile of fresh ash. I wondered what on earth I had set fire to the night before. I hoped it had been one of Dale's newspapers.

Soon I was down the stairs and back out the front door, squeezing again through the sideways boards. I closed the door behind me, quickly, in case someone saw me at that exact moment. I didn't want to admit I had been inside. Then I ran down the porch stairs and to the back of the house where I found my bike, cold and dewy, but where I had left it.

Back at the front of the house, I stared down my street. It looked different. Worse.

No one appeared to be up. It was a Saturday morning, not much later than 6:00 a.m., and silent except for a few distant birds. It occurred to me that Mom might be sleeping too. Even when drowning in self-righteous resentment I was still conscious of what it would mean to get in trouble for staying out all night. Perhaps I could sneak in and pretend I had been there the whole time.

Mom's blue Chevette was in the driveway. This comforted me, then in a flash it enraged me. Why hadn't she been out looking for her son? Was she really that clueless? Or did she just not care if I ended up in a ditch somewhere?

I hopped off the bike and let it fall with a dull clank onto our front sidewalk. I had a headache. My underwear felt gross and sticky. I didn't want to sneak in. I walked into my house defiant. I didn't want to take any shit from anyone. Yeah, I didn't come home last night, *so what?*

The screen door slammed behind me.

"Jimmy?"

This threw me a bit. It wasn't Mom's voice, but Grandma's.

"Yeah," I called back.

"Oh thank God, I'm so glad you're okay! Can you come up here, please?"

My insolence wavered a bit. I had no beef with my grandmother. I took a breath and climbed the stairs.

# THE PAPER

She was sitting on the edge of her bed. She seemed older, more gaunt than usual. A rosary sat on her pillow.

"Hey, Grandma."

She reached out to me so I stepped forward and gave her a quick hug.

"Jimmy," she said as I released her, "your mom went into labor."

"She what?"

"They took her in an ambulance late last night. She had started having contractions around midnight. I stayed behind to wait for you."

*You couldn't have made it down the stairs anyway.*

"Mom's not supposed to have the baby until the end of the month."

"Yes, I know. She came early."

I felt a bit of judgment on the word "early."

"You're saying this is my fault?"

"Where were you?" she asked, validating my question.

"Who gives a shit?"

"Watch your mouth, child."

This was too much.

"Fuck you, Grandma!" I saw her jaw drop, but I continued. "What, you think she was so worried about me that her body decided to push a baby out? That's a load of crap. I left because she made it clear that she *didn't* care. So don't go assuming I had anything to do with this. Maybe it was all the wine. Did you think of that?"

Her face had fallen now. She was more concerned than shocked. But this just made me angrier.

"Jimmy, where *were* you?"

Really? No comment on the f-word or the drinking? Or my claim that Mom didn't care about her son? Where was I indeed.

"I'll tell you where I was, Grandma. I spent the night in the Black House at the end of the block. Alone on an old mattress. And it was still better than being here!"

The color drained from her face, all concern replaced with horror. She tried to speak but couldn't.
*Good. Let that sink in.*
I stormed out of her room, crossed the hall into my own, and slammed my door.

You're probably wondering what the hell I was thinking. I get it. I was wondering the same thing. I just paced that tiny room of mine not sure whether to punch the wall or punch myself in the face. It was maddening, being so convinced of the virtue of my rage yet certain I was overreacting. I mean, as far as I knew, I had never raised my voice to Grandma in my life. Why did it feel so good to tell her off?

I should leave home again. No, I should shower. No, I should go to the garage and bash my drums until the skin on my hands peels off.

There was a soft thud somewhere outside my bedroom.

"Mom?"

No answer.

"Grandma?"

I opened my door. It took me a moment to process what I was seeing. Grandma was on the floor, blocking her bedroom doorway, her body spilling halfway into the hall.

I raced over and knelt down beside her. She wasn't moving. Her arms were stretched out in front of her, with bony fingers locked in little claws as if attempting to crawl, a plaster cast of a Pompeii victim frozen in time. Her eyes remained open but stared at nothing.

She wasn't dead. I could hear faint, shallow, raspy breaths. I needed to call for help.

*There's no hurry. Let her go.*

What, and claim I wasn't back yet? Then Mom would blame me for not being home when it happened.

*Maybe you didn't hear her fall.*

Too risky. I had to call the police. Besides, this was my grandma. I loved my grandma. What was the matter with me?

*Nothing's the matter with you.*

If I called for help, I could say I was home the whole

night. When I woke up, I found her like this and called the police at once.

*Unless Grandma wakes up and calls your story a lie.*

She was still staring blankly ahead. Was she conscious in there? Maybe she was wondering why I was stalling.

"You're going to be okay, Grandma," I said, and descended the stairs to the kitchen phone. This was before 911 was available in our area (hell, we didn't even have touch tone dialing yet), so I had to use the "local emergency numbers" magnet Mom had on the fridge. New Haven still had five-digit local calls, so I dialed 9-9500 and waited.

"Police department," said the woman. I gave my name and address and explained what had happened. They asked me if my grandmother was still breathing and I said that she was, but she didn't seem to be able to speak. They asked if my mother or father was around, and I said that my mom was at the hospital giving birth and my dad wasn't in the picture. The dispatcher's tone softened then, going into a spiel about how everything would be okay and what a strong, brave young man I was, blah blah blah. They also said they'd get ahold of my mother in the hospital and update her, too. Cool.

An ambulance and a police car came together and I greeted the responders on the front porch. The paramedics didn't really talk to me, but efficiently carried Grandma out on a stretcher. The cop was a young white guy in his twenties who had been briefed on the situation and said I could ride with him to the hospital.

I caught a glimpse of myself in the reflection of the car window. I looked like shit. I remembered I still felt and smelled that way, too. But the cop didn't care. He was letting me in the front passenger seat.

My first time in a police car. Part of me was thinking what a great article this would make.

*You're not on the paper anymore.*

Oh, right.

Mount Clemens General Hospital, as it was called at the time, had our nearest emergency room, about a twenty-minute drive under normal conditions. I don't know if it was considered a quality hospital or not because it didn't matter—it was the only option. I had been born there, as had my mom and probably everyone else I knew. Yet it still didn't dawn on me that we were walking to the maternity ward until the chatty officer asked if I was "excited to meet her."

"Who?"

"Your baby sister."

"Oh."

I hadn't thought about it. So, I guess I wasn't.

We parked and entered through the ER, but I didn't see Grandma. The ambulance had arrived before us and I figured paramedics had their own special doors for stretcher-bound people. I realized that I may have seen her alive for the last time, and only now did guilt set in for my earlier hesitancy in calling for help. I couldn't for the life of me remember why I had reacted that way. Yet was I feeling remorse, or just worried about getting in trouble? Everything was a bit of a blur.

I also didn't recall how we had made it all the way up here to my mom's room. But there we were.

"You have a brave son here," said the officer. "He may have saved his grandmother's life with that phone call."

Mom was in a bed, looking like hell. She was attached to at least one IV and a beeping heart rate monitor.

"Thank you," she said, and the officer left.

I glanced around the room. A pile of Mom's clothes were draped over a chair in the corner, and a tray of uneaten breakfast food sat on a wheeled cart by her bed. There was no baby.

Did that mean she hadn't had it yet? Or did something bad happen? Was I going to be an only child after all? I hated myself for hoping.

"Jimmy," Mom croaked. "Everything's going to be okay."

"I know," I said.

"Your sister was born a little early, that's all. She's in an incubator in the nursery." Her words were slurring. She sounded drunk.

"You don't look so good, Mom."

"They had to cut her out. I was in labor but she wasn't in the right position yet, so they had to do the Caesar thing. I'll be alright."

A nurse came in at that moment. A young, perky blonde. I was self-conscious of how I looked and smelled. I wanted her to find me attractive. Maybe we could make out on a gurney somewhere.

"Do you know how my mom is doing?" Mom asked.

"We don't know anything yet, I'm afraid," said Hot Nurse with what seemed like genuine concern. "But I'll have the doctor come in when we have an update."

"Okay."

She turned to me. "And this is your son?"

"I'm Jimmy."

"Nice to meet you, Jimmy. Your mom and sister are both fighters, so I'm sure your grandmother is a fighter too, okay?"

I tried to look brave. "Thank you."

She turned back to Mom. "Are you up to visiting Madeline?"

*Who the fuck was Madeline?*

"I need to rest a bit more," Mom said. "But you can take Jimmy."

I stiffened. Oh crap.

"Okay then, you rest," agreed the nurse. She turned to me and smiled, blue eyes sparkling. "It's time to meet your sibling!"

First, an aide came in and helped me place a hospital gown over my clothes. I also had to put on a weird little hat made of paper, a surgical mask, and latex gloves. I looked and felt ridiculous. Was all this necessary? Was my sister radioactive? Was she the Girl in a Plastic Bubble? But, absent alternatives, I did as I was told, and I soon followed the nurse out of the room to the nearby nursery.

There were a few babies in open glass cribs with white linens, and I thought at first one of them might be Madeline, but instead I was taken to the far back corner of the room which contained what I can only describe as a glass cage out of a research lab in a horror movie. It didn't help that this area of the nursery had its overhead light switched off.

I must have slowed in my approach because the nurse touched my shoulder in support.

"Don't be scared," she said, her words muffled through her own surgical mask she had applied. (Her eyes were still gorgeous.) "Preemies are just babies. She's in great shape. She'll look smaller than you're expecting, that's all."

I gathered my courage and continued forward, only to discover that Hot Nurse was a damned liar. The baby didn't just look smaller than I was expecting. She...it?...didn't appear human at all. The creature was a dusky red color, sickly and emaciated, naked and splayed on its back like the frogs we had to dissect last month in Mr. Archie's class. Worse, it was connected to a variety of wires and tubes like some sort of alien experiment, including a plastic corrugated pipe that seemed to have been shoved violently down its throat.

"This," the nurse claimed, "is Madeline."

I stared. I waited for something to happen. In movies, there was always a moment of connection a person would get meeting a new child or baby sibling for the first time. The spontaneous generation of a loving bond or some shit. But I felt nothing. This is what Mom was giving me up for? A piece of beef jerky?

I was about to say something but was interrupted by a loud beeping sound coming from the hallway. A blue light was flashing next to one of the rooms. Someone yelled "code blue in six."

"Wait here," said the unnamed nurse. "Don't worry, it's not your mother." Then she and another nurse in the room took off, leaving me alone with the creature in the cage.

I kinda feel this wouldn't happen today. There'd probably be some protocols, right? I mean, you don't leave a teenager alone in a nursery. I could have walked out with any baby I wanted. Not that I could imagine wanting any of them, especially not jerky-face over here.

There was a chart on a clipboard hanging next to the incubator. It was labeled "Logan, Baby Girl" and listed a birthweight of 4 pounds even. This seemed generous. A football weighs only a single pound, and it was hard to believe this baby weighed more than a football. The chart also listed her birthday as August 5th, 1989. Since the day before had been the 4th, Mom must havehad her baby after midnight.

I wondered why the document didn't say "Madeline." Maybe they were waiting to make sure it lived. I also noticed it only listed Mom as a parent—the space for the father's name was blank.

The creature rustled a bit. Until that moment she hadn't moved at all.

I leaned in closer to the glass. There was a fluttering happening underneath Madeline's red skin. I first wondered if she was shivering. But as I looked closer, the skin appeared to be bubbling, as if the blood underneath had begun a rapid boil. Soon spheres of crimson broke out over every inch of her.

I called for help, but no one came. Everyone must have been dealing with the emergency in room six.

I didn't know what to do. Something was horribly wrong, and I was all alone. I thought about running back to Mom's room, but how would she be able to help? So dazed and drunk and out of it. She probably wouldn't believe me anyway. Or she'd blame me. "You killed your sister!" she'd scream.

But I couldn't run to my mom because I couldn't move. I couldn't look away. As I stared, the pulsating spheres on Madeline's skin popped and sank inward like deflated bubble wrap. Just a few bubbles at first, and then all of them. Within moments she was a doll-shaped piece of honeycomb, a twitching mess of skin and holes. *My God so many holes.*

I staggered backward at this point, falling against a glass crib and knocking it to the floor. It crashed against the tile with such force it awakened other babies in the nursery, at least one of whom began to cry. I was on my back now on the ground, spinning around to see if the baby I had knocked over had been hurt. But I couldn't find a baby. I couldn't even find pillows. I became frantic, searching for the child who must have bounced or rolled away. It took several long moments before I realized the crib had been empty.

There were hands on my arms now, lifting me up. A strong man, not one of the nurses, brought me to my feet. A doctor? No, too young to be a doctor. Maybe a janitor or orderly. I didn't know. He was dark-skinned and bald and not much older than me, I thought.

"Are you okay?" he asked.

I couldn't answer. I was too busy passing out.

# Two

I didn't have any injuries from my embarrassing pratfall. It wasn't even serious enough to get me admitted to the hospital I was already in. Instead, they carried me to the recliner in my mom's birthing room where I awoke to a doctor with a brown beard shining a flashlight in my face. I rambled on about something being wrong with the incubator baby (I had forgotten her name), but they assured me that everything was fine with Madeline and not to worry. My apparent terror had freaked Mom out though so they helped her to the nursery to see for herself. She came back relieved, but annoyed.

"He must have been hallucinating," she said as if I wasn't there. "You can tell he didn't sleep at all last night. Who knows when he came home."

I said nothing, but I felt the shift in tension. The hospital staff had gone from being concerned for my well-being to viewing me as The Problem.

"Well," said the doctor, "you both need some rest." He turned to me. "Jimmy, you didn't seem to hit your head and I'm not seeing any signs of a concussion, so you're free to stay here with your mom or go back home."

"No one's at home," I explained. "Mom and I live with my grandma, but she's here too."

"She was admitted an hour or so ago," our nurse told the doctor. "We don't know much yet."

"I see," said the bearded man. "Is there anyone else you can call?"

"There's Mike," I offered, hopefully.

"We're not calling Mike," Mom snapped.

"Not even to tell him about his baby?"

Another shift in the air. I could taste it. All eyes were on my mom now, and she was fighting back rage. She, too, could feel the judgment flowing to her from the doctor, the nurse, maybe even the orderly. They were probably wondering what sort of white trash family they had gotten involved with here.

"I was going to tell him," Mom said through clenched teeth. "When everything had settled down."

"Well," the doctor interjected, "why don't you call him now, have him come and meet his daughter, and then he can drive Jimmy here back to your house. He's old enough to stay on his own a couple days, right?"

Mom looked like she wanted to punch the man in the face. I flashed her a smug smile.

*Did you hear what he said? We're old enough to stay on our own. What, do you think you're smarter than a doctor?*

Looking back, I don't blame my mom for being furious at the doctor for offering such a impudent suggestion. He didn't know our story. For all he knew, Mike was a domestic abuser we had just escaped from and she had every reason not to want to call him right away. But, this was the 1980s, when single mothers in maternity wards were afforded even less respect and grace than they are today.

She decided to call Mike. Probably since the alternative was having me stick around with her in the hospital.

Mike rarely worked Saturday shifts at the foundry, so he picked up right away and said he'd be there within the hour. When he arrived he gave my mom a hug and me a handshake.

"Congrats, big brother."

After he went to visit Madeline in the incubator, he came back beaming. He must not have seen the same thing I saw. No one could have been proud to have created that. Or perhaps unconditional love really was blind.

Before Mike and I left the hospital, we got an update on Grandma. She had suffered a stroke and had been placed in a medically-induced coma to give her brain the best chance to heal. I wanted to ask why they had to induce a coma when she seemed to have come in with a coma already, but thought better of it. Anything I knew about comas was from watching summer reruns of St. Elsewhere which I barely understood. Bottom line was that Grandma wasn't leaving the hospital anytime soon.

Mom could come home in a couple days, though, even if Madeline might have to stay a few weeks longer. She was born nearly a month before her expected delivery date and they needed to fatten her up or something. I couldn't tell if Mom was irritated or relieved when they told her she might not be able to breastfeed. I wondered if I had been a formula baby too. Then I decided I didn't want to think about the alternative.

Mike's Datsun had a decent sound system and neither of us were talkative, so we listened to a Mitch Ryder cassette the entire way home. I wasn't sure if he was going to come in the house or just drop me off. He wasn't sure, either. There was no protocol for this sort of thing. All three of my known blood relatives were at Mt. Clemens General. I'd be alone here for the weekend at least.

"Can I make you lunch, buddy?"

"I think I'm going to lie down." It occurred to me Mike didn't know I had been out all night, and I didn't want to tell him.

"I'll swing by tonight with pizza. We can watch a scary movie or something if you're up for it."

"You know I don't need a babysitter, right?"

"I know."

He seemed a bit hurt. I actually wasn't sure why I was being weird. Pizza and a movie with Mike sounded great. It also sounded great to have the place to myself all day to scream and eat junk food and play drums.

There was an itch inside of me. I couldn't quite place it. It's like something was bubbling under the surface of my skin trying to get out. I worried my arms would start breaking out into a rash like Madeline's.

"Sorry," I said. "It's been a weird day. I'll call you

later if I'm up for it, okay?"

"Okay."

I got out of his car and he left my driveway.

I went inside, walked upstairs, and stopped at the spot where Grandma had had her accident. But it wasn't an accident, was it? I had caused it. And then came close to not helping her at all. Why did I do that? I couldn't remember.

*Sleep.*

My legs felt heavy, weighed down as if my jeans were filled with rocks.

*Just a short nap.*

—

I opened my eyes. There was light coming in from my window, but not much. I guessed it was after 9:00 p.m. I had slept most of the day. I wondered if Mike had called.

I heard a sound coming from downstairs. Like furniture moving. It must have woken me up. I wasn't alone in the house.

"Mom?" I called out. No one answered. But, I hadn't been very loud. In case it was a burglar and all.

I got out of bed and crept into the hallway. I was a little foggy, and my vision was blurred a bit in the center. For a second I thought I saw Grandma's body lying there, but it was gone in a blink. The sounds from downstairs had stopped, too. I thought about calling "Mom?" again but decided not to risk it.

I descended the first part of the stairs and reached the landing. As I pivoted to the final steps, I saw a large, dark figure cross my view of the dimly-lit den. It seemed to make no sound. And it wasn't Mom.

I backed up against the front door. Maybe I could run outside. I wasn't wearing shoes, though. How far could I run barefoot? I held my breath and turned the knob.

"Jimmy?"

Mike's voice. I was an idiot.

"Oh, hi!"

He looked up at me from the bottom of the stairs.

"Going somewhere?"

"No," I lied. I let go of the doorknob.

"Sorry if I frightened you. I came by with food a couple hours ago but you were dead to the world and I let you sleep. Hope you don't mind if I ate some without you."

"Of course not. Pepperoni?"

"Yep. I'll heat some up."

Mike drank a Stroh's as I ate my pizza. It was a little awkward, and we didn't talk much. It felt weird to be alone in the house with Mike since I hadn't seen him much in recent weeks. I wondered if Mom knew he was here.

"I brought something for you."

"Oh?"

"Since you'll be cooped up here a couple days, I thought I'd loan you my cable descrambler."

"What's that?"

"It's basically a box that you plug into the cable line that lets you get all the premium channels for free. I know your mom just has basic channels, but now you can watch HBO, Showtime, Disney, all of them."

My eyes widened as my thoughts went to The Playboy Channel. I had totally tried watching Playboy even in its scrambled form. After all, sometimes you could still see bare breasts amongst the distortion. Any '80s kid knows exactly what I'm talking about.

"That sounds amazing. Is it illegal?"

Mike laughed. "I suppose so. A guy I work with was selling them for fifty bucks. I've had it for almost a year now and it works great. A normal cable box scrambles the channels you don't pay for by suppressing the horizontal sync signal so the picture can't be properly assembled. This box pretends you've purchased everything there is to see."

"Can't the cable company tell what we're watching?"

"Nah, it ain't like that. When you change the channel it doesn't change the signal coming in. It changes the piece of it you're watching. Cable TV isn't a switchboard. It's a one-way signal, just a big firehose of content flowing in. All homes are sent all channels at once, simultaneously. If you had fifty TVs and fifty cable boxes set up in the same house, you could watch all the channels at once."

This blew my mind. I had always assumed that when I changed the channel on the cable box, some signal got sent to the company that instructed them to send me the new channel I wanted.

"What are we going to watch?"

Mike grinned. "Well, I'm in the mood for crap."

We were in luck. The Movie Channel was having a marathon of *Joe Bob's Drive-in Theater*. From 1986 to 1996, comedian and film critic "Joe Bob Briggs" would spend 5-10 minutes introducing a film he had selected, mostly cheesy B-movie horror, and then come back on after the film was done for a funny conclusion and review. Sorta like Elvira if Elvira was a redneck in a bolo tie. I had seen a couple of these during sleepovers at Benny's house—he was the only kid on the block whose dad paid for premium channels, which I bet he got for free as a cable TV installer. It's how I had seen both *Maximum Overdrive* and *Surf Nazis Must Die* the previous summer.

Mike and I stayed up watching two of these "drive-in" movies. The first was *Friday the 13th: The Final Chapter*, which I remember almost nothing about. The second was *Scream for Help*, a truly bonkers 1984 thriller which to this day I remember *everything* about.

The story centers around a teenage girl who believes her stepdad is plotting to kill her mom. That's not a spoiler, by the way—the opening line of the film, even before the credits, is the protagonist narrating that exact suspicion. The movie at first teases the possibility that the paranoia may be all in the girl's mind, but soon it's clear that her intuition is correct, especially after a car-bike chase that takes literally three calendar days in the film's timeline.

"This movie is awful," Mike laughed at one point.

"Totally," I agreed. But concerned he would change

the channel, I added: "Let's see where it goes."

If you've seen *Scream for Help* (unlikely, I know), you might assume the only parts I would remember were the frequent and gratuitous shots of large breasts, both clothed and unclothed. At one point, our hero has a tight t-shirt emblazoned with the word "muffs" and for years I used "muffs" as a synonym for breasts, even if no one else knew what I was talking about. But it wasn't just that. I think some movies simply sear themselves into you on a single viewing. Even the inexplicably over-the-top orchestral film score followed my subconscious around for years afterward.

I wish I could say I was just an ironic fan of the campy filmmaking. Instead, the film electrified the dark, itchy feeling inside of me which had been consuming my recent thoughts. The paranoia that no one could be trusted. The dark fantasies about things I could do to my enemies, or friends who wronged me, or girls who rejected me. The idea that I had the power to control my life through my own actions, without empathy or concern for others at all.

In the final third of the film (okay, now these are spoilers), the evil stepfather and his associates lock the girl and her mom in the basement with a plan to kill them both at exactly 2:00 a.m. This creates an arbitrary ticking clock scenario which exists solely to give the women time to escape. Stupid, yes. Yet all I could think of were the missed opportunities. Couldn't they at least tie them up naked? If you're going to kill them anyway, why not enjoy yourself first? Bite them. Slap them. Fuck them.

*Imagine what you could do.*

Ah, there was the voice. Hadn't heard from him in a while.

*Imagine what we could do.*

I glanced down at my hands as the movie reached its climax. They had changed somehow. The flickering TV light emphasized wrinkles, divots, imperfections. I noticed veins for the first time. Pores. Hairs. These were not the hands of a child. They were a *man's* hands. They were strong. They could even kill.

I looked over at Mike. I wanted to show him my new hands. But he had fallen asleep in his chair.

I started to think of all the things I could do with my new adult hands. I could swipe his beer. I could strangle him. I could unzip his pants and check out the size of his dick.

*Is that what you fuck Mom with? Does she like it?*

Jesus, again, what was wrong with me.

*Nothing is wrong with you.*

I shouldn't be having these thoughts.

*Oh yes you should. This is growing up. These are grown-up thoughts.*

I shut my eyes tight for several seconds. But it didn't help. Rather than being plunged into a resetting darkness, I only saw the bedroom of the Black House projected against the inside of my eyelids. The soiled mattress, the peeling paint, the writing on the wall. But the words there didn't say "sleep" anymore. They didn't say anything. Just jumbled, random red letters. Indistinct and illegible, yet as vivid as if my eyes were open.

My heart was pounding now. I tried to focus my attention on the remainder of the movie, which was kind of lame but helped calm me down. When the credits started rolling, Mike woke up.

"I think I missed the ending," he admitted.

"It's time for bed," I said flatly.

He nodded and stood up. I stayed put on the couch.

"Alright, I'll take off. I know you slept all day, but try and go to bed now too, alright? Otherwise your internal clock will be thrown off for days."

*He's not your dad,* said the voice. *And he's only alive right now because you chose not to smother him with one of Mom's twenty couch pillows.*

"Okay," I said.

After Mike left, I debated my options. Part of me wanted to stay up and watch Playboy. A larger part of me wanted to ride my bike around at night looking for trouble. My logical side, though, saw the wisdom in

Mike's warning. I really should try to sleep.

*Pussy.*

—

I woke up hours later, drenched in sweat and painfully aroused. But I hadn't been dreaming about sex. I had been dreaming about torturing Dale. He was blindfolded and chained to a wall, stripped down to his underwear, and I was using a potato peeler on his chest to flay strips of flesh from his body, letting the pieces fall onto a cold concrete floor. It wasn't bloody, though. It was more like Dale's body was made of pink Play-Doh, which made soft little plops as each chunk hit the ground. Dale had tried to scream but couldn't—I had stuffed several wadded-up *New Haven Herald*s into his mouth. But I could tell in his eyes he was terrified, and that was the source of my lingering excitement.

I remedied the arousal. Then I stared at the dark ceiling.

It was strange being all alone in the house. Even if Mom was at work or shopping or something, Grandma's presence had been a constant since I was a child. It occurred to me that this might have been the first time I had spent the night alone.

My stomach lurched in hunger. It felt as if I hadn't eaten in days, even after all that pizza. I wondered if there was any left.

I crept down the stairs in my tightie-whities and turned on the kitchen light. The clock on the wall reported 3:30 a.m.

I opened the pizza box which was on the kitchen table. There was a single piece. I probably should have refrigerated it.

*TV time, Jimmy.*

I took the slice into the living room and switched on the cable. As I suspected, The Playboy Channel did indeed come in clear as day with Mike's magic box. Airing was a program highlighting the life of one of the bunnies, blonde and buxom, using a breathy Marilyn

Monroe voice as she described her turn-ons to the camera over B-roll of a recent photo shoot.

After a couple minutes of this, my stomach growled, and I realized I was still holding the untouched piece of pizza in my left hand. I had completely forgotten about it, distracted by boobs. I chuckled and took a bite. I had been worried that the slice had been left out too long, but it just tasted like normal, slightly stale pizza. The second and third bites, though, tasted sauce-heavy, as if all the cheese had slid off. By the fourth bite, I couldn't taste any crust. It was like biting into a water balloon filled with sweet, salty marinara.

I looked down to see what was wrong with the pizza, only to discover I wasn't holding a slice of pizza at all.

I was holding half a mouse.

I dropped it and cried aloud, jumping backward as if the bisected rodent was going to hop toward me anyway, just hind legs and a gaping, bloody torso. I felt around for a weapon, settling on the remote control. I clutched it in my right hand, and turned back toward the creature, but it was only a small slab of saucy pizza crust after all.

# Three

The next few days were more of the same. Mom was recovering in the birthing unit and Madeline and Grandma were still hooked up to machines. Mom tried to talk her sister Sharon into coming in from Pittsburgh to watch me for a few days, but I guess they had a big fight about it, each calling the other selfish, so it didn't work out. Instead, Mike swung by every morning and evening to make sure I didn't kill myself or whatever. We watched a few movies and played a couple games of chess, but he could tell I was distant and let me stay inside my shell. I mostly slept, played drums, and ignored the doorbell.

Eventually, Mom was able to come home, but Madeline needed more time to get strong before she could be released. It felt like I was still alone, though, since Mom spent every hour she could at the hospital and crashed the moment she walked in the door each night. I doubt we had a single meaningful conversation that entire week.

I missed writing for the paper, so I tried my hand at heavy metal song lyrics, but they all sounded gross and angsty. I found some of them while researching for this book:

> *I really did try my best*
> *But I still failed your test*
> *Get me out of this land*
> *I need your helping hand*
> *This world I do hate*
> *Let me articulate*
> *My pain's so very real*
> *Don't tell me what I feel*

Oh wait, and this gem:

*Why do we exist, subsist on this planet*
*Of death, despair—it just isn't fair!*
*Few clues to inspect, neglect and stupidity*
*Thrive every day—must be it this way?*
*Is there a Being seeing everything we don't,*
*and do, and grading us too?*
*Or is this a cell—a HELL—which we cannot escape*
*Inert, souls buried in dirt!*

I think a bit of Dale's pretentious vocabulary must have rubbed off on me for that last one. Or maybe it was ghostwritten by the voice?

Anyway.

Mom brought Madeline home on Monday, August 14th, earlier than expected. Mike drove them to the house but quickly left. Still no news about Grandma.

"You just left her there?" I asked.

Mom was annoyed. "There's nothing we can do for her. She hasn't woken up. She has to be monitored. But you know that."

"Yeah, I guess."

"Your sister is doing great, though! Do you want to hold her?"

"Not really."

Mom looked me up and down. "You need a shower."

"I'm fine." I wasn't. I had slept until 2:00 p.m. and was grimy even by the standards of a 13-year-old boy.

"No, go take a shower. Mike will be back in an hour with food."

I hoped it wasn't pizza. Hadn't been able to touch the stuff since the mouse thing.

"Are you two getting along okay?" I asked.

"Of course. Quit stalling."

As I walked upstairs I felt my skin turn itchy again. I supposed it was the germs.

The water felt good against my naked body. But it needed to be hotter. I kept turning the knob further and further to the left. Though I could see the steam, it felt lukewarm at best. I started imagining the water scalding me instead. I could picture my skin turning red, then bubbling, then splitting like the casing of a hot dog. I imagined blood and guts oozing out of my navel, my penis, even my toes. Soon the bottom of the tub would be covered in gore. But I knew it wasn't real. It wasn't a hallucination like at the hospital. I was in control this time.

After a while I used up all the "hot" water and it was too cold to continue. I stepped out, dried myself, and stared at my reflection in the foggy bathroom mirror. I looked older than I thought I should. If I was a little taller, I could pass for a tenth grader at least.

The front door opened. Had it been an hour? I had completely lost track of time.

"Come on down!" Mom called, either to me or Mike or both.

I sprinted to my room and threw on some cleanish clothes. Mike must have gone to New Baltimore, because the smell was unmistakable: White Castle cheeseburgers.

My stomach growled in anticipation. I loved White Castle. Their burgers came by the sack and you could eat eight or even ten if you were hungry enough. Sure, the fries were nothing special and the chocolate shakes were too thick to suck through a straw, but nothing beat those tiny little oniony burgers you barely had to chew.

Mike greeted me with a laugh. "You look excited, Champ."

"I am!"

He handed me my first burger and I inhaled it.

"White Castle? Really?" Mom wasn't amused.

"Oh come on, the boy loves it."

"It's junk food. It's not even *good* junk food."

"Sorry," Mike admitted. "I suppose it's not very nutritious."

This was true. In fact, White Castle hamburgers smelled the same coming out of you as they did going in: a sure sign the body absorbed nothing of value.

Mom didn't seem to notice Mike's apology. She was going through plastic bags from the pharmacy. It must have been the reason Mike had gone to New Baltimore. New Haven didn't have a proper drug store, so any time you needed something more complex than aspirin or antacids you needed to drive four miles to the next town.

"You got the Pepto?"

"Yes, it's there," Mike confirmed.

"And the heating pad, I see. And the vitamins."

"Yes."

I was finishing my second burger when Mom abruptly looked up.

"Where's the diaper cream?"

Mike froze. "Diaper cream?"

"I told you before you left! Zinc oxide diaper cream!"

"I don't...I'm sorry, I don't remember that."

"So, where is it?"

"What do you mean?"

"Where's the fucking diaper cream, Mike?"

"I...didn't get any. I must have forgotten."

Mom threw her hands up in exasperation.

"Oh, sure, you remember the *White Castle* but not the medicine for your own child! You want to see her in pain? Is that it?"

"I'm sorry, really. I don't recall you saying diaper cream and I remembered everything else..."

"Save it, Mike! You've made it very clear that you don't give two shits about anything or anyone in this family, so I don't know why I'm surprised."

I tried playing peacemaker. "Mom, I think..."

"Shut up," she spat at me. "Don't take his side. Take mine. And your sister's. She's the one who's going to suffer because of his incompetence."

"I can go back after dinner and get the cream. It's fine. Can we just eat?"

"It's not fine! You're not reliable. I have to do everything myself."

Mom grabbed her purse from the kitchen counter and tried to storm past Mike, but he stopped her.

"Look," he said. "I'll leave now, okay? You stay here. I can be back in twenty minutes."

"Get out of my way. You're not going to get the right kind."

"I'll get the right kind. Zinc oxide diaper cream."

"What *brand?*"

"You didn't mention a brand."

Mom laughed hard, biting, sarcastic. "Oh, you think it's all the same then? You're so fucking worthless. I'm going myself."

"Why don't you just tell me the brand you want?"

"I said I'm going myself!" She shoved him aside at this point and stormed up the stairs. Mike followed her, his patience waning.

"Jesus Christ, Nicole! Will you come back here and talk to me?"

They both went out the front door, out of earshot. I grabbed a third burger.

I began to hear a baby crying. But it sounded robotic, tinny. And inexplicably from the direction of the refrigerator. She wasn't in there, was she?

Nope. There was something new on the counter. It looked like a beige walkie talkie with Fisher Price emblazoned on the front. The same company that made Dale's camcorder. It must have been some sort of new way of monitoring babies. Madeleine was crying from her crib upstairs.

*You should go pick her up, big brother.*

The dark voice was sarcastic today.

*Maybe pat her little back. Play patty-cake. Give her a coo-coo-ca-choo.*

I ate another burger and ignored the voice. And the baby.

Eventually Mom came back in the house. Mike must have "won" the battle and was on his way to New Baltimore.

She didn't come downstairs but went right up to attend to the crying infant. I wondered if I'd get yelled at for ignoring the cries. I grabbed a final burger for the road and left out the back door.

I hadn't decided where to go, or whether I wanted

company, but saw Marco shooting hoops by himself in his driveway a few houses down.

"Hey, man," I said. He passed me the ball. I took a shot. Way short.

"You must be used to Dale's hoop," he teased. "Wanna go there instead?"

"What are you talking about? Dale doesn't play basketball."

Marco took a shot. He missed, too, but not as embarrassingly.

"Have you not been over there lately? Dale's dad installed a hoop on their garage. But he installed it at nine feet high instead of ten so it's more fun. I can almost dunk on it. It's wasted on Dale, though. He only knows how to play h-o-r-s-e."

I was flabbergasted. Not only at the idea that Dale would want a basketball hoop, but at the fact that Marco had been playing over there without me.

"Are you two friends now or something?"

"Uh, yeah, I guess. Aren't you?"

"We had a fight over a week ago."

Marco seemed surprised. "He hasn't mentioned it."

*He hasn't mentioned it? During all your long, intimate conversations?*

"How often do you talk to him?"

"Well, every day I suppose, since he got the new hoop. We've been writing some articles together too. Hang on, let me show you."

He tossed me the ball and ran into the house. I took a shot. It went in. Figures, since there was no one to witness it.

Marco returned with a sheet of *The New Haven Herald Jr.*

"It's the new page two," he explained. "There's a couple typos on it so it's not final. I just brought it home to show my mom. You can have it."

The left side had three short articles by Dale and an advertisement for Video Scene II. The entire right side was one long column entitled "Dale & Marco & The Movies" which was a shameless rip-off of the *Siskel & Ebert* TV show. There were a handful of movie titles followed by a review by Dale, then one by Marco, each ending in a thumbs up or thumbs down.

"Have you watched all these together?"

"Nah, we mostly picked movies we both had seen. *Weird Science* is one we all watched at your party, remember?"

I remembered.

"Speaking of parties, you're coming to Dale's right? On Friday?"

I had no idea Dale had a party coming up on Friday. I hadn't received an invitation and we hadn't spoken since the fight. I vaguely remembered that he was turning 12 this month but had given it no thought.

*Don't let him know you weren't invited to a nerd's birthday party.*

"Uh, sure," I said, folding the paper and stuffing it in my back pocket. "I'll be there."

"I got him Capsela toys. You know, those clear balls you connect with all the gears and motors inside."

I had seen the commercials but had never played with them in person.

"You think he'll like that?" Marco asked. "I hope so. I figure they're kinda nerdy and techy, like him. Apparently there's even a way to program them with a Commodore 64."

*You're concerned your gift isn't cool enough for Dale Dunkle? You're two years older than this kid, Marco. Don't be a fucking loser.*

"Why are you trying to impress him?"

Marco blinked.

"I'm...I'm not. I just know you know him better than me."

"No, it sounds like you two are *quite* close."

He got my insinuation.

"Don't be a dick, Jimmy. You spent a whole year trying to make me like the kid. You don't get to make me un-like him because you had a spat." He grabbed the basketball from the ground and chucked it at my chest. I caught it, awkwardly.

*Throw it at his head. Fucking traitor.*

"I'm just pissed at everything right now. Grandma's in the hospital and my mom brought home this…thing…that she claims is my baby sister but that I don't give a shit about. And she's being a total bitch to me and Mike, so I'm pissed at her, and Dale, and maybe you a bit for hanging out with Dale, and there's this voice in my head that is angry all the time and I just want to kick a fucking puppy until it's dead."

I dribbled once and took a shot. It was perfect.

I smiled at Marco. He didn't smile back.

"Jimmy, are you okay? This doesn't sound like you at all."

"I'm fine. Haven't you ever had a bad month?"

"Not bad enough to murder a puppy."

"Oh, come on. You're a pyro who loves to set action figures on fire. You're always bitching about racist teachers and the system being rigged and all that. And I know you're pissed about your absent dad. You're not filled with hate? Not even sometimes?"

"The world's fucked up, sure. Shit makes me mad all the time."

"So, let's do something about it! Slash a cop's tires! Burn down the school!"

Marco glanced around nervously. Then he chuckled. "Man, don't make me be the rational one here. That ain't my style. But you gotta get it together or you're going to get in trouble. Just chill."

*He's not your friend anymore, Jimmy. You've lost him.*

I could feel a rage building inside me, and began to see a strange, shimmering static flicker across Marco's face and body, as if dozens of gnats were floating in the space between us. It distorted his features ever so slightly, and I became convinced, for a moment, that this wasn't the "real" Marco at all.

*You lost him to Dale fucking Dunkle.*

I knew I needed to say something. Something hurtful. Biting. But I froze. Too angry, maybe. Or too scared.

I blinked. The jittering speckles retreated to my peripheral vision, then faded altogether. I looked down the street at the Black House half a block away. Even at this distance, I felt it staring at me, those two second floor windows like eyes judging my every move, looking for weakness, and finding it.

Marco's mom called him in for dinner and the moment passed. We said our "laters" and he walked into his house.

I stood on the sidewalk for a minute, deciding where to go next.

*Go play chess with Mike. It's the only way you have a chance of becoming a man, after all. You're sure not going to become one by being a whiny bitch.*

I set my gaze toward home. The floating black things surrounded my house now, too. Was nothing real anymore?

"He's not back yet," I whispered to nothing.

*Then go home and read the paper, Jimmy.*

"The paper?"

*In your back pocket, asshole.*

I had forgotten about that. I took the paper out and unfolded it. It, too, was surrounded by flitting, semi-transparent gnats. It made the printed words appear ephemeral somehow. Like they could rearrange themselves at any moment. It gave the task of reading them an urgency that a physical document normally wouldn't have.

I hurried home and raced upstairs to my bedroom. If Mom called my name or berated me for leaving, I didn't notice. I sat at my desk and started reading.

The first article by Dale was a boring piece about the New Haven Community Center, which apparently offered medical, educational, and counseling services to area teens. "With Program Director Mary Chessler at your side, you know that you're in great hands!" Lame. The second article was about the supposed dangers of red and yellow dyes in food. "Some red dyes like the ones in Jell-O or Triaminic can make children go wild, running around and acting crazy," Dale claimed. Okay. The third was barely an article at all, merely last semester's 7th and 8th grade honor roll kids. I was amused that the only student in the "ALL A'S" section for our grade was Emilia Jankowski. Even the great Dale Dunkle must have gotten a B somewhere. Probably in gym.

*Keep reading.*

Like I said, the entire right column was an extensive "Dale and Marco" review section, covering old and new films including *Weird Science*, *The Last Starfighter*, *Beetlejuice*, *The Golden Child*, and *Beverly Hills Cop*. I was a little surprised to see that last one, since I didn't think Dale was allowed to watch R-rated movies, then realized he likely watched it at Marco's house which made me want to punch a wall.

*Look harder.*

That was it. There wasn't anything more to read. I checked the back of the page to confirm it was single-sided.

*Don't be an idiot. There's a reason Marco wanted you to see this.*

I stared dumbly at the page. I stared at Emilia's name in particular, all alone there on her own line of All A's. Though it didn't actually say that. There was a typo. Dale had written "ALL A-S" with a hyphen where the apostrophe should be. (Don't get me started on why you need an apostrophe when it's plural not possessive—I'm as shocked as you.) But this struck me as strange. Dale never had typos, and certainly none bad enough that I'd notice. Could it have been intentional? Maybe...a shift cipher?

I studied the long review section. None of it was gibberish, so none of it could be decoded. But what about the left side of the text? The starting letter of each line? It looked like a message to me. U, I, Z, K, W.... what would that spell if decoded?

Starting with an A-S shift cypher, it spelled M-A-R-C-O.

I had figured it out. This couldn't be a coincidence. After all, why publish an honor roll over two months after school got out? It even explained why Dale was using unusual adjectives like "Zany" and "Kooky" in a review of *Weird Science*. I mean sure, *Weird Science* was zany and kooky, but this had to be planned.

I kept decoding. I decoded every first goddamned letter of that section, even as the cypher kept shifting. Then I stared at what I had uncovered. I could barely see the letters through the rage.

After adding spaces, it read:

*Marco is my friend now loser and I'm going to date Emilia.*

The gnats. So many dark, shimmering, trembling gnats.

# Four

The days leading up to Dale's party were filled with loathing. And planning. Not real plans, mind you. Not things I'd actually do. But fantasy plans. Like showing up wearing only wadded-up *New Haven Heralds Jr.* as underwear and taking a dump on his birthday cake. Or convincing Dale there was a special birthday present waiting for him in the Black House, but the present was chaining him up *Scream for Help* style, covering his nuts with honey and releasing a box of fire ants.

I wondered where I could get fire ants. Maybe somewhere in New Baltimore.

*Mike will have to drive you.*

Why would I say I needed the ants? Science class? No, the school year didn't start for another two weeks. Mike probably knew that. Maybe Dale had a pet that used them for food? That might work. Then I could claim the ants were needed as a birthday present, which they kind of would be, right? Not a *lie*-lie, then.

*You'll have to tape his mouth shut. Otherwise someone would hear the screams.*

Right, sure. Strong tape, honey, fire ants. Anything else?

*Bring a camera. Then you can hang pictures up at school.*

Wouldn't that make it easy for me to get in trouble?

*Who cares, Jimmy.*

Indeed. Who did care about me at this point. Mom sure didn't. She barely noticed I was alive anymore, except to yell at me for not helping with the little poop factory. She finally got me to hold Madeline at one point, to instill some sibling bond or whatever, but I felt nothing. Not a damned thing. It was kind of scary. What was to stop me from spiking the baby like a football? Fear of juvenile detention?

I ran into Benny and learned he, too, was going to Dale's party. Great. *Two* of my so-called friends would be in attendance. I supposed shitting on a birthday cake was impractical, but I bet I could piss in the lemonade. Just a little, so you couldn't tell at first. It might taste less sweet than normal is all, and there would be fun and laughter and balloons to distract you. Hell, maybe Dale's parents would have a clown. Only after everyone was properly quenched with little yellow mustaches could I reveal what I had done. Then they'd all barf all over themselves like in *Stand by Me* and I'd just laugh and laugh. A legendary way to end friendships that didn't mean anything.

*You don't need them. You have new friends.*

This was sort of true. I had recently smoked cigarettes with Pax, Derek and T-Too in back of the Black House. We didn't talk about anything important or serious, but it felt good to be accepted for who I was. No judgment, no bullshit. Just a few dirty jokes and laughing about what we'd do to the hot math teacher if we got the chance. At one point, that new kid Tony and his little brother were walking by and I demanded they buy treats for us if they were going to Huck's. The panic on their faces, man. I remembered being on the other side of that shit. I thought I could get used to this side.

The day of the party came at last. I had decided against any honey or urine-related activities and thought showing up uninvited was enough. I bet it'd be mostly his relatives anyway, aside from the couple of us from our street. Perhaps I'd throw some nasty comments his way, or tell jokes that would make people laugh at him for being a nerd or whatever. And if he asked why I was being an asshole, I'd take that decoded page out of my back pocket and shove it in his green-glassed face.

*Lame. You need to destroy him.*

Shut up, voice. I know what I'm doing.

*Do you, though?*

I wasn't sure. Maybe I was pulling my punches. Maybe I hadn't crossed fully over to the dark side yet. It felt good to be an asshole. It really did. But it still seemed to come easier to bullies like Pax. I had all the same contempt for other people that he did; the same rage at the world, complete with a melancholic certainty that I had gotten a raw deal in life. Pax was just more comfortable in who he was.

*But you know who you want to be.*

I went through my closet looking for an outfit I thought would suit my mood. Finding nothing clean, I dug through the dirty clothes pile by my bed. Even better. Nothing says "I don't give a fuck about your birthday" like a ratty, smelly Metallica t-shirt.

I went outside to get my bike when it was time, then thought it'd be better to walk. Let Dale see me coming. Slowly. Hoping I wasn't stopping at his house. Praying I'd pass on by.

Alas, no one was out front to see my horror movie approach. I heard voices, though. The party was in the backyard.

As I walked down the driveway, I got a look at the fabled nine-foot-tall basketball hoop for the first time. Christ, it was ugly. It wasn't even a real backboard. Had Dale's dad made it himself out of plywood? What a family of losers.

I saw the party when I rounded the corner and was shocked. The only family members seemed to be his parents and little sister. There must have been fifteen kids from school, including Marco, Benny, and even Zach. There were several girls from our class, too. How the hell did Dale know this many people?

*Who's the loser now, Jimmy.*

I opened the chain link fence gate and stepped onto the lawn. Dale saw me first. He looked momentarily stunned, then recovered and smiled, jogging over to greet me as if everything was normal.

"Presents go on the table over there," he said by way of greeting.

"Do you see me holding a present, Dale?"

His smile faltered a bit. "Well, no, but I'm glad you came!"

*Sure you are.*

Zach joined us. He was holding a *Ghostbusters* Ecto Cooler juice box. I noticed the streamers and decorations were similarly themed. There was even a green piñata in the shape of the character Slimer hanging from the willow tree in the back yard. I'd bet my left nut there would be a *Ghostbusters* logo cake too.

"Hey Jimmy," Zach said.

"What are you doing here?"

Zach glanced at Dale, confused. "Uh, I was invited, man. Weren't you?"

I didn't know how to respond to that. Was he implying that he thought I *was* invited or *wasn't* invited? Maybe he only came because he thought I'd be here.

*Bullshit. He didn't even come to your own party.*

He said he had a family thing.

*He's never been to your house, Jimmy. Not once. But here he is in Dale's back yard drinking Hi-C with your shitty friends.*

Dale's dad called Dale over for something. Probably to find out if it was okay that I was crashing the party. I watched to see if they were pointing at me, but they weren't.

"Marco said he's been writing more for the paper," Zach said. "That's cool I guess."

I eyed him sharply. "Dale hasn't talked *you* into writing anything, has he?"

"No," he said. I detected a "not yet" in his voice.

*Motherfucker.*

Calm down.

*Who else is Dale going to take from you?*

Benny and Marco joined us. They each held an Ecto Cooler as well. I hated how much those little green cartons were making me thirsty.

"This is the first time we've all been together since school ended," beamed Benny. "Are you excited about the new year?"

"Thrilled," I deadpanned.

"I got Mr. Fairley for Social Studies," said Marco. "Anyone have him yet?"

Zach nodded gravely. "I did. Last year. He's kind of a nightmare."

"How so?"

"Well, you know that girl Latisha? She happened to be the only Black kid in our class, and we were studying slavery. At least once each period Fairley would say something like 'imagine Latisha's a slave,' or 'Zach, imagine you owned Latisha as your property.' It didn't bother her at first but she seemed irritated after a while."

"Shit," agreed Marco, worried.

"Yeah. One time he was telling us about how freed slaves would carry paperwork with them proving they were allowed to have jobs and own property and stuff, but might sometimes run into slaveowners who would tear up their proof of freedom. To illustrate this, he picked up the top page of Latisha's class notes and ripped it into fourths right in front of her face."

*That's pretty badass.*

No, it isn't.

*You're no fun.*

"What did she do?" I asked.

"She tried to laugh it off, but I saw her crying by her locker at lunch."

"Man, I'm so sick of that school," Marco moaned. "I don't know who's worse: the bullies on the playground or the bullies in charge."

"Fight the power," Zach agreed, quoting the summer's Public Enemy song.

"Amen to that."

"Well hang on," I protested. "Your dad's the fire chief. He's part of 'the power' isn't he?"

Marco laughed. "My people have no problem with volunteer fire fighters, Jimmy. They're heroes."

"But you *love* fire."

"Yeah, and I know who to call when things get out of hand, don't I."

My back was to the fence gate so I didn't see who Zach was looking at over my shoulder.

"Holy crap, it's Janine!"

*Who's Janine?*

I spun around and my jaw dropped. Standing at the entrance to the backyard was Emilia Jankowski, dressed in the spitting image of *Ghostbusters'* Janine Melnitz. And not the frumpy Janine from the first film either. Oh no. Emilia was dressed as the *Ghostbusters II* version, which meant a poofy red wig, giant circular glasses, and what appeared to be a home-sewn version of the green and black dress Janine had been wearing when making out with Louis Tully in Dana's apartment. (I saw it three times in theatres that summer so don't question me on this.) She was even wearing the proper shiny black leather boots, too, despite the warm weather.

"I thought someone might recognize me!" Emilia cooed. My heart skipped a beat as she slinked over to us. I was summoning the courage for a hello when Dale beat me to it.

"Greetings, Emilia! You look amazing. Presents go on the table over there."

I hadn't noticed she was holding a bag. I had been too distracted by the flowing green skirt fabric hugging her legs as she walked.

*You look amazing, he said.*

My face fell. I was excited to see Emilia, but realized her attendance only confirmed Dale's hidden message. He *was* after my girl. The son of a bitch.

*He knew you wanted her, Jimmy.*

Had I ever even mentioned her to Dale? I couldn't imagine when or why.

*You must have. Maybe you told him she'd be a good writer for the paper. You were thinking it, weren't you? Or perhaps he saw the way you look at her in the hallway like a lovesick puppy.*

There's no way Dale had a chance with Emilia. He was turning 12 *today* for God's sake.

*But he's smart. And successful. She probably reads The Macomb County Chronicle, Jimmy. She knows who the real talent is. You're nobody.*

"Everything okay?" Benny could always tell when I

was upset.

"I'm fine," I snapped, as I distractedly watched Dale Dunkle introduce Emilia/Janine to his father.

*This is my girlfriend, daddy! Isn't she pretty? Can we go make out in my treehouse now?*

Yeah, you should let me up in that treehouse with you, fucker. One of us might have a little accident.

*That's not a bad idea, Jimmy. You could sneak over sometime and replace all the long, strong nails holding up the stair boards with short, weak little nails. Especially on the top boards which you put your whole weight on when climbing down. They'd look totally normal under they slipped out.*

I'll think about it.

*Who would ever know? You wouldn't even be there. The perfect alibi.*

I had to turn away from Dale and Emilia. Those wiggling black bugs were everywhere.

"How the hell does he know her," I vented.

Zach snickered. "Jealous, much?"

I must have shot him a look which chilled his blood because he held up his hands in surrender.

"Whoa, no harm meant, Jimmy. I don't know how they know each other. I bet through honor club or something."

"But I don't get it! Look at all the people here. And the popular kids, too!"

The blonde twins, Vicki and Sherrie, were the biggest surprise. Well-liked and well-off, I couldn't imagine that Dale would be friends with either of them, or why they'd have risked their social status by being seen with him. The truth came out while we were standing around a few minutes later, waiting to start hitting the piñata.

"How do you know Dale?" Emilia asked them.

"We're in a couple classes together," Vicki shrugged. "And his dad knows our mom."

Sherrie nodded in agreement. "Plus," after a quick glance around to assure no parents were in earshot, "our first school dance ever is in October, and mom said this party would be mostly boys."

Emilia sent a smile my way that I couldn't interpret, then turned back to the twins. "Looking at anyone in particular?" she asked.

*This outta be good.*

"I donno," Sherrie blushed. "The kid in the striped shirt is cute."

I looked around. Who was in a striped shirt?

*You've got to be kidding.*

"Benny?" I asked, incredulous.

Benny perked up at the sound of his name.

*That scrawny little twerp?*

I laughed, bitterly. He wouldn't have any popularity at all if it wasn't for me.

"What?" Sherrie insisted. "He has a nice smile!"

Benny. Benny! Jesus Christ.

"Isn't he your friend?" asked Emilia.

*Make them understand.*

"Yeah, I guess, but you're barking up the wrong tree there because he doesn't like girls." There were some giggles, and it was clear everyone could hear, so I continued. "He's a nice kid and all, but he's a faggot. Isn't that right Benny?"

Benny froze. He had heard me alright, and I stared him down hard. Daring him to challenge it. Daring him to accuse me as well. To bring up our time together the previous summer, squeezed into that old wooden spool in his backyard. Sharing secrets, holding hands, tickling each other's bodies, tasting the sweat off each other's necks. Running in sprinklers and then feeling each other's erections over our swimsuits. All of it. Even pushing him away at the end of the summer, telling him we were "too old" for that shit anymore, seeing the hurt in his eyes, trying to hide the pain in mine.

*You're not a fag, Jimmy.*

Wasn't I?

*You can prove you're not. If he runs his mouth.*

"Come on, Jimmy," Benny said eventually, his voice breaking. "Don't be mean."

Before anyone could notice that wasn't exactly a denial, Dale's dad sauntered up with a long wooden dowel.

"Piñata time!" he said, oblivious to the drama in the air. "Birthday boy first!"

The kids formed a circle with nervous energy. Finally, Dale forced a smile as his dad placed a blindfold on his head and spun him around. I was reminded of my fantasy from several nights ago.

*You're a Goddamned prophet, Jimmy.*

The kid took a swing and missed the giant paper mâché Slimer entirely. There were a few chuckles at this. He got to try again, this time making contact. Weakly.

Some kid I didn't know the name of went next. He didn't do much better.

*You're gonna pulverize that thing. Just imagine it's Dale's face.*

Benny's never going to forgive me.

*So what. You told the truth.*

Zach went third. He was pretty athletic and I expected a big hit, which he delivered. Not enough to drop any candy, but enough to dissipate any lingering tensions and get the crowd into the competition. He got some hoots and hollers.

Vicki followed, and missed her first hit so badly she fell onto the grass, laughing.

Someone tapped me on the shoulder. It was Dale.

"Hey," he whispered. "What's wrong with you today?"

*Why does everyone keep thinking there's something wrong with you, Jimmy?*

"Just enjoying your party, Dale."

"Really? Because you seem angry. Your teeth are clenched. And every time you look at me it's like you want to wring my neck."

*Perceptive little fuck, ain't he.*

"Alright, if you must know," I hissed between those accurately-observed teeth, "I got your coded message, asshole."

Dale put on a convincing air of confusion. "Message?"

I whipped out the page of *The New Haven Herald Jr.* from my back pocket, complete with my scribbled cipher key and translated text, and shoved it against his chest, holding it there with my hand. I leaned in closer so my soft, tight voice could echo in his head.

"You think I'm not smart like you, because I didn't go to your fancy high-IQ school, and I didn't skip a grade, and I don't own a computer or any of that bullshit. But I'm not an idiot. I will not tolerate you fucking with me, you little shit. Watch your back and stay away from Emilia." I shoved him backward a little, enough to show I was serious but not enough to be noticed by anyone around us, as they were all enthralled and distracted by the great Slimer beating.

"Jimmy, you're up!" called Mr. Dunkle cheerily. He hadn't noticed the tension between me and his kid. Or maybe he had, and that's why he was getting me away from him. Either way, I was done talking to that prick, possibly forever. Hell, this might be my very last moment in this backyard.

*Until you sabotage the treehouse steps.*

I was blindfolded and spun around. The thick dowel rod felt potent in my hands. The crowd began to cheer their support. They were with me. They wanted me to succeed.

*You can do this. Picture it.*

I couldn't see anything. Just blackness. And then, as if gaining a rudimentary x-ray vision, the blobby green shape of Slimer appeared before my eyes. The ghost of a shape, anyway. The ghost of a ghost.

I laughed. This would be a piece of cake.

But the ghostly shape wasn't done forming. It began to change and morph into different ghostly faces, first Mom, then baby Madeline, then settling on Dale. An ugly, green, distorted caricature of my nemesis, swaying back and forth in the breeze, surrounded by an undulating sea of black insects.

*Destroy him.*

My grip tightened on the two-inch maple rod. My forehead was sweaty. I flashed back to the time I had hit the game-winning home run in little league by slicing my bat through the air with the force of Indy's whip. I could do that again. I focused on the ghostly image of Dale's head, wound up my swing, twisted my midsection, lunged forward with my left foot, gave a primal scream, and swung with everything I had within my body and soul.

At the last second, the blindfold slipped down, and I saw not the piñata but Dale's dad right in front of me. He had a stupid, shocked expression on his face, and I knew I couldn't stop the swing even if I had wanted to. The rod cracked across the left side of the man's jaw with such force that I both felt and heard the bone splinter and explode against the makeshift bat. His front teeth were ripped out of his head in a pulpy mess—a lead pipe shattering a jar of chunky salsa.

As I watched the half-faced Mr. Dunkle fall to the ground in a sort of sick slow motion, I heard gasps and wails of horror around me. I became vaguely aware that I might get in trouble for this. Especially if the bastard died.

I dropped the rod. The screams were louder now. I was so transfixed by the blood and guts oozing out of Mr. Dunkle's face onto the grass that I hardly registered someone shaking me. Then I felt the blindfold being yanked from my eyes.

It was one of the kids I barely knew. And he was smiling.

"Nice hit, man!"

I blinked. I looked around. The blindfold had never slipped. The sounds around me had been shouts of joy. I had sliced the stuffed piñata clean in half. The ground was covered not in the blood and teeth of Dale's father but in Dum-Dum suckers and Hershey's Assorted Miniatures.

*They were cheering for you, Jimmy.*

A rush of excitement surged through my body. I glanced around at the small crowd. Most of the kids were starting to collect the fallen treats, but Benny's eyes caught mine. His head was cocked like a curious cat. I couldn't read his expression. He didn't seem mad, exactly, or even hurt. It was more like he didn't recognize me. It was irritating. Then, infuriating.

"What are you looking at?" I asked.

He opened his mouth to speak, but then his eyes darted to Emilia, who was walking towards me. With a wry smile, I knew what I had to do.

"Jimmy," Emilia began, but before she could finish, I pulled her into me and kissed her firmly on the mouth. It was electric. I was momentary lost in her smell, the taste of her ChapStick, the light tickles of red wig hair on my forehead, the feel of her body pressed against me, all of it. And as an extra, delicious bonus, I knew Benny was watching.

*A man takes what he wants.*

I broke the embrace and grinned. There were some woos from the kids around us, most notably from Vicki and Sherri, as if I was Zack Morris kissing Kelly Kapowski on *Saved by the Bell.* I glanced back at Benny, defiant, and caught him looking down at his shoes.

*Jealous, homo?*

I turned to Emilia, expecting her to look impressed. Maybe even swooning. But her expression was inscrutable. Shock, sure. But...good shock?

*Of course.*

Is she smiling? She's smiling, right?

*It doesn't matter.*

The voice was right. It didn't matter. None of this bullshit mattered. It didn't matter that Dale and his parents were giving me a stern look. Or that his little sister Debbie had her hands over her eyes. Or that Marco and Zach were glaring at me so strangely. Or that Benny seemed like he was about to cry. It was all so meaningless. I just wanted to smoke a cigarette with Pax in front of the Black House and make fun of the janky cars that would pick up Dale's party guests.

I laughed out loud. I was better than *all* of these losers.

"Thanks for the party, Dale," I said. "I'm out."

I flipped off the crowd, laughed with icy bitterness once more, and strode out the backyard with my head held high.

# Five

I decided to go straight home after leaving the party, which turned out to be a lucky call. As I walked in the front door I caught the tail end of a message being left on our answering machine. It was Dale's mom droning on about "Jimmy's strange behavior" and claiming to be worried about me. Mom was home but must have been napping or feeding Madeline upstairs and hadn't picked up the phone. It was a tape-based answering machine so I erased the message to make sure mom never heard it. Not that I was particularly ashamed of my behavior—or, at least I told myself I wasn't—but I didn't feel like being lectured. I didn't feel like much of anything.

"Is that you, Jimmy?" she called down.

I didn't answer. I flipped on the TV instead. HBO was playing some new Danny DeVito movie, but I wasn't in the mood. I wanted something violent. Maybe *Robocop* would be on later. After a few minutes I went upstairs.

"How was the party?" Mom asked from her room. She was sitting in a rocking chair nursing Madeline. I hadn't seen the chair before. Where did it come from? Ah, who cared.

"Fine," I said, averting my eyes. Breastfeeding was so gross. I thought they said Madeline would need bottles instead. Formula, I could handle.

"There's stew in the fridge."

"I'm not hungry." I wasn't. Which was weird. I didn't eat at the party and wasn't sure I'd eaten anything today at all.

"Mike's not going to be coming around anymore," she said.

I rolled my eyes. I had heard that before. She probably pissed him off again or kicked him out, but would call him back the second she needed diapers or some money.

*Jesus, lady. Sleep with him, don't sleep with him, who gives a shit.*

I don't know how I'll become a man without beating Mike at chess.

*Maybe you'll have to kill someone.*

"You need a shower," Mom said.

"Fine."

I didn't understand why she was so obsessed with me showering all the time. I never had to shower every day when I was younger, even when I was covered in dirt from playing outside. Was I really so much smellier as a teenager?

I stared at myself in the bathroom mirror. I looked different. Older in the face, perhaps. I didn't have stubble yet or anything, but there were crease lines around my eyes and mouth that I hadn't noticed before. My expression was weird, too. Like, I know I wasn't smiling, but it sort of *looked* a bit like I was smiling. Trying to hold back a smirk, at least.

*You're the man, Jimmy.*

I stared into my own eyes as I slowly removed my black t-shirt. I pretended I was taking someone else's shirt off as I did it. Benny's? Emilia's? Hard to say. But I bit my lip coquettishly when I was done, rubbing my fingers over my chest and nipples as I refused to break eye contact.

*Hey, handsome.*

I noticed some red spots on my chest. Mosquito bites, maybe. Or pimples? I wasn't sure. They didn't itch, but I scratched them with my nails anyway. It felt good.

I leaned into the tub and started the water. As it warmed up, I repeated my virtual mirror strip tease with my jeans and briefs. I eyed myself up and down. It wasn't a boy's body, but a man's. A man with agency and power and purpose. I could even see some muscle definition in my abs and along my upper arms.

There were a few more red spots on my legs. I scratched them, too.

I stared into my eyes once more and smiled. Or did I? I could *see* the smile. A full, attractive, seductive smile. A man's smile. I wasn't trying to smile, and couldn't feel the smile on my face, but it was clear as day in the reflection.

*People will follow that smile, Jimmy.*

The mirror was beginning to fog up, so I flipped the diverter and stepped into the shower. As the hot water cascaded over me, I replayed the afternoon's events. I was delighted to see how heroic I came across in the movie of my mind. I told off the traitors. I vanquished the green ghost. I even got the girl. Sure, Dale was pissed, but the others either wanted me or wanted to be me. I'd be the talk of the school. The badass. The rebel. The hero.

I had worked myself into a state of arousal by the time I got to my bedroom. I used the new lock Mike had installed and went right under my covers. I replayed the Emilia kiss over and over, then started thinking about the next time we'd be together, and how I could try an open-mouthed kiss like they do in the movies, or finally bite that collarbone.

My thoughts drifted to Benny, that beautiful, stupid face of his. And then the look of pain in Dale's eyes. And then Mr. Dunkle's chin cracked and splayed open on the grass. And then I saw myself standing there with the large bloody dowel rod, panting over his body, as if witnessing the carnage as an observer. Damn I looked amazing. So tall and strong, with sweat glistening off my forehead in just the right way, and a tear in my black t-shirt that showed some of my own perfect collarbone. And...

Something happened. I felt...oh my God. The thing Mike had warned me about.

Turns out I didn't need chess or murder to become a man. I just needed puberty.

I pulled back the comforter and gasped.

This can't be real.

*Of course it's real.*

What had come out of my body wasn't like liquid soap at all. It was a thick, maroon-colored tar. The substance covered my torso and my right hand. And it appeared to be moving, undulating on its own somehow, like fudge starting to boil on the stove.

I leapt out of bed and frantically tried to fling the substance from my skin. When that didn't work, I grabbed dirty clothes from the floor and used them as makeshift towels. The tar transferred to the clothes but remained on my skin as well, persistent and sticky as molasses. What the hell had come out of me.

*It's all real.*

There was a knock on the door.

I jumped. But it wasn't my bedroom door, thank God. Someone was out front.

"Jimmy, get the door please!" called Mom.

"Uh, I'm not dressed!"

"Then throw clothes on and get the door right now! I'm changing a diaper!"

I looked at my hand. The tar was mostly gone but the skin appeared stained as if from a permanent marker. A second knock snapped me out of my trance and I threw on an un-tarred pair of jeans and shirt, running down the stairs and opening the door before the person might leave.

It was Marco. He was pissed.

"What the hell is going on with you, Jimmy?"

How did he know? I flung my right hand behind my back. I didn't want him to see the stain.

"I'm, uh..."

*What's it to him?*

"Man, I've known you my whole life and you've never pulled anything like that. You know you're never going to be allowed back at Dale's. And I'm sure Benny never wants to see your ass again either. Oh, and what the hell was that with Emilia?"

"She's into me. What do you care?"

"Whether that's true or not, she sure didn't want to talk about what happened, even when the twins wouldn't shut up with questions. She was embarrassed and wanted to get out of there, but had to stay til the end of the party for her mom to pick her up. I felt fuckin' sorry for her, dude. First time I've ever felt sorry for a chick. That's how much of a dumbass you were."

I realized Mom could probably hear our conversation so I pushed Marco out the door, following him onto the small porch.

"Look, you don't know anything about what I'm going through, alright?" I had my finger in Marco's face now, and could still see the maroon stain on my palm and wrist. He didn't seem to notice. "Dale was just using me for the paper. Pretending to be my friend. He's using you too. If you're too fucking dumb to see that, well, I guess that's why they keep holding you back."

"Man, can you hear yourself?"

*Hell yes we can.*

"Why don't you go suck Dale's dick, Marco?"

"Why don't you stop acting like a piece of shit?"

I grabbed the front of his shirt.

"How about you get your dirty black ass off my porch before I call the cops?"

That did it. Marco's eyes became saucers and he punched me across the jaw before I could even inhale. I flew sideways off the concrete and into a small bush. I could feel the branches scraping my back, tearing my shirt as I fell. But he wasn't done. A full year older than me and quite a bit stronger, he pulled me off the bush and practically threw me onto the front lawn.

"You son of a bitch," he spat, and was about to kick me in the stomach when I grabbed his foot and twisted it, causing him to fall awkwardly onto my legs.

*He's going to kill you unless you kill him first.*

I sat up, pain shooting through my battered back, and tried to extricate my feet from his body to pin him down, but he was quicker than me, and managed to attack first. He sat on my crotch and attempted to punch my face again, but I grabbed his arm, pulled it toward my mouth, and bit down hard.

*Now* I was hungry.

He screamed in pain and jumped off me, floundering backward a bit, trying to flee but falling on his ass instead. I pounced, finally having the upper hand, and tackled him to the ground. I punched his chest and his right arm, but he blocked me from any direct hits to his face or head.

*Crush his skull, damnit! It's him or you!*

I tried once more but was blocked.

*Rip his eyes out of their fucking sockets, Jimmy! Squeeze them until your hands run with blood!*

Marco managed to knee me in the crotch. The pain was intense. I hadn't realized I'd been erect.

I fell to Marco's side and once again he straddled me, this time grabbing my t-shirt with both hands as if he planned to shake some sense into me. But as we stared at each other in anger, his expression cracked, and the hate drained from his face.

"Who...*are* you?" he almost whispered. I could see his gaze darting from one of my eyes to the other, intensely focused, prying. Then he gasped and jumped off of me.

"I..." I began, but the wind had been knocked out of me.

"*Who the fuck are you?*" he said, louder this time as he backed away. Then, once more, screaming, almost unhinged. "*WHO IN THE FUCK ARE YOU?!*"

Marco staggered onto the sidewalk. Then he ran toward his house.

I coughed a couple times, inhaled, and managed to get to my feet. The left side of my face hurt. I rubbed it cautiously.

What did Marco mean?

*He only knew the kid version of you. You're growing up. You're a different person now, Jimmy.*

He seemed scared.

*He should be.*

I walked to the center of my street and gazed down the block. I could see Marco's place. Benny's and Dale's as well, if I squinted a bit. The Black House at the end of the street, too, staring me down, though it was just a dark smudge at this distance.

I started to imagine a future without my friends.

Wouldn't I miss Marco and Benny? I couldn't remember a time when we weren't close. I'd even miss Dale, if I was being honest. Pax, Derek and T-Too were hardly an upgrade.

*Your new friends respect you. They like you. They're never going to be disappointed in you. They won't hold you back.*

Maybe.

*Don't deny who you are.*

I chuckled darkly. Who in the fuck was I, indeed.

I wiped some blood from my nose onto my left sleeve. Such a thing would have freaked me out last year. Not anymore.

A baby was crying in the distance. Probably Madeline, though I couldn't be sure. Not worth taking the chance going back inside. Besides, I didn't feel like explaining why I looked beat up.

I grabbed my bike from behind the house and rode down the center of Chennault, watching the Black House get larger and larger in my field of view. It was risky, given that I'd have to bike right past Dale's house and there might still be people around. But no, there weren't any unusual cars that I could tell. Everyone had left. Maybe my actions had made things clear out in a hurry. Or maybe I was losing my sense of time again.

Part of me was hoping Pax would be there, and he was. Just him.

I saw his cigarette smoke before I saw his shape. He was leaning against the front porch as if he'd been expecting me.

"Hey, Pax."

"You look like shit, Jimmy," he said. He had hardly glanced at me.

"Got in a fight."

"You want a cookie?"

"Sure."

Pax shot me a contemptuous look, then shook his head. I realized too late that his comment had been intended as an insult. There were no cookies.

I set down my bike and walked over to where he

was standing. Trying to be cool, I leaned against the house as well. The old wood felt good and cold against my aching back.

Pax offered a cigarette. I took it, lit it with my trusty Bic, and inhaled deeply. No coughing this time.

"You've been in there," he said. A statement, not a question.

"Yeah."

"Spent the night."

"Yeah."

Pax furrowed his brow and took a puff on his own cigarette.

"Then," he continued after a moment, "you started seeing things. Are still seeing things."

I froze. How the hell could he know that?

"And the voice," he went on. "You hear the voice, too."

Until that moment, I had been holding out hope that the dark voice was my own personality. Or at least I was lying to myself that it was. But it couldn't come from my mind alone if Pax heard it, too.

"Uh huh." I meant to sound strong, but it came out as a whisper.

Pax studied my face. His deep blue eyes were trying to bore holes into my brain.

"But you heard the voice first, didn't you. Before you entered."

I nodded. Trying to speak was pointless now.

Pax took another long drag, then stared off into space for a bit. I was trying to summon the courage to ask a question when he started up again.

"Do you remember a Black kid over on Stevens named Isaac? A year or two older than me, with small, fucked-up ears?"

I did remember him.

"Yeah, he used to hang out with one of Benny's older brothers." I had remembered seeing them smoke cigarettes by the Black House, just as Pax and his crew did today. Sometimes they'd give Benny and I shit as we walked by.

"But you don't see him around anymore."

"No, I guess not."

"He's in jail."

"Juvie?"

"No, real jail. Prison. He shot his dad in the face."

"Holy shit." I vaguely remembered rumors about such a thing, but no one had confirmed it, not even Benny.

"It was a year-and-a-half ago. They kept it kinda quiet, given that he was still a minor, and his dad didn't live in here in New Haven or nothin'. The dude was just coming by to give Isaac a damned birthday present."

"Did they get into an argument or something?"

Pax shook his head. "No, that's just it. Isaac had planned it out. He resented the shit out of his dad and thought he could kill him and get away with it. Claimed he could shoot him dead legally if he thought it was a burglar. Learned about it from his uncle. Some Detroit dentist back in the '20s proved it—it's called 'Castle Doctrine' I think. But Issac was sloppy. Greedy. It wasn't enough to kill his old man, oh no. He had to read him the riot act first, at gunpoint. Isaac was yelling so loud he didn't hear his mom come in the back door. She heard everything. So when the gun went off, she knew it wasn't an accident. Turned her own son into the cops. It was an open and shut case, even though they never found the gun."

"They convicted him without a murder weapon?" I had seen enough *L.A. Law* to know cops almost always needed to find the weapon.

"Yep. I was there when the cops took him away. He was screaming 'you said we'd get away with it!' over and over again. Some thought that 'we' meant him and his mom, ya know? Like, they had planned it together or something. But I knew the truth. He was talking to the voice."

A chill shot through my neck like an ice pick.

"Had you talked to him about it?"

"Nah," Pax said. "But I had already spent my first night up there at that point. Hell, I've heard that voice since I was ten. Even before it talked to me, I knew this place was magic. I'd walk over as a kid and stand in front and let the house just wash over me. I memorized every crack, every board, every nail. If you gave me a black crayon I could draw it in my fuckin' sleep."

The building creaked behind us. The wind, maybe.

"Mostly I'd stare at those upstairs windows. Especially that one." He pointed to the left room, where the mattress had been. "I had a feeling that if I concentrated hard enough I could make a light go on in there. After a while I was certain I was seeing one. So, I broke in. Just like you did. Spent the night."

"With Derek and T-Too?"

"Nah. They've hung out up there but it doesn't speak to them. You and I are special."

"Special," I repeated.

"You've felt it, right? There's a power inside you that wasn't there before. You don't take shit from anybody now. Not even me. Christ, look at you." Pax laughed. "The Jimmy I knew wouldn't fight back if he was getting his ass kicked. Now you're the one kicking ass."

Pax seemed almost proud of me. It felt good.

*Damned good.*

I tried to take a victory puff from the cigarette but it had burned out. I tossed it on the grass rather than lamely trying to relight it.

"How many kids do you think have been up there?" I was thinking of the different handwriting on the wall.

"Don't know, don't care," said Pax. "But think about who you know in town who has power. Money. A hot wife. They know they're the shit and treat others like shit to get their way. They're winning the fucking game, Jimmy."

I imagined some of the older bullies in my life, like Mr. Gilbert at school. How long had this house been vacant?

"I know you might be freaked out," he said. "I get it. But it's worth it."

He was right. Sure, the hallucinations were a pain, but I had felt more alive in the past few weeks than any time in the previous thirteen years. It felt tasty as hell to embarrass Dale. To kiss the girl. To tell off Grandma. To hit that bastard Marco. To be a goddamned man for a change.

"Life is like Nintendo, you mean."

"Oh?" he asked.

"Like in *Double Dragon*. You get points for fighting, not running. It's how you win."

Pax nodded. "Now you're catching on."

*Great things are coming for you, Jimmy.*

I had no doubt.

"But, the moral of your story is not to let the voice take over completely, right? So you don't end up like Isaac?"

Pax flashed me a twisted smile. There was a fire behind his blue eyes I had only seen once before, as his shoe stomped my face into the ground.

"No, moron. The moral of the story is not to get caught."

# Six

I woke up late, angry and horny as usual. It had been days since I'd left my bedroom except to eat and shit. After a quick shower to clear my head I decided I needed to get out of the house. I didn't know where I would go, since I was sort of on the outs with most people I would hang out with, and didn't really feel like being around anyone anyway. School was going to start up in a couple weeks so I'd be surrounded by those assholes soon enough whether I liked it or not. Might as well enjoy the me-time while it lasted.

Mom called out the window to me as I was biking down the driveway, but I pretended not to hear. I bet she wanted help with something. Too bad, bitch. Call Mike. Madeline ain't my problem.

I didn't want to ride around our subdivision, especially with the risk of running into Marco or Dale or even Benny. Instead, I rode downtown, then on some side streets. I think I went past the village limits here and there but I wasn't sure. No particular direction I was aware of. But perhaps my subconscious had other ideas, as after an hour or so I found myself in front of Kat's house.

It was a weekday, which meant there was a decent chance her dad was at work. Camp season had ended, so Kat was likely home.

*Go show her what you're made of, stud.*

I wiped sweat off my forehead. It was close to noon, and the August sun had been beating down on me during the entire morning ride. I probably smelled awful.

*She won't care.*

What about Emilia?

*First things first.*

I stared at the house for a bit. I needed to know she was alone before I knocked. Even with my budding self-cockiness I didn't think I could handle a parent answering the door. Hell, I didn't want to be seen at all.

I walked my bike up the grass of the side yard. It was a single-story home with a fenced-in back which aligned to the rear of the house. Did Kat have a dog? If so, I should probably stay on this side of the chain link.

Softly setting the bike on the ground, I risked peeking in the nearest window. It was a combination kitchen and dining room, but you could see the living room beyond it, too. No one was around. The lights were off, but that didn't mean anything this time of day. Someone could still be home.

A car drove by and I felt very exposed. What if someone reported a peeping tom?

*You have to try the back windows. Where the bedrooms are.*

I peered through the fence for evidence of a doghouse or dog toys. Finding none, I took a deep breath and opened the gate. As I turned the corner, I saw a stone patio in back and an old charcoal grill, and a back door with a broken screen door hanging off its hinges. Unlike the front, which had been recently mowed, the back lawn hadn't been touched in ages. I guessed they didn't do a lot of entertaining back there.

I pressed my body tight against the house to avoid being seen, flipping my ballcap backward so I could get as close as possible. I cautiously peered into the first window I came across. It was a bedroom, but not a girl's. There were men's clothes strung about and a giant Don't Tread On Me flag hanging on one wall. Thankfully, it was as empty and silent as the dining room.

I continued on, aware that I was getting further from my bike, my escape route—and also further from any plausible deniability if I had been caught. If I had been observed looking into a front window, I might have been able to lie and say I had knocked first but no one had answered, and had just glanced in to confirm no one was there. But that excuse doesn't work in a backyard. Especially one behind a fence.

Still, I had come this far. Adrenaline fueled me to the next window, which turned out to be a bathroom. Also empty, though with the light on.

*Maybe you just missed her showering.*

The last of the three back windows would be Kat's bedroom. I hadn't been in there, of course—Kat and I had hung out on the couch, not her room. But it was the only possibility left.

I was aware of some shimmering gnat hallucinations in my peripheral vision and ignored them.

*I bet she'll be naked.*

No, she won't.

*I bet she'll be excited you're looking at her.*

Maybe.

I walked past the back door, ducked down below the window, staying as close as possible to the siding, and slowly elevated my head to peer inside.

Kat was on her bed, propped on a pillow and sort of lying on her stomach, listening to music on a Sony Walkman with large gray headphones. She was wearing white cutoff jean shorts and a white t-shirt which showed off her slightly tan, freckled skin. She couldn't see me, as her headboard was against the far wall and she would have had to turn all the way around to face the window, so I was safe to stare at her legs as she fluttered them at the knees in tempo to a song I couldn't hear.

*She's all yours, Jimmy.*

I was so transfixed by the sight before me that I didn't register the back door opening.

"What the hell?" I heard.

I turned to see a large, muscular, beer-bellied man in an auto mechanic's uniform glaring at me from three yards away.

*Ha,* chuckled the voice. *Run.*

But the fence gate, and my bike, were on the other side of the man. I was trapped.

"I..." I began, but there was nothing to say. The man's face visibly darkened and his eyes narrowed to slits. He was putting together that I was staring into his daughter's room and was preparing to kick my ass.

Without delay, I bolted to the other side of the house, hoping to find a second gate to the fence. There wasn't one. This turned out to be a blessing in disguise as Kat's dad pursued me, since I was far faster at jumping over a four-foot fence than he was. As I raced around to the front of the house, I nearly ran face first into a pick-up truck in the driveway. He had probably stopped home for lunch. But again, luck was on my side, as I could quickly squeeze through the space between the front of the truck and the garage door, and he couldn't, having to run around the back of the truck instead. This bought me a few precious seconds to reach the bike, lift it up, hop on in a single motion, and get a full pedal in before he could have grabbed me.

"Get back here you fuckin' pervert!"

"Sorry!" I gasp-shouted back. Then, in what I thought was an inspired bit of misdirection, yelled "tell Kat that Dave said hi!"

He didn't try pursuing me in his truck, thank God. And I was sure Kat never saw me, either. I imagined she was still kicking her legs to the music, oblivious to it all, until her dad would storm in demanding to know who "Dave" was.

Now, I know what you're thinking. You're thinking I learned my lesson, right? Was humbled by the experience?

Not a chance.

If anything, I came away feeling invincible. I had done an objectively despicable thing and gotten away with it. The voice was right. I was special.

So special that, after riding around for a while making sure I wasn't being followed, I felt I deserved a reward.

I headed for Andy's Party Store. I had only a few quarters in my pocket but that was more than enough for a Faygo and a 3 Musketeers bar. As I opened the cooler for the pop, I noticed the cans of Colt 45, too.

Lando Calrissian's beer. I knew I wasn't old enough to *buy* one, but that didn't mean I couldn't *take* one.

I glanced at the counter. Andy (er, Not-Andy) had his back turned as he was retrieving a pack of smokes for the customer before him. No one else was in the store.

*Go on. You've earned it.*

In a quick motion, I grabbed a 16-ounce can and shoved it in the back waistband of my jeans, sending a shiver up my spine as it touched my skin. I made sure my baggy t-shirt covered it up before grabbing the Faygo Rock n' Rye I had come in for. I figured it would be less suspicious that I was stealing if I still made a legit purchase. I grabbed the candy bar too, and approached the counter.

"Hey, I remember you," Not-Andy said. "You're the kid with paper. Look here." The man gestured a bit further down the counter. To my disgust, there was a handmade newspaper box with the town's only paper inside. Dale had expanded distribution again. Was nowhere safe?

"That's right," I said.

"Are you coming to collect? I think there's at least a dollar in there."

I suppressed a smile.

"Sure am," I said.

He shook out five quarters from the container, I thanked him, then used three of those quarters to buy the candy bar and Faygo.

Fuck you, Dale.

*Damn right.*

Not-Andy thankfully turned away after I checked out, so I didn't have to attempt a suspicious sideways crab-walk to the door to conceal the condensating bulge in the back on my shirt. I had asked for a plastic bag for the quasi-legitimate purchases, though, so once I was safe outside, I just put the beer in the bag as well and hopped on my bike.

If I was going to drink a "fuck you" beer I needed a suitable "fuck you" place to drink it. I couldn't risk taking it home. Luckily, New Haven High School was viewable from Andy's Party Store parking lot, and that felt fucking perfect.

It was a little after 1:00 p.m. and the day had gotten even hotter. I had never tasted beer before, but somehow I knew it would be the right day to try.

I rode down the long driveway into the back of the school. As expected, there were no cars, and no people. The combination football field and track seemed an inviting place for a drink, so I rode right up to the metal bleachers and took a seat.

I started with the 3 Musketeers bar and the Faygo. I wasn't sure if I was putting off the adult beverage on purpose, to avoid getting in trouble if someone spotted me, or if I instinctively knew that malt liquor and chocolate wouldn't go well together. Eventually, though, it was time.

I inspected the can. Looked just like the commercials. It felt like a Coke can in my hand, except it was 16 ounces instead of 12. I popped the top and took a tentative swig.

"Wow," I said out loud. Not because it was good. I couldn't believe this is what adults preferred to drink over pop. This musky dishwater was one of the finer things in life? You let me down, Billy Dee.

*Would you prefer a juice box, princess?*

I learned in elementary school that each part of the tongue was for tasting a different flavor. As this now-debunked theory went, the tip of the tongue was for sweet and salty things, sour flavors were captured on the sides, and bitter flavors were detected by the receptors on the very back. I reasoned that might be why college guys in movies seemed to be chugging beers straight back into the throat, bypassing most of the tongue. For the next sip, I tried that instead, and it did improve the experience. Barely.

Clouds had covered up the blazing sun, which was likely a good thing. I would have chugged the whole thing in minutes if the sky had been as intense as it was an hour ago. Instead I got to "savor" the bitter drink as I thought about all the ways my life had sucked in the past few months. I had been fairly past-obsessed in recent days, replaying every slight and disrespect I had ever received from others. Must be what it's like to be Mom, I thought. No wonder she's always pissed. But unlike her, I really *did* deserve so much more than I was getting. That little demon baby had to go, for starters. My friends better start pulling their weight too if they want me to spend time with them. And hubcaps for cymbals? What was I, a starving kid from a Sally Struthers commercial?

As the can got lighter in my hand, I alternated between feeling sorry for myself and confident in my superiority to everyone and everything, including this lame-ass school. I began to notice how shitty the football field looked. The uprights hadn't been painted in years, and there wasn't a proper scoreboard. Even the track was in bad shape, and track was the one sport we were supposedly known for. The bleachers were stained and old. There was garbage strewn about, too. No one gave a shit about this place, so why should I?

As I stood up, I felt...funny. I hadn't noticed any effects from the alcohol until this moment, but now my world was in a bit of haze. It didn't feel bad, exactly. In fact, I started laughing. It reminded me, not unpleasantly, of coming off a spinning carnival ride like the Tilt-a-Whirl or the Gravitron.

I tossed my garbage on the ground before inspecting the trash to look for quarters or anything valuable. It was largely candy wrappers, cigarette butts, that sort of thing. But something unusual caught my eye. A syringe. It still had an orange tip covering the needle, so it might never have been used. Looking back, it probably had an innocent explanation, like falling from the jeans pocket of a diabetic parent or something. At that moment, I saw it as evidence of New Haven's rot.

I put the syringe in my pocket, a trophy of the afternoon. Could be useful to fuck with Mom a bit. I could leave it in a conspicuous place to see if she gave a shit about my health anymore, or if I was a lost cause. Or I could give it to Madeline to play with.

As the clouds darkened I could feel the day turning

muggy. Wouldn't be a good idea to bike on Gratiot if it started to rain. Especially after 16 ounces of a beverage that "works every time."

I got on my bike, peddled about three feet on the gravel surface, and fell right over, skinning my right knee and elbow. It hurt like hell. But I just lay there and laughed for five solid minutes, on my side in the gravel and dirt, my bike between my knees, belly full of beer.

Eventually, I righted myself, crossed Gratiot, and rode to the north entrance of The Heights. As I approached Shirley Ann St., I saw two kids I thought looked familiar.

*Oh, this is your lucky day.*

"Hey there," I said, slowing my bike. "Tony and Jason, right?"

The kids froze. They remembered me. They thought I was a scary bully. Well, maybe I was.

"Answer me," I barked.

"Yeah, that's us," said the older one. I couldn't remember who was who.

A sly smile crept across my face.

"Hey, I got something for you."

The two brothers looked at each other. Probably deciding whether to run home to mommy.

"What is it?" the younger one asked.

With a showman's flair, I reached into my pocket and produced the syringe.

"It's...*cocaine*," I said.

The fear in their eyes. Holy shit. Those *Just Say No* commercials had done a number on us all. They thought merely being in a drug's presence would destroy their lives in seconds.

The boys started to run towards Stevens where they lived. I leapt off my bike and chased them down, waving the syringe like a madman.

"Come on, kids! Don't be pussies! Everyone's doing it!"

I almost caught the younger one. In my mind I planned to tackle the kid and make his brother watch as I plunged the empty needle into his arm. But I didn't feel so hot. My vision vignetted a bit and my stomach flipped. I dropped the syringe, put my hands on my knees, and vomited beer-drenched chocolate nougat right there in the road.

The boys were gone after I had looked up. I suppose I had to get out of there before they blabbed to a parent. I wiped my mouth, grabbed the dropped syringe, hopped back on the bike, and made it home.

"Jimmy! Where have you been? I need help with the baby!"

*Ignore her.*

I stomped upstairs to the bathroom and slammed the door.

For a while, I just leaned over the sink, uncertain if I was going to throw up again. Then I raised my head and stared at my reflection.

I looked years older than I expected. There were bags under my eyes. And my pupils were dilated something awful.

I was thinking of those Stevens kids. Such wimps. How were people so weak? How could they stand it? I wasn't weak. I was strong. I was brave.

I didn't remember taking the syringe from my pocket, but there it was, in my right hand. I had always averted my eyes when doctors gave me shots and wondered what the needle tip looked like. I pulled off the protective orange cap and examined the impossibly thin steel, about half an inch in length. Would you even feel it going into your flesh? I held it close to my eyes, fascinated by its elegance. It had a sloped tip, and you could tell it was hollow.

*Your pupils are huge, Jimmy.*

They were indeed. I could see them.

*Huge, cavernous holes.*

I felt time slow into a dreamlike slog. What was I doing?

*You've got this. Your hands are steady.*

In the mirror, I saw my hand rotating the syringe to align with my right eyeball.

*Don't look away.*

The needle tip was too close to focus on now. I'd

have to use the mirror to guide me.

*In and out. One time. To prove you're in control.*

It should be easy. As long as I didn't look away. The hole was wide enough. The needle could go right in and come out without touching the iris. It wouldn't take any unusual skill. Just bravery and a calm hand.

*Here we go.*

There was barely a millimeter between the needle tip and my eyeball when I noticed a reflection of the bathroom light on my eye. The pupil wasn't a hole. It was reflecting light, too. Jesus Christ. I had almost punctured my cornea.

I tossed the syringe away from me. It clattered against the toilet.

The dark voice laughed. It was the second time today it had laughed at me, but this time was different, dripping with derision and contempt.

"Jimmy!" yelled a frustrated voice from downstairs. "I need you to watch Madeline!"

"I don't feel well!" I shouted, voice cracking a bit. And I didn't. The adrenaline boost had made the nausea return with a vengeance. "I'm going to lay down!"

Would Mom even care that I was sick? Would she check on me? Probably not. She only worried about Madeline. Nothing mattered except for Madeline.

*Nothing matters at all, Jimmy.*

I found the syringe, wrapped it in toilet paper, and shoved it to the bottom of the garbage can. Then I stumbled to my room and passed out.

—

My eyes fluttered open a few hours later. I was on my back, fully clothed. I hadn't even removed my shoes. My head was pounding and my throat was dry. I could hear rain beating against my bedroom window. And a crying baby.

My dreams had been intense, filled with violence and blood and pain. Like the dream of torturing Dale, but far worse. I had to shake the images from my mind. I couldn't be capable of those things. No sane person could.

*But you could.*

The crying was getting louder now. Where the hell was Mom?

I stood up, a bit too fast, for it felt like my brain smacked against the front of my skull.

I wandered into the hallway. Nothing felt real. Was I delirious? Was this just another dream? Even the crying sounds were coming from everywhere all at once, both inside and outside my head.

"Mom?" I called out. No answer.

I went to Mom's bedroom. Madeline was in her crib, on her back, kicking her legs as she wailed. When she saw me, the crying intensified, becoming screams. We had once had a dementia-riddled old cat which had screamed like that. Shrill, ear-piercing yowls that wouldn't end. It had been Grandma's cat, Daisy. It was a relief when she had to be put down. It was the only way to shut her up.

"Mom!" I shouted. "Where are you?"

Lightning flickered in from the window. It cast ragged, shifting shadows on the walls like a failing florescent bulb.

I backed away from the screaming thing. Mom must be downstairs. How could she not hear this?

I had to lean on the railing to make it to the living room. My feet kept planting just a few inches off from where I expected them to. It felt as if someone had rigged the home with hydraulics.

Mom was on the floor with her mouth open, snoring. An empty wine glass and a tipped over bottle lay beside her on the carpet. She was in a bathrobe which was bunched up a bit, exposing her thighs.

*If only Pax could see her now.*

Shut the fuck up.

"Mom?"

The caterwauling continued upstairs.

I glanced at the clock. 7:30 p.m. That bathrobe meant she hadn't gotten dressed today. What the hell was the matter with her. I knew she didn't care about me anymore but apparently she didn't care what happened to her precious Madeline, either. At least we had that in common.

*You have to stop the screaming.*

I knew I did. Mom was useless. I was enraged. I had to take care of everything, didn't I. The only one of the family worth a damn.

A lightning flash triggered a new round of stabbing head pain. I shut my eyes tight for a moment and felt the ground shift underneath me like I was standing on loose gravel. When I opened my eyes, swirling black dots swarmed from my periphery and into the center of my vision. The gnat-like creatures weren't just floating in front of me this time, but seemed to be actively surrounding Mom's body, contouring to the shape of her, pecking at her cheeks, even flying into her mouth.

*You have to stop the screaming.*

I stumbled backward and almost fell, but I couldn't look away. I watched helplessly at some of the larger creatures began borrowing into the flesh of her pale thighs, leaving deep, black holes.

*You have to stop the screaming, Jimmy.*

The what?

Everything was in a fog now. But the voice was right. The screaming upstairs was getting louder. More alien. It was louder than the rain and thunder. It had to be stopped.

I raced up the stairs on all fours, panting and feral. When I reached Mom's room the screams were deafening. WAAAH. WAAAAAAH. WAAAAAAAAAAAH. There were undertones of an earthly growl in that voice. Something more animal than human. Desperate. Pleading.

I looked down at my hands. A man's hands. They were holding a pillow, one of many from Mom's bed. I hadn't remembered picking one up.

*No one will know it was you.*

WAAAAAH. WAAAAAAAAAAH.

The gnats were swarming the child. She was trashing about, all arms and legs, as if trying to shoo them away as they crawled over her skin. But those gnats were the least of her worries.

*Stop the screaming, Jimmy.*

None of this was real anyway, was it? It was only a nightmare. The sooner I did what the voice commanded, the sooner I could wake up.

*Do it.*

My fists were gripping the pillow so tight I was surprised my fingernails hadn't torn right through the fabric. I took a step toward the crib. Clusters of black holes now covered the creature's arms and cheeks. I raised the weapon.

Lightning flashed through the windows again. But this time, the flicker brought a moment of clarity. The gnats vanished. There were no holes in her exposed skin. Even the screaming seemed more human. She was just a small, helpless baby.

Madeline. My sister.

*Do it.*

"No," I whispered.

*Do it now.*

My head pounded. I let the pillow fall to the ground.

For the second time today, the voice had almost convinced me to do something awful—first to myself, then to a baby. What would be next? Pax' story of Isaac shooting his dad replayed in my mind.

I backed away from the crib. I needed to get Mom.

*I don't have to let you stop.*

The room appeared to twist and turn in on itself. In a flash, I was standing over the crib again, pillow in hand, ready to strike.

I willed my body backward, throwing the pillow across the room. I had to get out of the house.

I had made it down a single stair toward the front door when, *again*, I seemed to jump over seconds in time and was back at the crib, pillow in hand, this time already pushing it downward, smothering Madeline's face, her tiny arms and legs kicking futilely beneath me.

The gnats were all around me now, acting as giant

hands pulling me toward the crib, forbidding my escape. I was conscious but paralyzed. It took every ounce of strength I had to try to resist, to pull back, to break through the crushing embrace of the gnats. I attempted a scream but no sound came. But I tried again, and again, and soon I could hear my voice, and the grip on the pillow lessened, and I broke free, and found myself on the floor, screaming the loudest shriek of my life.

It was enough to wake Mom. She raced up the stairs, disheveled and confused.

"Jimmy, what the hell?"

I had stopped screaming. But Madeline had stopped screaming, too.

Mom followed my gaze to the crib. The pillow was still over the baby's face, but only partially, and, thank God, her arms and legs were moving.

"Damnit, Jimmy! You can't put a pillow in a baby's crib. What the hell is the matter with you? Don't you know *anything*?"

I felt my hands become fists without my consent.

*I don't have to let you stop.*

Another lightning crash bathed the room in harsh, angular shadows, and again there was a moment of clarity, everything frozen like a photograph. I saw Mom holding Madeline. I saw a laundry hamper in the corner. I saw the dresser topped with pictures of me from years ago. I saw the clock. The *time*.

There was a chance to end this.

And then I was on my bike, pedaling my heart out toward the Black House. I didn't remember leaving. Why couldn't I remember leaving? What had I done? But it didn't matter now. I was focused on a singular, obsessive goal.

I stared down the house as it got larger and larger, those top two windows staring right back at me, the giant, dark eyes of a violent soul. I was tempted to crash right into it at full speed. But the house wasn't my destination. And it knew it.

*You can't escape me.*

Oh yes I could.

It would be close. A left turn onto Clark, a half a mile at top speed, and I'd be free. A pancake, perhaps, but free.

The rain clouded my vision, and made the ground seem to crackle and undulate all around me. My head and heart were pounding. I feared I was going to pass out.

I remember approaching the stop sign and deciding not to slow down. If a car happened to hit me, I'd just get my wish a few minutes early.

Someone yelled "Jimmy!"

I was distracted. I lost control.

The next few moments are hazy.

I remember finding myself on the wet pavement, seeing my bike a few feet away. I remember an intense pain in my ankle as I stood to lift the bike up. I remember seeing the mangled back tire, knowing it wouldn't be rideable. I remember trying to run, only to crash down to the asphalt as my leg gave out.

It was a girl's voice who had called my name. Incredulous, I looked up to see the kid from the corner house staring at me, rain beating down on us both, soaking her little white dress. What the hell was she doing outside? And how did she even know my name?

"Why did you do that?" I howled at her. "You don't understand! You ruined everything! I could have made it! I could have ended it!"

*No you couldn't have.*

Far off in the distance I heard the whistle of an approaching train, cementing and mocking my failure. I buried my face in my hands, screaming "no" and "why" into them at the top of my lungs.

My vision began to darken, a movie fading to black. I barely understand what happened next.

A small hand touched my forehead.

A deep, wailing moan flooded my ears.

My legs began to tremble uncontrollably, which spread to my torso, my arms, and then my head, my body seizing and thrashing in the road.

I saw light. It was getting closer. Brighter.

I cried out for my mom.

# Seven

A doorbell rang.

The front door opened.

A muffled conversation followed, then footsteps.

It was daylight. I was in my bed, on top of the covers, in a clean t-shirt and pajama shorts. I had no memory of getting home or changing. Plus, there was a bandage on my right knee and, when I looked around, one on my right elbow as well. I could see some purple bruising on my ankle, too, but when I rotated it it didn't hurt much.

Mom knocked gently, then poked her head in.

"Jimmy?"

"Yeah, Mom?"

"Dale's here. I told him you were in bed but he was worried about you. Do you want to get dressed and come down for a bit? It's almost 11:00."

I couldn't believe it. Dale, of all people. Worried about me.

"Uh, yeah. Can he wait downstairs for a minute?"

"Of course. I'm going to put Madeline down for a nap."

"Alright."

A beat.

"How are you feeling?"

I wasn't sure how to answer. The last few days had been such a blur. I didn't know what had been real. My own actions seemed not to have been committed by me, but an actor playing me. Even my memories, fuzzy as they were, were from a third person perspective in my mind.

"Better, I think." And it was true.

"That's good."

Mom lingered a moment, as if she wanted to say more, then just slowly closed the door. I got up and threw on jeans and shoes.

Dale gave me a smile as I reached the living room. He was holding the PXL 2000 camcorder and a black plastic box.

"Hey," I said, uncertain.

"Hi, Jimmy. You doing okay?"

"Yeah, you?"

"I'm alright."

I knew I owed him an enormous apology but didn't know how to start. I also still didn't know why he was in my house, and the camcorder was making me nervous. He must have caught my worried expression and shook his head.

"Oh, no, I didn't bring it to make movies. I wanted to show you something. Can I plug it in?"

"Sure."

Dale fished an adapter out of his plastic box and fiddled with the back of our television for a bit. When he was done, he played the tape in the camcorder. The image was dark for a moment, and then flashes of lightning appeared. Based on the angle, I guessed the footage was taken from his bedroom window.

"I was getting b-roll of the storm, in case I needed it for a movie later. Cool, huh?"

"Uh, yeah."

"I had already stopped filming when I saw you riding your bike down the street. I watched you crash your bike on the turn. When you began screaming, I started recording again."

Interesting that his first instinct was to film me and not help me, I thought, though I suppose I wasn't his favorite person at that moment.

There was a break in the footage, and then there I was, lying on the ground. The shot was from far away, of course, and the PXL 2000's 8-bit resolution was so poor that you couldn't make out that it was me specifically. I was just a couple lighter grey pixels on a dark grey road. But it matched my memory. Guess it hadn't all been a dream.

"Now, watch this," Dale said, pointing to the right side of the screen.

As Dale panned his camera to show the Black House, the footage became scrambled, with giant waves of distortion filling the screen, undulating in a psychedelic pattern that was vaguely familiar. When Dale panned back to me on the ground, the distortion went away. Soon, Mom's car drove into view, the headlights illuminating my small, collapsed body. Dale caught her running out into the road, picking me up and carrying me to the car. The picture stopped.

"Your mom left your bike in the road," Dale explained. "I went out with an umbrella and dragged it back to my place if you want to fix it."

"Thank you," I said, touched, not just by Dale's thoughtfulness but at Mom coming to find me. "But, why did you want me to see this?"

"Remember when I said the footage we got at the Black House didn't work out? I thought it was a problem with the tape. Now I don't think so. The distortion only happened last night when the camera was focused on the house. And it was the same distortion that happened in almost all our footage of that day."

Dale took the previous night's tape out of the PXL and put in a different cassette labeled "bad." The images on the screen were unwatchable. You could hear us talking and laughing pretty well, but the visuals were all over the place. It occurred to me what it reminded me of.

"It's like trying to watch a scrambled cable channel," I said.

"Huh. Is it?"

"You never tried to watch Cinemax or Playboy?"

Dale looked horrified. "Of course not!"

Maybe when he was older, I thought.

But I had an idea.

With Dale's permission, we ran a coaxial cable out from his PXL adapter and into Mike's fancy descrambler box. The automated settings didn't help the image much, but Mike had mentioned something about horizontal sync being important, and fine tuning those buttons started to bring things into focus. It wasn't pretty, but the distortion was now intermittent rather than constant, and you could make out the house for the first time. It appeared different, though, as the siding didn't seem to be black anymore, which I assumed to be a glitch related to all the settings we were tweaking.

"Let's rewind it and start from the beginning," Dale urged, so we did.

The video progressed more or less as I remembered filming it a couple months ago. We walked up to the front. I asked if Dale could zoom in to read the writing on the upstairs walls, and he explained the camera didn't have a zoom. But something was different.

"Wait, rewind that," I asked.

Dale did.

"Do you see it?"

Dale's eyes widened. "The front door. It doesn't look boarded up."

"But it was. I'm sure of it. It has been since we were kids."

The video continued as we walked around the back. Again, the house wasn't quite right. The painted wood siding was lighter in the video than real life, and even with the terrible picture, the place simply looked newer. Even the vegetation around the house appeared to have changed. And the giant "No Trespassing" sign neighborhood kids had ignored for years was missing.

At the back of the house, I tried the locked door, and began my fake television reporter narration.

"Folks, we're standing here in the back yard of what neighborhood kids call the Black House..."

We watched until the end, looking closely for details about the house that didn't match reality. Unfortunately, the final minute consisted of me talking in the center of the frame, the house relegated to the background.

After I had completed my monologue, you could hear Dale laughing, and then panning the camera to the left before shutting it off. A frame there, in that last second pan, stopped me cold.

"Play that back."

Dale rewound and replayed the final couple of seconds. It was blurry, but it was definitely something.

"Is that..." Dale began.

"I don't know. Can you pause it right before the video cuts off?"

Dale shook his head. "No, there's no pause button I'm afraid. But if we recorded the signal onto VHS tape first, we could!"

I had to borrow another cable from the TV to daisy chain the system together, but after a few minutes I was able to record the input from the PXL, through the descrambler box, into the VCR, and back to the TV. It took a couple attempts to pause at just the right time. Once we did, even with the impossibly fuzzy picture, we both saw the same thing.

"I don't understand," Dale said in a near-whisper. "The tree we're looking at here doesn't exist. I'm sure of it."

"Yeah," I agreed. "And even if it did, we sure as hell would have noticed that body hanging from it."

—

Over the next hour, I confided in Dale part, but not all, of what I had been experiencing in the past month, including the night spent in the Black House, the dark voice urging me to do horrible things, and even the discussion with Pax about his own experiences, including being there when Isaac was taken away by the cops. I sanitized some of the past 24 hours, though, when I saw him getting freaked out. No reason to give the kid nightmares for life. I'd have enough of those myself.

"So I guess you were right with your story pitch," he remarked after a bit.

"How so?"

"That house," he said. "It's fucking haunted."

It was the first time I had heard the great Dale Dunkle use the F word. I laughed out loud. But he knew I wasn't making fun of him. I was impressed.

"Think we should write an article about it after all?" I asked. "Raise awareness, and all that?"

"Oh, you want back on the paper already?"

"I bet you never took my name off the masthead."

Dale smiled. "It's true. Didn't have the heart."

This appeared to remind him of something, and he produced the draft page of the paper that I had shoved in his face at the party. He smoothed out the folds and wrinkles and pointed to the "message" I had decoded.

"There's no pattern that can turn these letters into the message you thought you saw," Dale explained.

"Uh, I think I had convinced myself, or had been convinced, that it was a shifting cypher, so every few lines started with a different letter shift."

"But that would make no sense. You could make any series of letters say anything you wanted it to if you changed the shift cypher every line."

"I get that, now." I gave him a sheepish look.

Dale nodded with, I thought, a touch of exaggerated solemnity.

"So let's do it," he decided.

"Do what?"

"Write the article about the house. Though, I'm not sure how much credibility a kid's newspaper has. And grown-up journalists would never believe us."

It was true. I thought for a moment.

"You're going to think I'm nuts, but I think I know someone we can call."

I ran upstairs, grabbed a random copy of *The New Haven Herald Jr.*, and found the ad:

*Al Horner | Historical Restoration & General Contracting*

I held the phone sideways between our heads so Dale and I could both hear. Al answered on the first ring.

"Hey, um, Mr. Horner," I said. "It's Jimmy Logan and Dale Dunkle."

"Ah yes," he said. "From the paper."

We smiled at each other. *The paper.*

"Do you remember when you and I talked about old buildings? You said some places can be evil. Do you really believe that?"

"What's this about, kids?"

Dale piped up. "We're doing a story on a local haunted house."

"Why do you think its haunted?"

I wasn't sure how much I wanted to reveal. I settled on: "It's making people hear voices."

"Voices?"

"Well, *a* voice, anyway. It encourages certain individuals to do bad things."

The line was silent on the other end. Dale whispered, in a way he thought Al couldn't hear, "I don't think he believes us."

"No, I believe you," Al said.

"Okay."

"You guys are, what, 13?"

"Yeah," I said. Dale, who had just turned 12, didn't correct me.

"My dad passed away when I was your age," Al said. "I was an only child but a bit of a handful. My mom needed help, so we moved up to stay with her cousin Lin in East Lansing. Do you know where that is?"

"Sure," I said. "Michigan State." I didn't know much about college, but Big Ten sports were fun to watch. I guessed from Dale's confused expression that his Commodore didn't have any NCAA sports games.

"That's right," Al continued. "It was only supposed to be for the summer, but we stayed through the fall as well. 1978. They enrolled me in eighth grade, but Mom didn't want me alone after school, so I spent a lot of afternoons at the MSU Library where Lin worked. I was already quite obsessed with old buildings and local legends and all that on account of some recordings I had found of my grandfather's, so having access to a big college library just fueled my obsession further. And then students started going missing."

"At State?"

"Uh huh. It was weird. The papers didn't talk about it much, but Aunt Lin seemed to know *a lot*. See, Lin lived alone in this little house on Lexington, about five blocks north of campus. Mom slept upstairs and I had the finished basement to myself. But it meant I could hear every conversation Lin had in the kitchen or living room, on the phone or in person. Sometimes she'd be whisper-shouting things like 'you have to fix this!' or 'I've already told him to stay away.' Then at one point, a college kid showed up sobbing that he had stabbed his best friend because 'the tower' told him to. He wanted to destroy the building with dynamite."

I swallowed hard. This was hitting a bit close to home.

"So what happened?" asked Dale.

"Well, obsessive, nosy me started doing a bit too much research and asking too many damn questions. Lin freaked and kicked Mom and I out. We ended up back in Detroit. I don't think either of us have talked to Lin since. Though, obviously no one blew up the clock tower, as it's still standing."

"Do you think the tower was talking to your Aunt, too?"

"I don't know," Al admitted. "But it made an impression on me, along with my grandpa's recorded rantings and the books I was reading about schizophrenic serial killers. Since then, I've learned to *listen*. To believe local legends. And, to answer your earlier question, yes, to believe that some places can indeed be haunted. Or evil."

"What's the difference?" asked Dale.

"Well, I suppose a building that's haunted has an evil spirit inside. A building that's evil is itself a sort of spirit. What do you think you're dealing with?"

"We don't know," I said. "We think the house may have made a previous owner hang himself. But, I guess it's possible the person who was hung is haunting the place."

"Interesting," said Al. "Do you have an address? I can do some digging."

"There aren't any numbers on the house, but it's

right where Chennault ends at Clark. Does that help?"

"That'll do. Can you narrow down a time period for me?"

"Not really," I admitted. "I know it was originally owned by a farmer with the last name of White, and I don't think anyone lived there after him. It's been boarded up for decades at least."

"It might be hard with so little to go on," he said. "But if I find anything out, I'll send it your way."

"Thanks, Mr. Horner."

"Don't mention it. It was good to talk with you two. In the meantime, probably best to stay away from the place, okay?"

He didn't have to tell us twice.

—

For the record, I did apologize to Dale, sincerely, before he left that afternoon. I don't remember what I said exactly, and I'm sure it was inadequate given how I had behaved at his birthday party. Dale said he forgave me. I doubted I would have forgiven him if the roles had been reversed. I still didn't know how much of my behavior could be blamed on some supernatural voice, and how much was my own petty asshole insecurities. Either way, I wondered how far someone's compassion and empathy could extend to the person who did them wrong.

Mom and I had dinner together. It was pleasant, if a little awkward, like old friends who hadn't seen each other in years and weren't sure what they still had in common. I owed her an apology, too, and suspected she wanted to give me one as well, but neither of us went that far. I imagined it was hard for teenage boys to stay close with their mothers even under ideal circumstances, and these were decidedly not those. I was just grateful for the lack of raised voices, nagging, and eyerolls that had become our usual routine.

At the end of the meal she came over to my side of the table and gave me a little one-armed hug. It was the first form of physical affection she had shown me in more than a year. I sat there for a while afterward, remembering my childhood, when it was just me and Mom against the world. How had we both become so disappointed with each other all the time? I supposed we were both disillusioned at the distance between where we wanted our lives to be, and where we actually were.

As I lay in bed for the night, it occurred to me that it had also been the first full day in over a month without hearing the voice. I almost didn't want to think about this, for fear of jinxing it. But the voice didn't come back, even when I caught myself thinking the words "hello?" and "are you there?" I felt relief, and also a sense of loss. I thought about what might have caused it to abandon me. Had it been the little girl who had touched my forehead? Or had that been Mom? Whoever it was, did that action release the spirit? Or was an attempted suicide too much for the voice to bear? Nothing seemed to fit, and I drifted off with more questions than answers.

Then came the nightmare. Oh my God.

It started with a greatest hits reel of my recent misdeeds, but this time I was in the victim's point of view, and Pax played the role of Jimmy Logan. He forced a kiss on me at Dale's party, and punched me in my front yard, and tried to suffocate me while I lay helpless on my back in a giant, wooden cage. Then things started to turn around, and I was kicking a woman (was it Grandma?) down the stairs, and putting out cigarettes on the cheeks of a grade school boy, and bashing a stranger in the head with an aluminum bat. I started to have fun with it. I stopped being horrified. It became a sort of lucid dream, where I knew I had the power to change my actions and my surroundings. I immersed myself in unspeakable, cruel delights. Then I could hear the voice returning, far away at first, as if shouting at me from a distant cavern. I began to tremble as the voice got closer, louder, angrier.

*I'm not giving up on you, Jimmy.*

Jesus, make it stop.

*Because I fucking own you.*

The next thing I knew I was on the floor of my bedroom, panting. There were tears on my cheeks. It was daylight.

It had been a nightmare, sure. Deep down, though, I knew. Yesterday had been a reprieve, but the voice was going to find me again. It was going to make me do things. Maybe some of the dream's elements were glimpses into my actual future. It was only a matter of time.

I walked downstairs to the kitchen and dialed Dale on the phone.

"Good morning, Jimmy! What's up?"

I took a big breath. It was a big ask. But it was either this or the train.

"We have to destroy the house."

# Eight

Dale and I spent the morning at his place, planning. After he was fully on board, I decided to recruit Benny next. I hoped I hadn't sabotaged my friendship with Benny as much as I had with Marco, even with how I acted at Dale's party. I somehow felt Benny might be more likely to believe my story, too, especially when I shared what I knew about Isaac, his brother's friend. Still, I asked Dale to come with me to talk to him, perhaps to show that if Dale could forgive me, Benny could, too.

"You'll have to prove that you're genuinely, deeply sorry," advised Dale as we walked over.

"I am," I said.

"I know you are. But he's allowed not to want to talk to you. Now, or even forever. Apologizing doesn't mean anything if it's a quid pro quo for pretending nothing happened."

"What's a 'quid pro quo'?"

"It's Latin. Real, not pig. It means a favor in exchange for a favor."

"In other words, I need to apologize without any expectations for forgiveness, or it doesn't mean anything."

"Right."

I thought about fights Mom and Mike had had, where he angrily said things like "I *said* I was *sorry*" and she still refused to talk to him for a while. I had always assumed Mom was in the wrong, because you're supposed to accept apologies, aren't you? Mom herself never said she was sorry for anything, even when she should have been. But now I wondered if maybe Mike was in the wrong, too, for demanding forgiveness just because he asked for it.

We arrived at Benny's front door. I was too nervous to knock. Dale rang the bell, and Benny answered.

"Hey," he said, curtly.

"Can we talk?" I asked.

I must have looked like I was about to cry, because Benny's expression changed in an instant from guarded skepticism to puppy-dog pity. He stepped out onto the front porch and gave me an unexpected and undeserved hug. I caught Dale shooting me a look of surprise.

"Marco told me about the other day," Benny said after ending the embrace. "I don't think he's going to be as understanding."

"Can I tell you what's been going on?"

"Please do."

I did. We sat on his back porch and I walked him through it all. Dale chimed in near the end with confirmation about the distorted video footage, and what he had seen the night I tried to kill myself. Benny listened intently, wide-eyed, but believing.

"Do you think that house affects everyone?" he asked.

"What do you mean?"

"Like…you know."

Dale didn't get it, but I did. Benny was wondering if perhaps there was a reason his parents and older brothers were so cruel to him. Why his older brothers in particular seemed to enjoy causing him pain and embarrassment. I thought about all the times I had been there for Benny, consoling him when he had been bullied or beaten, telling him it would be okay and even, once, that I loved him. And then I replayed in my mind the look on his face when I destroyed him at Dale's party. I wanted to throw up.

"I don't know," I said, my speech weak. "I guess I hope so."

"Me too," he said.

Dale could sense that we were sharing a moment and asked to use the bathroom. After he was out of earshot, I promised Benny that I would never hurt him again.

"You can't promise that."

"Yes I can."

He just shook his head, smiling but sad. I reached over and held his right hand, squeezing it for a moment, before pulling it back.

"Jimmy, I believe you about the voice. I do. But part of you wanted to be an asshole, too. It's like my dad. When he drinks, he gets mean. Violent. Says and does horrible things he would never do sober. Mom once said that alcohol doesn't *change* who you are, it *reveals* who you are. What if, deep down, you *want* to be that guy?"

"And I'm only using the voice as an excuse?"

"Not that, really. Just that you were enjoying yourself. You didn't seem like someone being forced to be an asshole against their will."

"Just because it felt good in parts doesn't mean I want to feel that way again. It's why we want your help. And Marco's. And Zach's, too, I think."

"Zach's important," Dale said from the doorway. I wondered how long he'd been there. "Or, at least his dad is."

Benny realized we weren't just there to apologize.

"Help for what?"

We told him.

As Benny had predicted, Marco was the tougher sell. Not on the plan itself, of course. He loved the plan. His eyes got all sparkly and he started making a list of necessary items on a piece of paper. But it was harder for him to accept the idea of being friends with me again. "I'm still bruised up, you dick," he said at one point. And he was.

Eventually he agreed to help not out of loyalty to me, but "to the town." I told him we'd take what we could get.

"You really think a place can be evil, huh?"

"Yes," I insisted. "We talked to an expert in Detroit about it."

"Well, I suppose someone in Detroit will have seen

more shit than most," Marco said. "But you're going to have to do as I say for this to work. I don't want to hear any complaining when I'm barking out orders."

"I trust you completely," I assured him.

Marco narrowed his eyes. The feeling did not seem to be mutual. He rubbed his arm where I had bit him.

I thought Zach would be the easiest one to convince, given that he "owed me" the most and I had never cashed in, but when we called him, he was shocked at the request.

"You don't have to join us," I insisted. "It's better if you don't. It would just really, really help if you could buy us time if someone happens to call it in."

"I don't think I can buy you as much time as you need," Zach explained. "My dad has something called a Plectron device that turns itself on when there's a fire. I think it has battery backup too."

"No pager or anything, like doctors have?"

"No."

"Do all the firefighters have a Plectron?"

"I'm not sure. I don't believe so. I've heard my dad make calls when he's gotten an alert. He uses a private line in his office, calls one or two people, and they use a phone tree to reach the rest. Sometimes dispatch has called him on that line as well to make sure he heard the report. If they can't reach him, I assume they call the next guy on the list."

"But if they do reach your dad, *he* calls the next guy on the list?"

"I think so."

"How much do you sound like him?"

In the end, Zach agreed to try and turn down the volume on the Plectron, and ensure the private line was disconnected for a couple hours. He couldn't commit to impersonating a fire chief on the phone, though. Something about not wanting a felony on his record. I told him to do his best, and no matter what happened, any debt he had to me for saving his life from that giant mower would be long forgiven.

The hardest part of the plan was figuring out how

we could all be together at night. We ended up concocting a "sleepover" for the upcoming Friday where Dale, Benny, and Marco got permission to stay overnight at my place, but because we didn't want to be loud for the baby, we agreed to sleep in tents in my backyard instead. I was relatively certain Mom wouldn't leave the baby alone to check on us in the middle of the night, and of course we *would* be in the tents most of the night anyway even if she did. All parents gave permission, with a little pleading. "But it's one of the last weeks of the summer! Pleeeeease!" Mom was happy to confirm with all the parents that this was okay, since she was still thrilled we were getting along at all. She did cock an eyebrow at the enormous duffel bag Marco lugged over, but on the fly he came up with some bullshit about needing both his sleeping bag *and* all his favorite pillows, which, as a pillow hoarder herself, Mom accepted without question.

Since the rainstorm on Monday, the weather had been unusually hot and dry, and we were grateful the ground wasn't muddy. We set up two tents, side by side, with entrances facing away from my house. We figured this way the four of us could sneak out, walk behind the detached garage, and come out the side yard in a way unseen by any window in my house, in case Mom happened to be looking outside at the wrong time. We huddled together in the larger of the tents and prepared our strategy.

"I made a map," Dale revealed. He pulled out a graph paper pad with a decent overhead drawing of the Black House property, with Clark St. on one end and the woods behind the house on the other. "Each square on the paper is approximately two feet in length. I walked it after dinner before coming over."

"Huh," Marco said, impressed. "What's the big circle surrounding the house?"

"Ah," said Dale. "That's what I consider the safe zone. If we're outside this circle, we shouldn't get hurt by falling boards."

"Just don't ask him to figure out the circumference," I teased.

Dale beamed. "Are you sure? I have a super easy method!"

"We're good."

Benny piped up. "What's the plan if someone sees us?"

Dale pointed to his sketch of the woods. "That's the beauty of the property. If we run straight back, the house will shield us from view. Then we can run through the woods to the creek, follow it under the bridge, and end up in my backyard. If we think we're being followed, we could even sneak up into my treehouse."

Good thing I didn't sabotage it.

"Or," Benny said, "we could keep going up the creek and cross over at the vacant lot across from Jimmy's, right back into our tents where we've been 'sleeping' the whole night."

"That does mean we'd have to cross Chennault, which might expose us for a moment," I said.

Marco dismissed this concern. "By then, if anyone's out, they'll be looking in the other direction."

—

The plan was to rest a few hours and walk over to the house at 2:00 a.m., when we figured everyone would be asleep and off the road. But of course none of us could attempt heads on pillows. The adrenaline was too great. And, for me, there was the added fear that the voice would reach out in my dreams again. It was like having my own personal Freddy Krueger.

Dale's calculator watch started beeping, and we knew it was time.

Marco, Benny, Dale and I silently made our way to the road. Marco had his duffel, but the rest of us had nothing. The night was clear and the neighborhood felt deserted. The Black House was invisible this far away. The moon had already set, which let the overhead constellations shine. Stars sure seemed brighter back then. Or maybe New Haven in the late '80s had less light pollution than any city I've lived in since.

"See the big sideways W?" whispered Dale, pointing.

"Yeah."

"That's Cassiopeia. The bright star it's sort of pointing to is Polaris. Due north. So we know the house is directly underneath that star."

Marco chuckled. "Does everything have to be a lesson with you, Dale?"

"Just making sure we don't get lost."

Dale smiled at me. I smiled back. He was just trying to break the tension. I realized that this might be the first time he had ever done anything, well, bad. Certainly anything illegal. And he was doing it, in large part, out of loyalty and friendship to me. A friendship I had actively tried to destroy only days ago. I hoped I was worthy of it.

The house faded into view as we got closer. My heart began to beat stronger in my chest. There was no turning away now.

"We should go to the backyard," Marco advised. "In case a car passes."

We snuck behind the house. Marco got out his flashlight and opened the duffel bag. Methodically he removed two quarts of lighter fluid, several Bic lighters, three cans of Aqua Net hairspray, and a variety of sparks-shower firework cones.

"These are silent," he had explained in the tent. "No whistling noises or explosions. Nothing flying in the air. But they last a long time."

Dale had given Marco a handful of draft pages from *The New Haven Herald Jr.* to use as kindling. I had expressed concern that such pages might be used as evidence against us, but Marco assured me that the paper would be burned into ash so thoroughly that nothing would remain.

"I like the poetry of it," Dale explained. "The Paper helps take down the Haunted House. Just as you wanted, Jimmy!"

Indeed. Though I was starting to feel a tension spasm developing in the back of my neck. This mission was not without risk.

Benny and I were tasked with applying the lighter fluid. We each took a container, doused the rear first, then separated, Benny taking the east side of the house and me taking the west. We had a couple pages to wad up as Marco had directed, which we would shove inside rotted holes and cover with more butane. Marco had told us to spread the fluid evenly across the lower couple of feet of wood siding, making sure not to leave any gap in coverage. We made it to the front of the house at the same time, and emptied the rest of our cans onto the wooden porch and the boarded windows.

"It's done," Benny confirmed as we joined the others. Marco and Dale were already placing several firework cones a few inches from the back of the house, using rocks to secure and angle the cones toward the most promising areas. The idea was to concentrate the greatest amount of pyrotechnics on the back side of the house as it was less visible from the road.

"Okay," Marco said. "Dale, you're on lookout duty. If you see any cars approaching, any headlights at all, yell out to us, then run."

"Got it."

"The rest of us get blowtorches." He passed out the lighters and cans of aerosol hair spray. As children of the '80s, we knew exactly what to do. We popped the tops and shook the cans like spray paint.

"Ready," I said.

"Me too," Benny confirmed.

Marco nodded. "Okay. The key to making this work without getting caught is to light up as much as possible, as fast as possible. Ideally we'd do this from the inside, but I'm sure as fuck not going in there. I'll concentrate on the back, including the fireworks. You two start with the front, finish with the sides, and meet me back here. If Dale sees someone coming, or when we're sure the blaze isn't going to go out, we run straight back into the woods."

"Jesus, Marco," said Benny. "It's almost like you've done this before."

A broad grin spread across his face. "Only in my dreams, man."

Dale moved into position near the front of the house so he could observe Chennault and both directions of Clark. Marco nodded to both Benny and I, then walked briskly to his starting position by the fireworks.

I peered up at the Black House. The siding really was in terrible shape. Pitted, even, in a way I had never noticed before. As if it had been shot up with bullets, and was now covered in holes. So many holes.

"On three," Marco said.

I saw Benny walking to the other side of the house. Another pain shot through my neck and the base of my skull.

"Three... two..."

I raised the lighter in my left hand to eye level, a couple feet in front of me, while gripping the Aqua Net with my right hand, index finger on the trigger.

The moment I heard "one" I flicked on the flame.

# Nine

It was suddenly very quiet. The air had changed. All I could see was the lighter flame, eerily still in total darkness. I raised my right hand and found it was empty. Had I dropped the can?

I looked around. I was alone. Inside the Black House.

I heard the dark voice from far away, deep and echoing, as if calling out from the end of a long hallway.

*Jim.*

I spun around, flame still held out in front of me as a shield. I was standing in the threshold between the living room and the study with the empty bookshelves.

*Jimmmm.*

The voice had never come from a *direction* before. It had always originated from inside my own head. But now it was coming from a room to my left. Or was it?

*Whaaaat do you think you're dooo-ing.*

The voice came from the right this time, like it was circling me. I spun around again, taking a couple steps into the empty space.

"Leave me alone," I said, trying to sound strong despite my voice cracking.

*I need....*

I had to get out of here. I saw the front door, but when I took a few steps toward it, I was back in the study. The house seemed to be transforming around me, blocking every direction I stepped toward.

The flame was beginning to burn my thumb, but I dared not let go of the lighter since the darkness would be absolute. Yet there was motion in the darkness. The longer I looked around in panic, the more the walls appeared to be vibrating, as if covered in millions of black insects.

Then I saw a flicker of light. And heat. It appeared part of one bookshelf was momentarily ablaze. I dropped my left hand to my side, and was shocked to see my right hand was now raised, holding a flaming aerosol torch.

*Neeeed....*

The voice was behind me again. I turned sharply, and I was back outside in the nighttime air, my Aqua Net torch shooting flame not inches from an empty bookshelf, but from the face of a terrified Dale Dunkle. I attempted to drop the can but couldn't.

"Jimmy... no..." Dale pleaded.

I felt the voice rise up then, deep from within my bowels, and screamed the word, not in my own voice, but in the rich, terrifying tone of the monster in my mind.

"*Neeeeeeeeed!*"

I felt my body lurch upward, a marionette pulled by a string, seeming to hover in the air so that I now towered over Dale by nearly a foot. The blowtorch flame intensified too, fueled by more than mere over-the-counter propellant, but by a thick, oozing hate I had never felt before or since. More than I thought it was possible to feel, to be honest. I was going to burn Dale's face off. I could see it clear as day. His flesh would liquify and melt down his shoulders, and I'd feel heat radiate off his skull like hot stone.

The wet, growling sound of a hungry predator escaped my lips.

"*This bastard will be the first to die.*"

A shower of bright sparks caught my attention, and my eyes darted to the house. While Dale had been trying to distract me, putting himself in harm's way, Marco had lit the fireworks.

"*Stop!*" I screamed in the voice, and tried sprinting towards Marco, forgetting my feet weren't touching the ground. Instead, I found myself falling forward for a moment, before a great weight crashed into my left side. The hairspray can fell to the ground, instantly extinguishing itself, and I realized I, too, was now on the grass, with Benny straddling me, pinning my hands.

"I'll hold him!" Benny shouted. "Finish it!"

I struggled, writhing beneath his body, panting and shrieking like an animal. Somehow, Benny held firm. I was vaguely aware of Marco and Dale running around the house with their makeshift torches, setting the perimeter of butane-soaked century-old wood ablaze. At one point Marco even shoved a lit, spark-showering firework into a gap in one of the boarded-up windows. The acrid smell of it all began to overpower me, and I could taste the flames inside my throat as if I was being burned alive.

Again I tried to force Benny off me, and again I was pinned back to the earth. Benny clutched my wrists and pressed his chest against my own, his face inches from mine, staring intently at the fiery reflection in my eyes.

"It's going to be okay," he said.

I could feel the voice trying to growl through my throat, to respond, to threaten. But no words came.

My mind became flooded with images, tense moments from my past, including events of recent weeks but older stuff, too, like the first time I got in trouble in grade school, and my first fight, and stealing money from Mom's purse. But they were jumbled with memories that weren't mine at all—slapping a woman's face, being hit with a bottle at a bar, and staring down a pair of men who had come to kill me.

"It's okay," I heard Benny say once more.

Then the outside world collapsed again, and I was on the hard floor of the Black House study, still on my back, but with the face of a new person looming over me instead of Benny. The stranger was an older Black man with chiseled wrinkles on his forehead and literal fire in his eyes. A quick glance around proved the fire was a reflection of the walls and shelves burning all around us.

"Jimmmm," the man roared under his breath, and then his skin began to shimmer, fading into another man's face altogether. This new man was white, with broken wire-rimmed glasses and a sneering mouth of crooked teeth.

"Why?" I cried out.

But the new face couldn't answer, and wasn't done changing. It morphed and blended into at least three other distinct men, all strangers to me, all holding me down as the flames reached the ceiling. The newest face opened its mouth as if to speak, but its gaping mouth revealed nothing but fire, as if the back of his head had already burned clear off.

Then, in another flash of swirling gnats and fire, I was back outside. I was on the ground, but I was alone. It was dusk, and I could see Chennault, a dirt road now, with only a single house on its corner. The Black House was still beside me, but it was now a light grey. I felt a great tearing beneath my flesh, as if my chest had been ripped apart, organs scattering to the winds.

And then I was once more underneath Benny's sweat-soaked body, his labored breaths mingling with my own in the thick, smoky air.

"Benny," I croaked, and realized the voice was my own.

"Is that you?" he asked.

"I think so."

His grip loosened a bit.

I looked around. The flames were lapping the second story, now. I heard a grinding, creaking, moaning sound, and couldn't tell if it came from the burning house or from my own body.

The dark voice wasn't gone completely. Not yet. I could hear it shouting my name from far, far away. But it had lost its rich, resonant, commanding tone. It was now just the choking, gurgled screams of a dying man.

Benny let me sit up, though he stayed on my legs, ready to pounce if I tried anything foolish.

Marco and Dale had stepped back from the house, watching with awe.

It occurred to me that no one was on lookout duty.

"Guys," I said. "We need to get out of here."

They all stared at me. Could I be trusted?

"We weren't quiet," I continued. "We've been shouting. Someone's bound to have called it in."

Dale and Marco glanced at each other. Benny rolled off me and helped me to my feet. Marco nodded, grabbed his empty duffel bag, and hurried toward the safety of the woods. We followed close behind.

At the tree line, I turned back to see the entire house aflame.

—

Our walk through the woods was the only time any of us ever talked about what had happened, even to this day. Some things were subject to debate. Benny swears he saw me float like magic in the air, a foot off the ground at least, just hovering there before them. Marco was certain I had stepped backward onto the old stump which made me artificially taller. All had seen me snap and try and use the makeshift blowtorch on Dale rather than on the house, though. And all agreed the house caught fire much faster, and burned much hotter, than any had anticipated.

"It will be ash by morning," Marco assured me. "If not sooner."

We heard sirens just as we crossed Chennault. The Black House was still ablaze at the end of the street. I wanted to stand there and watch it cook, but my friends ushered me back to our tents.

You'd think the adrenaline of the night's events would have left us wired. You'd be wrong. I don't even remember crawling into the sleeping bag. I just remember waking up hours later, the tent bathed in morning light, my aching body covered in dew and dried sweat, with Benny asleep in his own bag beside mine.

I unzipped my tent and walked over to the other. Dale was inside, alone, writing in a notebook.

"Hey, Dale."

"Good morning, Jimmy!"

"Where's Marco?"

"He left a bit ago. Said he smelled like smoke and needed to get home to shower. I bet we all should do that."

Good call. It probably wasn't the best idea to smell smoky after committing arson.

I nodded toward the notebook. "You're not writing about any of this, are you?"

"Don't worry," he smiled. "It's not for the paper. It's only for me. I promise no one will ever see it."

I believed him.

"What do we do now?" I asked.

"How do you mean?"

"Like, how do we know if it worked? Burning down the house."

Dale grinned, and we both sang, in unison: *"Burning down the house!"*

"Keep your voices down, guys," a sleepy Benny called from his tent. "I'm not going to jail for you bastards."

"Benny's right," Dale said. "We can't even joke about it."

"Okay. You get home and shower. We'll meet up later." And then, louder, "you too, Benny."

Benny grumbled in response. I heard rustling as he gathered his things.

"To answer your question," Dale said, closing his notebook, "we'll know it worked if you're back to normal."

Normal. A weird thought. I wasn't sure what normal was anymore. Obviously, the last few weeks had seen a major escalation in my assholery, to put it mildly. But I wasn't sure I had been the best person *before* entering the house, either. Or even before hearing the voice in my head for the first time. If it's true that the voice "caused" much of my bad behavior, and the voice was now gone, then it's also true I'd have no excuse now if violent thoughts lingered within me. I guess I'd have to wait and see.

I was thinking of this in the shower after rolling up the tents and saying goodbye to the guys. I wondered what Grandma would say if she was here. Something about trying to live in the present and not the past. And slowly it dawned on me that I may never see her alive again. Mom hadn't mentioned her in recent days. Was no news "good news" when someone was in a coma? Or did each day in a coma make it less likely you would ever wake up?

I tried to replay our last conversation. My words to Grandma might have been the last thing she'd ever hear, and I had yelled at her. Or had I? Honestly, trying to remember most events of recent weeks was like trying to relive a dream. Even today, decades later, I sometimes wake up in a cold sweat, worried that I had said and done far worse to people during that time than my subconscious will let me accept.

"Jimmy," Mom's voice called from her bedroom. "You're taking an awful long time in there!"

Christ, she probably thought I was masturbating.

I shut off the shower.

After getting dressed I went into her room. She was rocking baby Madeline on the chair by the bed. The sun was coming in through the far window and hitting them just right. It was the first time in ages that I thought my mom looked pretty. Exhausted, too, but pretty, and content.

"How was your sleepover?"

"It was uneventful," I lied. "We stayed up too late reading comic books and telling ghost stories."

"You didn't get woken up by sirens?"

"No, why?"

"That house at the end of the street burned down."

Friends, I could have won an Emmy for my shocked reaction.

"Oh my God!"

"Yeah. Probably those mean kids who are always smoking back there. You should never smoke, Jimmy. It isn't safe."

"You smoke."

"Sure, but I'm trying to quit."

This was news to me. But, Madeline seemed supportive of the plan, and let out a soft, soothing coo. It made me smile.

"Do you want to hold her?"

"Yes," I said.

I sat on the edge of the bed and accepted the tiny, living bundle. Madeline was awake, barely. Her eyes fluttered open a bit, and saw her caretaker had changed, but didn't object. I intuitively bounced her in my arms with a tenderness I hadn't expected from myself. Her miniature pink mouth opened for a silent yawn, and then she drifted off.

"It won't be so bad being a big brother," Mom said.

"You're a big sister, right?" I asked.

"No, your Aunt Sharon's older. And doesn't let me forget it."

"Oh, yeah."

"But it will be different with you two. Sharon and I were so close in age we were always in competition. She didn't watch out for me the way you'll watch out for Madeline."

"Mom," I said, carefully. "I will try to be a good brother. I will. But I want to live my life, too. I don't want to be a dad to her. She has Mike for that."

I was worried this would set her off, but instead she nodded.

"That's what your grandma said, too."

"Have you heard anything from the hospital?"

"No," Mom admitted. "We should go down there tomorrow. Maybe being around you and Madeline will wake her up. I just want to bring her home, even if time is short. Like she always says, she was born in New Haven and wants to die in New Haven."

Something occurred to me.

"This house is pretty new," I said. "She didn't grow up *here.*"

Mom laughed. "No, of course not. Down the street, though. You pass it all the time, on the corner. It's the only house other than the black one that's that old."

I had no idea, and said so.

"Here, I think I have a picture. You've seen it."

Mom walked over to her bedroom bookshelf and retrieved an old brown photo album, the kind with sticky pages and cellophane. She flipped through the first few sheets before turning it around to me.

"There," she said, pointing.

It was a black-and-white image, of course, and a bit fuzzy. But it was indeed the same house on the corner of Clark and Chennault.

The only person in the picture was a little dark-haired girl, maybe five years old, standing on the front porch, wearing a white play dress.

—

I talked with Zach on the phone later that day. He had been successful in delaying the fire department, at least for a few minutes. He'd turned the Plectron volume all the way down, and remembered to unplug his dad's private phone line, but hadn't thought to disconnect the family line.

"When it started ringing around 2:30, I panicked," he explained. "I heard my dad pick up and I knew what it must be about. So, I ran to the bathroom and popped two Alka Seltzer in my mouth and started chewing."

"Wait, what?"

"Yeah, it tasted awful, but it filled my mouth with foam. Then I made a big bang sound and lay on the bathroom floor and started shaking my body, you know? Like I was having a seizure."

"How did you know Alka Seltzer would do that?"

"Eh, I had bit down on one a year or so ago thinking it was a chewable painkiller. Anyway, the trick worked, Dad dropped the phone and ran to me, and woke my mom up, and they called the hospital, but I played it off like I must have been sleepwalking and eaten the tablets by accident, then happened to have fallen. They believed me, otherwise I'd probably still be at the hospital being brain scanned to death. Or grounded."

See, Mom? Not "just a school friend."

I asked Zach if he could get a ride down to see the house, the fruits of his labor, but he said they were going to dinner out of town. For the best, I imagined, since it might be hard to explain to his dad why he'd want to drive out to a pile of rubble without arousing suspicion. Dale, Marco, Benny and I had agreed to meet up at 5:00, though, to make our peace with the smoldering remains. In our case, we figured it might be suspicious if we *weren't* interested.

It was strange seeing a landmark of our childhoods destroyed. At first we just gawked at it. The late afternoon sun painted angular shadows across the skeletal remnants and charred boards. It played tricks on your eyes when you looked too long, as if you couldn't quite bring it into focus. Marco broke the silence.

"Any voices in your head today, Jimmy?"

"Just my own."

"Do you really hear your own voice in your head?" asked Benny.

"Well, sure. Don't you?"

"I don't think so."

"I do," Dale interjected. "It's called an 'internal monologue.' Not everyone has one."

"Well that sounds terrifying," said Benny. "You mean you hear your own voice in your head, just telling you what to do all day? How do you know it's not some outside spirit messing with you? No offense, Jimmy."

It was a fair point. Until recently, I would never have given it a second thought. But now I wasn't so sure.

I was about to respond when I *did* hear another voice. From behind me.

"Did you do this?"

We spun around. It was Pax. T-Too and Derek were with him. The classic bully troika together again.

"My mom thinks it was *you*," I told him, deflecting but not exactly denying.

"You know damned well it wasn't me." He scanned our faces. "It was one of you fuckers. I just know it."

Pax wasn't doing well. He looked like he hadn't slept in weeks. He was trembling, like he was cold, or maybe filled with rage. For me, losing the voice was a weight off my shoulders. I didn't want it. I didn't need it. Perhaps Pax did.

"It will be okay, Pax. Really," I said.

"Tell me," he said through gritted teeth, "who did this."

When none of us spoke, Pax pulled a handgun from a front pocket of his shorts. Really. A fucking handgun. I had never seen a real gun before. The weapon glinted in the sun the way no toy pistol ever did. It shocked all of us, including T-Too and Derek, who exchanged a look of panic. Whatever they thought the plan had been, this wasn't it.

"Tell me," Pax repeated. "Now."

My eyes kept darting from the steel barrel of death to Pax's equally cold gaze. He wasn't aiming at any of us yet. He just sort of held the thing close to his body, making sure we could see it, but not attracting undue attention until he had to.

T-Too dared to speak. "W-where did you get the gun, Pax?"

"Jimmy knows," Pax said, never taking his eyes from mine. And, somehow, I did.

"It was Isaac's," I answered.

"That's right."

"You said they didn't find his gun."

"Yeah. 'They' didn't. I did."

A little birdie told him where to find it.

"Pax," I began, but he raised the gun and pointed it at me before I could come up with a cogent thought.

"It's fuckin' daylight, man," Derek protested. "What the hell are you doing?"

Pax ignored him. He just steadied his aim.

"Who. Did. This."

They say your life flashes before your eyes in moments like these. Maybe my life hadn't been long enough at that point, for I saw nothing. Time slowed as still as a photograph. I had no idea what to do. Where was a dark, bossy spirit when you needed one?

"I did," answered a meek voice to my left.

"Fine," said Pax, pointing the barrel toward my friend. "Bye bye, Benny."

Now, don't freak out, reader. I know it's bad enough this novel doesn't pass the Bechdel Test. I'm not going to Bury My Gays, too.

I'm also not going to invent some undeserved heroic flourish on my side. I mean, it's *tempting* to take some liberties, to make you like me again after 100 pages of me being a despicable creep and a prick to those I cared about. I could say I dove in front of Benny and saved his life, even taking a bullet for him in the process, because I had finally learned true empathy or the meaning of friendship or something. And you'd say "wow, that Jimmy Logan redeemed himself in the end!" and I'd earn an extra star on Goodreads.

What actually happened, though, is poetic enough.

Pax pulled the trigger. But a split second beforehand, I saw T-Too (yes, T-Too) knock Pax's right arm down with a sort of karate chop. It sent the bullet to the road instead of Benny's chest, landing inches from his shoes and ricocheting off somewhere. I saw Benny flinch and fall on his ass, but I knew he hadn't been hit. When I looked back to Pax, incredulous, I saw T-Too had wrestled the gun away altogether. It toppled to the ground beside them with a satisfying metal clunk.

A man from a nearby house, the one next to Dale's, ran out of his front door. I think his name was Mr. Williams. He assessed the situation instantly, ran toward Pax, kicked the gun a few feet away from the scene, and helped T-Too restrain the shooter.

"I'll kill you!" Pax screamed. "I'll fucking kill you!"

I recognized in that moment that we were seeing the real Pax. Nothing external was guiding him. This is who he was without the dark voice. Perhaps who he had always been.

By now a few others were racing toward us. Not Derek, though. He was thoroughly freaked out and had made a break for it.

I helped Benny to his feet.

"What were you thinking, man? You could have been killed! Why would you risk your life for me?"

We stared at each other for several long seconds. He didn't answer. He didn't have to.

The police arrived in record time. They took turns

asking us questions, and since all witnesses agreed Pax had tried to kill a kid, they confiscated the gun and arrested him at once.

"Are you kids going to be okay?" the lead cop asked. "We will have to follow up with your parents, you understand. You may have to testify."

"My parents live right over there," Dale pointed. "But they aren't home. Our number's here on my business card if you want to try later tonight!" He handed the bemused officer an Owner & Editor card from his pocket.

Benny looked miserable. "My folks will probably blame me no matter what you tell them." I thought my mom might, too.

The cop nodded. "My old man was hard on me as well. But give your parents a chance. I bet they love you." He turned to Dale, Marco, and T-Too as well. "*All* of you. Tell them what happened. I'm sure they'll be happy to know you're safe."

Mr. Williams and a couple onlookers went back to their homes. As the police drove away, I saw T-Too was still standing around, shuffling his feet.

"Thank you for what you did," I said to him.

"Yeah, well."

Marco spoke up. "No really, man. That was brave as hell."

"I d-don't think Pax is going to be happy with me."

"Join the club," I said.

T-Too seemed to consider this, as if it was an actual offer.

"Nah," he replied after a beat. "You're still a bunch of losers."

I chuckled. Maybe we were, maybe we weren't.

T-Too spun around to walk toward Stevens. After a few steps, he started making a loud, long "pssssss" sound. I didn't get it at first, but Dale sure did.

"It was chocolate milk!" Dale called out, laughing. "You *know* that!"

T-Too didn't turn back. He just gave an elaborate "who, me?" shrug and kept on toward home.

# Ten

It was the final Friday of summer vacation. Dale was working hard to complete the September issue of the paper, which he planned to get to stores Monday morning. Michigan schools generally open back up on a Tuesday, the day after Labor Day, and I found myself both terrified and excited to start eighth grade. Rather than channeling this apprehensiveness into more emo poetry, I decided to write an article instead, whether Dale had room for it or not.

That evening, I was at his front door holding a piece of paper.

"Hey, Dale."

"Hey, Jimmy! What's that?"

I handed it to him.

"I don't know if you can use this on such short notice, but I'd love to know what you think."

"It's typed!" Dale said, impressed.

I nodded. "Wrote it by hand first, but it was messy. It took forever to type this on my mom's Smith Corona. I don't know how you do it."

Dale began to read.

```
THE MIND OF A BULLY
By Jimmy Logan
    I've heard that bullies treat people
badly to hide that they're insecure. That's
what the school assemblies say. And maybe
that's true sometimes. The punk who knocks
your books down in the hallway to make up
for his dad being poor, sure. There's a
pain inside him. He's filled with self-
doubt. He knows he's a loser, he can't take
it, and he lashes out.
    But the scariest bullies are those
filled with a different kind of darkness. A
```

voice that convinces them that they are special. That the rules only apply to others. New Haven High School has such bullies, and not just among the kids. It's this darkness that makes the math teacher ridicule the nerd until he cries, or the history teacher rip up the notes of a Black girl just for laughs. It's when you lose what my grandma calls empathy. It's what happens when you think you're the star of not only your own movie, but everyone else's.

I'm not ashamed to admit that I've been bullied. I've been called names, had my money stolen, rocks thrown at my face, and worse. But I AM ashamed to admit that, for the last couple months, I let a dark voice inside my head change the way I behaved toward others. I hurt people, including family and the friends I care about the most, especially B.R., M.P., D.D., and E.J.

I wish I could say it wasn't my fault. But I let it happen. Maybe it started with feeling sorry for myself, like the first type of bully, but soon I was filled with hate instead, and there's power in hate. I didn't tell the voice to leave. I liked it. I wanted it to stay. Until I didn't. By then, I found it was hard to break free.

I hope the voice never comes back. If it does, though, I'll be ready. Because in the end, each of us has to decide the kind of person we want to be. It felt good to be a bully. It feels better to be a friend. And you can't be both at once.

Dale seemed to be taking his time. It occurred to me that he was reading it twice.

"You don't have to publish it," I wavered. "I just wanted to get my thoughts down, you know?"

Dale finally glanced up.

"It's great, Jimmy. Best thing you've written. Probably the best thing we'll ever publish."

"I wouldn't go that far. What about my *Ghostbusters II* review?"

"Fair enough." He thought for a moment. "Sure you're okay with sharing this?"

"I am."

"Okay. I'll shift some things around and get it in tomorrow's printing." Dale studied it again. "I might change 'I was filled with hate' to 'I was consumed by hate,' though. Sounds a bit better."

I must have given him quite a look, for he immediately backed down.

"Sorry," he said. "Force of habit. I won't change a word."

"Thank you."

He scanned the article once more.

"I don't want to assume, but, I'm 'D.D.' right?"

"Yeah," I smirked. "Double Dork."

"Clearly, the evil voice is controlling you again."

I smiled. "No, that's just my standard inner asshole."

On my way home I stopped by Benny's house. At first I thought he wasn't there, but I found him in that giant spool "clubhouse" behind his backyard. I squeezed in beside him.

"This might be the last time we both can fit in here," I said. Amazing that up to four of us used to sit inside.

"We're getting old, Jimmy."

"Eighth grade," I observed.

"Eighth grade."

We sat in stillness for a bit, our legs touching as they dangled out of the entrance hole.

"I wrote an article about what it felt like to be a bully," I said.

"Yeah?"

"Yeah. It comes out Monday."

"I don't think I could ever be a bully."

"I don't think you could, either."

He smiled at this. "Thanks," he said.

"I'm sorry for what I called you at Dale's party."

Benny turned to me. "Even if it's true?"

"Yeah."

He looked away. "But you're not one, are you. You like girls."

It was true. I did like girls. But I also liked Benny in the same way. I just didn't know what to do with those feelings. I still don't.

I didn't have the courage to speak, so I put my arm around him. He rested his head on my shoulder. We said nothing for what must have been an hour. I wouldn't have traded it for the world.

—

The paper was distributed on time Labor Day morning, except for the library, which was closed for the holiday and would have to wait. Dale bumped two of his own short articles in order to have my longer piece on the front page. I thought this was rather sweet of him, though the prominent placement made me nervous. Someone at the high school might get upset at my mention of teachers being bullies. And that's exactly what happened.

Halfway through seventh period on the first day of school, Dale and I were called down to the Principal's Office. We weren't in class together at the time, so we arrived separately, which means we didn't have a chance to get our story straight before we were escorted into the room. Not that it would have mattered.

"Take a seat, boys," said Principal Bartlet, a stern, balding man I had never said a word to.

We did.

Bartlet sat down behind his cherry wood desk across from us. Then two other grown-ups entered the room. There were seats available, but they chose to stand and glower instead. One was the scraggily-bearded Vice Principal whose name I can't recall, and the other was the school counselor Mrs. Loughlin.

"Some kids were passing this around in math class," Mr. Bartlet said, brandishing a copy of our paper as if it was a signed confession. "I'd like you to explain this article."

Dale spoke up first. "Which article, sir?"

That was ballsy. He knew damned well which article.

"This one," Mr. Bartlet said, pointing. "It claims New Haven High School not only has bullies, but that some of the *teachers* are bullies. This is a serious accusation. If you got one of our educators fired, you could be sued for libel."

"Only if it wasn't true," Dale said, sitting up a bit straighter, preparing for a fight. I could tell it took Bartlet by surprise.

I spoke up. "I didn't use any names. Not of teachers or anyone else."

"But everyone knows which two teachers you're referring to," interjected the Vice Principal.

"If it's true that everyone knows who I was talking about, then you must know who your problem teachers are."

Mr. Bartlet stiffened. "I have known Mr. Gilbert and Mr. Fairley for years, if indeed those are the men whose reputations you are meaning to besmirch, and trust them both completely, as teachers and as Christians. I also know for a fact that neither of you have had Mr. Fairley yet, which means you can't have any first-hand account of anything that has gone on his classroom."

"I haven't," I began, "but I trust—"

Dale interrupted me before I could share Zach's name. "We don't reveal our sources, sir. That's how journalism works."

"You don't know how journalism works, boy, because you haven't had a journalism teacher."

"I have too," Dale protested. "At Roeper. But this school won't let me into journalism class until I'm in tenth grade, so we had to start our own paper."

"An editor would have caught this and stopped you from publishing something inappropriate," Mrs. Loughlin chimed in. "You boys can't keep distributing this thing without a proper editor."

"Dale's the editor," I snapped. "And our paper has fewer typos than the school's."

"Look," said Mr. Bartlet, his hands raised in mock surrender. "I'm not saying what Dale has accomplished isn't impressive. And the damage is done for this issue, so I'm not saying you have to take them all down or anything. But you're going to have to run all future issues by the administration here before publication. That's non-negotiable."

Dale was appalled. "This is not a school project. You have no authority to do that."

"Try me," said Mr. Bartlet. The Vice Principal gave a dark, sycophantic chuckle.

"There may be another way," suggested Mrs. Loughlin. "Can you boys excuse us for a moment?"

Dale and I were sent to the waiting area. The normally-friendly receptionist shot us a look like we had been caught with weapons, so we didn't say anything in her presence for fear of self-incrimination.

When we were ushered back in, Mr. Bartlet was all smiles.

"I think we've found a solution," he said. "Dale, Mrs. Loughlin informs me that we have an opening in journalism this year. I can grant an exception to the grade level requirement and let you in."

"You would have to give up band," the counselor added, "as they meet at the same time. But only for this year. High school band is at a different period so there wouldn't be a conflict next fall."

Dale's eyes seemed to sparkle. To be in journalism class is all he had wanted. And giving up band was icing on the cake. He had never enjoyed it. The only offer that would have been better is if he could have avoided gym.

"Of course," Mr. Bartlet said, "you can't write for two newspapers at once."

"Double jeopardy," claimed the Vice Principal.

"So I'd have to shut down *The New Haven Herald Jr.*, just like you want me to."

"Unfortunately, yes," the Principal confirmed.

Dale turned to me.

"What about Jimmy? Is there only one slot available?"

"That's right," said Mrs. Loughlin. "Besides, even if there were two openings, one of the prerequisites for the class is having passed Grade 9 English. Dale, you've done that. Jimmy hasn't."

Dale shook his head. "No. Jimmy and I started the paper together. It's either both of us, or no deal. It wouldn't be fair." I saw him begin to tremble. Soon he was bound to do his scrunched-up ear-scratching tic. I put a hand on his shoulder to calm him down.

"Dale," I said. "It's okay. It's a good offer. You should take it."

Dale was stunned. "You're kidding."

"This is what you wanted all along. It was an honor to be able to write for your paper—"

"—*our* paper," Dale corrected.

"Our paper," I agreed. "It was great. I learned a lot. I had fun. But honestly, I'd much rather go back to writing heavy metal songs."

Dale laughed out loud. But his eyes were wet.

Mr. Bartlet leaned back in his chair. "Do we have a deal?"

We did.

The bell rang, signaling the end of seventh period and our first day of eighth grade.

As we left the office and joined the sea of students scrambling for lockers, I couldn't resist a gentle ribbing of Dale Dunkle.

"Ninth grade English? As an 11-year-old?" I had known he was in a different class than me, but I had always assumed he had been in *eighth* grade English, not *ninth*.

Dale merely shrugged.

"What can I say," he said. "I have a thing for naughty books."

A voice called my name, and I whirled to see Emilia. When I turned back to Dale, he was grinning.

"Go on," he encouraged. "I have to get to the bus." And with that, he skipped out the door.

Dale thrived in journalism class, by the way. *The New Haven High School Rocket Report* published its first issue of the school year in October, and the kid had more articles than any other student. The one that I remember most was the first one I read, about the Village of New Haven formally adopting a new town seal and flag. Back in 1973, a high school student named Cathy had won an art contest to design a village seal, but it had only been used once and had long been forgotten. In 1989, the seal was rediscovered and officially implemented, and provided a source of pride for a community dedicated to positive race relations. It's quite lovely: white and Black hands clasped in unity, surrounded by the words "Pride and Peace of Our People" and "The Enlightened Truth of the Common Good."

Sorry, I'll quit stalling.

I took a breath and strode over to where Emilia was waiting. She looked incredible, as always. Cute new haircut, with a hint of a summer tan, sporting a fitted black t-shirt that was far too fashionable for this place.

"Hey, Emilia. How was your first day?"

"Good, and yours?"

"Not bad."

"I heard you being called down to the office on the intercom."

"Yeah," I admitted. "Dale and I got in trouble for my article about bullies."

"I figured," she said.

"Wait, you read it?"

"Someone in third period had a copy. They were asking if I was E.J."

I felt my face flush with embarrassment.

"Uh, yeah."

"Jimmy, I wanted to let you know that I appreciated what you said. I think it's mature to admit when you've hurt someone."

"I really am so sorry, Emilia. I wish I could take it back more than anything. I was such a jerk. I'm better than that, I swear."

"I know," she said. "And I accept your apology."

This was such a relief. I had only seen her once today, in math, our sole class together this year, but had avoided making eye contact. I had been wondering if I would have to steer clear of her the entire semester out of shame.

"Do you think," I said, cautiously, "that we could hang out sometime? Maybe get ice cream after school or something?"

Emilia gave me the saddest smile I have ever seen. The kind you'd muster for a child to tell them their dog had passed away.

"No," she said, warm but firm. "I accept your apology, because I believe it is sincere, and my faith calls me to forgive the sins of others, as I too hope to be forgiven someday. But that is different than moving on as if nothing happened."

"I'm not saying—"

She held up a hand. "Jimmy, I don't know if guys think about this stuff as much as girls, but you have to know that I've been dreaming of my first kiss since I was watching Disney movies as a little kid. I had an idea of how I would wait for the right guy, and we'd be holding hands, and we'd know it was time, and we'd share something special. You stole that from me. For the rest of my life, whenever I think back to my first kiss, or someone asks me about my first kiss, it will be of it being forced on me before I even knew what was happening. I know you're sorry. I do. But that doesn't change how I feel. I just can't imagine wanting to hang out with you. Ever. I'm sure you understand."

I did. I told her so. And I watched her walk away.

The buses began to leave, and a silent stillness crept over the school grounds as I filled my backpack with books from my locker. Mike had fixed my busted back tire, so Mom had given permission for me to bike instead of bus, as it was a nice day and I was an eighth grader and all.

Without really planning to, I found myself taking a long way home, circling the town and riding by many of the locations that had been so important in the past year: Huck's, Andy's, St. Clair Studio, the abandoned train depot, even the library. I was sad about the paper shutting down, but I suppose one chapter has to end before another can begin. That's what Grandma says, anyway. Yet it dawned on me for the first time how lucky Dale and I were to live in a community like this. From the local advertisers, to the people we interviewed, to the hundreds of residents who purchased an issue of *The New Haven Herald Jr.* and read our words, this village had really come together to support the dream of a couple seventh graders they didn't even know. Not all towns would have done that. It made me proud to be from New Haven—then, and now.

I thought about the dark voice, too. It hadn't made a peep since the house was destroyed, yet I still felt him in there somewhere. Suppressed, but adding color to my emotions. When I first heard the voice months ago, I had assumed it was my subconscious. An alter ego of my inner monologue, as Dale called it. But I should have known it wasn't coming from my own mind. It called me Jimmy, after all. It tried to trick me into things. It lied to me. For a few minutes, it could even control me. For what I did to Emilia, Marco, Kat, and others, I probably should have been arrested. And I had been just getting started. What would have happened to Madeline, or my mother, or myself, had I let it continue? The voice was a poison flowing through my veins. Like, I imagined, a drug. Yet even at that moment, I missed some of the strength the poison gave me. If only there was a way to harness the good power of the poison without losing control to it.

It was strange coming up on Chennault and seeing a pile of ash and rubble where the Black House should have been. It had been the anchor of the subdivision. Now it wasn't.

I hopped off my bike and slipped under the caution tape. Soon, I assumed, they'd come and clean all this up. It was likely toxic. Or some kid could step on a rusty nail and need a tetanus shot.

At my feet there were small pieces of burned up wood. I picked one up and examined it. It was charcoal on one side, black and crumbly, but if you turned it over and held it at just the right angle, it looked like healthy, untouched pine.

*I should take this,* I thought. *A souvenir.*

I tucked it into my backpack and hopped back on my ride.

I passed Dale's house, then Benny's. I saw Marco on his front porch reading a textbook. I waved and he waved back.

Mike's car was in our driveway, and I realized it must be later than I expected. Where had the hours gone?

"Hey, sport," Mike greeted as I entered the front door. He was holding Madeline. "Just in time."

"How was your first day, honey?" asked Mom.

She had made goulash. It smelled spectacular.

"Pretty good, actually."

I leaned over to peek at Madeline. She was drifting off to sleep, but seemed to recognize me, and appeared quite happy, though it might have been gas.

My mind began to picture what she might be like as an older kid, able to think and talk. I imagined her first at age five like Dale's sister Debbie, a wide-eyed chatty little information sponge. I realized I'd be a high school senior then, perhaps planning for college, or at least preparing to branch out on my own somehow. Will I have been a good role model for her during those years together? I suppose that was up to me.

Then I thought on, wondering how our relationship would be into adulthood, me in my 30s and Madeline in her 20s. I suspected we would each move out of New Haven and make our respective claims on the world, but hoped we'd stay in touch, at least to complain about Mom together. Looking down at her doll-sized fists, it was difficult to see how this tiny child could ever become a grown-up. But I was starting to be able to envision myself as one.

Mike gingerly lay Madeline down in the small crib we kept in the living room, then returned to join us for dinner. I told them both about my new classes and what I was excited for. I left out the part about Emilia, but did explain about the paper being over. Neither were upset or even surprised, though Mom wasn't amused when I mentioned the shakedown from the school administrators. Still, she didn't overreact or threaten to give Mr. Bartlet a piece of her mind or anything. I was grateful for that.

"I'm sure you'll find something new to do," she said.

I agreed, helping myself to seconds.

When dinner had ended, we sat in the living room talking softly as not to wake the baby. After a while, the phone rang, and Mom excused herself to answer.

"So," I whispered to Mike, "what's the deal? Are you guys back together or what?"

Mike shook his head. "No, I think that ship has sailed."

I must have looked disappointed.

"Hey," he said. "Your mom and I didn't work out. It's true. But I'll always be in your sister's life. Which means I'll be in your life."

"I'd like that."

I heard Mom's voice from the kitchen. She was asking "how many visitors" and ended with "okay, we'll be right there." She came back to the living room looking excited.

"It's about your grandma," Mom explained. "She's waking up."

"Can we go see her?" I asked.

"Yes, you and I can, if Mike can stay with Madeline."

"Works for me," he said. "Tell her I'm thinking of her too."

"We will."

Mom and I drove to Mt. Clemens General at once. On the way, Mom warned me not to expect too much. Grandma might not be able to speak yet, and certainly wouldn't be coming home anytime soon. Selfishly, it occurred to me that her not speaking might be a good thing. After all, my behavior may have sent her into a coma in the first place. Her first words might be to tell Mom what an asshole I had been.

We made it to Grandma's room. She was awake and relatively alert. A young doctor was asking her to follow his pencil with her eyes, and she was able to comply.

"Do you know your name?" he asked. "How about the year?"

Grandma didn't answer. She opened her mouth as if to speak, but nothing came out.

"It's okay," the doctor said to us. "Give it time."

We pulled visitor's chairs up to the hospital bed. Mom took one of Grandma's hands in hers, careful not to disturb the IV attached to her paper-like skin.

"We're here," Mom said.

"Do you know who's sitting next to you?" asked the doctor.

Grandma turned and looked at Mom, then over at me, and smiled ever so slightly in recognition.

"My grandson," she said.

I had so many questions. Had she known she had been asleep nearly a month? Did she remember collapsing by the stairs? Had she really grown up in the house on the corner? Did she have an opinion on whether ghosts could travel back in time?

Of course, I asked none of these things. In fact, I never would, not once in the three full years she lived afterward. From my perspective, those were concerns of the past. And I was thinking of the future.

# Epilogue

I know, I know. Epilogues probably aren't much better than prologues. The story's over, right? What's this coda for?

Yet you're still reading.

Maybe you think I'm going to provide *Breakfast Club*-style notes on what became of all my friends. "Benny Roberts is presently an interpretive dance instructor in Seattle. He has three cats: Stacey, Mitch, and Aloysius." Yuck, no. Just because this is a true story doesn't mean you get closure on everything. Especially in a work of fiction.

Or, maybe you want to learn what happened with Al Horner's research into the Black House. Unfortunately, if he uncovered anything, he kept it to himself. Al had sent Dale his regular five dollars for the monthly ad buy, along with a note that he was still researching our question. Dale mailed the money back explaining he had shut down the paper, and we never heard from Al again. Maybe it's better not to know.

No, I get why you're here. You're wondering why I never resolved the central tension of the story, the Kasparov's Gun of it all: when did I beat Mike at chess and "become a man."

Well, that's *exactly* what an epilogue is for, because this novel is about the late 1980s, and I didn't beat Mike at chess until the 1990s. Ten minutes into the '90s, in fact.

Mom had invited Mike to spend New Years Eve with us, and he had brought champagne for the grown-ups and sparkling cider for me. We played board games together and took turns feeding and burping Madeline, who had taken a special liking to her big brother for some reason. Mom made a passive-aggressive comment or two about that, but I didn't let it get to me. I had learned to understand her better in recent months and we found ourselves in a good place. Grandma had moved back in with us by then, so we spent some time in her room as well, though her days of staying up until midnight were over. "Sleep," Grandma explained, "is never overrated."

Mom went to bed right after the ball drop, but I was wired. (Sparkling cider might not have alcohol, but it's *loaded* with sugar.) When Mike grabbed his coat, I stopped him.

"Aw, don't go! Let's watch a cheesy horror movie!"

Mike laughed. "Tomorrow's a workday, Jimmy."

"On New Year's?"

"Things need to be foundered every Monday."

"Oh."

He took pity on me and set his coat down on the couch.

"Okay, one game."

Now, I don't know if I had really gotten better or if Mike had consumed a bit too much champagne, but about halfway through the match I got the sense that I was in control of the board. I could anticipate his strategy. I could stop what he was trying to do. And slowly, move by move, I developed an advantage.

My heart thumped in my chest as I positioned the final piece into place, half-certain I had miscalculated, scared to release the bishop from my fingers which would lock the move in forever. But, I had him, and he knew it.

"Checkmate," I whispered.

Mike leaned back in his chair, crossed his giant arms, and studied the board for a long time. Then, a glint appeared in his eyes. He leaned forward and placed his right elbow firmly on the center of the chessboard, a cupped hand raised in challenge as he stared me down.

"The day you beat me at arm wrestling..."

## Author's Notes and Acknowledgements

The real *New Haven Herald, Jr.* ran from February 1988 through March 1989. My best friend John Lochbihler was involved from day one, and all early articles were written by one or both of us. Later, John Rogan joined the team and would continue through the entire run. Several other kids submitted articles or helped with layout in later issues, including Tony Hamilton, Michael Hinkley, Paul Fontana, and Patrick Roberts. While most characters in *The Paper* aren't intended to match up with specific real-life counterparts, I think it's safe to reveal that Dale Dunkle was based on me. But, perhaps, not *just* Dale.

As in the novel, no grown-up was involved in the creation, writing, layout, or distribution of the paper. But it would not have gotten noticed without the support and advocacy from several prominent community figures such as Ron Huck of Huck's Party Store, Judy Roberts of St. Clair Studio, and Jean Waterloo of the Lenox Township Library. These adults and so many others took a chance on a nerdy 10-year-old's dream and helped it come true.

I'd also like to thank the local Macomb County media for their pieces on *The New Haven Herald Jr.*, particularly "NHHS Student is Boy Publisher" by Jeanette LaVoy, published in the *Anchor Bay Beacon* on November 9th, 1988, and "Paper's Editor Soon to Turn 12 Years Old" by Shirley A. McShane, published in *The Macomb Daily* on April 18th, 1989. They were both wonderful, flattering articles, but as you may have surmised, I always felt guilty at how the paper was portrayed as a solo operation. I could not have done it without my aforementioned friends, nor would I have wanted to. That lingering guilt inspired this book.

Speaking of press, I also feel bad about never completing the planned May 1989 issue, especially after *The Macomb Daily* piece had generated so much interest. The real reason that issue was shelved has been portrayed more-or-less accurately in the book. The administration at New Haven High School was indeed upset about a piece I published in the March issue about bullying, called me into the office, and warned me against writing anything like that again. When I explained that it was an independent project, since I couldn't even be in journalism class until the tenth grade, they made an exception. I wrote for the school newspaper my entire eighth grade year, the youngest student ever to be given the opportunity, under the editorial direction of Vivian Henegar. Both Mrs. Henegar and her husband Thomas were among my favorite teachers at New Haven. And although this novel begins after I'd already left Roeper, I have to give shout outs to Diana Elshoff, Emery Pence, Terry Rudman and others from my magical formative years there.

Of course, as in all things, I wouldn't have had any of my childhood experiences without my supporting and loving family, especially my mother Linda Addis, an accomplished local journalist herself who inspired me to be a reporter in the first place; my father John P. Addis, an English teacher and avid reader who helped me become a storyteller; and my grandmother Eleanor Addis, who saved everything I ever wrote, good and bad, giving me the pride and confidence to attempt new things, knowing I'd always have at least one fan.

I must lastly give a special heartfelt thank you to Leah Addis, for her support and patience with my obsessive babbling about this novel during the time I was writing it, and peppering her with a hundred questions after she became the first person to read and copyedit the first draft. I'm sure it is a bit exhausting to live with an occasionally manic creative person, even if she would never admit it.

As of this writing, I have no idea if *The Paper* will connect with a large audience the way my first novel

*The Eaton* did. This is, after all, a remarkably personal and autobiographical story. It means a great deal to me, but the horror elements I've become known for are largely subdued here, even allegorical. I wanted to tell a story in which everything was both discernibly true, in fact or in feeling, *and* wholly made up. Being a pre-teen is hard, and not everything makes sense at the time, or even decades later. So whether to treat this story as a literal autobiography or a puberty parable is ultimately up to you.

*Dale        Jimmy        John*

Article use by permission of *The Macomb Daily*.

333

## About the Author

John K. Addis is a writer and marketing professional from Lansing, Michigan. When not advertising the products and causes of his clients, Addis enjoys crafting suspenseful tales set in Michigan locations. His award-winning first novel, *The Eaton*, was an Amazon and Audible bestseller.

## About the Artist

Ryan Holmes is an award-winning artist also from Lansing, Michigan, known throughout the region for acrylic paintings and chalk art. He is a lover of all things '80s and has been active as a local Ghostbuster for more than 20 years. This is his first book cover commission.

# Copyrights and Attributions

Pages 73-74 120, 124, 131, 178, 315-316:

Text adapted from articles by John Addis, John Lochbihler, and John Rogan, originally published in *The New Haven Herald Jr.*, 1988-1989. All rights reserved.

Page 155:

**Welcome Home (Sanitarium)**
Words and Music by James Hetfield, Lars Ulrich and Kirk Hammett
Copyright © 1986 Creeping Death Music (GMR)
International Copyright Secured All Rights Reserved
*Reprinted by Permission of Hal Leonard LLC*

*Special thanks to Yundi Hal at Hal Leonard for assisting me with obtaining these permissions.*

Page 333:

McShane, Shirley A. "Paper's Editor Soon to Turn 12 Years Old." *The Macomb Daily*, April 18th, 1989, p. 3.

*Special thanks to Don Wyatt with MediaNews Group Michigan for assisting me with obtaining this reprint permission.*

*Also Available:*

## *The Eaton*
by John K. Addis

Spanning more than 100 years of mid-Michigan history, but told in the gruesome style of '80s horror classics, The Eaton tells the story of Sam Spicer, who purchases the dilapidated Michigan Central Railroad Depot in Eaton Rapids with the dream of opening a hot new martini bar. But when he and his friends unearth an abandoned underground hotel directly beneath the property, they must discover what happened to the original guests—before their own time runs out.

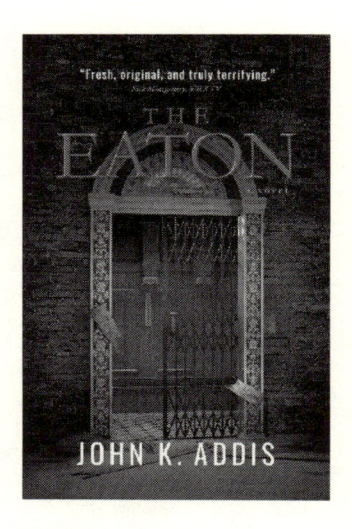

**An Amazon and Audible Best-Seller**
**Over 1,000 Four-Star and Five-Star Reviews**
**A Readers' Favorite Book Award-Winner**

"*The Eaton* is the best kind of horror." – *Midwest Book Review*

"*The Eaton* will hold you captive." – *Jenn Carpenter, Violent Ends Podcast, Author of Haunted Lansing*

"Rich, well-developed characters." – *FangFreakingTastic Reviews*

"*The Eaton* is a must-read." – *Portland Book Review*

"Out-and-out thrilling." – *ReadersFavorite.com*

## *Journey to Cassiopeia*
*by John K. Addis*

When her father comes home late as usual, eight-year-old Cassie has wisdom to share beyond her years.

*Illustrated by Daniela Olaru.*

**A Readers' Favorite Book Award-Winner**
**A MarCom Award-Winner**

"Hauntingly beautiful." – *Kory M. Shrum, USA Today Best-Selling Author*

"A heart-tugging, first-of-its-kind children's book for grown-ups." – *Kirk Montgomery, ABC-TV*

"A remarkable tale [that] shines a light on our own mortality." – *Rosie Malezer, Readers' Favorite*

## *The New Haven Herald Jr.*
*Complete Archives 1988–1989*

This collection contains all six original issues of the kid-run newspaper *The New Haven Herald Jr.*, along with history, commentary, and more.

*Coming Soon:*

## The Bells of Beaumont Tower
### The Complete Scripts
by John K. Addis

In Fall of 2003, East Lansing's public access station aired a four-part mystery-horror series which reimagined Michigan State University's famed Beaumont Tower as the heart of a strange student cult. As new episodes debuted through the winter, local students became invested in trying to solve the mystery before the final episode aired. This printed collection contains all shooting scripts for this bizarre local phenomenon, along with the original rough plot sketches, behind-the-scenes details, and facts about the production.

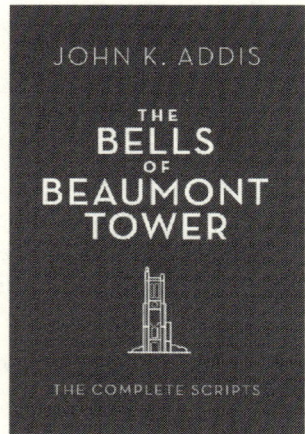

## Bob & the Birds
by John K. Addis
with Sophia Magyar

Based on an improvised series of nightly bedtime stories told to Addis' daughter when she was between the ages of four and ten, this illustrated collection of magical tales will span at least three books.

Made in the USA
Columbia, SC
25 June 2024